THE

BOYHOOD DAYS OF JACK STRAW;

OR,

THE SWORD OF FREEDOM.

COMPLETE.

BEAUTIFULLY ILLUSTRATED.

LONDON :
"BOYS OF ENGLAND" OFFICE, 173, FLEET STREET, E.C.,
AND ALL BOOKSELLERS.

THE
BOYHOOD DAYS OF JACK STRAW.

"AS THEY LOWERED HIM INTO THE DARKNESS A CRY OF HORROR ESCAPED THE MAN'S LIPS."

THE

BOYHOOD DAYS OF JACK STRAW;

OR, THE SWORD OF FREEDOM.

An Historical Romance.

By the Author of "Dark Deeds of Old London," "Armourer's Son," &c., &c.

CHAPTER I.

INTRODUCES SIR GUIBALD LE MANDUIT, HIS SON, AND HIS COMPANIONS, MARK TREVOR AND BASIL TREMAINE.

To the right of the village of Dartford, in Kent, and not a dozen paces from the River Darrent, stood, at the time our story commences, the remains of Dartford Abbey, which, built by the Monk Hestel, nicknamed the Black Knight, during the reign of Edward the First, was attacked and almost destroyed in that of Edward the Second.

On the left, and almost entirely surrounded with noble trees, which formed a kind of park, stood the stately castle belonging to Sir Guibald le Manduit, a haughty nobleman, who was heartily hated by all whose misfortune it was to have been born in the lower scale.

Sir Guibald was rich—excessively rich—but he took especial pains to keep his wealth to himself.

His hand was never extended in charity, but was ever ready to authorise the arrest of some poor serf whose means did not allow him to pay what was due to his landlord.

At the time when this history commences, Sir Guy had attained his fiftieth birthday.

He was tall, and with a fine presence, but this was marred by the fierce look of his eyes.

Sir Guy married, when thirty years of age, Maud, only daughter of Sir Lion Steele, but whether because he loved her, or because of the large sum of money she brought with her, was not exactly known.

Two years after the marriage a son was born, who was christened after his father—Guibald.

Some persons said it was a *mysterious* birth, but, at any rate, a year afterwards Lady Maud died—some said of a broken heart—and left her beautiful boy to the tender mercies of his indifferent father.

What did Sir Guibald do?

Well, something very simple.

He sent for one of his tenants—a young woman with a large family—and to her he said—

"Listen to me. You are poor?"

"It is indeed so, Sir Guibald, And who should know it so well as you?"

"Into that matter I am not prepared to enter," replied Sir Guibald, with a haughty wave of his hand. "But if you will listen to—"

"Your pardon, for my anxiety overpowers me," interrupted the poor woman; "but you will tell me that you have not sent for me to say that I, my husband and family, must begone?"

Sir Guibald smiled grimly.

"Nay, 'tis not that," he said; "though I am informed you are at present indebted to me in a large sum of money. But I will let that pass. I am informed you are an excellent nurse?"

The woman made a low curtsey.

"See my children," she said, "and judge for yourself."

"It is not necessary. You are aware that my lady is dead, and that I am left with her child on my hands."

Her child, mark, not *our*.

"I am," replied the woman. "May the Virgin take her to her breast, and may Heaven watch over her dear little boy."

"Tush!" cried Sir Guibald, impatiently. "List to me, and make no such remarks. What is now the number of your family?"

"Eight."

"Eight! By my troth! a goodly number indeed. Well, are you prepared to make your family nine? I would place in your care my son."

"Ha!" cried the woman, joyfully, "willingly would I take charge of the son of thy late noble lady. But my means are very—"

"Let not that trouble you. If you take charge of my son, you will, henceforth, be my servant, and as such I will pay you your dues."

"I thank you, noble sir."

"You will at once take charge of him?"

"I will, at once."

"In that case you shall live rent free while he is under your care; and, besides that, you shall receive twenty nobles per year."

The woman curtsied, and murmured her thanks.

"All is then settled," Sir Guibald said, with a look of relief, as he rang a bell at his side. "The child shall now be placed in your arms, and you shall have ten nobles with him."

A servant entering, she was desired to bring the child and place him in the woman's arms.

The servant wonderingly obeyed these, as she considered, strange commands.

In a few moments the pretty baby, fast asleep, was placed in the charge of its new nurse.

The ten nobles was then paid her, and she departed.

On the threshold of the door she paused.

"When shall I prepare for your visits, honoured sir?" she asked.

"Make no preparations whatever," replied Sir Guibald. "I shall not often trouble you, depend upon it."

Thus it will be seen that at the age of twelve months, Sir Guibald thrust, as it were, from his door his only son and heir.

Years passed away, and when the son had attained his ninth birthday, he was sent to Canterbury, and placed in charge of an eminent scholar.

He remained there until he was sixteen, when he was sent to the castle.

For six years Sir Guibald had not so much as set eyes upon his son, and when he entered the castle and stood before him for the first time, he simply bestowed upon him a look of utter indifference.

Yet one would have thought he would have been proud of such a son.

He was a very handsome youth, tall and powerful, and wonderfully daring.

To his astonishment, Sir Guibald told him that, on the following day, a learned divine would call for him, and would take him to Rome.

Though, at these callous words, Guibald's lips trembled, and a tear or two rolled down his cheeks, he made no reply.

Bestowing a glance of scorn upon his hard-hearted father, he left the room.

The learned divine did call, and Guibald left with him, his father never seeking him to bid him farewell.

For two years he remained in Rome, during which time he, and two of his companions, named Mark Trevor and Basil Tremaine, both English youths of good parentage, made themselves particularly notorious.

The daring of these youths was extraordinary, and such a pitch did it reach at last, that the three of them were expelled the city.

These proceedings reached the ears of Sir Guibald, and he swore that he would do nothing further for his son, forgetting that it was all through his own folly in not having the boy under his own command, and teaching him which was the right, and which the wrong road.

It is here that our story properly commences.

The night of the 13th of June of the year 1359 was a most lovely one.

In those days people retired early to rest, and at ten o'clock very few persons were abroad.

The village was very quiet when the hour of ten struck.

Suddenly this silence was disturbed.

From the extreme end of the village came sounds as of the tramping of horses' hoofs, mingling with the sounds of merry laughter.

Then a bright voice sang the first verse of a hunting song, and was joined in the chorus by two others.

Many persons left their beds, and looked out of their windows.

Such a thing as a hunting song sung in the village at such an hour, was undoubtedly a remarkable occurrence.

Well were they rewarded for their curiosity.

From the shadows of the trees emerged three horsemen.

And not one of these horsemen had reached his nineteenth birthday.

Each was mounted on a powerful animal, and from their bearing, it was evident that riding had long been one of their accomplishments.

Each was well attired in a short, richly-embroidered jerkin, and wore tight-fitting, high-legged boots.

They rode abreast, thereby taking up all the roadway.

The horseman in the centre was the most noticeable of this group, being a head taller than his companions, his dress somewhat richer, and instead of the soft velvet cap worn by his companions, he had a cap made of leather, richly and daintily embroidered with a falcon's wing on its right, fastened with a gold buckle.

Each was armed with sword and dagger.

The youth in the centre was Guibald, only son of Sir Guibald le Manduit; the one on his right was Mark Trevor, while the one on his left was Basil Tremaine.

They had returned from Rome, and this was the third day of their arrival in England.

When in front of the "Royal Arms," Guibald cried "Halt!"

The party drew rein.

"Why do you pause?" asked Basil Tremaine.

"This," replied Guibald, "is the village inn, the host of which has the audacity to call it the 'Royal Arms,' ho, ho! Well, friends, comrades, brothers, I am athirst, and would partake of a measure of wine or ale. I am not particular. What say you?"

"I am with you," cried Basil, "for I know I am parched, and cannot join thee in a song again, unless I clear the dust from my throat."

"Nor I," said Mark Trevor; "but, if I mistake not, the house is closed."

"'Tis so," replied Guibald; "but see, a light is within, or no doubt the host has not yet retired. What ho, host! what ho!" he shouted.

"What ho!" roared the others.

In a few seconds the door was cautiously opened.

"What want ye, my masters?" asked the hoarse voice of the host.

"Drink, and at once. We are weary travellers, and are athirst. So, hurry, my friend."

"'Tis late, young sirs," replied the host, eyeing the three suspiciously; "however, if you have the money, I will supply you with the refreshment you desire. I am always paid first."

"Take your money, then, varlet," cried Guibald, as he flung a gold piece at the landlord's feet, "and hurry, mark you, or 'twill be the worse for you."

"Wine or ale, my masters?"

"Wine, since you have there money enough to pay for what we shall drink of it. See that it is the best, or look to your bones."

"And supply it in cups worth drinking from," cried Basil.

"And see that the cups are brimming ones," shouted Mark, with a loud laugh at the landlord, who in his haste nearly broke his neck over the step of the door.

The host brought out a wooden

platter, upon which he had placed the silver cups, each of them brimming over with wine.

Each of the youths took one.

"Your healths," said Guibald, holding aloft his cup.

"And yours," was the answer of his companions.

"And long life and prosperity to you at the castle," said Basil.

"You know that I shall not be welcome there, Basil," said Guibald. "Nay, I much fear me I shall be turned from it directly I enter."

"Say not so," said Mark. "Mayhap things may be better than you imagine."

Guibald shook his head.

"No," he said, "I shall not be welcome there. Besides, if I were allowed to stay, I should, no doubt, be confined there like a dog. Against that my soul revolts. I would be free—free as the birds of the air. I have always felt that my life is to be a life of adventure. I trust such may be the case. I ask for nothing better."

"Well," said Basil, with a laugh, "if you are thrust from your father's roof, such a course is the only one open to you. As for us—well, we shall not dare to return to the parental roof, and must follow your lead."

"And for me," said Mark, "of course such a life as you speak of is a dangerous one, but what matters that? All must die sooner or later. Well, all but one, Guibald le Manduit, ho, ho! 'Tis certain *he* will never die a violent death. Forget it not, Basil, Guibald carries in his bosom the single straw he plucked from St. Peter's dungeon at Rome. 'Twill guard him against such a fate ; at least, so 'tis said, and Guibald devoutly believes it. Is it not so, comrade?"

"It is. I feel certain that while I carry this sacred straw I am safe from such a calamity."

"I believe it also," said Basil. "And if Guibald *is* turned from his rightful home, I propose that he adopt the name of Straw. What say you, Mark?"

"'Tis not a bad name. What say you to Jack Straw, Guibald?"

"JACK STRAW be it!" Guibald replied.

"Then, in anticipation of your adopt-ing that name, I quaff the remainder of my wine to your good fortune."

"And so do I," cried Basil.

And the three emptied the remainder of the wine down their thirsty throats, and handed the cups to the host, who wishing them a good-night in the surliest tones he could master, retired and closed the door with a bang.

"Where is the castle?" asked Basil.

"Yonder," replied Guibald, pointing to the towers which, in the distance, stood out clear and distinct in the moon's rays.

"Shall we await you here?" asked Mark.

"Yes, pray do so. For there is no doubt I shall return. But look across the river there on your left. What do you see?"

"What looks like a ruined abbey," replied Basil.

"That is what it is. Take your horses about a hundred yards along the bank, and you will be able to ford the river and reach the abbey, where you will find shelter in plenty. Fear not, I shall return to you ere long."

Bidding them adieu for awhile, Guibald rode off towards the castle, while his two friends made their way to the abbey.

Directly Guibald left his companions he became thoughtful.

His hand slackened on the reins, and the horse took advantage of it and walked as slowly as an animal does in a funeral procession.

Guibald at length reached the castle.

He found the drawbridge raised, and not a soul to be anywhere seen.

Of course he was not expected.

Indeed his father had not the slightest idea as to whether he was in England or a thousand miles off.

Guibald had a wonderfully powerful voice, however, and he could use it to advantage when he thought proper.

Rising in his stirrups he shouted as loudly as he could—

"What ho! What ho!"

The gate at once opened and an archer appeared.

"What want you?" he growled.

"Admittance, and at once," replied Guibald.

The man replied with a loud laugh of derision.

"Laugh not, fool!" cried Guibald. "Know ye who I am?"

"Nay, nor care," replied the man.

"I am Guibald le Manduit and your master. Lower the drawbridge at once, or 'twill be the worse for you."

"Are you, indeed, my young master? By Our Lady, I crave your forgiveness."

"'Tis granted. Lower the drawbridge."

Assisted by a comrade, the man soon lowered the bridge, and Guibald passed into the courtyard.

Here he was met by the steward.

"My father does not expect me," said Guibald. "Has he retired to rest yet?"

"He has not, young sir; he is in his study."

"I pray you have my horse taken to the stables, and—"

"Nay," interrupted the steward, as he shook his head, "if you will be advised by me, you will have the horse remain where he is. If I am not mistaken you will require him very shortly."

The significant tones in which this was said convinced Guibald that no friendly reception awaited him.

"Well, then, let him remain," said Guibald, carelessly; "but see that he is provided with water and food while I am within the castle."

The steward, having instructed one of the men near him to see to this, requested Guibald to follow him to the reception room.

"Follow?" cried Guibald, drawing himself erect, "follow? Am I not in my father's house? I know his study, and can proceed there alone."

The steward bowed.

"Your pardon," he said, "but days, nay, weeks ago, your father, Sir Guibald, instructed me that whenever you thought proper to make your appearance I was to announce you."

"Is that indeed so? Well, do as you have been bidden."

With another bow the steward departed.

In less than three minutes he returned.

"Sir Guibald will see you," he said; "pray proceed to the study."

"A nice reception for a son, by my faith!" muttered Guibald, as he went along the stone corridor leading to his father's study, his spurs ringing loudly on the pavement.

There was no door to the study, the entrance being covered simply by a pair of dark, heavy curtains.

Drawing these aside, Guibald entered, and doffing his cap, flung it on the floor.

Sir Guibald was seated in a carved, oaken chair by the table, which was covered with papers.

At his feet crouched a pair of huge bloodhounds.

He did not rise as his son entered, but placing down his pen and crossing his legs, he stared hard at Guibald.

There was no doubt that he was somewhat startled at the change his son had undergone in two years.

He never thought he would have grown, in that short time, into such a tall, muscular, and fine-looking youth.

But he did not betray any surprise.

In low, deliberate tones, he said—

"And so you *have* returned? I was thinking that, perhaps, after what you must have known has reached my ears, you would not have entered the castle again. I suppose you have come to ask my forgiveness?"

"I have not," replied Guibald, boldly, as he advanced a few paces and folded his arms across his broad chest, "and I was prepared for this reception."

"That is well."

"You are my father."

"Unfortunately, yes."

"Unfortunately?" cried Guibald, bitterly, "*unfortunately!* What a word for a father to use to his only son! But I thank heaven I have no mother to overhear you say so. That dear mother! I have heard of her goodness, but heaven snatched her from me. I never knew a mother's love—I never knew anything but a father's hatred. Why do you hate me so? You have hated me from my birth. I am certain of it."

"I am not compelled to give you any explanation. If I never hated you before, your conduct at Rome was sufficient to cause me to do so now."

"To say the most, 'twas all boyish folly."

"Not in my eyes. However, your conduct and the conduct of your companions has reached even the ears of his majesty, who is naturally indignant. I told him that you were no longer my son."

"Do you then, disown me?" cried Guibald.

"I do. And however you may beseech me to do so, I will never change my resolve."

"Beseech you? *I* beseech you? Never! I would rather die on the road-side than either beseech you not to disown me or beg from you so much as a crust that you would fling to those dogs."

"I admire a bold spirit, but you have not the means to sustain it."

"I will get them."

"How?"

"That shall be a matter for my future consideration."

"Hum! Well, of course I have expected that you would return one of these days, and I have had ready for you the sum of a thousand crowns. There is the bag by your side. Take it and trouble me no more."

Guibald reached out his hand and took the bag.

"Am I at liberty to do with this as I may think proper?" he asked.

"Of a surety. 'Tis thine. Do with it as thou wilt. But no more shall you have of me."

Guibald deliberately untied the string of the bag, and going to the window, opened it, and threw out the whole of the money.

It fell into the moat like a shower of rain.

Sir Guibald started to his feet with a loud cry of rage.

"Mad boy!" he shouted. "What have you done?"

"Given the money to the mud at the bottom of the moat."

"Away with you! Never more—not even if you were starving—would I bestow upon you so much as a single piece! Go! leave this castle, and never dare to enter it again. You are disowned and disgraced. Go! go! and take unto yourself another name, for mine you shall no longer bear."

"Fear it not," replied Guibald, picking up his cap. "I will never trouble you, and I *will* take another name. I have already one, and shall assume it at once."

"What is it?"

"JACK STRAW!"

"Ah, 'tis like thyself—common."

"No matter for its commonness. It is a name that you shall frequently hear, and shudder at."

"What then is your intention? To still further disgrace me?"

"That shall be *my* secret. I bid you farewell. This interview has convinced me that what I have often thought is right."

"And that is?" asked Sir Guibald; but his voice was low and trembling now.

"*That you are not my father!*"

A strange look overspread the face of the knight.

"Pshaw!" cried Sir Guibald. "Those are but the words of a lunatic. Begone!"

Without another word, Guibald turned, and strode haughtily from the room, and in less than another five minutes he had crossed the drawbridge, and was riding in the direction of the ruined abbey.

CHAPTER II.

WHAT TOOK PLACE AT THE RUINED ABBEY—THE DESPERATE FIGHT—JACK STRAW DRAWS HIS SWORD FOR THE FIRST TIME IN DEFENCE OF THE PEOPLE.

BASIL TREMAINE and Mark Trevor forded the river safely, and soon reached the ruins of the once noble abbey.

They drew rein before what had been its principal entrance, and seemed to be transfixed with wonder and admiration.

Certainly the scene which met their eyes was grand in the extreme.

The soft rays of the moon lit up the

right side of the abbey, showing the sadly broken and disfigured stained-glass windows.

Through the break in the massive stone walls the remains of the once grandly-carved marble pulpit were plainly seen, as also the wreck of the altar.

"Alas!" sighed Basil, "what ruin and desolation! Oh, that I had to deal with the caitiffs who thus destroy the noble edifices which are built for the worship of the Almighty. By the Blessed Virgin! none should escape me. Every one should be hung alive in chains for the foul birds of the air to feed on."

"Ay, ay," replied Mark, much touched at the sight, "'tis sad in the extreme! And observe the interior. How grand even the ruin is! Let us enter, Basil; Guibald said we should find plenty of room here. Let us enter and bring our horses with us."

"Good. They require rest."

The pair, dismounting, led their animals through the ruined entrance.

The sound of the iron hoofs of the horses was answered by a mournful echo, and more than one owl uttered a scream of dismay at being thus disturbed.

"See," said Basil, "here are the remains of what was the vestry. There is plenty of room here to stand the horses. As to their food and bed—well, we must wait for Guibald."

Having removed the heavy saddles from the animals—who immediately lay down—the two sat themselves on the ground in such a position that, by the aid of the moon, they could see each other, and commenced to talk of their prospects.

Half-an-hour passed away, and no sound had reached their ears but the hoot of the owl or the flapping of a bat against one of the pillars.

Suddenly, however, Basil leant forward.

"Hist!" he whispered, "I could swear I heard voices."

He was right.

As both listened, the sound of subdued voices in conversation reached their ears.

Then there was a sound as of the hurried tramp of several persons.

Looking through the doorway, the pair saw at the entrance about a dozen men.

One was clad in a long, dark cloak, and he was conversing with another attired as a monk.

The remainder, who were somewhat rough-looking fellows, and well armed, stood at a respectful distance.

"Eh!" whispered Basil; "what means this, I wonder? From the way they are conversing, it would seem that they are on some secret mission."

"List! we may, perchance, overhear what they say."

"My lord," said the monk, "I have only to once more assure you that all is properly arranged."

Basil pressed Mark's arm. "Didst hear that?" he whispered. "The one in the long cloak is addressed as 'my lord.'"

"And we are far away from any habitation, you say?" continued the cloaked stranger.

"We are, my lord. Even did she resist and shriek, as she may do when she discovers the imposture, her voice would not be heard."

"Good! I trust you as I ever did. Have you the links?"

"They are here."

And the monk took from beneath his robe two links.

"Then go to the altar, light the torches, and prepare your books. But, by the Virgin! what an altar! See, the moon's rays rest upon it. I much fear me that that will at least shock the nerves of Mistress Dorothy Leighton."

"Fear it not, my lord. See here"— and the monk produced a long, white cloth—"I will conceal it with this. Observe, that upon the front is an embroidered cross."

"I see it. Well, prepare. Ha—ha! Mistress Dorothy, never were you more deceived than you will be this night!"

The monk lit the torches and went down the ruined aisle towards the altar, while the individual he had addressed as 'my lord' went without, and seemed to be giving some instructions to his armed men.

"What think you of this?" asked Mark.

"'Fore heaven!" replied Basil, "an

unholy crime is about to be committed?"

"What crime?"

"It is evident, that that man attired as a monk, is no monk at all. I can see through the whole of this. There is to be a false marriage. Some unfortunate girl is to be brought here under the impression that she is to meet her lover. This man who is addressed as 'my lord' is, no doubt, an unsuccessful suitor."

"My own impression. And if she shrieks her voice cannot be heard—eh? We shall see that! What say you, Basil?"

"*We* shall hear her, I'll warrant me!" replied Basil. "And if foul play is intended, as I suspect, let them look to it."

"Unfortunately, there are four to one."

"No matter for that. I will not see an outrage committed without drawing my sword."

"Nay; nor will I. Let us wait. But I would Guibald were here."

"Well, he may be here ere it is too late."

"I trust so. I am not afraid of being opposed to more than one man, but I should feel safer with Guibald for a leader."

"You speak truly. But observe—the monk has spread his white covering over the altar and has placed a book upon it— Aye, and he has found a place for his links. He is a long way off, but— an' I make no mistake—there is a cunning smile upon his ugly face. And hark! I hear a murmuring—what means that?"

"His 'lordship,' whoever he is, is giving more hurried instructions to his men. Ha! something is advancing. Keep back in the shadow."

At this moment his "lordship," with all the men but one, entered the ruined edifice and concealed themselves in various recesses.

In a few seconds the sound of horses' hoofs was heard, and there came up to the entrance three riders.

Two were elderly men, and between them, almost completely enveloped in heavy wrappers, was a young and most beautiful lady.

The two elderly men dismounted, and assisted the lady to her feet.

The man his "lordship" had left came forward, and making a low bow, said—

"I pray you, Mistress Dorothy, to enter. As you observe, if you look, all is prepared."

The lady looked, and a startled cry escaped her lips.

"What, then, is this?" she asked, in trembling tones.

"Dartford Abbey."

"But 'tis in ruins! Do you tell me that Master Edmund intends to marry me *here*? I did not complain at the hour, but I dreamt not that I should be taken to such a place. Ha!" she cried; "where is he?—where is he? Edmund! Edmund! come and assure me that all is well."

"I assure you that all is well," replied the man. "Master Edmund is at the altar; pray follow me."

Gathering up her skirts, the lady followed.

When before the altar, a piercing cry left her lips.

Starting back, she said—

"Betrayed!"

The person who had been addressed as "my lord" stepped beside her, and in deliberate tones, said—

"Yes. Did I not tell you that a time would come? I swore that you should marry me, and you shall!"

"Never!" cried the lady, drawing herself erect; "never! Ah, my Lord Rochester—so far I see you are successful. Fool that I was to be so deceived by the letter, which was, no doubt, forged by your hand. And do you think that I will marry you? No."

"By the Blessed Virgin, I say you shall. Here all is in readiness."

"For a mock marriage, and in a ruined abbey. My lord, I see all plainly."

"'Twill be no false marriage. This man at the altar is—"

"A villain like yourself," interrupted Mistress Dorothy. "But to your followers, I appeal, as men, to let me depart in peace."

Rochester—for that young lord it certainly was—folded his arms and smiled grimly.

"You are here," he said; "and you do not depart hence except as my bride. Come forward to the altar, or I shall be compelled to make you."

"Oh, heaven!" cried Dorothy. "Am I then entirely abandoned by all? I will *not* come forward. Nay, sooner would I die a thousand deaths than consent to take part in such blasphemy. See!" she cried, as suddenly throwing back her cloak she snatched a dagger from her girdle, "I am armed, and if you attempt to seize me, I will drive this dagger into my heart!"

And she raised the glittering weapon aloft.

Hardly had the young girl drawn her dagger ere one of the men behind reached over her shoulder and seized her wrist.

Rochester darted forward and wrenched the dagger from her grasp.

"Fool!" he cried; "think you that I will be baulked? You *shall* be my wife. Come," he added, as he took Mistress Dorothy by the arm, and attempted to force her forward; "come to the altar."

"No," replied Dorothy. "Help! help!" she screamed; "is there no one who will rescue me?"

"No," replied Rochester, fiercely. "Come! No help is here—"

"It is false!" shouted a loud ringing voice; "help *is* here!"

And Basil, sword in hand, ran out of the vestry, followed by Mark.

"Let her go!" said Basil; "let her go, villain, or you die!"

"Who are you, fool, who dares to interfere with me?" asked Rochester, but without letting go of Dorothy's wrist.

"It matters not who we are. We have accidentally overheard what you said. We are of the common people, as you are pleased to call them. Let the lady go."

"Cut these wretches down!" yelled Rochester, as he swaggeringly drew his sword.

Instantly his men surrounded him; but Basil dragged Dorothy from him.

Seeing that help had come, the two men who had accompanied Dorothy, placed themselves by the side of Basil and Mark and drew their swords.

Rochester smiled, but it was a very faint and forced smile.

"Listen, robbers," he said, "for such from your attire I take you to be; to attempt to defend this lady is utterly useless. Those men you see before you are trained soldiers who, at my command, will hack you in pieces."

Basil replied with a loud laugh of derision.

"Trained or not," said Mark "they have no terrors for us. Take the lady," he added, to one of the men by his side; "we will cover your movements."

"Have at thee, madman!" cried Rochester, attacking Mark furiously. "Cut them down, I say; cut them down."

Rochester's men advanced.

"Stand firm!" cried Basil; "stand firm. Let us see what courage can do against cowardice. Ha!" he exclaimed, as the man he had attacked slipped. "Thy death lies at thine own door!"

With this he swung his heavy sword round his head and brought it down with fearful force on the man's skull.

With a deep groan he fell—never to rise again.

This had the effect of rousing the other men.

Uttering loud yells of rage they pressed closer to Basil and the two men—Dorothy's servants.

Poor Mistress Dorothy!

She had fled to one of the pillars, and crouching down beside it, placed her hands over her ears.

But the fight—the battle on her behalf—a battle being fought in her defence by utter strangers—had a kind of horrible fascination for her.

As Basil, with that one powerful sweep of his sword, cut down one of the men, she tried to shriek, but her tongue clove to the roof of her mouth.

Fiercer and fiercer became the fight.

Cries of mortal agony, mingled with the clash of steel, rang throughout the ruined building.

To add to the confusion, one of the links had gone out, so that the place was only faintly illuminated.

The monk still stood beside the altar. He seemed to be rooted to the spot.

His face was ashy pale, and he trembled in every limb.

Basil still fought on—his dagger in his left and his sword in his right hand.

But the two men who had accompanied Dorothy were now lying dead by his side, and across their bodies lay two of Rochester's men.

Rochester, who was an excellent swordsman, and Mark, had been fighting without a pause.

Both were wounded, but neither offered to give in.

Suddenly a loud clattering of horse's hoofs was heard, and a horseman, with a ringing shout, dashed into the building.

It was Guibald.

Without pausing he urged on his horse, then drawing his sword he cried—

"What ho! what means this?"

"Help us," cried Basil, at once recognizing the voice, "in heaven's name, help us!"

Guibald did not require to be urged twice.

Dashing forward, and raising himself in his stirrups, he brought his sword to bear upon Basil's opponents, and with such effect that in a moment two men were cut down.

The rest, seeing that to fight further would be absolute madness, turned and fled.

At this moment Mark had obtained the upper-hand of Rochester, and had stricken him down.

His arm was raised in the act of driving his sword through Rochester's heart, when Guibald stayed it.

"Hold!" he cried, "whom have we here? What is the name of the knave? I know nought of this quarrel, so prithee tell me what it means."

Basil did so, and as briefly as possible, concluding—

"And there is the lady."

"Come forth, mistress," said Guibald, "we are all thy friends."

Dorothy staggered forward without hesitation.

"What is thy name, lady?" asked Guibald.

"Dorothy Leighton, an it please thee, kind and brave sir."

"And yonder villain lying there is really the 'renowned' Rochester?"

"Ay, sir."

"And he would perform a mock marriage with you against your will, is that so?"

"It is, sir. He sent me a false letter —a letter which I thought came from my lover whom I have not seen for a length of time. That letter was a forgery."

"And whence came you, fair mistress?"

"From London."

"Good!"

Turning to Rochester he said—

"Rise, knave."

"Not at a robber's bidding," replied Rochester.

"Mark it well! Rise, and at once, or thou art a dead man."

Rochester, seeing the determined look on Guibald's face, slowly rose.

He was badly wounded, his cloak being covered with blood.

Guibald surveyed him steadily for a few moments, then he said—

"'Tis you who profess abhorrence of the common people, my lord?"

"I am not bound to answer you," replied Rochester, proudly.

"Nay, 'tis true thou art not bound to reply to me, but it will be better for you if you do. Answer me, and at once!"

"What, answer a boy like thee?"

"Trifle not with me, my lord. 'Tis true I am not much more than a boy in years, but if it were likely I should become a man like thee, I would choose to die now. Answer me—you profess abhorrence of the common people?"

"I will answer thee, because now I am powerless to do otherwise. Yes, I *do* hate the common people; and were the power to do so mine, I would crush them as I would crush a worm beneath my heel!"

"Your reply shows your true nature, my lord. You, like others I wot of, are a coward. But think not that you, and nobles like you, will in future be allowed to crush the people of this land. A champion will arise and will defend them."

Rochester smiled.

"A champion," he sneered; "what care we for champions? No champion that the people may select will have any terror for us. Bah! thy words are but the words of an ignorant and boastful youth."

"Not so. But list ye. For a moment I thought it would be as well to make an example of you. But I will not now do so. I will spare you awhile. There," said Guibald, pointing to the altar, " is the villain who was about to perform this unholy rite. Is that not so, my lord ? "

No answer.

" Is that not so, I say ? " thundered Guibald.

" It is."

" And you admit that not only is the hour of midnight a forbidden time for the performance of the marriage ceremony, but also that the ceremony was to have been a false one ? "

Again no answer.

" By the Holy Virgin ! " Guibald hissed, fiercely, " if you do not answer my questions, I will cleave thy lordly skull in twain."

" I admit it," said Rochester, in surly tones.

" 'Tis well," said Guibald, springing from his saddle. " An example shall be made of the knave who dares to stand beside an altar to perform a mock ceremony, when his face proclaims him to be, not one of the Lord's anointed, but a villain."

With these words he darted upon the supposed monk, and dragging him forward a few paces, snatched his robe from him.

He rent it in a dozen fragments.

Then he looked into the man's terrified face.

" Your name, villain ? " he asked.

" Rokeby Lynn," gasped the man.

" Are you a servant in the pay of this precious lord ? "

" I — I — came —" stammered the man.

" You are a servant—eh ? Yes ? 'Tis well. Out on you for a blasphemous wretch ! List ye ! For attempting to perform a fearful crime in what was once a sacred house of prayer, I pronounce sentence upon you."

Rochester laughed.

" Laugh not, my lord," said Guibald, " or I may pronounce sentence upon you. Lord Rochester, deliver up your sword and dagger."

His lordship hesitated a moment ; then, seeing that resistance would be useless, he handed his weapons to Mark.

Guibald now took from under his saddle two stout straps.

One of them he handed to Basil, saying—

" Tie his lordship's hands behind his back."

" I will not suffer this indignity ! " cried Rochester.

Guibald held the point of his sword to his breast.

" Tie his hands behind his back," he repeated ; " and if you move, my lord, I swear that I will send this good blade through your heart."

Basil soon completed the pinioning process.

" Now," said Guibald, " take this strap and tie *that* villain's hands behind him."

And he pointed to the supposed monk.

This operation was also quietly completed.

" Mercy ! " cried the man, " spare me ! spare me ! "

" You deserve no mercy from me," said Guibald. " Bring him this way, Basil."

" Oh, sir ! " cried Dorothy, rushing forward with clasped hands, " what would you do ? "

" Punish him."

" Spare him this once—spare him."

" Nay, fair lady, I will not spare him. But I do not mean to kill him. I pray you not to interfere with me."

With this Guibald walked towards the back of the altar.

Stooping down he inserted his hands in a huge, iron ring, and, exerting all his strength, pulled up a large flag.

A hole as black as pitch was revealed.

The supposed monk uttered a loud cry of horror.

" Do you intend to bury me alive ? " he said.

" Silence ! " replied Guibald, as snatching up what was left of the link, he held it aloft in his left hand, while with his right he held his sword within an inch of the man's back. " See, there is here a rope."

And he pulled one up from the hole.

" We will tie this about your body thus "—slipping a noose round the man's waist—" and we shall lower you down there, and then cut the rope."

Another howl of horror left the man's lips.

His cries for mercy might have been

called pitiful, but they made no impression upon Guibald.

Calling upon Basil to assist him, the monk was lowered into the hole.

Down, down he went, until he had dropped quite twenty feet.

The rope had run out, and with his sword Guibald cut the top.

"Now, my lord," he said, "that man is your servant, and, therefore, one of the common people. You will have to rescue him, or there he remains till the Judgment Day."

"How am I to rescue him?"

"I neither know nor care."

"Heartless wretch."

"Nay, *you* are the heartless wretch. You, my lord, are at liberty to remain here, or return whence you came."

With this Guibald seized the iron ring again, and dragged the stone to its position.

"I will remain here," said Rochester.

"Do so then. As for myself and my companions, we will return to London with this lady and see her safely to her home. Come, comrades."

Sheathing his sword, Guibald took his horse's bridle with one hand and gave his other to Dorothy.

When they reached the vestry, Guibald turned.

"I trust your lordship will not forget me," he said, "and if ever you hear the name of Jack Straw, remember that it is he who now speaks to you."

His lordship made no reply.

Sitting down on a block of stone he moodily watched the departure of Dorothy and her rescuers.

CHAPTER III.

THE ARRIVAL IN LONDON—JACK STRAW OVERHEARS A STRANGE CONVERSATION, AND, WITH HIS TWO COMRADES, OBTAINS POSSESSION OF ENORMOUS TREASURE—WHAT BECAME OF THOSE WHO WERE ABOUT TO SEIZE IT.

THE roads, in the days of which we write, were dreadful for travelling. The State never dreamt of putting them in repair.

Notwithstanding the fact that Jack Straw, his companions, and Dorothy Leighton were mounted on powerful and fleet animals, the party did not arrive in London until the afternoon of the following day.

When crossing London Bridge Jack Straw said—

"And now, Mistress Dorothy, tell me the exact whereabouts of thy residence."

"It is in the Strand, kind sir."

"Ah! the Strand. And what is thy father?"

"He is a goldsmith and jeweller to the Court."

"Then, if I mistake not, that is how Lord Rochester became acquainted with you?"

"It is."

"And your lover, Edmund?"

"Is one of our apprentices."

"Soh! I see, I see. 'Fore Heaven, he is a most fortunate youth. And you have not seen him for some time?"

"Nay; he was despatched on some private and urgent business by my father, but whither I know not."

"Is it likely he may now have returned?"

"I cannot tell."

"You will pardon me if I say that your love is not approved of by your father?"

"Such is the case. Alas! that it should be so."

"And when you received that letter you were under the impression that it was from him?"

"Ay, asking me to marry him secretly, because he has so often asked me, and I have consented."

"Take my advice then, gentle lady, and do not consent again. Secret marriages, I have heard say, generally end in serious complications. Two loving hearts are sure to come together in the end. But see here, we are now rapidly approaching the Strand. And since it would be as well if we were not seen, I would advise you to proceed to your father's house alone. You must lay all the blame on Rochester."

"That I will not fail to do, kind sir."

"And when you tell your lover of it do not fail to say that it was Jack Straw and his comrades who rescued you. The name of Jack Straw is not very well known at present, but it will be ere long."

At the commencement of the Strand, the three bade Dorothy adieu, and set off in search of a tavern in which to obtain refreshment and rest, which all three stood so greatly in need of.

They soon found a place.

It was called the "Three Bells," and stood on the spot where now stands Danes' Inn.

It was a rickety and tumble-down hostelry, and noted more for its dirt than its wine.

"Have you room for three men and three horses?" asked Jack Straw.

"Ay, or for a dozen, noble sir. We have bedrooms for fifty people, but as for the horses, they are generally placed in the stables."

"No doubt, no doubt. Well, then, my worthy host, do you order our horses to be at once placed in the stables. See that they are well supplied with good food, and in addition, what is quite as important, good beds."

"They shall be supplied as you direct —that is, if you have the money to pay the score when it is presented to you."

"Fear it not," returned Jack, as he took a bag from his pocket and clinked it upon the table. "The ring of this will inform you that we are well supplied, eh?"

"I am quite satisfied, your honours, and your animals shall be at once attended to by my orders, while I myself will attend upon your honours."

"And look you," said Jack, "have you a room containing three beds?"

"Ay."

"Then we will occupy that, for we always like to be together."

"Ay, ay. Well—ah! I had forgotten."

"What?"

"Well, you see, noble sir, I must tell you that this house is free to all comers with money."

"So it should be. Proceed."

"The room which contains the three beds is by the side of one which has been taken by four somewhat strange-looking characters."

"That will not matter to us."

"But, sirs, for all I know they may be robbers."

"Aye," laughed Jack, "they may be so of a surety, but what will *that* matter to us? We have sufficient only to pay for food and rest. If while we are asleep you fancy that they contemplate robbing us, your assurance that we are poor will quite satisfy them. Go, host, and lead the way."

Thereupon the host, having given his ostler the necessary instructions, took a key from a bunch hanging at his belt and led the way up a narrow flight of wooden stairs.

Pausing on the landing of the first floor, he inserted the key in the lock of the first door he came to, and throwing it open, said—

"That, gentlmen, is the room. Is it quite comfortable enough for you?"

"Yes, quite," answered Jack. "Send up the best refreshments you have at once."

"And when do you wish to depart, gentlemen?"

"Not until night, but we may stay until to-morrow morning. It all depends how we have rested."

The host bowed, and retired to prepare and send up the refreshments.

This took but a short time, and the three hungry and thirsty travellers proceeded to make short work of what was placed before them.

Very little conversation took place during the meal, and what was said was in whispers.

They could hear the sound of muttering, however, and concluded it came from the room occupied by the four persons of whom the landlord spoke.

But presently the mutterings took shape, and a word or two was very distinctly heard.

At last something reached them that caused Jack Straw and his companions to leap to their feet.

That something was "Rochester!"

"Hist!" whispered Jack, "don't move from where you now are. I will find out what connexions of Rochester's they are. Stay here."

"Nay, don't go," said Basil. "You know not in what den we really are. You may probably be killed if you are discovered."

"That I must risk. But something seems to tell me that Rochester will be somehow mixed up with my future career. I *must* find out what they have to do with him."

Seeing that it was useless to try to dissuade him further, Basil and Mark let him go.

Opening the door cautiously, Jack crept out, walked quickly along the passage, and soon found the door of the other room.

At the side of it was a deep recess—evidently a place used for depositing lumber. The voices were here quite distinct.

Into this Jack crept, and looking about him, saw that a few feet above was a small, round hole.

Carefully placing a barrel under it, Jack Straw applied his eye to the hole.

Imagine his great astonishment when he beheld four well-dressed men, of middle age, seated round a table, upon which, mixed up in a glorious and totally indescribable state of confusion, were a number of wine bottles and drinking liquors, dice, cards, and last but not least, several piles of gold pieces.

From their dress he immediately concluded that they were of the class known as swashbucklers.

"Oh, oh, my merry men," thought Jack, "ye certainly are carousing in magnificent style."

"*But*," cried one of the men, as he brought his fist down with violence upon the table, "since he failed to give us our own share we shall now *take* it. What say ye?"

A roar of assent was the answer from the other men, who banged down their fists upon the table in imitation of their comrade.

"What's the total amount of the treasure?" growled one.

"One hundred thousand marks."

"Oh, oh! a nice little sum, i' faith! Why, a quarter is a fine fortune for each of us."

"Yes. With it each of us can set sail for glorious Spain, and end our days in ease and contentment."

"A very fine resolve, my merry men," thought Jack. "That is if you can carry it out."

"Now, let me see," said the first speaker, as he drew forth a sheet of parchment and spread it upon the table; "this mark here is Blackheath, this is the copse to which the treasure was carried, and this is the tree under which it lies buried."

"Ay, ay! But you have not borne in mind the fact that Lord Rochester may already have carried it off."

"Fear it not. On the night when we lowered the bags down the hole and filled it in again, I placed a handful of oats near the surface. When I looked this morning they had taken root, and the blades were through the mould.

"Thus, there can be no doubt but that the treasure still lies where it was hidden."

"Ay, ay!" replied the others. "You speak truly. May the fiend take his lordship. *We* will have the money! And in good truth we have as much right to it as he has, seeing where it came from. It is a puzzler, though, what has become of Rochester."

"It is," said the man with the plan, "but we care neither where he is nor anything about him. When we have the money in our possession we shall be quite as rich as his lordship. So let's drink to our success."

Each man filled his horn, and raising it over his head, shouted "Success!"

They then drained the contents.

"Now," said the man who had first spoken, "let us consider. All we require are pickaxes and a spade. There are four bags, so that we can fasten one to each horse."

"At what hour do you propose lifting the treasure?"

"At midnight—so now to snatch a few hours' rest ere setting forth upon our journey."

Jack Straw waited to hear no more.

Descending from the barrel, he made his way back to his comrades, who were eagerly awaiting him.

By the look of his face they at once concluded that he had made an important discovery.

Drawing both close to him, he, in hurried tones, made them acquainted with all he had overheard.

They were astounded.

"What do you intend to do?" asked Basil.

"'STAND BACK!' CRIED THE LEADER, 'THE TREASURE IS OURS,'"

"Do? Obtain the treasure for ourselves."

"A right proper object. But you did not hear him say the precise position of the tree under which the treasure is buried?"

"Nay; but that matters not at all. We must rest for two hours only, and then, if we at once to horse, we shall reach Blackheath before them. We must conceal ourselves and watch their proceedings, and when they have brought the bags to the top, pounce upon them, and take them away from them."

Basil and Mark laughed outright at this daring proposal.

"There are four to three," Jack said; "but leave it to me, and all will be well. Now, as I have said, we must obtain a little rest and—"

"As for me," interrupted Basil, as he commenced to impatiently pace the apartment, "I can obtain no rest until this vast treasure is in our hands. 'Fore heaven, it seems as though such a thing must be but a wild dream. Nay, I cannot rest."

"Nor I," said Mark.

"For my part, I could rest very well," said Straw; "but since you say you cannot, why I will keep company with you. We will sit and partake—moderately—of the wine, and draw up our plans for the future. I will also tell you all about the interview with Sir Guibald, and will explain to you why I have arrived at a certain conclusion with respect to my parentage, and why I have resolved in the future to adopt the name of Jack Straw and no other."

*　　*　　*　　*

As soon as darkness had set in, the horses were ordered.

Jack was careful to ascertain whether the four men had gone, and finding that they had not, he felt well satisfied that he, Basil, and Mark would be at Blackheath long before them.

Blackheath!

What a long string of historical events that heath calls up before one!

At the time of this history, Blackheath, and the country for many miles around it, was nothing but a wild wilderness of black brushwood and large clumps of tall poplars and fir trees, and it was interspersed with narrow, deep and muddy little canals, many of which were hidden from view by tall grass and rushes.

It was close upon the hour of eleven ere Jack Straw and his comrades reached the Thames.

"We are opposite now," said Jack, looking about him; "but, on my soul, I know not how we are to cross. Ha, yonder is a boat. Dismount."

All dismounted.

Jack Straw went down the bank a few yards, where lay a large wherry, with two men standing in the bows.

"What ho!" cried Jack. "We want a boat."

"Well, we did not say ye did not," growled one of the men.

"And would hire yours."

"It is already hired."

"Hum," thought Jack, "it is evident, I should say, that the four men have hired it."

"Well, friend," he said aloud, "can you tell me how we may cross?"

"Marry, I cannot. There is no way of crossing except by boat or fording. But," he added, "a few yards off there is a raft which will hold a goodly burden, yet it would be dangerous to cross without an experienced hand to guide it."

"I will pay you well if you will undertake the task."

"Nay, young sir," replied the man, shaking his head; "we have been paid to remain here, and here we *must* remain."

"As that is so I must try my own hand at guiding a raft. Where is it?"

"Yonder."

And the man pointed to a large black-looking object, floating on the water a short distance from him.

Jack approached it, waded into the water, scrambled on to it, and closely inspected it.

"It looks a powerful raft," he thought, "and quite capable of sustaining the weight of three horses and men. Yet no doubt it will be dangerous to attempt. Bah! No time must be lost in idle thought. There is the treasure to be thought of, and by my faith! if I can get it I will. To secure such a right noble sum, a little danger is nought."

Seizing hold of the long hook, he

drew his sword, and severed the rope which held the raft fast to the shore; and then, plunging the hook into the water, he pushed the raft into the middle of the river.

Now running to the other end, he, with might and main, worked the raft with great swiftness through the water, and gained his object.

The other end of the raft went with a rush on to the shore.

"Now," cried Jack, "lead the horses, while I hold the raft. Quick!"

Basil and Mark led the horses down, and Jack, taking each by the bridle, led them on.

At first they were somewhat terrified, but a little patting and words of encouragement soon made them quiet.

"Now," said Jack, "you two keep close at their heads. Are you ready?"

"Ay, ay!"

"Good! Then away!"

With this, Jack once more seized the hook and plunged it into the water.

In another moment the raft was slowly moving off in the direction of the other side of the river.

It was a lucky thing that Jack Straw was possessed of enormous strength, and plenty of coolness and courage.

Time after time the raft swung round with such frightful velocity as almost to send the whole of them off their feet.

When near the shore, Jack gave the raft an extra push, let go the hook, ran to the other end of the raft, and taking the rope, sprang ashore.

While he held the rope, Mark and Basil led off the horses.

But, when that had been safely completed, Jack let go the rope.

"Ho!" cried Basil, trying to plunge after it. "The raft will be lost."

"Never heed it," laughed Jack. "There are plenty more rafts in the river. That one will be an addition to the German Ocean. Come!"

Each sprang into the saddle, and at once prepared to push on.

"As I live!" cried Jack, looking back, "we are none too early; for see, four horsemen are speaking to those in the boat."

Such was the case.

"That is bad," said Basil, "for they may be suspicious. We shall follow them, or how are we to know the whereabouts of the treasure?"

"I am ready for that," said Jack. "We must dismount again, and lead the horses. See yonder dense wood? In that we must hide. Fortunately, the moon is not at its full, so we have not much chance of being discovered."

The three thereupon dismounted and walked their horses, Jack leading the way.

They soon reached the centre of a clump of fir trees. It was perfectly dark here.

"Now let us remain," said Jack. "At any rate they must pass near here."

Twenty minutes went by, and no sound had reached their ears.

At last, however, they heard loud voices in conversation.

"They come!" said Jack.

He was wrong.

Up a narrow path, and at a good round pace, came three horsemen, whom from their attire Jack at once recognised as men in the king's guard.

It was evident that they were bent on some important arrest, and they soon passed out of sight.

"I could have sworn they were the men we— Hist!"

Another sound met their ears from an opposite direction.

The sound of horses' hoofs.

Then four riders rode up to within a few feet of where Jack and his comrades were concealed.

They were the four men Jack had seen at the "Three Bells."

Jack and his friends were on the track of the treasure at last!

Jack mounted his horse, stood upon the saddle, and watched them until they were lost to view.

"Come," he said, "I see the direction they have taken, but we had better lead the horses."

Along the path went the three. They moved cautiously for fear of a surprise, and, moreover, they found that they had to keep a careful watch upon their footsteps; for, as we have before remarked, the place was full of little hidden canals.

At last they came out into the open, and Jack went forward.

"I see them," he said. "They are now crossing a horsepond by the side of what looks like a dismal copse. In the centre of it is a huge tree. That must be the one mentioned. Now we will lead our horses right round, and come on them from the opposite side."

This, after some difficulty, was accomplished, and the three found themselves within forty feet of the four men.

The thick, damp grass had prevented their footsteps from being overheard.

"Hold the horses," Jack said, "and I will go forward and watch. When you hear me shout, run to me at once. And, above all things, keep your swords loose in their scabbards."

The men had commenced digging as Jack crept close to them.

And they worked with a will too.

So hard, indeed, that the perspiration began to pour down their faces in torrents.

"There is a great mystery in connection with this money," Jack thought. "I wonder where Lord Rochester got it from? Well, it matters but little to me."

Clash! clash! went the picks, and thud! thud! went the spades.

Suddenly a thought struck Jack.

Sinking upon his stomach he crawled to where stood the four horses, and taking out his dagger he cut the saddle bands of each, removed the saddles, and one by one dropped them gently into a narrow, muddy ditch.

Then he returned to the men, who for several more minutes, continued digging.

Suddenly one cried out—

"Hold! here is the first."

Each man dropped his implement, and stooping, they dragged up a goodly-sized and weighty bag.

In a few more seconds another came to light, and was lifted to the edge of the pit they had made, then a third and a fourth.

A cry of delight escaped the men's lips.

"And now," said he who evidently acted as leader—"now that we have worked so long, and so laboriously, let us partake of some well-needed refreshment. Here, my merry men," taking a flask from his pocket, "drink. It will put fresh life into your veins."

He was about to take the first pull himself, when Jack came forward.

"Hold!" he shouted, drawing his sword—"hold, ye robbers!"

Instantly the flask fell with a loud crash to the ground, and the men, starting back, snatched their swords from their scabbards.

"Who cries hold?" asked the leader.

"I!"

"Who are you?"

"One who knows that you are taking away that which does not belong to you. Thieves! that treasure belongs to Lord Rochester."

"And what if it does?"

"I tell you to replace it, or go and leave it just as it is."

"A likely thing. You had better be off, young sir, or, whoever you are, we will make short work of you, and leave you in yon pit."

"Ho!" cried Jack. "Ho! come forward."

Mark and Basil at once joined him.

"The horses!" cried the leader, frantically—"the horses!"

Two of the men ran round, seized the animals, and brought them to the edge of the pit.

Then it was that they saw the saddles were gone.

Uttering loud cries of astonishment and consternation, they endeavoured to lift the bags.

But before they could do so Jack Straw and his companions stood before them.

"Let them alone!" roared Jack. "Let them alone, I say!"

"Never!" cried the leader. "Stand back! stand back! The treasure is ours, and we will defend it with our lives."

"I warn you that, if you do not at once seek safety in flight, you shall *lose* your lives."

"Stand on your guard, companions," roared the leader, flourishing his sword. "Death before being deprived of our treasure!"

"Death!" replied his companions.

Jack Straw snatched his dagger—a long-bladed one—from his girdle, and flung himself with terrific fury on the leader.

Basil and Mark followed, and soon a fierce and terrible fight raged over what, in those days, was considered a mighty treasure and vast fortune.

The four men were somewhat heavy fellows, and certainly powerful; and they were experienced in the use of the sword.

On this occasion they wielded their weapons with great fierceness and determination, but it soon became evident in whose favour the battle would turn.

Jack and his companions were lithe, active young fellows, and thoroughly versed in the use of arms, which the four swashbucklers soon found to their dismay.

They seemed to be here, there and everywhere at one and the same moment.

Fiercer and fiercer became the fight.

The clash of steel could have been distinctly heard far away over that wild and gloomy-looking heath.

Suddenly the leader shouted out—

"Make short work of them! Spare not one of them. Oh!" he yelled, as just as the last words had left his his lips, Jack cut off his sword hand fair at the wrist; the next instant our hero's dagger was buried to the haft in his breast, and the leader fell with a loud thud into the pit he had so recently assisted in digging.

There was a pause for a moment, and only a moment.

With redoubled fury the fight was resumed.

Though, so far, Jack Straw had escaped, Basil and Mark had not been so fortunate.

Each was wounded, though not desperately.

Having disposed of his opponent, Jack assisted his comrades, and soon two more of the men lay dying by the side of the pit.

One man only was now left, and he was grievously wounded.

Jack advanced to him, but the man lowered his sword.

"I cry you mercy," he said. "I would fight you, but I am too weak."

"Mercy you shall have," replied Jack; "but on one consideration."

"Name it."

"That you divulge the name of the person to whom this vast treasure belongs."

The man hesitated.

"I thought you knew," he said. "Are you not a friend of Rochester?"

Jack laughed.

"*I* a friend? Nay," he said. "Who could be a friend of Rochester, I should like to know?"

"Then, young sir, perhaps you will tell me how you came to know of the whereabouts of this treasure, and also how you knew that we were about to get possession of it?"

"Nay, nay," replied Jack, "'tis I who will ask questions, not you. To whom does this treasure rightly belong?"

"To the king."

"To the king! To the *king*, say you?"

"Ay, to the king."

"By our Blessed Lady! Who could have dreamt that? Then, pray, how did Rochester obtain possession of it?"

"Ah, how!" replied the man. "Methinks I may as well resume the fight, and be killed like my companions; for, did I tell you, and you were to inform upon me, it would not be long ere my carcase hung in various parts of the city."

"I swear I will not inform upon you, my friend. Come, speak the truth, and mark you, if you will agree to join me, you shall have a fair share of the booty."

"Rochester had charge of a litter bringing this amount to the Royal treasury at Greenwich. Now, of course, you know that Rochester is a somewhat poor—"

"Bah!" interrupted Jack, "I know nought of his poorness. I have heard of him as a grinder down of the poor, and *know* him as a great knave."

"Ay, ay. You are not far out there, young sir. Well, as I have said, Rochester was entrusted with the charge of this treasure. Two horses carried it, and it was guarded by two of the Royal troops."

"And where was Rochester?"

"Within the litter."

"Go on."

"Previous to his departure Rochester called on us, and arranged that we were to surprise the litter when crossing this heath, slay the men in charge, and then bury the bags until a favourable opportunity came for dividing the spoil."

"On my life, a nice courtier is Lord Rochester. One of his majesty's most faithful servants, in very truth! But go on."

"We did as he directed. We attacked the litter, slew the men in charge, and buried the treasure. Finding that his lordship made no attempt to settle with us ·we determined to take the lot."

"A wise plan, ha! ha! The next time you arrange to get possession of a booty be sure you are not overheard."

The man started.

"Where could we have been overheard?" he said.

"That I cannot tell you," replied Jack. "But you *were* overheard, hence our appearance."

"And you offer me a share?"

"On consideration that you join me—yes."

"But I know not to whom I am speaking. Are you and your companions men of the highway?"

"Nay. That is, not yet. Probably we shall have to be so—more or less—in order to keep up appearances. I will tell you who I am. Would you have me tell you?"

"Yes."

"Well, then, I am one who is acquainted with the wrongs of the poor. I have heard their cries; and though I myself come of a noble family, yet I have resolved to draw the Sword of Freedom in defence of the people. Mine be the task to lead and to guide; and in the days to come, when peace and prosperity are restored, many will remember him who fought for them with such determination—whose name was simply Jack Straw!"

To this speech, the man listened, and when Jack had concluded, he seized both his hands and pressed them upon his heart, and in a voice full of emotion, said—

"With all my heart and soul will I join you! Some years ago I owned a farm near the Royal Palace at Windsor, and out of the profits of it I maintained my poor old father and mother. The property belonged to the king, but its management was placed in the hands of Earl Stanhope. This cruel lord imposed fearful taxes, I was unable to pay, and the consequence was that one day, just after my departure to London, where I was to stay a week, my parents were thrust from the home. When I returned I discovered they had been found dead—locked in each other's arms—in Windsor Forest."

"Fear it not," said Jack, grimly; "you shall have your revenge. Such fiendish acts are punished sooner or later, and your time shall *come*. Now let us away. But, first, to bury these unfortunate men."

The four set to work, and in a short time the three men were laid in the pit and covered up.

The saddles belonging to the four horses were then brought up and replaced on the animals.

Jack selected the strongest horse, and on him were tied two of the bags, and two others had one bag each. Thus there was one horse for the man Jack had spared.

In a few moments the whole four were mounted.

"One moment," said Jack. "You have forgotten to tell us your name."

"Ay, ay," said the man; "well, my name is simply Simon Sampson."

"A mighty strong name, too. Now, are ye all ready?"

"Ay," replied Basil; "but whither are we bound?"

"To Dartford. This is Blackheath, and somewhere there is the main road. If we reach that, Dartford is in a straight direction."

"Follow me," said Simon, "and I will lead you straight to it."

CHAPTER IV.

ELIAS LEIGHTON, THE "STRAND MISER"—THE SCENE IN THE BULLION
VAULT, AND THE ABDUCTION OF DOROTHY LEIGHTON.

AT the time of this history the houses in the Strand were few and far between, and business was carried on in a very careless way.

The tradesman who was known to be the most wealthy, was Elias Leighton, who was called the "Strand Miser."

In about the centre of his house—a rickety, tumble-down wooden structure —was fixed a hand holding a mallet as if about to strike.

This sign showed that the proprietor was a goldsmith.

Elias had been a goldsmith in the Strand for many long years, and, besides that, he was one of the Court jewellers.

He was not a money-lender, unless the interest was enormous ; but he was frequently heard to chuckle over the large amount the king owed him.

On one occasion, when he had an interview with the king, his majesty had said—

"You are a right worthy citizen, Master Leighton, and your daughter, 'tis said, is a beauty. Well, fear it not. Ere long she shall be presented to us, and shall take her place in our Court. So keep your eyes open, friend Leighton, and I will see what can be done in the way of a titled husband for your daughter."

This, delivered in the king's most gracious manner, gladdened the heart of the ambitious goldsmith ; and he was about to tell the king that he thought Rochester was smitten with his daughter's charms, but, after a moment's consideration, he thought he would delay it.

And it was well he did.

His daughter's account of how Rochester was about to force her into a mock marriage, at once kindled in the breast of the goldsmith a bitter hatred against Rochester, and he swore that he should never have the chance of again seeing her.

Yet he could not forget that his daughter had left her house, as she confessed, with the intention of being secretly married to his apprentice, Edmund Gaston.

The first thing the goldsmith did was to lock up his daughter in her room.

When Edmund returned—which he did two days after Dorothy, the goldsmith treated him to a long lecture, in which he was pleased to point out that it was utterly ridiculous for Edmund to think of ever marrying Dorothy.

"You are penniless," he said, "while Dorothy will, at my death, be worth an enormous fortune. I intend her to marry a title."

"But, sir," replied Edmund, "I cannot see how a titled gentleman will marry a tradesman's daughter."

"Eh, you cannot see it? Money, my son, dispels all differences of rank ; and, besides, the king will find Dorothy a husband. So, there, there—no more of the matter. Your road and Dorothy's lie wide apart. All that you have to do is to attend to your business, and one day you may be rich enough to cut a respectable figure."

Dorothy remained in her room a week, carefully watched by the old housekeeper ; and Edmund had no opportunity of communicating with her.

One night, however, Edmund caused a note to be sent to the goldsmith, setting forth that his presence was required in connection with his business at Whitehall.

The goldsmith at once obeyed the summons.

The next thing Edmund did was to send the housekeeper off on a wild-goose chase.

Thus, the two being out of the way, the road was clear.

Upstairs went Edmund at once.

Knocking at the door, he whispered—

"Dorothy."

"Who calls ? Surely that voice is Edmund's ?"

"It is, darling—it is Edmund. Open the door, beloved, and let us pass at least one blissful hour ere your father returns."

"Is my father not at home?"

"No."

Dorothy at once opened the door, and the lovers were clasped in each other's arms.

That happy meeting—that happy hour they passed!

The last hour on this earth!

It was close upon the hour of ten when the old housekeeper suddenly burst into the room.

"Caught," thought Edmund, "and she will tell the goldsmith."

But, as it seemed, the old woman did not appear astonished at what she saw.

Her face was deathly pale, and the muscles of her mouth worked convulsively.

Seizing Edmund by the arm, she gasped out—

"Robbers are in the house!"

"Robbers!" repeated Edmund, incredulously. "Nay, that cannot be, since I have myself seen to the fastenings of the house."

"I tell you 'tis so. Not long since, when looking from the window at the back, a shadow crossed my path. I took no notice of it, but in a few moments another shadow glided past, then another and another, until there were four. I watched and listened. Soon a strange noise fell upon my ears, and I knew that, by some means or other, robbers—for they can be nothing else—had gained an entrance. At this very moment they are in the vaults."

"What!" cried Edmund. "In the vaults, say you?"

"Ay, in the vaults. Quick, my son. Save your master's property, and trust to it he will reward thee with Dorothy's hand."

Edmund turned swiftly.

"One second, dear Edmund," gasped Dorothy. "For my sake be careful of your life."

"Fear it not," said Edmund, hastily kissing Dorothy. "For your dear sake I will not recklessly risk my life."

Rushing to the goldsmith's room, he snatched from over the fireplace a heavy sword, and lighting a link, he held it over his head and commenced to descend the narrow stone stairs which led to the vaults.

It was a long and tortuous passage, and black, slimy, and slippery in the extreme.

Every now and then Edmund paused and listened.

Could the old woman be mistaken?

Was it possible that what she saw was seen in a dream?

It looked like it.

Suddenly a loud noise, as of the clanking of heavy chains, fell upon his ears.

"Who is there?" cried Edmund, in loud tones. "Who is there? Speak."

Lower and lower he went, and as he descended the more he became convinced that several men were below, and from the dense smoke which came circling up the stairs, it was evident that they were burning three or four links.

Just as Edmund reached the bottom, some words were uttered in low, deep tones—tones which froze the very marrow in his bones.

He recognised to whom they belonged.

"Speak!" thundered Edmund. "Speak, robbers! Why are ye here?"

The last word had barely left his lips, ere the torch he carried in his left hand was dashed to the ground.

A brilliant light now burst upon the scene, and Edmund saw before him, not four, but six masked men, each carrying a drawn sword in his hand.

Not a word was uttered by any of them.

Only for a moment did Edmund pause.

Drawing his dagger from his girdle, and keeping it with an iron grip in his left hand, he attacked the man nearest him with terrific fury.

The passage was too narrow for him to be surrounded.

The man Edmund attacked was a big, burly fellow, but roused to desperation, Edmund was more than his match.

Getting close to him he raised his heavy sword, and brought it down with all his might upon the man's head.

The blow clove his skull in twain,

and, with a gurgling cry, he fell upon his face—dead.

With one foot upon his body, Edmund commenced to attack the next, and he soon got an opportunity of delivering a blow upon the fellow's body.

The man fell, to all appearance grievously wounded.

Little did Edmund dream that this was arranged during the fight with the first man. But so it was.

Leaping over his body, Edmund commenced to attack the next man.

It is certain that he would have made short work of him had he been allowed so to do.

While hotly engaged with him, the man whom Edmund supposed to be mortally wounded crawled to his feet, drew his dagger, and creeping close to Edmund raised it aloft.

"Die, dog!" he hissed.

Down came the dagger, and it was buried to the hilt in poor Edmund's back.

A deep groan left his lips as, staggering back, he leaned against the wall and fixed his eyes upon a man—the tallest of them all—at the end of the passage.

"Ah!" he gasped, "I thought I could not be mistaken. You are Lord Rochester. I knew your voice. Oh, that I could have got you within reach of my arm! Holy Virgin! I am dying, dying! Assassin! Cowardly assassin! Though your arm did not strike the blow yet you are the guilty one, and Heaven will punish you."

"A long time ago you defied me," said Rochester—for Rochester it certainly was—"and I swore that your life should pay the forfeit."

"Robber!"

"Not so. To enter these vaults was but a ruse to get you within my grasp. The gold shall remain untouched. Your death was all I asked for—it will take place in but a few moments, and, despite all, Dorothy Leighton will yet be mine!"

The mention of Dorothy's name once more roused Edmund.

Raising his sword he staggered forward.

But the effort was too much for him.

With a wild, bitter cry he fell face downwards upon the ground.

"He is dead," said Rochester, "but we had better make sure."

"What shall we do?" asked one of the men.

"Had I better drive my sword through his heart?" said another.

"No, no! He has already a dagger in his back. Turn him over."

Edmund was turned upon his back.

His eyes were closed, his form was rigid.

Certainly he looked a dead man.

Rochester looked into his face for a few moments, then he said—

"He is dead, sure enough. Good! He, at least, will trouble me no more."

"Since we have done what you required," said one of the men. "I suppose we may help ourselves to what the vault contains?"

"No, *no!* I tell you. I have said several times that I will handsomely reward you all, and I will. Now for the— Ha! see, she comes."

Down the stairs a white figure, holding a small lamp, was gliding.

It was Dorothy.

Despite the terrified expression upon her face, she looked gloriously beautiful.

Rochester with his own hand extinguished the torches, so that the passage was in darkness.

"Edmund," cried Dorothy, "where are you? Oh, speak, if you love me, speak!"

No answer came.

"Oh, Heaven!" moaned Dorothy, as she entered the passage and held aloft the lamp, "what is the meaning of this silence? Methought I but this moment saw a light. Edmund, dear Edmund, where are you?"

At this moment her foot touched the body of the man Edmund had first stricken down.

Uttering a wild cry she started back.

"Ha! heaven!" she cried, "murder has been done. Edmund has been murdered!"

"Not so," said a deep voice, "he was killed in fair fight."

"Killed!" repeated Dorothy, with a piercing shriek. "Dead! dead! Oh, my heart! my heart! And you—you who speak—his murderer?"

"Nay, one who loves you; who has come to take you hence; who will live only to fulfil your every wish."

And Rochester stepped forward.

Dorothy raised the lamp, and for an instant scanned his features.

There was a pause—an awful pause of a few moments.

Such a terrible look was upon Dorothy's face, that, even the men, scoundrels though they were, gazed at her in astonishment and admiration.

They looked at the parted lips, the dilated nostrils, the scornful eyes and the heaving breast, and wondered what she was about to say.

Presently she said in low, trembling tones—

"I am not dreaming! This is not some hideous nightmare? No! no! Once again, and in my own father's house, I am face to face with the ruffian Rochester."

"A dainty, pretty speech to make, on my faith!" replied Rochester, with a sneer. "Very pretty for a maiden. Such lips should never be opened to let such words pass."

"I am aware that whatever words I may utter would fall on ears which would heed them not. And so *you*, my Lord Rochester, are the murderer of my lover?"

"I did not say so."

"No, but I feel that you are. You say he is killed; let me look upon his dead body, and so satisfy myself."

"Nay, such sights should not greet a lady's eyes. He is dead, that I swear."

"Coward, coward! I know why you and your hired bravos are here, my lord. But mark it well, the king shall hear of this, and your punishment will follow. Oh, that I had a dagger! My abduction should never be effected. Ha! what is this?"

Her eyes had rested upon a blood-stained sword at her side.

She was about to seize upon it, but Rochester caught her arm.

The next instant a cloak was thrown over her head.

Scream after scream escaped her lips, but they were soon stifled.

Two men seized her, and poor Dorothy was carried upstairs.

"This time she shall not escape me," muttered Rochester. "And, fortunately, the old man will not know that her disappearance has anything to do with me."

The lamp one of the men had snatched from Dorothy burned with a feeble flicker upon the ground.

Rochester looked at it a moment, but he passed up the stairs without extinguishing it.

Yes, the lamp burned very feebly, but its feeble rays revealed a terrible scene—a scene sufficient to appal the stoutest heart.

The old housekeeper, paralysed with terror, watched the villains as they brought their horses up, and, mounting them, rode off.

Her heart told her that the muffled figure they carried between them was Dorothy, and that her master's apprentice lay cold in death downstairs.

From the window she watched for the return of the goldsmith.

The minutes slowly dragged themselves along. Lower and lower burned the lamp in that blood-stained passage.

Suddenly a deep groan echoed along it.

The figure of Edmund Gaston moved. Once, twice, thrice! The eyes opened, the lips parted, and another groan left them.

Edmund Gaston was not dead, though the hand of death was fast settling down upon his pale brow.

"Water," he moaned, "water! Oh, for one drop of water to moisten my parched lips! Dying! There is no hope for me—no hope! Dying, and so young, too! Oh, that I had someone to avenge me! Who could avenge me? Ah, heavens, I have it! He who wrested Dorothy from Rochester's grasp. His name—his name? Jack Straw! Ay, Jack Straw. But my strength fails me, I am sinking fast. If I could but write a few words, the goldsmith would see that it reached the hands of this strange youth. But I have no pen."

Once again his head dropped, and for some few seconds he was lost in thought.

Suddenly he raised himself, and by a great effort turned himself over.

Then he crawled to the lamp, seized it, and placed it by the door of the vault.

Now slowly, painfully, he dragged himself within the vault, and placing his hand upon the handle of the drawer of a small cabinet, he pulled it open.

It was full of rolls of parchment.

Taking one, he slowly crawled back with it.

Stretching it upon the ground, he placed his finger in a little pool of blood, and after a great deal of labour he traced these words—

"I am dying. By Lord Rochester's instructions I have been assassinated. Dorothy told me all about Jack Straw, and upon him I call to avenge my death. Dearest Dorothy, farewell !
        "EDMUND GASTON."

His strength failed him directly he had signed his name, and as he fell back, with the parchment in his hand, the lamp went out.

Alone and in darkness, but with the parchment in his grasp which showed who was responsible for his death, Edmund Gaston died.

CHAPTER V.

SHOWS HOW JACK STRAW PAID A VISIT TO THE ROYAL PALACE AT GREEN-WICH—HIS INTERVIEW WITH THE KING ON THE TERRACE, AND WHAT THE KING SAID TO HIM.

TWO weeks passed away, and during that time Jack Straw had made himself so notorious, that his name and his daring deeds began to be spoken of all over the country.

The poor began to idolise him—the rich to curse him for his extraordinary audacity.

Jack Straw—who had purchased the old Blackfoot Castle, a mile distant from Dartford—and his companions, who now numbered at least a score, made themselves masters of the road between Blackheath and Canterbury, and they levied a tax on every traveller of importance who happened to pass.

Owing to his superior education, this wonderful youth was looked up to by his companions as a fit and proper leader.

Though Jack was of a kindly and very generous disposition, he was very strict and stern as regards his orders.

Whatever he commanded to be done, those who had joined him knew he would see carried out.

Blackfoot Castle, which, as we have said, Jack Straw had chosen as the residence of himself, was a noble pile.

It was built of solid stone, and was surrounded by a deep moat.

It was a somewhat gloomy-looking place on the outside, and no less gloomy was it within when the fires were extinguished, for the lower portion of it was full of narrow, vaulted passages, secret doors, and treacherous wells.

One fine morning Jack caused the horn to be sounded an hour earlier than usual.

It instantly brought Mark and Basil to his side.

"List ye," said Jack. "I am about to depart on a short journey, and shall be absent probably the whole day. In your charge I leave the castle and our comrades. Do not, on any account, quit the place. Towards evening have the banqueting-room well prepared. To-night I can promise you all a magnificent repast."

"We always have magnificent repasts," laughed Basil.

"Yes, that is true. But on this occasion it shall be a repast off Royal venison."

"What mean you ?" asked Mark, starting. "You surely do not mean that you are about to visit the Royal palace ? "

"Of a truth I do. I am going to have an audience with the king."

"Impossible ! "

"Not at all."

"An audience would not be granted you. Nay, 'tis likely enough that if the king heard your name, he would give instructions for your instant arrest."

"No doubt he would, if he were told who I was by anyone, but I will tell the king myself who I am. At any rate, I am resolved, and will run the risk of any danger that may threaten."

"But," said Mark, "the reason you seek an audience ? "

"To speak with him respecting that which is nearest my heart. To speak to him of the wrongs of the people, and get his promise to redress them."

Both Basil and Mark shook their heads very gravely.

"Heaven knows the object you seek is praiseworthy," said Basil, "but even if fortune so favoured you that you got an audience of his majesty, your words, however skilfully delivered, would assuredly fall on deaf ears."

"That I must risk. Fortune *does* favour me, and I am certain that it will so far favour me this day that I shall speak with the king."

"Then there is no persuading you not to undertake this dangerous journey?"

"There is not."

"And you will have no attendant?"

"Yes, one."

"We recommend you to take with you Simon Sampson."

"Nay, I shall not need his services. The only one I shall take with me will be Egbert."

Both Mark and Basil uttered a cry of astonishment.

"You are surely jesting?" said Basil.

"Nay, I was never more serious."

"Oh, Jack!" cried Mark, "will it not be wrong to subject him to such danger?"

"Nay, where I go he goes. Ask him which he had rather do—stay here or go with me."

"That would be useless, seeing that he loves you so well."

"Well, then, that— Ha! yonder he is. He is coming this way. What ho, Egbert, what ho!"

In a few moments they were joined by the object of their conversation, Egbert—he had no other name.

He was a youth of about nineteen, with a beautiful face, remarkably feminine in look.

This womanly appearance was considerably heightened by his large, almond-shaped, jet black eyes; his two rows of small, pearly white teeth, and his long, thick, wavy black hair.

Added to this he had a figure of striking gracefulness, which was set off to great advantage by the tight-fitting hose he wore.

His head-dress consisted simply of a small cap, in which was placed a single white feather.

His arms were a short sword and small poignard.

"Egbert," said Jack, "I am about to visit the Royal palace. Will you go with me?"

"Willingly," replied Egbert, joyfully. "But pray—an it is a fair question—what is the object of your visit? Is it to the king himself?"

"It is."

"To be knighted?" queried Egbert, with a merry laugh.

"Holy Mary! no. I would not be knighted under any circumstances; but I will tell you more of my errand anon. Get yourself ready at once. We depart in an hour."

In much less than an hour the pair were ready and mounted—Jack Straw upon an immense jet black horse, Egbert upon a small white one.

The pair formed a curious and striking contrast.

Egbert's attire was altogether different from Jack's. Mounted and ready for the journey, Egbert only carried, besides his sword and dagger, a light crossbow and a small quiver of arrows.

These hung at his saddle.

Jack Straw wore a doublet of Kendal green, a small cap with a heron's feather stuck in it, and boots of French leather, which fitted closely to his legs, and ascended above the knee.

His arms were a long, broad-bladed sword—which weapon he, being of prodigious strength, as we have before remarked, could wield with terrible effect—a long poignard, and, attached to his saddle, a heavy, glittering battle-axe.

In those days firearms were not thought of.

Amid the cheers of their companions the two set out.

To have seen them as they proceeded along the country roads, one would have taken them to be lovers instead of companions-in-arms.

They lost a lot of time in loitering, and two hours had elapsed ere they arrived in sight of the Royal palace at Greenwich.

They were passing a dense shrubbery when a mounted knight, attired in glittering armour, approached them.

"Halt, Egbert," said Jack, as he pulled up his powerful charger, "here is one of the Court knights. I wonder who *he* is?"

"An ill-favoured knight, whoever he is," replied Egbert.

"As I live," muttered Jack, "it is Rochester!"

At this time Jack Straw had not heard of the terrible tragedy at the house of Elias Leighton.

"Well, fellow," said Rochester, haughtily, as he bent an insolent glance upon Jack, "how dare you place yourself in my path?"

"How dare I?" sneered Jack. "Why, I dare do anything?"

"Insolent! Out of my way. Know ye who I am?"

"Right well. You are the villain Rochester."

With a cry of anger Rochester was about to draw his sword.

His hand was upon the hilt, but he took it off again in haste.

Egbert had disengaged his crossbow, fitted an arrow to it, and had levelled it at Rochester's throat.

"And," continued Jack, "unless it has pleased you to have a new set of eyes placed in your head, you should recognise *me*."

"Ha!" ejaculated Rochester, "you are the robber, Jack Straw."

"Robber! Well, if it pleases you to so call me, well and good. I am not a robber, though. I am a despoiler of the rich, that I may give to the poor."

"You are in my way. Stand aside. Your punishment shall come one of these days. I trust it will be by my hands."

"And," continued Jack, calmly, taking no notice of this speech, "since you are one of the rich, who so cruelly ill-use the common people, as they are called, I demand a tax from *you*."

"From me?"

"From you."

"Then you will not get it."

"I shall. I demand a tax from you."

"I will hand you nothing."

"Then I shall be compelled to take it from you."

"I will defend my property with my life!"

"You would be very foolish to do so now. I should not hesitate to do battle with you, though you are clad in armour, while I have none."

"My honour would not allow me to fight with a robber."

"Honour!" sneered Jack; "honour! Have you any honour about you? If so, in the name of the Virgin, in what particular part of your body do you secrete it?"

"I will no longer bandy words with you."

"Your purse, my lord," cried Jack, drawing himself erect, and raising his battle-axe. "Your purse, I say. Deliver it up to me at once, or I swear it will be the worse for you. Whatever its contents may be, rest assured that I will most faithfully distribute it among the poor and needy."

"My bitter curse rest upon the poor and the needy."

"And theirs upon you, say I!"

For only a few seconds did Lord Rochester look upon Jack's stalwart frame and resolute face, then he looked at Egbert, whose arrow was still levelled at his throat.

He saw that any hostile movement on his part might be fatal to him.

Taking his steel-chain purse from his saddle-bow he held it towards Jack Straw, who at a glance saw that it was well filled.

But Jack did not attempt to take it. He signed to Egbert, who advancing, took it from his lordship and affixed it to his own saddle.

"Am I now free to depart?" asked Lord Rochester, glancing around as if he thought help was near at hand.

"Ay, villian, you can go now."

"We shall meet again," said Rochester through his set teeth as he moved forward.

"I sincerely trust so," replied Jack, "and I hope that on the next occasion I shall not have to rescue an unfortunate maiden from your lordship's clutches. Until next we meet, my lord, farewell. Pray remember Jack Straw in your prayers—that is, if ever you recite any, which I much doubt."

As Rochester passed Egbert he looked hard into his face.

Then as he rode on he muttered—

"*If that companion of this daring robber Jack Straw is not a girl, then my name is not Rochester!*"

* * * *

Arrived in front of the palace, Jack Straw drew rein.

"Our adventure will be told to his majesty by Rochester, I should think," said Egbert.

"Nay, I do not think so," replied Jack. "If he told it to the king, his majesty would tell it to the Court, and Rochester would assuredly be laughed at."

"But not by all, I trow," laughed Egbert.

"Why not?"

"Well, methinks Rochester would not be the only one whom thou hast stopped and taken toll from. For instance, there is the proud Duke of Somerset, whom you compelled to take off all his armour and throw it in a ditch."

Jack Straw burst into a loud roar of laughter, in which he was joined by Egbert, whose silvery tones sounded strangely different from Jack's.

"We must not venture into the lion's mouth without due precautions," said Jack. "Now this will be the wisest plan. We will take the horses and conceal them behind yonder trees. There they will not attract attention. Yet we will not tie them up, in case we may be compelled to beat a hasty retreat. Then— Ha! what is that?"

The sound of several horns being vigorously blown burst upon their ears.

Then the loud baying of dogs.

"'Tis the huntsmen's horns," said Egbert. "The king is no doubt about to hunt the boar in the forest."

"He is. Hasten, hasten, or we may lose our opportunity."

Leaving the horses behind a group of tall trees, Jack, with Egbert at his side, stepped forth.

Going a somewhat roundabout way so as not to be observed, they at length reached the broad terrace in front of the palace.

"Do you really mean to enter the palace?" asked Egbert.

"Ay, that do I. But if you have any fear, go and await me at—"

"*Fear?* You know I have no fear. Where you go, there go I."

"You are as true as the sword I carry. Kiss me, Egbert."

"Not here, Jack. We may be observed, you know," smiled Egbert. "But go on; I long to see the king. Ha! who are they standing on the terrace steps."

Egbert pointed to a tall, youthful figure, clad in a blue velvet mantle, lined with ermine, embroidered all over, and fastened with a diamond clasp.

The velvet cap upon his head was studded with wonderful brilliants, which flashed and sparkled as almost to dazzle the eyes.

By his side stood a beautiful lady of some twenty summers.

This was the renowned Duchess of Chelmsford.

"It is the king," whispered Jack. "We are fortunate, for see, there are no courtiers about. Follow!"

Up the broad steps went Jack, followed closely by Egbert.

When before the youthful king, Jack Straw doffed his cap and bowed.

But he did not bend the knee.

The king stared at him in wonder, as also did the duchess, who surveyed his picturesque attire with much curiosity.

"Well," said the king, "who are you?"

"One who craves a few words with your majesty."

"With me, knave?" cried the king. "Didst ever hear the like, your grace?"

"Never, sire!" replied the duchess, with a smile. "But, mayhap, this youth desires to be one of your majesty's foresters, or, perchance, a keeper of the bloodhounds."

Jack replied to this with a scornful look at the duchess.

"Say your say, sirrah!" said the king, "since you have had the audacity to make your way to us. But, first, who is your companion? Come forth, young sir," added the king, who fixed his eyes in perplexity upon Egbert's beautiful features.

Egbert stood forward, his face covered with a deep blush, as he saw that not only the king's but the duchess' eyes were fixed full upon him.

"What is your name?" asked the king.

" Egbert, may it please your majesty."

" Egbert ! I should have thought that it would have been Editha or Winifred, or some such name. What says your grace."

The duchess only smiled.

" 'Tis certain this youth was cast in the wrong mould," went on the king, as he gazed admiringly upon Egbert, and utterly forgetting Jack's presence. "He certainly should have been a girl, eh? On our lives, we never beheld such handsome proportions for a boy. He would make us a capital page, your grace, eh?"

The duchess nodded.

" Would you like to be one of our pages, young sir?" asked the king.

" Nay, your majesty," replied Egbert. " I would acknowledge *no one* as my master."

" Not even your king?" smiled the duchess.

" Nay, not even the king."

" Certes ! the youth has spirit as well as beauty," laughed his majesty. "And why is it you would acknowledge no master?"

" He will answer you, your majesty," said Egbert, pointing to Jack, " if so be you will listen to him."

" Ha ! we had actually forgotten his presence. Don't frown, sirrah !" he said, as he noticed the fierce look upon Jack's features, " but say your say."

" Sire," began Jack, drawing his supple figure erect, " I have sought an audience for the purpose of laying before your majesty the many grievous wrongs under which the poorer classes are now labouring. Your majesty—"

" Stay but a moment," interrupted the king. " Who is this who addresses us on the wrongs, as they are called, of the common people? Why, by the Blessed Virgin ! you are but a youth."

" True, sire," answered Jack, boldly ; " but nevertheless I have mastered all the particulars respecting these oppressed—"

" Pish ! silence !" commanded the king, waving his hand ; " we cannot listen to such idle talk ! What have *we* to do with it all? We are not the council who arrange such matters. We cannot investigate the circumstances of the common people."

" And why, sire ?"

" Why ? *why* ? Can this youth be aware of the peril he is in to address us so? Dost think so, your grace?"

" The youth is bold of speech, your majesty," replied the duchess ; " but will not your majesty ask who this is who dares to address you in such insolent tones?"

" Have I not already asked?"

" His dress, his features, and his bearing remind me of a daring robber (described by my husband the duke), who stopped him at Blackheath, and compelled him to pay a heavy toll ere he would allow him to pass."

" What is your name, sirrah?"

" Jack Straw !"

" Heavens ! the very name," almost shrieked the duchess.

The king started back with a smothered exclamation.

" *You* Jack Straw?" he cried.

" Yes, *I* am Jack Straw."

" Then your life is forfeited. What ho !" he shouted, " what ho !"

" Quick, for our lives," cried Jack, seizing Egbert by the wrist. " Quick, or we are lost. See, some of the courtiers have heard the cry and are running along the terrace."

About a dozen courtiers, who at the cry from the king had drawn their swords, were running pell-mell along the broad terrace.

At the end of them, not being able to run so fast on account of his heavy armour, Jack's quick eyes detected Rochester.

Jack was a wonderfully fleet runner, and so also was Egbert.

The courtiers halted a few moments in order to learn what had happened, then all, with the exception of Rochester, started off at full cry after the daring pair.

Very soon Jack and Egbert reached their horses, and, vaulting into the saddle, they dashed forward.

But one of the courtiers, a tall, thin young fellow, had outdistanced the others, and had reached the head of Jack's horse.

" Hold !" he shouted waving his sword above his head, " hold, and surrender, or you die !"

" Let go your hold, fool !" cried Jack, in a voice of thunder. " Let go I say !"

"ANOTHER HOUND FELL DEAD, THE ARROW BURIED IN HIS BODY."

CHAPTER VI.

TREATS OF THE MANNER IN WHICH ROCHESTER ATTEMPTS THE CAPTURE OF JACK STRAW AND EGBERT—THE KING AND JACK ONCE MORE FACE TO FACE.

"SURRENDER, I command you," cried the courtier.

"Pshaw!" cried Jack, "what are your commands to me? Let go, I say," he added, as he drew his sword.

The courtier, who was no other than the young Lord of Ferras, made a stroke at Jack's head.

The blow was cleverly avoided, and the next moment Lord Ferras lay bathed in his blood upon the ground.

"Draw your sword, Egbert," said Jack, "but strike only in defence of your life. See, the others are nearly upon us—ha! what was that?"

A startled exclamation fell from Egbert's lips.

An exclamation left Jack's, too, as he saw that an arrow had been shot and had buried itself deeply in Egbert's saddle-bow.

"Quick!" cried Jack, as he seized the arrow, and, withdrawing it, threw it furiously upon the ground. "Quick! for your life!"

The two horses plunged forward.

The courtiers did not attempt to follow.

Looking back, Jack saw they were devoting their attention to Lord Ferras.

"We are safe enough here, I should say," said Egbert.

"Not so," replied Jack, "we must push further on. I am not afraid the courtiers will pursue us, but independent of them, we may have to encounter dangerous enemies."

"What mean you?"

"The king may order us to be tracked down by his fierce bloodhounds."

"Heavens!" cried Egbert, shuddering. "You really do not think the king would adopt such a course?"

"I certainly do. Besides, Rochester is such a great favourite, and he may advise it. By Saint Mary! I would rather encounter any number of men, than a horde of bloodhounds, such as the king keeps."

"For what purpose does he keep them?"

"For hunting. And these dogs, Egbert, are trained to hunt men as well as animals. They are terrible creatures, yet I would not fear to do battle with them were I and my horse clad in true armour. There—hark! as I live, that is the horn of the huntsmen!"

Both drew rein and listened intently.

Again and again they heard the distant winding of the huntsman's horn.

Jack turned quickly in his saddle, and glanced at Egbert.

But no trace of fear was to be seen upon his beautiful features.

Jack dismounted, and placed his ear to the ground.

In that position he remained for several seconds.

Suddenly starting to his feet, he cried—

"'Tis as I thought. I hear the deep baying of dogs. The bloodhounds have most certainly been put upon our track."

"Let us fly, then. No time is to be lost."

Jack shook his head gravely.

As he once more leapt into the saddle, he said—

"It is of no use attempting to fly. The bloodhounds can make their way through the forest twice as quickly as we can."

"What, then, do you advise?"

"*Face them!*" replied Jack, grimly, as he drew his sword and loosened his dagger. "Fit an arrow to your bow and discharge it—not at the dogs, but at him who has charge of them. I have heard that the principal person who has to do with them is Baron Locke, a cruel and bloodthirsty tyrant. If he is not clad in armour your shaft should find its way to his dastardly heart. But be careful, dear Egbert, to let me cover your movements. Sooner should the bloodhounds tear me in pieces ere you should suffer injury. You believe me, Egbert?"

"With all my soul."

"If aught happens to me, Egbert—if I should be killed—"

"Talk not of death," interrupted Egbert. "Near your heart do you not still carry the sacred straw? Yes! and that will assuredly protect you from a violent death. But if, in this hour of trial, Heaven forsakes you and you are killed, this dagger shall also deprive *me* of life. I could not live without you. But hist! I hear the dogs now. Oh, Jack, that they were men instead of dogs. It seems so horrible—horrible!"

Nearer and nearer came the baying of the hounds, and above that was heard the loud tones of a man urging them on.

Presently, with a rushing sound, they came into view—six of them.

Behind them rode a knight, clad in glittering armour.

It was Rochester!

Strange to say he was alone.

The nearest dog, an enormous and ferocious-looking anmal, with a low, deep growl, sprang at the throat of Jack's horse.

Jack raised himself in his stirrups, and as the animal leapt he brought his sword fairly down upon it.

The bloodhound was cloven completely in twain.

Egbert saw that to discharge an arrow at Rochester would be loss of time, for the villain was too well protected by his armour.

He therefore directed it at one of the dogs, and with so good an aim, that the hound, after a wild leap into the air and a fearful yell, fell dead, the arrow buried half-way in his body.

With loud, frantic cries Rochester urged on the now maddened animals, but by dexterous manoeuvring of his horse, Jack managed to avoid them.

They certainly did not relish the look of the glittering sword which continually flashed before their eyes.

Presently another hound fell dead, he also being pierced by an arrow from Egbert's bow; then another, who rushed up to Jack's side, fell with both his fore feet severed by our hero's sword.

The other two, despite Rochester's cries, drew back, their foaming jaws wide open, and after giving vent to several melancholy howls, rushed madly away.

Another second, and Jack was at Rochester's side.

"Coward!" he cried, bitterly, "you said not very long ago that we should meet again. We *have* met. And so *you* use bloodhounds—the king's bloodhounds—my lord? Dastard! Every time I encounter you I learn more of your true character. Listen, my lord. Although you are clad in armour, were I not afraid that pursuers will be upon my companion, I would at once do battle with you. Go. Remember that one day I shall be even with you."

Rochester did not hesitate.

He turned and fled, but as he did so Egbert fitted an arrow to his bow and discharged it at him.

It struck the armour with a crash and then fell to the ground.

"I would I had your strength, Jack," said Egbert. "I warrant me one of my shafts should find an opening in his armour or make one itself."

"Hist!" said Jack, "I hear the winding of the huntsman's horn again. Ha, as I live, there is the stag, look! but where are the riders?"

"I can just discern them through the trees," said Egbert.

"How many of them?"

"I see but two, and from the flowing robe of one, the rider is a lady."

"Are you sure?"

"As I am that I am a—"

"Peace!" interrupted Jack. "See, the stag advances at a rapid pace, and will be here in a few moments. Fix an arrow to your bow. Quick, Egbert!"

"Good, that is done. For whom is the arrow intended, the riders or the—"

"The stag. I have promised our companions at the castle a feast of Royal venison, and they shall have it."

On came the stag at a tremendous pace.

When within ten yards Egbert sent his shaft speeding.

The arrow plunged into the brain of the animal, and it fell dead.

In a few moments the riders came up.

"By the Virgin!" cried Jack, in amazement, "it is the king! He has become separated from his courtiers.

But I have heard he is a splendid rider. Now! what will he say?"

Yes, it was the king sure enough, and with him the duchess.

His majesty drew up before the dead stag and the mangled dogs, and surveyed them for some few moments.

Then he looked hard at Jack and his companion.

His face went white with rage, and it was some time ere he could speak again.

Jack sat upon his horse, immovable as a statue, and returned the king's look with interest.

At length his majesty, drawing himself erect, said—

"Dastard! robber! have you then not quitted my domain?"

"It does not look like it, sire," replied Jack, boldly.

"Was it you who slew my hounds, caitiff?"

"It was. I was attacked by them, and had I not defended myself, I should have fallen a victim to them. It is everyone's duty to defend himself."

"Sire," said the duchess, in a voice which fairly trembled with rage, "since your courtiers appear to have missed you, I would suggest that *you* should effect the capture of this audacious robber."

"Nay, your grace," replied the king, in great perplexity, "I cannot soil either my blade or my hands by bringing them in contact with such a worm as this!"

"Worm!" cried Egbert, in tones of intense passion. "Worm would be a better word if applied to your courtiers, sire, for do not they crawl to *you?*—you who, like us, are descended from one common mother—Eve!"

"I would willingly allow this robber to depart in peace," whispered the king to the duchess, "if I could but effect the capture of this pretty youth—*youth*, bah! I am more than ever satisfied that this youth is *not* a youth but a girl. There is a mystery here, your grace, which I should well like to fathom."

This speech, delivered in tones which left no doubt as to their sincerity,

seriously offended her grace, who urging on her horse a few paces, said, addressing Egbert—

"How *dare* you speak in such tones to your king?"

"We do not acknowledge him as *our* king," said Jack, with a loud laugh. "We require no king to govern us— we can and *will* govern ourselves."

"By heaven's grace!" cried the king, "this surpasses all we ever heard! But fear it not, your capture shall be effected. And mark it well, when you *are* captured a long rope shall instantly be your portion."

"I am obliged to your majesty," sneered Jack, "and trust that *you* will never come to a more sudden death. But I will detain you no longer," he added, as he dismounted. "This Royal stag will—"

"Touch it not," cried the king. "On your life touch it not!"

"And why, sire?"

"It belongs to the crown."

"I am aware of it. To the crown in one sense, to the people in another. Your majesty, I promised my companions a feast of Royal venison, and, as you may learn ere long, Jack Straw never breaks his word. That being so, I am compelled to break your commands."

With this Jack stooped, and raising the stag in his muscular arms, he swung it across his saddle-bow, and then, remounting, raised his hat.

"Farewell, sire," he said, "and let me express one fervent wish. It is that your majesty's counsellors will give you better advice in the future, or ill-fortune may come to you. See at once what can be done for the people, *or they may rise, wrest the crown from your grasp, and trample it under their feet!* Once more, farewell."

With this, Jack and Egbert turned, and putting spurs to their horses, were soon lost to view.

The king sat for some time motionless upon his horse, and no words of the duchess elicited an answer from him.

At last, with a deep sigh and a sad look at his favourite bloodhounds, he turned and rode slowly towards the palace.

CHAPTER VII.

WHEREIN IT IS SEEN HOW JACK STRAW OBTAINS THE INFORMATION OF DOROTHY'S ABDUCTION—HOW THE GOLDSMITH JOINS IN THE FEAST— AND HOW TWENTY HORSEMEN SET OUT FOR LONDON.

THE sun was setting when Jack and Egbert, tired and hungry, arrived in sight of the gloomy-looking Blackfoot Castle.

They were descried from the battlements, the drawbridge was at once lowered, and the two entered, being greeted with loud shouts of delight by their companions.

Mark and Basil came to the front, anxious to learn all that had occurred.

"All in good time," said Jack, gravely; "when the feast is over I will relate all that has happened. Have you the fire ready for cooking this Royal venison?"

"Yes. A fire large enough to cook an ox."

"Let the stag be at once taken to the kitchen and prepared. Is there anything of importance to tell me?"

"Ay. We have been joined by ten men."

"Ten?"

"Yes."

"Who are they?"

"They belonged to the Royal troops, but being dissatisfied with the treatment they have been receiving, they have deserted."

"Good. Have you sworn them in?"

"Yes."

"On what?"

"On the sword."

"'Tis well. They shall join us at the feast. Anything more?"

"Yea. Something of more importance than this."

"Ha! speak."

"There is in the kitchen an old man who craves an audience with you. He is a stranger to us, and there seems a deep mystery about him."

"Did he not give a name?"

"He did. It is Elias Leighton."

"Leighton? Leighton? Methinks I have heard the name before."

"You have. But you had better enter the kitchen. He has awaited you some hours."

"Stay. Was not Leighton the name of the girl we rescued from the clutches of Rochester?"

"It was."

"And can this be her father?"

"It is so."

Jack waited to hear no more, but vaulting from the saddle he strode into the castle, being followed by Egbert.

Traversing the long and narrow passages, he at length reached the kitchen, an enormous, lofty apartment, adorned with a fire-place broad enough to have cooked an ox entire. Many specimens of these can be seen at the present day at the South Kensington Museum.

A log fire blazed on the hearth, and in various parts of the kitchen men were preparing the evening meal, which on this occasion was to partake of the character of a feast.

Strange enough did these bronzed and bearded, muscular men look, with their bare arms and their swords and daggers dangling at their sides instead of cooking implements.

But the appearance of these men sank into insignificance by the side of a figure sitting on a stool by the fireplace.

The figure of an old, bowed, grey-haired man, who for hours had been rocking himself backwards and forwards, alternately praying, cursing, and imploring. He would answer no one who spoke to him.

His only words, uttered in whining, child-like tones, were—

"Has Jack Straw returned?"

For the hundredth time he had asked this question and had been answered in the negative, and he was just about to ask it again, when Jack strode into the kitchen, his huge spurs rattling merrily upon the stone flags.

Standing in the doorway, his tall, commanding, and picturesquely-clad figure erect, he surveyed the old man for some moments in silence.

Slowly, laboriously, as if it were a torture for him to stand, Elias Leighton rose, and looking hard at Jack, said—

"My heart tells me that you are the man I seek—you are Jack Straw?"

"I am. What would you? Your name, I understand, is Leighton?"

"It is, it is—the goldsmith of the Strand, the father of the girl you rescued, good sir."

"What is amiss that you should seek out me, who is now, or generally thought, a robber and an outlaw?"

"Oh, sir," cried the miser, clasping his hands fervently together, "she whom I valued more than my life, more than all the gold I have been at so much pains to scrape together, has been abducted."

"Abducted?" cried Jack; "from where?"

"My own house."

"Know you by whom?"

"Ay, ay, by the court villian, by the assassin, Rochester."

"Holy Mary!" said Jack, starting forward, "you must be crazed, old man."

"Nay, nay, 'tis even as I say, young sir. 'Twas Rochester who abducted her beyond question. Though I have no positive proof of it, I am certain 'twas he. He came to my house with several of his hired bravos; my apprentice, Edmund Gaston, attacked them in the bullion vault, and he was assassinated."

A cry of horror left Jack's lips.

"Go on, go on!" he said, eagerly.

"I found him dead upon the stones, with a dagger in his back. In his hand was this parchment."

And Elias Leighton took from his doublet the parchment, which he handed to Jack, who opening it, carefully read it.

"Written with his own blood," he said, "and he calls upon me to avenge him. Old man, he shall not call in vain. Would that I had known of it this morning. And when did this happen?"

"More than two weeks ago."

"Heaven's mercy! how was it you did not seek me out before?"

"Alas! young sir, the terrible tragedy and the abduction of my daughter—the only one in the world I have to love—prostrated me, and I have been confined to my bed. It was only by the skill of an eminent physician that my life was saved, but it was at a great cost, nigh upon a hundred nobles."

"No matter what it cost. The loss of a few nobles should not trouble a man of your wealth. But tell me, how is it that you did not lay these particulars before the king?"

"I have, I have. That is, I got my physician to do so."

"And what was the king's reply?"

"That he could not interfere. Mark it well! oh, mark it well!" moaned the old man, "and I have advanced him large sums of money."

"I am sorry to hear it; for there can be no doubt you will never get it again."

"Oh, don't say that, don't say that," cried the miser. "All my scrapings of years to—"

"What is all your scrapings of years to do with the safety and the honour of your daughter? Pah! Gold, accursed gold, you have indeed much to answer for. Old man, where is your daughter confined?"

"Alas! that I know not."

"You know not? Have you not endeavoured to ascertain?"

"I have, and I can form no other conclusion than that she is confined in Rochester House. I have bribed the servants during Rochester's absence, for you may be aware he is with the king?"

"I am," replied Jack, grimly.

"I bribed them, they willingly took the bribe, and then they laughed at me."

"Hem! No doubt of that. But there can be no question about her being confined there, I should say. From what I can see she is a most unfortunate girl. Listen, old man, I am tired and hungry, and must eat and rest awhile. Though sleep is what I most urgently require, yet I will not lay me down until I have marched to London, and have endeavoured to find out whether your daughter is within Rochester House."

"May Heaven's choicest blessings descend upon thee, noble sir! The blessing of a lone, old man be upon thee!"

And stretching forth his long, withered hands, the old man fell upon his knees, and bowed his head until his flowing beard almost touched the ground.

"Rise!" said Jack. "Kneel not to me, kneel not to the tyrant king; kneel to no one but the Almighty. But, listen. Are you athirst?"

"I am parched."

"Then you shall be provided with wine such as has never yet graced the table of his majesty. Are you hungry?"

"The pangs of hunger have been upon me for days, but I have had no inclination to eat."

"Could you eat now?"

"But a morsel."

"A huge platter full shall be placed before you anon, and you can eat as much as you think fit."

At this moment the stag was brought in by a couple of men, who, throwing it upon the flags, drew their daggers, and commenced to skin it.

"There is part of the feast, old man," said Jack, "and you may, perchance, get an appetite, when I tell you that it was taken from the king himself. It is the first, but by no means the last. Ho! ho!"

"Ho! ho! ho! ho!" echoed the men.

"There is no telling," said Jack, "one of these days we may take the king himself. But now at once get the feast ready, my men, for to-night some of us will have a hard ride, and, mayhap, some hard work to do."

During this conversation Egbert had amused himself with arranging different articles upon the table.

But directly Jack had strode off, he turned, and walking up to the old miser, who had now resumed his seat and mutterings, he said, as he folded his arms—

"Old man."

Elias Leighton looked up wonderingly.

The sound of the voice, which was so different to what he had heard, at once impressed him.

"Old man," repeated Egbert, in low tones, "is your daughter *beautiful?*"

"Beautiful! Ay, my son. Very—very beautiful!"

He did not notice that his answer caused Egbert's eyes to flash fiercely.

"And she is young?"

"*Very* young."

"Has she had a lover?"

"None, my son, none," answered the old man, looking hard into the great fire.

At that moment his thoughts were of Edmund.

"Has she ever had a lover?"

"She—" he paused.

"Go on," said Egbert, impatiently. "Had she ever a lover?"

"She had."

"And he?"

"He is, as you have heard me say, dead."

"Then this apprentice, who was assassinated, was your daughter's lover?"

"He was, though not with my consent."

"You do not know whether your daughter loves Jack Straw?"

"What!" cried the old man, rising suddenly—"what! Are you mad, boy, or are you endeavouring to torture me? Love Jack Straw! Why, she never saw him but once, and that was when he rescued her from the clutches of Rochester!"

"Sometimes, old man," said Egbert, in quivering tones, "love comes at first sight!"

"Away, boy," shouted the old man, stamping his foot. "Are you not a comrade of Jack Straw's? And from what little I have heard of him, Jack Straw has little time to devote to love-making, even though he had the opportunity. Why do you question me? And why do you look at me thus?"

Egbert took hold of the miser's arm, and whispered in his ear—

"Because I have the right to question. Do you hear me? The *right* to question. *I* love him with all my heart and soul, and did I know that he was beloved by any woman—"

"Ay, ay, my son."

"I would find out that woman, and—and *kill* her!"

The miser fairly trembled as he looked into the large, fierce, black eyes, which seemed eating into his very soul.

He looked at Egbert curiously—fearfully, as though regarding and listening to, a man whose reason was unsettled.

At last he said—

"My son, my years are over three

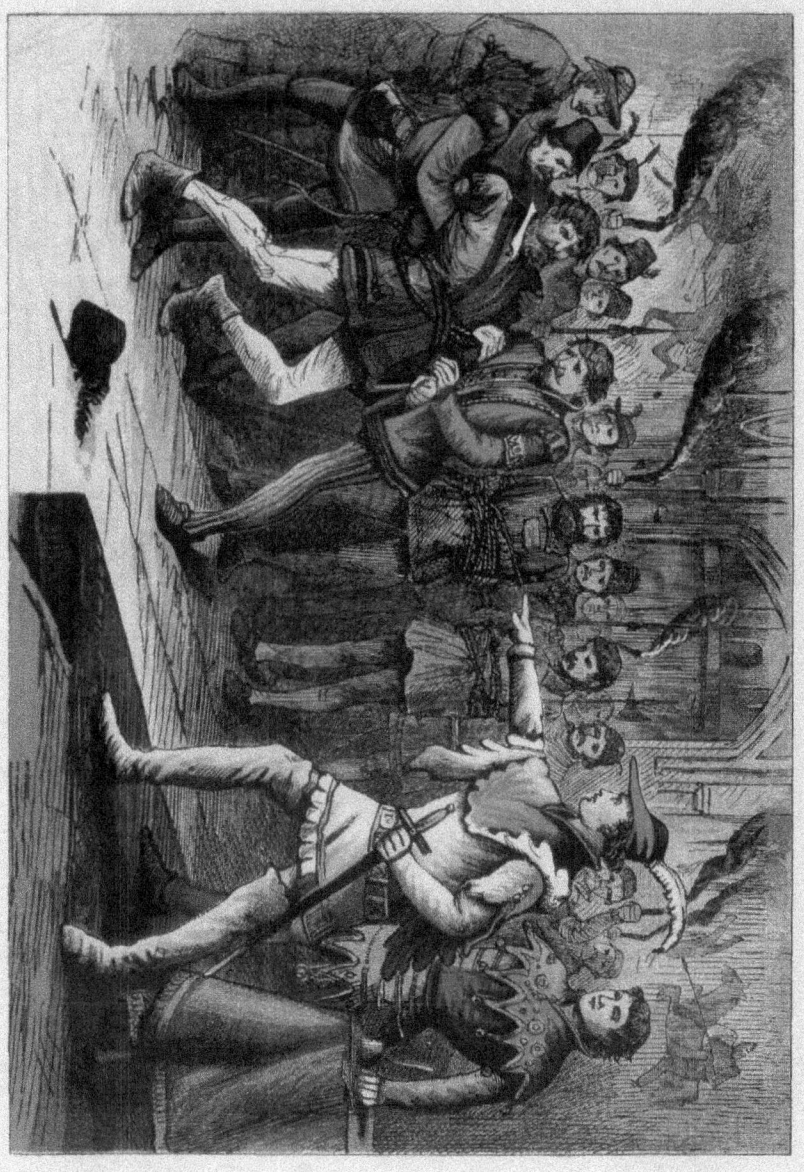

"'DO YOU DARE TO SENTENCE US TO DEATH?' SHRIEKED THE LEADER."

score and ten—more than the space allotted by the Almighty to man—and in the course of these years I have passed through much. I have mixed with many strange men, I have heard strange things, but the words you have just now uttered are the strangest I have ever heard in the course of my long life. I fail to interpret your meaning."

"I tell you that I *love* him!" said Egbert, as his delicate fingers firmly clutched the old man's arm.

"I have no doubt of it," said the miser—"no doubt whatever of it, my son. It is but natural that you should love such a fine, powerful, commanding, and fearless youth. You are his comrade, and you have the right, as you say, to love him. But—"

"But! Go on, go on."

"Though you love him as a leader, as a friend, as a brave youth, you cannot love him as a woman would you, as a youth cannot have the feelings of a woman."

"Can I not? can I not?" replied Egbert. "I *have* the feelings of a woman?"

"*You?*"

"Ay, *I*."

"Go, my son, go. I much fear me you have been indulging in wine. Yet stay, stay," added Elias Leighton, seizing Egbert by the hands and looking hard into his face. "A thought strikes me. Listen."

He whispered for a moment in Egbert's ear.

"Yes," said Egbert, "you are right. But it is a secret, and must so be held."

"It shall be so with me," replied the miser, as he again sank into his seat. "Go, your love will not be misplaced. Love on, my son, love on; and Heaven guard you and him!"

"And will you not give me your blessing?" asked Egbert.

"With all my heart. Kneel, my son. I am but a poor old man—a man people call a miser; but a blessing and advice from me can do you no harm."

Taking his cap from his head, Egbert knelt.

The men, busy preparing the meal, saw the movement (and our readers must remember that in those days an old man's blessing was reckoned as good as a priest's), and doffing their caps, they, too, knelt down.

Once more rising, Elias Leighton raised his hands over Egbert's bowed head, and in low and impressive tones, his really noble-looking face turned upward, he said—

"May all good angels guide you now and hereafter. May the choicest blessings of our Heavenly Father guide you. Oh, my son, guard yourself carefully. Let not your passions rise without cause; let your heart for ever be turned in sympathy to those in sorrow or in suffering. Be ever cautious; be ever wary, lest the snares of the world lead you into the wrong path. Be strong, be brave; but yet be forgiving, as ye hope to be forgiven. But—and let this not slip from your mind—forget not that, under this king the poor are fearfully oppressed. Do not interfere needlessly with those who think it their duty to make outrageous laws; but if the hour comes when tyrants trample upon the serf, draw at once the Sword of Freedom, and cry, not 'For the king!' but '*For God and the People!*' Rise, my son; you have my advice, warning, and blessing."

Soon after this the great bell was rung in the hall.

This announced the important fact that the meal was ready.

Egbert conducted Elias Leighton to the banqueting-hall, the tables in which groaned beneath the weight of food of every imaginable description.

At the end of the centre table, on a sort of raised dais, the massive arms of which represented a couple of lions in a crouching attitude, sat Jack Straw.

He saw the look on Elias Leighton's face and smiled.

"What think ye of this, old man?" he asked.

"'Tis fit for a king," cried the old miser, rapturously; "it is superb. Ay, ay, 'tis fit for a king!"

"Ay, you are right. But 'tis better fitted for Jack Straw and his comrades. What say ye all?"

The men in the room—numbering at least two score—gave vent to a cheer.

"And the gold and the silver!" said Elias, as he took up a cup and weighed it in his hand. "Yes, 'tis worth a great deal of money. Shall I estimate its value for you, brave sir?"

"Bah! Estimate its value? No! what care we for its value? These vessels belonged to a certain noble lord. He was conveying them across Blackheath, and going in the direction of London; no doubt he was about to raise money on them—"

"Mayhap he was about to come to me," interrupted the miser.

"Probably. We did not ask him for any particulars. We knew him as a man who utilised his leisure time in drawing up cruel laws, which at convenient moments he placed before the king. We knew him as a man who trampled upon the common people. One half of his gold and silver we broke up, melted down, and distributed the pieces among the poor—"

"Oh!" cried Elias, "broke up such beautiful plate?"

"Yea," continued Jack, "and as I said, we distributed the pieces among the poor, according to the number of the family. But now take your seat on my right, and you, Egbert, on my left."

This having been done, and everyone else having taken their seats, the platters were filled and passed round the tables, as was the wine.

Elias took his cup, and was about to drain it, when Jack said—

"Wait a little, old man. You have not joined us in our toast. Though we do not expect you to eat as we shall do, yet, no doubt, you will drink the toast I shall propose."

Jack thereupon stood up and raised his cup aloft in his left hand.

His action was followed by everyone present.

There was a brief pause, during which, the dropping of a pin might have been heard.

Suddenly, Jack placed his hand to his side, and instantly forty swords flashed in the air.

High over their heads the men held them, while Jack, in a loud, passionate voice, cried—

"For God and the People, and death to tyrants!"

"Death to tyrants! Death to tyrants!" was the hoarse response.

Another moment and the goblets were empty.

Elias Leighton repeated the words, evidently to Jack's satisfaction.

But the sight of the naked—and some of them blood-stained—weapons caused him to shudder visibly.

The swords were sheathed, and the men sat down. Soon nothing was heard but the clatter of platters.

"On my soul!" cried Jack, "when next I meet the king I will not fail to tell him that we found his Royal venison delightful eating. Eat away, my men, for such a number of us should contrive to eat at least a Royal stag. Ha! ha!"

"Ha! ha!" echoed the men.

"How do you like Royal venison, father Leighton?" asked Jack of the miser, who was very busy with the contents of his plate.

"It is fine and fat of a surety," replied Elias. "It is no wonder the king and his courtiers look so well when they feed off meat like this whenever it so pleases them."

"Nay, there you are right. But since we intend to partake of Royal venison in future, it is certain that the king and his courtiers will have but little."

The meal being concluded, the men rose, and Jack explained to Mark and Basil all that had occurred, and announced his intention to proceed to London, and, if possible, discover the whereabouts of Dorothy.

"But why not delay the journey till the morrow," asked Basil. "You want rest, and if you persist in making long journeys, you will assuredly be laid upon a bed of sickness."

"In this case there can be no further delay. The unfortunate girl must be rescued. I admit that I should not think so much of it, having so many important matters to think of, had not this poor youth been assassinated. With his own blood he wrote the paper which calls upon me to avenge him. Such an appeal should be attended to with as much despatch as possible. I have already rested sufficiently."

"If it be indeed your intention to set out at once," said Basil "I pray you let Mark and I accompany you with the others."

"Nay, that must not be. I will take with me twenty men only."

"And I will ride by your side, Jack," said Egbert, pleadingly.

"You shall, Egbert."

"And I shall be allowed to go with you, brave youth?" said Elias.

"No; you must stay here. Your presence would only impede our movements."

Twenty men were selected, and each having provided himself with a cross-bow and a quiver of arrows, in addition to his ordinary arms, the horses were saddled and brought into the courtyard.

Darkness had now gathered over the country, but it was not profound, the moon being at the full.

All being in readiness, the small troop sallied forth amid the cheers of their comrades, in the centre of whom stood Elias Leighton, invoking a blessing on Jack and his companions, and praying heaven to return his daughter to him safe.

Jack was armed as he had been in the morning, but at his saddle-bow he carried a long coil of stout rope.

Weird in the extreme did the cavalcade look as they crossed the country, the moon's rays causing the helmets of the men to glitter like mirrors reflected in the sun's rays.

The only sound they made as they proceeded was the rattle of arms, for the heather effectually muffled the sound of the horses' hoofs.

Thus, on the road to London, on an errand of courage and mercy, we leave them for a time.

CHAPTER VIII.

IS OF WHAT BEFELL DOROTHY—OF ROCHESTER'S PERSECUTION—OF THE FATE OF FRIAR KISH, AND OF THE SUDDEN APPEARANCE OF A NOTED CHARACTER.

We must now, for awhile, turn back to the night on which occurred the terrible tradegy at the house of Elias Leighton in the Strand.

Dorothy was carried, totally unconsious, to Rochester House, near Westminster Abbey.

It was an old, rambling structure of enormous size, and built partly of wood and partly of stone.

Rochester, though he kept within it a numerous train of servants—the number being considerably over two hundred of all grades—seldom occupied it, though for what reason no one knew.

Probably he had many unpleasant recollections connected with it—or perhaps he did not like its appearance, which certainly was as forbidding within as without.

To this undesirable residence Dorothy was carried.

When within the courtyard she was placed in the arms of a brawny, muscular woman, and by her conveyed to an upstairs apartment, a splendidly-fitted room, which was occasionally occupied by Rochester.

Here she was placed upon the bed, and a restorative administered to her by the woman.

Directly, however, Dorothy showed signs of returning consciousness, the woman noiselessly left the apartment and locked the room.

"Well, woman?" asked Rochester, who was waiting on the broad landing.

"She is rapidly recovering," replied the woman, in harsh tones.

"Then I will have an interview with her."

"Better delay it until the morrow."

"'Twill not do. I may have to attend upon his majesty, and when that occurs there is no telling when I may return."

"You will not get her to listen to you to-night, my lord, whatever you may say."

"I will try. Give me the key and retire for awhile."

The woman did so, and went down the stairs.

Rochester placed the key in the lock and flung the door open.

Dorothy at the same moment leapt from the bed, and looking wildly around her, cried in loud tones—

"Heaven, what is this? Where am I? Where am I? Oh, my mind wanders! I am going mad—mad! What place is this? Ah, I remember. Rochester—the murder. Rochester, the villain—the—"

"He is here, dear girl, to answer for himself," sneered Rochester. "Although you are pleased to shower such compliments upon me, I cannot feel it in my heart to be angry with you. You had now better listen to reason," he said, locking the door inside and seating himself. "You are in my power, and—"

"Answer me, monster. Where am I?"

"At my noble residence, Rochester House. I repeat, now that you are in my power, you had better listen to reason. If you will consent to be mine, all that is here—all that I have shall be yours."

"Villain! I scorn your proposals. Sooner—far sooner would I be carried to my grave than stand at the altar with you. You, my lord, are indeed a coward. But since it seems that I am your prisoner, and that I must remain here until Heaven raises up a deliverer—"

"Bah!" interrupted Rochester. "He would be a bold adventurer indeed who attempted to effect a deliverance from Rochester House."

"Coward! I feel that I am not the first poor girl whom you have, against her will, brought to this house."

Rochester turned pale, but he made no reply.

Dorothy continued—

"Since it seems that I am to remain here your prisoner, I say, I tell you to begone. Go! Rid me of your hateful presence."

"This, I again tell you," replied Rochester, "is my residence, and that being so, I claim the right to remain as long as I please in any part of it."

"You would remain here to torture me," gasped Dorothy, her hands clenching themselves so tightly that the nails gradually embedded themselves in her delicate flesh.

Rochester smiled tauntingly.

"Torture you!" he said. "How can my love for you be called torture? Ha, ha, ha! by the Blessed Virgin, I do swear that you look more beautiful than ever when you are angry. Come, my lovely—"

He did not complete the sentence.

With a heartrending cry, Dorothy seized a heavy stool, and with a spring she rushed upon Rochester, then raising it, she brought it down with all her force on his head.

So sudden and unexpected had been this attack, that Rochester had no power to defend himself.

He attempted to rise, but Dorothy, clutching the stool with both hands, dealt him another blow, and with sufficient force to send him bleeding and senseless to the floor.

Though greatly exhausted, Dorothy did not lose her presence of mind.

Seizing Rochester's sword, she drew it from its sheath, but immediately let it fall, its weight was too much for her.

Falling upon her knees, she unbuckled his dagger, and concealed it under her dress.

Then she wrenched the key from his clenched hand, and inserting it in the lock, turned it, and opened the door.

"Heaven have mercy upon me!" she gasped, as she raised her hands above. "Guide me in this, my hour of need. Free, so far, but alas! I fear there is no escape."

She was right.

Crossing the broad passage, she reached a flight of stone stairs.

Cautiously descending, she was about to turn round a pillar, when she felt a firm grip upon her wrist, and a hoarse voice cried—

"Ha! what is this? Where go you?"

It was the voice of the brawny serving-woman we have before spoken of.

"Unhand me!" cried Dorothy, endeavouring to wrench herself free. "Unhand me, if you are a woman. Let me go! let me go!"

But the woman's grip only tightened on her wrist.

"Return with me," she said fiercely. "Return, and let me see what has happened."

"Let me go, I say!" screamed Dorothy, as by a powerful pull she succeeded in freeing herself. "Let me go, or I will free myself even at the risk of committing a crime for which I may hereafter be sorry. Away!"

And, springing back, she took the dagger from her dress, snatched it from its sheath, and held its glittering blade aloft.

But the serving-woman's blood was up. To be defied by any woman was not what she could stand.

With a terrible oath, she rushed upon Dorothy, who, without hesitation, brought the dagger down with all the force she could master upon the woman's breast.

But her strength had left her.

True, the dagger buried itself about an inch in the woman's bosom, and the blood instantly began to trickle down her broad chest, but the woman snatched it out, and flinging it upon the stairs, sprang upon Dorothy, and bore her with a crash to the ground.

With a series of horrible imprecations, she dashed poor Dorothy's head upon the stones, until a little stream of blood began to trickle down the stairs.

Twice the woman's hand wandered to the dagger, and once she had actually raised it to plunge it into Dorothy's breast; but she thought better of it, and finally hurled it from her.

Dragging Dorothy out of the way, she descended the stairs, and in a few moments returned with a number of retainers.

But as they reached the landing, Rochester came from the room.

His face was covered with blood, and he looked bewildered.

"Fetch me help," he said, "and do one of you fetch me a cup of wine."

Then, catching sight of Dorothy, he asked what had occurred.

The serving-woman told him, adding that Dorothy had sworn to murder her, and pointed to her bosom.

"Had I not felled her to the earth," she said, " of a surety she would have accomplished her purpose."

The surgeon (one was constantly on the premises), was summoned, and after he had administered restoratives to her, he ordered that Dorothy should be at once taken to a room, where she was to be kept quiet for a time.

"That is your advice?" asked Rochester.

"It is, my lord," replied the surgeon, with a low bow.

"Then let me tell you it shall not be followed," said Rochester, sternly.

"You are quite right, my lord—" began the serving-woman.

"Silence!" cried Rochester. "Listen to me. Take her within that room again, and lock the door."

This was done.

"You are sorely wounded, I see, my lord," said the surgeon. "Pray let me attend to you."

"You shall attend to me anon," continued Rochester, as he took a large cup of wine offered him by a pretty page. "At present I cannot afford the time. Listen to my orders, and let them be carried out to the letter. When she has sufficiently recovered to be removed, let her be taken to the Black Vault—"

The surgeon uttered a cry of amazement.

The serving-woman, as well as the retainers, merely grinned.

"It will kill her," said the surgeon.

"She must take her chance," replied Rochester, "but my belief is, that a short confinement there will bring her to her senses."

"If she dies," said the serving-woman, grimly, "she will not be the first."

"Take my advice," said the surgeon, addressing the woman, "and let not your tongue wag so much, or his lordship may take offence, and order you to be hung from the highest battlement; and, as you are aware, *you* would not be the first who has been so served."

"Well said, well said," said Rochester. "And the advice is most excellent. I would counsel you to follow it, woman."

"Do you seriously mean to have her confined in the Black Vault, my lord?" asked the surgeon.

"I do. I know the girl well. She has a most violent temper, and, as I have said, my opinion is that a short confinement will have the desired effect."

"When are your orders to be carried out, my lord?" asked the serving-woman.

"In four hours. I shall, no doubt, remain in the house until to-morrow night, by which time I trust she will have been brought to her senses."

With these words Rochester rose, and beckoning to the surgeon to follow him, strode away.

The retainers followed, and as soon as the serving-woman heard their footsteps die away in the distance, she entered the room and stood for a long time contemplating the fair Dorothy as she lay, to all appearance, lifeless on the bed.

At length she went away, muttering that the four hours would soon pass.

"But, by the Virgin," she thought, "I trust his lordship will not alter his mind."

*   *   *   *

Rochester did *not* alter his mind, though he was appealed to by the surgeon to countermand his order.

It was very early in the morning when, once more, the serving-woman entered the room in which Dorothy lay, and rudely awakened her from the light slumber into which she had fallen.

Directly her eyes fell upon the stern, nay, brutal face of the serving-woman, she started violently, but no cry left her lips.

No mercy nor pity could she expect from *that* quarter.

In stern tones the serving-woman ordered her to rise, and Dorothy obeyed.

"What would you with me?" she asked.

"Silence!" was the reply. "Ask no questions. If you do, expect no answer from me. *Follow* me!" she shouted.

"Where?" asked Dorothy.

"I tell you to ask me no questions. Follow me."

Dorothy did so.

Outside the room her tearful eyes rested upon a dozen retainers, who, with drawn swords in their right hands and flaming links in their left, and looking like a number of frowning statues, awaited her.

One, a tall, terribly fierce, ugly-looking brute, and evidently the leader, said, in sneering tones—

"Follow me, *your* ladyship."

Dorothy looked at the man for a moment, then crossing her hands upon her heaving bosom, she slowly followed him.

"I am going to my death," she thought, "but I fear not. Rather let me thank heaven for my deliverance! Rochester finds that I will not give way to him, and he will avenge himself by murdering me as he did poor Edmund."

Here a half-suppressed sob escaped her lips.

"You wil have something to sob over ere long," cried the brutal serving-woman. "Move yourself a little faster, or the point of a sword will make you."

"Be assured heaven will avenge me," said Dorothy, fixing her eyes upon the woman.

"Ay, ay, let that be your belief. It may do you good, and assuredly will not hurt me!" replied the woman with a sneer.

Down one flight of stone stairs, then another and another, went the party, until at last Dorothy began to wonder whether there was any end to them.

In a few moments she became aware that the atmosphere was very damp, and that the walls in many places ran with slime.

A violent shivering took possession of her.

At length they reached a long, narrow corridor, the stone floor of which was covered with thin mud to the thickness of at least half-an-inch.

"Where am I?" asked Dorothy.

"That matters not to you," replied the leader of the men, gruffly. "You will probably find out soon enough."

With this he selected a key from a bunch hanging at his girdle, inserted it in the lock of a low narrow door, and pushed the latter open.

A slight scream escaped Dorothy's lips.

"That is your apartment for the future," said the serving-woman.

"'Tis a living tomb," ejaculated Dorothy.

"You are not the first who has said so," said the leader of the men. "Enter without further delay."

Dorothy entered, and found herself in a small, square cell, the walls, flooring and ceiling of which were of stone, and as black as ink.

The only furniture it contained was a low wooden pallet and a stool; and, strange to say, these articles were *also* as black as ink!

It was no wonder that Rochester had christened it the "Black Vault."

All this Dorothy was enabled to see by the aid of the link which the leader of the men held, and she did not fail to notice that there was no window.

Looking slowly round, she said—

"If this is to be my prison, I pray heaven to release me from it ere another day shall dawn."

"You will not know whether the day dawns or not," said the serving-woman. "You will be enabled to see nothing here."

"Ha! am I then to be left without even a link?"

"Pah! link! Why, yes! Think you that his lordship grants such a thing as a link to any one he makes a prisoner? No!"

"Before we go," said the leader, "have you anything to say?"

"Nothing; except it is to call down heaven's most bitter curse upon you all."

"Thanks, my *lady*, thanks! But we are all so used to curses of every description, that one from pretty lips can do us no harm. Ho! ho!"

"Ho! ho!" echoed his companions.

"But," continued the man, "have you any *commands* to give us? Have you no message for us to take to his lordship? I can tell you of a message, which, if you give it to me to convey to my Lord Rochester, will cause you to be instantly released from this dungeon. Is it not so?" he asked the serving-woman.

The woman nodded her head.

Dorothy hesitated a moment.

"Name what the message should be," she said, "though methinks I can guess it."

"It is that you accede to his lordship's wishes. Would it not be better to reign in this grand house as Rochester's queen, as others—"

He stopped abruptly.

"Silence!" cried the serving-woman, "or mayhap his lordship may hear of what you have said."

"You would say 'as others have done,'" said Dorothy. "Ay, I mark well your words. Go! Sooner would I remain for ever here than look once more upon Rochester's villainous face!"

The man made no reply to this. Seizing the ring of the door, he pulled it to with a terrific crash, and Dorothy was alone in profound silence and darkness.

* * * *

Two weeks passed away. It seemed like the greater part of a lifetime to Dorothy; but, of course, she had no knowledge of how long she had been in her prison.

The days and nights seemed alike to her.

But, once in every ten hours, a loaf of bread and some water were brought to her by the serving-woman, who, without a word, deposited them upon the floor, and after a brief contemplation of Dorothy's rapidly-changing features, departed.

Rochester, as our readers have seen, had been summoned to attend upon the king, and that was the reason why Dorothy never received a visit from him.

Now, on the very morning that Jack Straw had had an interview with the king, Rochester had instructed Friar Kish, a bloated, drunken scoundrel, attached to the Court, to proceed to Rochester House, and endeavour to preach a "sermon" to Dorothy, with the object of bringing her to her senses.

Friar Kish received these instructions with secret satisfaction.

It was not his first errand of the same kind, and he had heard much of the beauty of the goldsmith's daughter.

But Rochester's instructions had been overheard, and by no less a person than Silverbell, the king's principal jester, so called on account of his attire, when standing behind his majesty's chair, being profusely decorated with silver bells.

He was acquainted with the goldsmith, and more than once had seen Dorothy, of whose abduction he had heard; and now that he knew where she was confined, he resolved to do what he could towards frustrating Rochester's designs.

And very unfortunate was it for Rochester's designs that Silverbell had overheard the instructions given to Friar Kish, for he knew every inch of Rochester House; indeed, as will be seen, he knew more—far more of the secret passages of the mansion than did those who occupied it.

In the evening Friar Kish had his mule saddled, and set off for London, where he would not arrive for some hours, he being a heavy man, and by no manner of means addicted to fast riding, though he was much addicted to strong wine, a huge flask of which he carried at his saddlebow, and "refreshed" himself with it every few moments.

Silverbell gave him two hours' start, and caught him up at Whitehall.

He was in the act of taking a long pull at his flask, when Silverbell came noiselessly up to him, and snatching the flask from him, drained it, much to the astonishment and great indignation of Friar Kish, who, raising himself in his stirrups, and clenching his fist, cried—

"May all the saints—"

"Stay your curses, good Friar Kish," interrupted Silverbell, handing back the flask. "You see, I should not have taken your wine, only I happen to know that it is always of the best."

"Eh, *you* know, do you? Well, you rascally knave, you know my name, that is evident enough; but how do you know that my *wine* is always of the best?"

From the thickness of his speech it was quite evident that the friar was more than half intoxicated.

"Well," replied Silverbell, "I said *your* wine, but that was a mistake."

"Eh? How, thou lying knave?"

"I meant the king's."

"Oh, oh! Out on ye for a lying fool! What mean ye by saying that the wine I carry is the king's?"

"Because I have seen you take it from his cellars; and, moreover, I have seen you, on more than one occasion, drunk between his barrels."

"What!" cried Friar Kish, in pretended indignation, "*I* drunk between the king's barrels? *I*, a good friar? Ho, ho! The jest is ill-timed, friend. But since you know, or pretend to know, so much of me, pray let me ask who *you* are. Ah, on my soul! Why, 'tis Silverbell!"

"Right, Friar Kish."

"Eh? Ha, ha! ho, ho! What a

merry jest. But what means this disguise? Why do you wear a long cloak? Where is your motley?"

"Under it."

"*Under* it! Ha, ha! ho, ho! What a merry jester is Silverbell. Are you not, Silverbell?"

"Ay, a *very* merry jester, Friar Kish," replied Silverbell—"as you may find out ere long," he muttered.

"It was a huge jest to drink my wine, Silverbell; but seeing that I, like thousands more, love you, I can't complain. You won't say aught about the wine, Silverbell?"

"Nay, not I."

"It would be a dreadful thing for me if Rochester thought I partook too freely of wine."

"At this moment you look as if you were in the habit of doing so. Your face proclaims you a drinker, and on no small scale."

"Ha, ha! ho, ho! *What* a jester you are! But, Silverbell, an' it's a fair question, whence go you?"

"To Whitehall."

"You are there now."

"I know it. Here my journey ends."

"I am sorry for that, for I like your company right well."

"Whence go *you*?"

"Ah, dear Silverbell, *I* am on a visit to my aged parents."

"Indeed!"

"Ay, I frequently visit them."

"They ought to be proud of such a son," sneered Silverbell. "Well, I bid you adieu."

"Farewell! The Virgin protect you."

"May all good saints defend us!" muttered Silverbell, and he turned his steed round, as if going in another direction. "Of all the lying friars I ever encountered, surely Friar Kish is the biggest."

Drawing into the shadow of a huge oak, he waited until the friar had vanished, then, putting spurs to his horse, he went towards Rochester House in a different direction to the one the friar had gone.

Friar Kish made no more pauses, but went straight on to his destination.

He was instantly admitted.

NOTICE.—*Another Coloured Picture is Given Away with this Number.*

"WITH ALL HER FORCE DOROTHY BROUGHT DOWN THE STOOL ON HIS HEAD."

The first thing that Friar Kish did was to order a supper to be placed before him.

This was done in a very short time.

Do not ask what sort of supper the friar made.

He could eat quite as well as he could drink.

When he had finished, he placed his hands upon his huge stomach, gave vent to a deep sigh, which meant that he was sorry he was compelled to stop, and then, eyeing the serving-woman, said—

"You have guessed my errand?"

"Of course I have."

"It's a sad, *sad* task."

"Well, *you* don't think it so."

"I do, and I don't. The fact is, I love the dear creatures."

"*Love* them?"

"Well, the Church says—"

"Don't tell me what the Church says, or what it don't say. My advice is—though I bear her no good will myself—to go and see the girl and use your arguments with her at once."

"Is she in a bad state?"

"A *very* bad state."

"Give me a link and the key, and I will go at once."

"Alone?"

"Ay, alone. Have I not been alone before?"

"You have, but you have not always won them over."

"True. But in this case, seeing how long she has been confined, I think I shall have but little difficulty."

A link and the key were procured, and with them Friar Kish, who knew the way right well, went off.

It was certainly a wonder, though, that he did not break his neck, for in going down the stone steps he stumbled times enough.

Opening the door of the Black Vault, he found Dorothy upon her knees.

In low, trembling tones she was praying—for death.

"Rise, daughter," said the friar, placing the link in a staple. "Pray not for death, but life."

"Who are you?" asked Dorothy, rising, and shading her eyes from the rays of the link.

"My daughter, my name is—that is, I am called the good Friar Kish. I have come to—"

"By whose authority are you here?"

"My dear daughter, by whose authority but the good Rochester's? Ah, daughter, if you only knew his lordship's real nature—"

And he advanced nearer to Dorothy.

"Away!" cried the maiden—"away! I *do* know his real nature. Ay, and the nature of those in his pay. Away, I tell you. Approach me not. Already I loathe the sight of you. *You* a good friar? *You?* You, who are already under the influence of strong drink? Away, I tell you, and let me die in peace."

But the wine had obtained the upperhand of Friar Kish.

Dorothy's reply, uttered in tones which left no doubt as to their meaning, caused him to become enraged.

"I *will* speak to you!" he cried, starting forward and suddenly seizing Dorothy's wrists. "You *shall* listen to me."

"'Tis no use calling for help here," gasped Dorothy, "that I know right well; but, if you are a man—if you have the least right to the garb you wear—unhand me."

"No. I tell you I am sent here by Rochester to—"

"To what?"

"To bring you to your senses, girl; to—to press upon those lips the kiss of peace—to—"

A long, piercing scream escaped Dorothy's lips as she struggled to free herself.

Round and round the cell they went, Friar Kish trying hard to get her to stand still.

At length, by a brutal push, he forced her to her knees.

Dorothy, by this time, was exhausted, and could only look what she would have said.

The friar still held her firmly by the wrists.

Suddenly there was a low, rumbling sound. A huge stone in the corner of the cell revolved with a click, and a dark figure dashed through the aperture.

Dorothy saw a glittering blade raised for an instant in the air—the next it was plunged into the friar's heart.

"Ah!" cried Dorothy, starting up, but drawing back at the sight of a dagger dripping with blood.

"Who—who are you?" she asked. "Hist! Silence for your life!" was the answer. *I am Silverbell!*

CHAPTER IX.

SHOWS WHO SOUNDED THE ALARM AT ROCHESTER HOUSE, AND WHAT BE-CAME OF THE RINGER AND THE BELL—THE DISCOVERY—SILVERBELL AT BAY—JACK STRAW ONCE MORE TO THE RESCUE.

"SILVERBELL?" whispered Dorothy, inquiringly.

"Ay, Silverbell, the king's principal jester. Mayhap you have heard of him?" said Silverbell, as, stooping down, he wrenched the key of the cell from the hand of the dead friar, and locked the door. "If you have not, your father has. Fear not, I am your friend. My face, so people have said, was created for nothing but laughter. They are mistaken. Silverbell can be serious and determined when he likes. Come, follow me at once, or all may be lost."

Seizing the link, he took Dorothy's hand and led her to the aperture.

"It is no nice thing for a lady to do, I trow," said Silverbell; "but, to escape, you will have to crawl upon your hands and knees."

"Anything, so that I escape."

"I will go first."

Casting himself upon his knees, and holding aloft the link, Silverbell passed through the narrow aperture and was closely followed by Dorothy.

When both had left the cell, Silverbell said—

"Can you feel the stone with your foot?"

"I can."

"Give it a sharp kick."

Dorothy did so, and the stone revolved to its proper position, and fastened itself with a loud click.

"They cannot enter from the cell," said Silverbell, "even if they found us out, which is not likely, for I'll warrant none of them know of this secret passage."

"Will you tell me—" began Dorothy.

"Let us preserve silence," interrupted Silverbell. "I will tell you all anon. I can only say now that, if we can reach the moat, to which this leads, we shall be safe. It is not a dark night, but we can manage to escape observation. It is a long, narrow, filthy, and tortuous passage, and— Ha! that is the first misfortune," he added, as the link flickered, hissed, and went out. "But no matter; keep close to me, and all will be well."

* * * *

The serving-woman waited until nearly half-an-hour had elapsed, but the friar not returning, she became alarmed, and summoning the brutal leader of the men, together with about a dozen of his followers, repaired to the vault with them.

As our readers know, it was locked.

"What ho!" shouted the leader. "What ho, holy friar! What ho! I say."

To each of his "What's ho's," he delivered upon the massive door a loud whack with a small axe which he took from his girdle.

Echoes were the only replies.

"Heaven's mercy!" cried the serving-woman, "what can have happened?"

"Mayhap the holy friar is so engaged in praying," ventured one of the men, "that he takes no heed of your knocks."

Once again the leader banged upon the door, this time louder than before.

No reply, of course.

"Of a surety something serious has happened," said the serving-woman.

"'Tis exactly as I think," replied the leader.

"She has escaped, perhaps," said one of the men.

"How can that be, fool," replied the leader, "when there is no escape whatever this way? Besides, you being one of the guards on the round staircase, if she has escaped that way, why you would be to blame for it."

"No one has passed me," replied the man, in surly tones.

"You are sure the friar did not pass?"

"Ay; if he had attempted to do so, what would have been the result? Your orders were that I was to cut down any who tried to pass without the password."

"Except the friar and our men."

"Friar or no friar, I should have slain him, had he not given the password."

"In so doing," said another of the men, "a deal of our lord's good wine would in future have been saved."

This caused the men to burst out into a roar of laughter.

"This is no time for jesting," said the serving-woman. "That something serious has happened there can be no doubt. And woe to me if there has, for I shall be answerable to his lordship."

"What do you advise?" asked the leader.

"That the door, not having a second key, should be instantly battered down."

Thereupon the leader gave the word for a battering-ram to be brought.

The great lumbering instrument was fetched, and the whole of the men brought it to bear upon the door.

For a long time the latter resisted all their efforts, but at last the lock was smashed, and the door flew open.

The leader instantly rushed in, but he was in such haste that he fell over the dead friar, and his link was extinguished.

So frightened, for the moment, was the coward, that he howled for mercy.

His companions raised him, white and trembling, to his feet.

"By the soul of the Virgin!" he cried, "who is this?"

"Ha!" cried the men in chorus, "it is the friar."

"And dead," added the serving-woman, as she deliberately turned him over on his face.

"Ay, and dead," echoed the man.

"But where is the girl?" shrieked the serving-woman.

There was no reply to this.

All the men looked superstitiously round the dismal cell, and seemed as if they should like to flee from the spot.

"Where is the girl, I say?" repeated the woman, tears of mingled rage and fear gathering in her eyes.

"Heaven knows!" said the leader, in hollow tones. "She is not here, and she cannot have escaped—that would have been a matter of impossibility."

"Go at once!" cried the serving-woman. "Search the corridors—search everywhere. I myself will sound the alarm; she cannot have gone far, if she did get out of this cell."

Away went the serving-woman to sound the alarm.

It was a long way to the bell-turret, and the staircases, with the exception of where the moon's rays pierced the narrow apertures called windows, were very dark.

But the serving-woman knew the way, and rage and despair lent wings to her feet.

As she dashed through the doorway leading to the roof, the moonlight fell full upon her, revealing a face of fiendish fury.

Her hair—of raven blackness, and as wiry as that of a horse's tail—had escaped from its combs, and flew about her face and shoulders in wild confusion.

Rushing to the bell-rope, she tore it from its fastenings, and exerting all her strength, tugged furiously at it.

But the serving-woman had made a fearful mistake, and, too late, she saw it.

She had taken the whole length of the rope from its staples, instead of only half.

The result was that, as the ponderous mass of metal gained its full velocity, it dragged her hither and thither.

The more it swung her, with greater tenacity did she cling to the rope.

Wider and wider became its scope, and suddenly the serving-woman, with a gasping cry, *seized the bell-clapper itself* as it swung towards her.

The result was horrible.

The heavy clapper dashed her head against the bell and smashed it; and her weight—no light one—broke the ring, tore the bell from its position, and both went flying over the battlement, and fell with a loud splash into the moat, the tremendous weight causing the water to rise into the air like a waterspout.

The retainers, awakened from their sleep by the clangour of the bell, had dressed, and arming themselves rushed into the courtyard, where they were witnesses of this awful calamity.

But they paused only for a brief space. Whoever had fallen into the moat from such a height, they thought, had been most assuredly killed, and, at present, they could pay no attention to the circumstance.

They had been ordered by their leader to watch the edge of the moat very closely, and they carried out these instructions to the letter, for with flaming links, held high above their heads, they well examined the sides.

"Above all things," said the leader, "if you catch sight of any moving object don't discharge an arrow, for if the girl is killed it would not be well for us."

Round and round the moat went the men, their eyes fixed upon the dark walls of the castle, but for some time they saw nothing.

At last, however, a hoarse yell burst upon the air, and a rush was made to the spot whence it proceeded.

A score of links were held aloft, causing so great a reflection in the sky, that persons at a distance must have imagined that some residence was on fire.

This great flare was observed by a party of horsemen, the leader of whom gave the word for the horses to be put to the gallop.

"What see you ?" cried the leader of Rochester's men, peering in the direction indicated. "Ha," he shouted, "two figures, as I live! One is a woman, I swear. Hold! Stir not, but keep your bows ready, for I see that one is a man."

By the side of the wall crept two figures, Silverbell and Dorothy.

"What ho!" shouted the leader, drawing his sword with a flourish. "What ho, there, I say! Surrender, and no harm will be done ye. Refuse, and you die."

"We are discovered," said Silverbell, "but would you not rather die than languish in that horrible dungeon, or become the mistress of the villainous Rochester ? "

"Sooner, a thousand times."

"Take, then, this dagger. I have here my sword. 'Tis a weapon I seldom carry, but 'tis a true blade, and I know well how to handle it. This, as you see, is a broad moat and deep, but I can easily swim it with you in my arms.

"Mark it well : if we are set upon on the other side, use your dagger as freely as your woman's arm will let you. Rochester—"

"What ho! What ho!" again shouted the leader. "Surrender."

"Never, vile caitiff ! " cried Silverbell. " I have taken this poor girl under my protection. I have rescued her from Rochester's vile clutches, and sooner than I will deliver her or myself up to you, I will die."

"Then die thou shalt, thou hell-hound," almost shrieked the leader.

The words had barely left his lips before Silverbell, placing Dorothy over his left shoulder, plunged into the moat.

"We shall have them directly they reach here," said the leader. "Holy Mary! who can this man be? and how did he contrive to enter the house ? "

"'Tis not how he contrived to enter the house," replied one of the men, "it is how did he reach the Black Vault ? "

"Ay, ay! When we capture him we will wring the secret from him, or wring his neck. Certes ! how he swims, and with his cloak on and a girl on his arms."

Just as Silverbell reached the bank, a great rush was made to seize him, but he showed them that they had a desperate man to deal with, for with a clean stroke he cut down the man nearest him, and, in the confusion which followed he, with Dorothy, scrambled on to dry ground.

Here he made a bold stand.

"Surrender yourself," said the leader. "You see that you are surrounded by armed men. A dozen arrows are pointing at your breast."

"I fear them not," replied Silverbell. "Discharge them an' you like."

"We prefer to take you alive, so that my Lord Rochester may interrogate you, and see who and what you are."

"You will never take me alive."

"Do you defy us ? "

"Ay, I do defy you. Neither—"

At this moment a loud shout rent

the air, and the party saw a number of horsemen rapidly advancing.

"Hurrah!" shouted the now excited leader, "'tis my Lord Rochester—'tis my Lord Rochester. Hurrah!"

"Hurrah!" echoed the men. "Rochester! Rochester!"

But they were very much mistaken.

In a few seconds the horsemen rode up.

"Who shouts for Rochester?" asked a somewhat deep voice. "By Our Lady! he who led such a shout deserves to have his tongue cut from his mouth."

The leader of Rochester's men looked up, and saw before him a youthful though powerfully-built figure.

Suddenly a great cry—a cry of surprise and joy burst from Dorothy's lips.

"Ah!" she cried, "heaven has heard my prayers! *It is Jack Straw!*"

Rochester's men drew back with loud murmurs.

They had heard a great deal of this daring youth, but had never before seen him.

And, to tell the candid truth, they did not like the look of him.

The leader of Rochester's men drew back a few yards, and his followers surrounded him.

"I have heard he is Rochester's most determined enemy," he said to them, "and a heavy price would be paid for him, dead or alive. Archers, draw!"

"Listen, thou follower of England's most accursed noble!" said Jack Straw. "If you order those men to shoot a single bolt, I will burn you alive before the gates of this house. What if your men outnumber mine by a few score? Think you that those who surround me are all that I command? Within call of this horn are *hundreds* of brave hearts, who at my bidding would hack you and your men in pieces, and raze this mansion to the ground."

This, of course, was a deliberate falsehood, but Jack was well aware that he stood at a great disadvantage.

Rochester's archers, at their leader's command, had fixed their arrows, but at Jack's speech they lowered them, and looked inquiringly at each other.

"Look you, my men," said Jack, rising in his stirrups. "No doubt many of you have heard of me. It is said that I am a robber. That is a lie! a dastardly lie! I am but a sympathiser and liberator of the poor. I would crush oppression and tyrants. What is he you call your master? What is he but a tyrant—a cowardly knave and murderer? Ay, ye know it well. How long will you serve such a master? Join *my* banner, and you shall have freedom and plenty. *Who shouts for Jack Straw?*"

A dead silence reigned for some moments.

The men whispered among themselves; then, suddenly, one, stepping forward, cried—

"I am for Jack Straw."

"And I!" "And I!" "And I!" was repeated again and again.

It was in vain that the now exasperated leader raved, swore, and cursed; the men heeded him not at all.

One by one they crossed over, until at last only two remained by the side of the leader—two brutal-looking scoundrels, who were really assassins, paid by Rochester to do his bidding, whatever it might be.

"'Tis well," said Jack. "On our return to Blackfoot Castle, all of you shall be sworn in. But I will place in your hands my first order. Arrest those three men."

With an oath the leader called upon the two men to defend themselves, but they were wise enough to see the folly of so doing, and they therefore threw down their arms and allowed themselves to be secured.

The leader had his sword wrested from him, and by Jack's orders, his arms were tied behind his back.

And now, for the first time, Jack's eyes rested upon Silverbell and Dorothy.

The latter, who came forward, he instantly recognised, and a cry of astonishment escaped his lips.

"Are you not Dorothy Leighton?" he asked, slightly raising his cap.

"The same, brave Master Straw," answered Dorothy.

"Then, in the name of heaven, what are you doing here?"

"I was so far rescued when I and my rescuer were set upon by orders of yon villain."

And Dorothy pointed to the captive leader.

"Ha! Why, as I live, I and my comrades had come all the way from Dartford to rescue you, and we left your good father praying for our success and your safe deliverance."

"My father!" cried Dorothy, clasping her hands. "My dear father! Oh, sir! what agony must he have suffered. He is safe and well?"

"Ay, within the walls of my castle."

"Heaven be praised!"

"But see here, Mistress Dorothy, who is your would-be rescuer? Is that he who stands there like a dark shadow?"

"Yes."

"His name?"

"I dare not utter it."

"Oh, oh! Come forward, sir," cried Jack, "and let me look at you."

Silverbell obeyed.

"Prithee, tell me your name, sir," said Jack, eyeing him curiously, "though, methinks, I have seen you before."

"If ye will stoop in your saddle, I will tell you."

Jack did so.

"My name is Silverbell, the king's principal jester."

Jack started, and eyed him with astonishment.

"Silverbell!" he repeated to himself. "Holy Mary! what a blow to the king if I could win this man over to our side."

Addressing Silverbell, Jack said aloud, "I have heard a great deal of you, Sir Jester, but until this moment I was not aware that you devoted any portion of your time to rescuing unfortunate maidens, or that you were in the habit of drawing the sword."

"I am not in the habit of doing either, but a time comes when any man, no matter what his occupation, is justified in attempting to defend those who cannot defend themselves."

"Well said, Sir Jester, well said. Well, I will not now ask you to give me all the particulars, but I will anon. What ho, Egbert!"

"Here," replied Egbert, coming forward.

"I prithee dismount, and take under your charge that young girl. She requires your attention."

Egbert at once dismounted.

"Now," said Jack, "lead the way into the castle, and we will see what is to be done with these three villians."

The men, so recently under the banner of Rochester, led the way across the drawbridge, the leader and the two men went next, and Jack Straw and the remainder followed.

CHAPTER X.

IS OF HOW JACK STRAW HELD A "COURT" IN ROCHESTER'S OWN HOUSE— OF HOW HE SERVED THE LEADER, AND THE TWO MEN, AND HOW SILVERBELL JOINED HIM.

THE principal reception-room at Rochester House was a very splendid apartment. The ceiling, walls, flooring and furniture were of carved oak, and the entrances, of which there were four, were hung with heavy damask curtains, the gold embroidery upon which must originally have cost an immense sum of money.

Around the walls, and very artistically placed, hung pieces of armour and weapons of almost every description. These had been worn and wielded in various battles by Rochester's ancestors, and inscriptions on gold plates beneath the trophies told the name, the date, and so on.

All were in a state of excellent preservation, and as Jack Straw entered this gorgeous apartment, in which kings and peers of the realm had been entertained, and his eyes rested upon this great display of armour and arms, he uttered an exclamation of delight.

At the extreme end of the room, and opposite the principal entrance, was a raised dais, which was decked with cloth of silver and gold.

Over it hung a most magnificent suit of Damascus steel-chain armour, an elaborately chased battle-axe and a steel cap, in the centre of which was placed a large diamond, and this was surrounded with quite a little crowd of rubies.

Jack Straw, who was followed into the apartment by the whole party, looked at this for a moment; then calling one of his men, he bade him take it down.

"On your life, touch it not!" cried the leader. "That armour is the property of the king."

"The king?" said Jack. "Then how comes it here?"

"That I cannot tell you, but it is the property of the king, and neither you, nor anyone else, dare tear it from its position."

"Say you so?" cried Jack. "See, then, that Jack Straw *dares* to take it from its position."

So saying, he mounted the dais, and reaching over, dragged the whole down with a loud crash.

"My Lord Rochester shall know by whose hand that armour—sacred in his eyes—was torn down," said the leader.

"Sacred in his eyes, say you?" shouted Jack. "Holy Mary! I should much like to know what is sacred in the eyes of Rochester. Ho, ho! But mark ye, knave, I think it unlikely that *you* will have the opportunity of telling Rochester by whose hand it was torn down."

With these words Jack, to the intense astonishment of the leader, took his seat upon the dais.

Then he told the men with the links to range themselves round the room, at so many paces from each other, after which he bade the man he had called forth hold up the armour.

This was done, and Jack said—

"The property of the king, or any-one else, is of little importance. So far as this armour is concerned I like it much, and I can see that it will fit my person right well. This time to-morrow, an' I live, I will wear it."

"And by Our Lady," laughed a number of the men, "it will become you far better than the king."

"Now," said Jack, "let Egbert come forward."

But Egbert was nowhere to be seen.

"The youth of whom you spoke," said Silverbell, "is attending Mistress Leighton in another apartment."

"It is what I was about to instruct him to do," said Jack. "They will be well together. Now bring forth yonder fiendish-looking knave."

And Jack pointed to the leader.

He was seized by two stalwart men and thrust in front of the dais.

"Look up, sirrah," shouted Jack.

The man looked up defiantly.

"You are Rochester's leading retainer?" asked Jack.

"I am," replied the man, in insolent tones, "and as such I shall decline to answer any questions which you may think proper to put to me."

"You will, will you? Well, it will be a matter of but little moment. We found you in the act of attempting to recapture an innocent girl, who was forcibly taken from her father's house by your accursed master. Look here," pointing to Silverbell, who stood on the right of the dais, "here stands one witness against you. And let me tell you, his word can be relied upon, for know that he is no less a person than the king's principal jester, by name— Silverbell!"

At these words Silverbell threw back his cloak, disclosing the magnificent attire always worn by the leading jester.

All present, as may be supposed, were thunder struck, and loud and long were the murmurings in the room.

Silverbell told all he knew, which, as our readers are aware, was something of importance.

When he had concluded, Jack complimented him on his courage.

It was quite laughable to see how the leader's eyes opened when Silverbell spoke of the secret passage, and he longed to be free, if only to ascertain whether all the jester had said was true. Dorothy was now sent for, and she, amid breathless silence, told of the cruel manner in which she had been treated by Rochester, the leader, and the serving-woman, whose absence now began to cause some surprise among those who had been Rochester's followers.

As Jack listened his brows became knitted, and it was easily seen that the fate of the leader would soon be decided.

When Dorothy had concluded, she became so faint, that Egbert had to lead her away.

There was now a pause for a few moments.

Suddenly Jack rose, and calling to one of the men, said—

"At my saddle-bow you will find a long coil of rope. Bring it hither."

The man departed on his errand.

To another Jack said, "Fetch me pen and parchment, if such things are to be found within these crime-stained walls."

These happened to be handy, and a small table being wheeled in front of him, Jack took out his dagger, cut the parchment in three pieces, and taking the pen wrote on each—

"By Order of Jack Straw."

All eyes were anxiously bent upon his hand as he traced these words.

When he had finished this, the man brought in the rope, and a long and thick coil it was of a surety!

Beckoning to several more men, who came forward, Jack said—

"First cut sufficient to bind the arms of these men to their sides."

A loud howl of horror now left the lips of the leader and his two comrades.

"In the name of the Virgin!" cried the former, whose face had turned to ashy paleness, "what is about to be done to us?"

"You will see anon," replied Jack, and in such calm tones that those who heard them shuddered.

The arms of the men having been tied to their sides as directed, Jack ordered a piece of parchment to be placed on each man's breast.

This was also quickly done.

Jack, surveying the three trembling wretches, said in stern tones—

"You three, as I am now assured, are hardened villains in the pay of this bloodthirsty Rochester. Heaven alone knows of what crimes you have been guilty. But, for your treatment of this poor girl, who could not defend herself, you deserve death, and a speedy death will therefore be your portion."

"Do you dare to sentence us to death?" shrieked the leader.

"Of a surety. That is the sentence I pronounce. If there are any here who do not approve of my judgment, let them come forward."

But no one stirred.

"Take the three," continued Jack, still in the same calm tones, "to the highest battlement, and let the sentence be carried out directly you hear a blast from a horn."

Resistance was useless. The former retainers of Rochester led the way up the various stone staircases, and at last reached the top.

Jack, with several of his men, went into the courtyard, and there watched what was going on above.

"Ye are true comrades," cried the leader, "to desert me and assist in executing me."

"We have joined Jack Straw," replied one of his late companions "and must now carry out his orders."

"May my most bitter curse rest upon ye all."

But no reply was made to his ravings.

A portion of the coil of rope, nearly ten feet in length, was cut, one end placed in a slip-knot round his neck, and the other round a beam—one of six—projecting from the battlement.

The other two were served in the same way.

The preparations being completed, the men awaited the signal

It was a weird and awful sight—these three men standing thus, in the full glare of the moon's rays, on the brink of eternity, and without having received absolution for the numerous crimes they had committed.

The leader continued to rave and curse, but his two companions seemed to have fallen into a state of partial insensibility.

Suddenly the loud blast of a horn was heard, and before its echoes had died away, the three miserable wretches *were pushed over the battlements!*

Down they shot like lumps of lead and hung quivering over the moat.

Backwards and forwards they swayed for several minutes, but at last they were still.

"'Tis a warning for Rochester," said Jack, "and for those who follow in his footsteps."

Being joined again by all the men, Jack gave instructions that the whole of the arms and armour were to be carried off from the reception-room, together with every article of value that could be found.

These orders were carried out with alacrity. The men liked this sort of work, and very soon everything of any importance was brought out and placed in the courtyard, and it certainly formed an extraordinary and valuable collection.

The horses from Rochester's stables, to the number of twelve, were then saddled and brought forth.

But the collection of plunder was so extensive, that it was found necessary to load nearly every horse that Jack's comrades had ridden.

The next thing ransacked was the wine cellar. Several barrels were brought up, tapped and partaken of by the now thirsty men, and what was not drunk was thrown into the moat.

Silverbell watched all these proceedings with great attention.

At last Jack turned to him.

"Sir Jester," he said, "I make no doubt it is almost useless to ask you, but will you join my banner? Your pay, as principal jester to the king, may be large, but I would make it larger, and you would be as free as the birds of the air. What say you?"

Silverbell hesitated but an instant.

Holding forth his hand, he said—

"I am with you."

Jack shook hands heartily with him, and then shouted—

"Mark it well! Silverbell, the king's jester, has joined us. Greet this acquisition with a loud cheer, my men."

Three loud cheers the men gave, and accompanied them with waving of hats and weapons.

Jack gave orders for a horse to be placed at Silverbell's disposal.

"And ride by my side," he said, "for I would converse with you on matters connected with the Court."

There being few horses to spare, Dorothy was mounted behind Egbert, and all being in readiness, the whole cavalcade moved off at a walking pace.

CHAPTER XI.

SHOWS HOW THE KING WANTED TO BORROW SOME MONEY—HOW ROCHESTER AGREED TO LEND IT—HOW HE AND LORD WALWORTH SET OUT TO GET IT—HOW IT WAS TAKEN TO WALWORTH HOUSE—AND WHAT THE BAGS CONTAINED.

HIS MAJESTY was mightily troubled.

One thing and another had gone entirely wrong lately. The doings in France and Spain annoyed him, and now he found that the people were beginning to grumble at the way they were oppressed and ground down by his nobles.

To add to this the name of Jack Straw was beginning to be spoken of by the people as their future deliverer. His name was mentioned at Court with a shudder.

When, however, the news reached the Court of what had taken place at Rochester House, a cry of horror at Jack's daring was raised, and the king swore that he would hunt him and his followers to death.

A week after the events narrated in the previous chapter, his majesty was pacing the broad terrace before his palace at Greenwich.

His head was bent upon his breast, and it was evident that he was greatly agitated.

Several of his favourite courtiers were on the terrace conversing in groups, and if any attempted to approach him, the king waved them off.

But suddenly he caught sight of two horsemen riding slowly up the avenue, and, calling to Lord Tempest, who happened to be standing nearest him, he said—

"Look yonder, my lord, and tell me if that is not Rochester."

"It is, sire."

"I thought so. And who rides with him?"

"It is Walworth, your majesty."

"Hum! They seem to be inseparable companions lately. Can you tell me why, my lord?"

"Nay, sire. Neither Rochester nor Walworth are pleased to entrust me with his secrets. But—"

He paused abruptly.

"Proceed, my lord," said the king.

"Mayhap they are putting their heads together, and endeavouring to think of the best way to capture the now redoubtable and much to be feared Jack Straw."

As he said this, however, a grim smile lurked in the corners of his mouth.

The king at once noticed it.

"You are satirical, my lord," he said. "But fear not that *I* will find a way to capture this youth, who is pleased to call himself Jack Straw. I have sworn it on the Cross. But if what I have heard is correct, *you* have not much reason to complain of this Jack Straw."

"Nay, sire, that is indeed true."

"I have heard a little of the incident, but perhaps you will be pleased to give me the full particulars?"

"With pleasure, your majesty," replied Lord Tempest, with a low bow. "Two nights ago, sire, I, with her ladyship and a dozen followers, were crossing Dartford Common."

The king nodded.

"We had arrived at about the centre of the common," continued Lord Tempest, "and on account of the night being very dark, I had just issued orders that the men should be placed on guard, when we suddenly came to a halt—"

"Eh?" interrupted the king.

"A halt, sire."

"But were you not on horseback?"

"No, sire, but in the litter with her ladyship."

"Proceed."

"We suddenly came to a halt. I put my head out with the intention of ascertaining the reason of the stoppage, when I beheld what I, at first, took to be a mass of dwarf trees. I looked round, and then saw that we were completely surrounded by a large number of armed men.

"Quite romantic!" said the king, with a slight sneer. "I presume your lordship immediately fainted?"

"Nay, sire; your majesty knows I have been present at several battles, and have never flinched from my—"

"Pray proceed, my lord," laughed the king. "I did but jest."

"Before I had time to enquire what all this meant, a loud, commanding voice cried out, 'Halt!' I asked, 'Who cries halt?' and the answer was, 'Jack Straw.' Knowing, sire, that this same Jack Straw is in the habit of extracting toll from whosoever might pass his way, I, of course, thought that we should have to make him a present of all our jewellery. But, in the first place, he called a man to his side—I heard the name distinctly, it was Sampson—and after a few moments' conversation, this Jack Straw called out, 'Who is within this litter?' I replied, 'Lord Tempest and his lady.'

"Jack Straw then came to the door of the litter on horseback—and I may remark to your majesty, that he is, in good truth, a fine youth—opened the door, and said, 'It has been told me, my lord, that on more than one occasion you have befriended the poor and needy, and that being so, I allow you, and those who accompany you, to depart in peace.'"

"Was this all he said, my lord?"

"Nay. He said, 'Act always kindly to the poor, my lord, and when you want a friend, fear not that you will find one in me. No man shall want who is kind to the poor, but when he acts otherwise, let him beware. Our watchword is, *Death to tyrants!*'

"The last words had barely left his lips when there arose a wild shout—a shout that seemed to shake the vault of heaven. It was, '*Death to tyrants!*'"

The king started, turned pale, and for a few seconds paced the terrace with rapid strides.

Pausing, he said—

"And this was all, my lord?"

"All, sire," replied Lord Tempest bowing. "We were allowed to proceed without further interruption."

"And you cannot guess the number of men who surrounded you?"

"Nay, sire, the night was too dark, but the number must have been great."

"And did all appear to be mounted?"

"All, your majesty."

"Hum! By the Holy Virgin! this

is, indeed, assuming serious proportions. But here is Rochester. We will consult him, though I much fear he is too dejected to converse on any important matters."

But Rochester certainly did not appear dejected.

On the contrary, he was laughing and chatting with Walworth. Yet any close observer would have seen that his laughter was cruelly forced.

Dismounting, and leaving their horses at the foot of the steps, the two lords ascended to the terrace and bent their knee before the king.

"Rise," said the king. "Rochester, I am glad to see you thus early. My Lord Walworth, I pray you retire."

Again bowing lowly, Walworth retired some few yards, and was soon engaged in conversation with Lord Tempest.

"Now I look closely at you, my lord," said the king, "I see that you do not bear upon your face any very great expression of regret at what has lately taken place at your house."

"Sire," replied Rochester, "during the past few months I have met with so many misfortunes, that this last has failed to make any great impression upon me. I am content to wait. Your majesty, I live now but to wipe out the insult this boy has done me. And I will wipe it out in his blood."

"You mean, my lord, that if you had a chance, you would do battle with him?"

"Precisely."

"Hem! Do nothing of the kind, my lord."

"And why, sire?"

"Because you would assuredly meet with your death. Remember, that you are not like your ancestors. Your father fought side by side with many brave knights on the battle-field, and as one who kept a watchful eye upon him, I am bound to say that he was ever brave and fearless. He was never known to flinch even under such a storm of arrows that the air was darkened."

"Sire, you do honour to my illustrious parent, and cover me with shame!" said Rochester, in low tones.

"Nay, 'tis not so. I warn you, and it is for your own safety. Latterly I have heard a great deal of this extra-ordinary youth, and I learn that he is a thorough master of every weapon. That he is such a complete master of even the horse he rides, that he guides it with his voice. I have heard also, my lord, that, in the midst of the greatest danger, he never flinches. That being so, my lord, youth or man, he is not one for you to try your strength against. There is another thing which puzzles me amazingly. This Jack Straw appears to have the power of appearing and disappearing at his own will. Can you account for that, my lord?"

"Nay, sire."

"Nor anyone else. But the mystery shall shortly be unravelled. And I think you said that the armour, which hung over the dais, and which really belongs to our armoury, has also been taken?"

"It has, your majesty, and I make no doubt that at this present moment it graces the person of this villainous outlaw."

"Does he dare—"

"He dares do anything, sire."

Once again the king paced the terrace with excited strides.

Stopping suddenly, he said—

"Look you, Rochester, many things have lately occurred to diminish to an alarming extent the money in our treasury. Of course, since we have offended that miser, Elias Leighton, it is useless to think that he would advance us any. Now, do you think it possible that, by any means, a sum of fifty thousand crowns can be raised?"

Rochester started.

"'Tis a large sum, your majesty."

"But a small amount compared with the sum taken from us by accursed robbers."

"True, sire. Well, your majesty, I believe I can raise the amount, but not from one individual."

"It matters not to me how many lenders there be, so that the amount be raised."

"And the security, sire?"

"You shall have one half the royal jewels."

Rochester bowed.

"With that security, your majesty," he said, "I venture to think that I shall have no difficulty in obtaining the sum. When shall I set about the matter?"

"At once. I am greatly in want of the money for many purposes. Get the fifty thousand crowns, and any favour—I should say, any favour in reason—we will grant you."

Rochester bowed himself almost to the ground.

He had a great many favours to ask.

At this moment a large number of courtiers were seen advancing, the proud Duke of Somerset in their midst.

"What has happened, your grace?" asked the king.

"Sire, I regret to say that I have bad news for you."

"Heaven's mercy!" cried the king, "what, bad news again? Holy Mary, defend us! When are we going to have any *good* news, your grace?"

"I know not sire, but—"

"Pray let us know what the bad news this time is."

"Sire, you are aware that Silverbell has been missing for some days."

"Of a surety. I trust his dead body has not been found? I think we treated him rather hardly, for such a merry fellow as he was."

"He deserves no sympathy!" cried Somerset. "We have at last discovered his whereabouts."

"Ha! And that is?"

"With Jack Straw."

The king started back as though an arrow had pierced his breast.

"Impossible!" he gasped.

"Nay, sire, 'tis *not* impossible. We have it on good authority."

"Whose authority?"

"A man who but an hour ago was captured. He is one of Jack Straw's band. We questioned him as to the number of men Jack Straw had, but he refused to say. He, however, mentioned that the king's jester was attached to Straw's company."

"And that was all he would say?"

"All sire."

"Let him be again questioned, and if he refuse to answer your questions, nail his ears to a wall and cut his tongue out."

The king waved his hand, Somerset bowed, and, with the courtiers who accompanied him, departed to carry out the royal commands.

It was evident that this last intelligence was a great blow to the king. Folding his arms, he stood looking moodily across the park. Rochester's presence was forgotten, and visions of Jack Straw, surrounded by a multitude of armed men, rose up before him.

Gliding, snake-like, down the steps, Rochester strode towards the other end of the terrace, and sought out Walworth.

"I have some important news for you, my lord," he said.

"If it is good news it is right welcome," replied Walworth.

"It *is* good news. But come, let us mount and ride through the park, and as we ride I will tell you the purport of my interview with the king."

The two were soon mounted, and they rode off through the park.

The king saw them, but he was too much occupied with his own thoughts to take any notice.

"Now for the news, Rochester," said Walworth, when they were some considerable distance from the palace.

"Ay, I will tell you now, but—"

"What are you looking about for, my lord?"

"What I have to say must not be overheard, and you know that the followers of this accursed Jack Straw are almost everywhere."

"We are now in the open, my lord," replied Walworth, "and unless Jack Straw's spies can transform themselves into birds, they cannot escape our notice."

"True! Now, my lord, what I am about to say is of so important a character, that before I tell you I must ask you to swear on this crucifix that you will not divulge one atom of the secret."

"It is, then, a secret?"

"It is. I want you to assist me in carrying out an important work. If you will agree to do so you will be richer by ten thousand crowns."

"Holy Mary! Am I awake or dreaming?"

"You are wide awake I should say."

"Ten thousand crowns, you say."

"Ten thousand crowns!"

"And what is to be undertaken, my lord? I am not very particular, as you are aware. Ho! ho! How many murders are to be done for this sum?"

"None."

"*None*, say you? Then, on this crucifix, I swear to assist you and to keep the secret."

Kissing a small crucifix Rochester held towards him, Walworth listened with great and anxious attention.

"The king," said Rochester "wants to borrow fifty thousand crowns."

"Ha! ha! impossible. Who, my lord, does he think will trust him?"

"I am going to get it for him."

"You?" cried Lord Walworth, in great and genuine astonishment. "Why, I thought that you, my lord, were as poor as am I."

"So 'tis generally thought."

"I presume you intend to borrow—"

"Tush!" interrupted Rochester. "You will remember, my lord, that some time back robbers stole four bags of money which—"

"The Blackheath robbery, do you mean?"

"Ay."

"*I* remember! *A most mysterious* affair, my lord, eh?"

"Very!"

The two looked at each other for an instant, and then broke out into a roar of laughter.

"I understand it all perfectly," said Walworth, "and, therefore, it is quite unnecessary for your lordship to enlighten me. Still, I may as well ask you where you concealed it?"

"On Blackheath."

"Buried it?"

"Exactly."

"A wise plan, my lord. Then you actually intend *to lend the king his own money?*"

"Of course."

Walworth indulged in another loud and hearty laugh.

"It is a huge jest, my lord," he cried. "A very huge jest, on my soul! You are, indeed, a man of many resources! By the Virgin! I don't believe that even merry Silverbell could have imagined a better jest."

"Now," said Rochester, "in order to get these bags, it will be necessary that we go to the place at midnight, and disguised."

"Of course."

"We will go disguised as peasants, but under our disguise we must be well armed, for probably some of Jack Straw's spies may be abroad."

"They would not interfere with peasants."

"True. But I mean they may be on the watch somewhere near the spot. However, we must risk that. There is one comfort in the fact that the bags are not very deep in the ground."

"A most comforting assurance to me, my lord," replied Walworth, "for I am no hand at digging."

"All is then settled," said Rochester, "and to-night, my lord, you may depend upon being a richer man by some thousands of crowns."

"But where do you propose to take the money after getting it? I suggest that we take it to my residence, which, as you know, is at Deptford."

"Agreed. We can then arrange as to the king's loan."

Having thus settled the matter, and entirely to their satisfaction, the pair rode off as if about to take the road for London.

* * * *

The remainder of the day was spent by Rochester and Walworth in completing their disguises, and, to tell the truth, they were very good indeed.

Midnight came round, and the pair set forth, stole to the stables and got their horses.

Across the back of each horse were strung two bags, as much like those which had contained the money as Rochester could remember.

These were filled with oats.

All being in readiness, they went off, leading the horses, and taking the high road to Blackheath.

They met several peasants, who greeted them with a "Good e'en" and "The Lord save you."

"Even Jack Straw could not penetrate our disguises, Walworth," whispered Rochester.

"Nay, and a blessing it is that we are assured he could not, otherwise an arrow from one of his men would probably penetrate our bodies!"

The spot on Blackheath, where the money was buried, was entirely deserted, save for a few villainous-looking owls, who as the two advanced, hooted and hissed in a loud and defiant manner, and a few blind bats, who tried as hard as they could to smash themselves against the trees.

"Hist!" cried Walworth, suddenly seizing Rochester's arm, "look yonder, someone approaches."

And he pointed in the direction of what appeared to be a small light advancing towards them.

"Bah!" exclaimed Rochester. "'Tis only a jack-o'-lantern. Look, there are now some dozens of them."

"True. For a moment I had forgotten. But I like them not."

"Why?"

"They say it means ill-fortune."

"I do not believe in such childish prattle. Come, take this spade and throw up the earth while I dig."

The two set to work with a will, but they paused every few moments and listened.

Ere long the bags were revealed.

Now, our readers will be pleased to remember that Jack Straw took these bags away, and that the dead men were thrown down the hole.

That being so, how came the bags there? We shall see ere long.

One by one the bags were brought forth.

Then they were tied together and put across the horses' backs instead of those containing the oats—this, of course, being in case they met any of the same people on their return journey.

The oats were flung down in their stead, and the earth was filled in.

"Hark at the merry jingle!" chuckled Rochester.

"Ay, ay," replied Walworth, "but we shall have to proceed at a snail's pace, or the merry jingle may be heard."

"On my life! I tremble somewhat as I think of what would become of the money and ourselves, if this accursed Jack Straw suddenly came upon us."

"Fear it not, my lord; Jack Straw and his cut-throat companions are no doubt holding high revelry at one of his numerous places of retreat. Are you ready?"

"Quite."

"Then come, and cautiously."

Strange to say, on the return, they did not meet with a soul, and this, of course, was a matter of great delight to them.

Arriving at the stables, they led the horses in, and then the pair, taking each a bag, Walworth leading the way, entered the house by a narrow, secret passage.

So narrow was it, indeed, that Rochester fell with a crash. He relieved his feelings with a bitter curse. Walworth, however, indulged in a quiet chuckle at his misfortunes.

At last they reached a wooden staircase leading to Walworth's bedroom.

"Be careful, my lord," said Walworth, as he paused, produced a tinder-box, and lit a link, that was stuck in the wall, "this staircase is somewhat rotten, and with your weight, and the weight you carry, it may give way."

"May the fiend fly away with the staircase!" hissed Rochester; "how is it you do not repair your premises, my lord?"

"In good truth, because I have not the wherewithal to defray the expenses of so doing. I should require skilled workmen, my lord, and skilled workmen require to be well paid. There is not a serf on the whole of my estate who can properly drive a nail. But this way, my lord, and tread lightly."

In a few more moments the bags were deposited in the room.

The other two were then fetched, and they were ranged in line.

"Verily!" cried Rochester, "a good night's work. Now for the money."

"Now for the money," repeated Walworth.

With trembling hands the two lords untied the mouth of the first bag.

Suddenly a loud howl left Rochester's lips. It was a howl of dismay.

The bag toppled over and fell with a crash to the floor, the contents being scattered in all directions.

Rochester, with another yell, fell upon his knees. His eyes seemed starting from their sockets as he looked upon the contents of the bag.

No crowns were to be seen. No!

Instead of crowns were some hundreds of round brass plates.

"See!" cried Walworth, suddenly stooping and snatching up a piece of parchment tied with a silk cord. "What is this?"

"THE DAGGER WAS PLUNGED INTO THE FRIAR'S HEART."

"Give it me," said Rochester, starting to his feet, and snatching at the parchment.

With a volley of imprecations he tore off the cord and opened the parchment.

Directly his eyes rested upon the contents, he let it fall as if it were a red-hot coal, and starting back, fell into a chair with a deep groan.

Walworth picked up the parchment and spread it out.

There, in large letters, were the words—

"BY ORDER OF JACK STRAW!"

Walworth, in turn, dropped the parchment.

Looking hard at Rochester, he said—

"Beaten again by this accursed and most mysterious Jack Straw. My lord, this is becoming most serious."

"In the name of the Virgin!" shouted Rochester, leaping to his feet, "how did he obtain the knowledge that the treasure was concealed there? Ha, I have it!" he added, with an oath. "One of the men who assisted me."

"That you did not compensate?"

"Ay."

"My lord, you should never have allowed any man with such a secret, to slip out of your sight. Had I been in your place, I should have slain the men, one at a time."

"'By order of Jack Straw,'" muttered Rochester, looking thoughtfully at the parchment.

"Ay, 'tis plain enough," said Walworth, "whoever wrote that must be a fine penman."

"'Twas Jack Straw who wrote it, I will be sworn!"

"How know you that?"

"'Tis similar writing found on the bodies of the men whom Jack Straw hanged from the battlements of my own house. May all the fiends seize upon him, say I."

"With all my heart!" ejaculated Walworth, "for he has made the large sum I contemplated having in my keeping vanish completely."

"Walworth," exclaimed Rochester, "since it appears impossible, owing to the immense number of men with which he is surrounded, to get hold of Jack Straw, suppose we set a trap for him?"

"A trap?"

"Yes."

"I am afraid that, if you set any number of traps, and have them well baited, you will never catch Jack Straw. He is mystery itself, and even the king's men converse in whispers about him."

"Fear it not, we *may* catch him! Oh, that we could, and could carry his dead body to the king!"

"Ay, that would be a fine stroke of business, indeed; but that would not be lending the king the money he requires."

"'Tis no jesting matter, my lord. Let us think of a plan to trap him. Have you any good wine, Walworth?"

"Plenty. I will place some before you, and, as payment, will accept yonder brass plates. Ha, ha! Though I am annoyed, your lordship, I must have my little jest. Ha, ha! but we have not examined the other three bags."

"They also contain brass plates, I'll warrant me."

The other three were opened, and their contents were found to be as conjectured.

"By heaven!" said Walworth, "to look at such a vast number of these plates, one would fancy that Jack Straw must have purchased the stock of every 'Merry Andrew' in the kingdom. Well! well! his majesty has been exceeding dull lately, but if he knew the rights of this, what would he say?"

"Talk not of his majesty," said Rochester, impatiently, "but produce the wine, my lord, and let us endeavour to form some plan—some trap. We are older than this Jack Straw, who is but a boy; and surely two heads like ours should be able to form a plan to entrap him."

"Though I detest the accursed outlaw," replied Walworth, "I must say that, boy though he may be, he has wonderful powers. He must be peculiarly gifted, Rochester, since everyone admits that he commands the utmost respect from every man under him."

"Robber chiefs generally force that from their followers," replied Rochester. "No doubt his men think it better to assume respect, since, if they did not, it is probable they would not receive a fair share of the booty he is always capturing."

"Well, let us try to forget our disappointment in draughts of good wine," said Walworth, who then disappeared.

It did not take him long to fetch a small barrel of wine, then placing it upon the table, the head was knocked in, and the two lords drank draught after draught to each other's good health, and confusion and death to Jack Straw.

For several hours the two sat in that room, and before they separated, they had fixed upon a plan to entrap Jack Straw—a plan which, if properly carried out, seemed almost certain to prove successful.

The most peculiar thing in connection with this plot was that the chief performer in it was to be a lady !

CHAPTER XII.

WHEREIN IS SEEN HOW JACK STRAW RECEIVES AN IMPORTANT SUMMONS TO LONDON—HOW HE OBEYS IT, AND HOW HE FINDS HIMSELF ENTRAPPED —THE FEARFUL FIGHT, AND JACK'S MIRACULOUS ESCAPE FROM THE SAVOY PALACE.

JACK STRAW and his followers reached Blackfoot Castle in safety.

The cavalcade met with not one mishap, with the exception that twice on the road Dorothy fainted; but this was not to be wondered at.

On the following day, Dorothy and her father, in company with four men to act as a guard, returned to their home in London, where Jack Straw promised to visit them on a future occasion.

Their departure was a source of great comfort to Egbert, who, notwithstanding the fact that during the short time she had been with him he had treated Dorothy with great kindness, regarded her presence in Jack's castle in the light of an intrusion.

Some days elapsed, and nothing of any great importance occurred.

Men of all classes wishing to join Jack Straw's banner presented themselves at the castle, which was now almost packed with armed and determined men.

It was a strange sight to see dozens of poor serfs creep to the gates, and crave to be allowed to join the banner of he "who lived for the poor."

Jack turned none away who upon the cross swore he had no wife or children, or other relatives who could make a claim upon him.

"For," Jack said, "we are almost daily passing through some danger, and sometimes several men are either killed or maimed for life. If, therefore, I allow any married man to join my banner, and he was killed, his wife and helpless children would call down Heaven's curse upon my head. And that I would not have for the whole of England."

Besides the wonderful secret corridors and cells in the castle, and of which we have previously spoken, a subterranean passage, which led to the edge of Blackheath, had been discovered.

This was, of course, of vast importance to Jack.

Though, when discovered, it was lumbered with gigantic stones and rubbish of every imaginable description, besides the skeletons of men and horses, Jack's men soon cleared it, and on one side accommodation was provided for no less than two hundred horses, which number was placed there directly the passage was fit for their reception.

Nearly all these horses—fine, powerful animals — were kept constantly saddled in case of emergency.

Jack's own beautiful black steed was kept in a large room by the side of that in which its master slept.

One fine evening, Jack, with Egbert at his side, was standing on one of the battlements surveying the lovely expanse of country before him.

He was, as was usual with him, fully armed; and he wore the splendid suit of chain armour he had taken from Rochester House.

The diamond in the centre of his helmet, glittered and flashed in the sun's rays.

Jack was thoughtful, and had been thoughtful for some hours.

"You are sad, Jack," said Egbert.

"Sad? Nay, nay, not sad. Why should I be so? Think you I could be sad with all this music about me?"

"Music?"

"Yes."

"I hear no music."

"Nay! Can you not hear the clatter of arms? Can you not hear the hearty laughter of our brawny comrades? Can you not hear the merry ring of the blacksmith, as he puts fresh rivets into loose armour? That is the music I mean. Take instruments from every Court under the sun, and place them in the hands of skilled players, and they could not produce—to me—sweeter music than this."

"If you are not sad you are troubled—you have some trouble upon your mind which you have not confided to me?"

Jack made no reply to this.

His gaze wandered across the country to the towers of the palace.

But suddenly turning, he saw that Egbert was quietly weeping.

Placing his strong arm round the youth's waist, Jack drew him to his side.

"Why do you weep, dear Egbert?" he asked.

"Because I have guessed why you are so thoughtful."

"Have you indeed? Then tell me what you think."

"It is because Dorothy Leighton is no longer here."

Jack laughed softly.

"Jealous again?" he said. "Nay, let me hasten to assure you, my pretty Egbert, that such is not the case."

"Ah, that I were assured."

"Listen Egbert. You know what it is I hold as my most sacred possession?"

"I do. It is the sacred straw you brought from Rome."

"True. 'Tis here."

Placing his hand beneath his armour he drew forth the case containing it, opened it and took out the straw.

Placing it to his lips he kissed it reverently, then he took hold of a small silver cross hanging at Egbert's girdle, and kneeling and doffing his helmet, he kissed that, saying—

"I swear before Heaven, that I have no other feeling for Dorothy Leighton, than that of a brother towards his sister. The promise I have so often made to you, shall be kept when I have accomplished my object. If Heaven spares us both, I swear *I will make you my wife!*"

The next moment Egbert was in Jack's arms, and was clasped closely to his breast.

"But," said Jack, "your real name, and the fact that you are a girl must be kept a profound secret. Though no doubt numbers of the men believe you to be a woman, they keep their knowledge to themselves. All is well, my pretty Egbert—all is well."

"Hark! what is that? As I live, 'tis the horn announcing arrival."

Casting his eyes around the various narrow roads below, all of which led to the drawbridge, Jack saw an elaborately attired and well-mounted page slowly advancing.

After a short parley with the guard, the drawbridge was lowered, and the page passed into the courtyard.

"Who can he be from, I wonder?" said Jack.

"May it please your royal highness," interrupted a merry voice, "there has arrived a messenger who has brought the Crown of England with him, and who desires your acceptance of the same."

And Silverbell, his face beaming with smiles, bowed so repeatedly, that the bells upon his cap jingled most merrily.

"The Crown of England, Silverbell?" smiled Jack.

"On my soul, yes!" replied Silverbell. "I have the crown under my cloak."

"Indeed! Produce it, and I will see whether it fits *me*," cried Jack, with laughter.

Silverbell gravely threw back his cloak, plunged his hand into his pocket, and brought forth a crown piece.

Jack burst into a roar of laughter.

"Well, your royal highness sees that this is the Crown of England," said Silverbell.

"*One* of the crowns, Sir Jester," replied Egbert, smiling. and snatching the piece out of his hand; "and though it will not fit my head, 'twill fit my pocket—thus."

"Who has arrived, Silverbell?" asked Jack.

"A very pretty, prettily-spoken, prettily-dressed, prettily—"

"Of a truth, did you ever see such a flatterer?" cried Egbert.

"I assure you," continued Silverbell, with a rattle of his bells, "that though he is but a page, he is a right *noble* youth—"

"Did he have the audacity to tell you so?" asked Egbert.

"He did."

"He comes of a right noble family, say you? Who is his father?"

"A London weaver, by name Eric *Noble;* thus——"

"'Tis useless to argue with Silverbell," said Jack. "He will assail you at every corner and find an opening to poke his fun. Speak now seriously, Silverbell. Who has arrived? Whence comes this page?"

"From London."

"To what lord does he belong?"

"That I cannot glean. I questioned him, and Mark and Basil questioned him. But all he gave was his own name, his father's name, and a packet. In return we gave him a portion of a boar's head and a measure of wine."

"You did well," replied Jack, "and the packet?"

"Is here."

And plunging his hand in his doublet, Silverbell drew out a small packet heavily sealed.

Withdrawing a few paces, Jack broke the seals, and opening the packet, which proved to be a neatly-folded piece of parchment, he read these lines—

"To MASTER JACK STRAW—

"GREETING.

"May heaven preserve you and prosper you in the good cause you have undertaken. You are a noble defender of the unhappy poor, who are ground down by the iron heels of unprincipled nobles! As you value

that sacred word 'FREEDOM!' come to me at my residence to-night. Come disguised, and give your name as Louis Lemar (the name of my dear cousin), and you will be safely conducted to my presence at the Savoy Palace. I would confer secretly with you, and endeavour to co-operate with you. Into your hands I will place the sum of five hundred crowns for distribution among such of the poorer classes as you may think fit. Let such of your companions as you may select accompany you as an escort, but they must not be admitted to my presence. May all good saints protect us.—Thine, MARGARET

"(Duchess of Lancaster)."

"Duchess of Lancaster!" muttered Jack, hastily folding the parchment, and thrusting it in his breast. "By the Blessed Virgin! can this be so? Can this powerful lady wish to assist me? An' I gained her to my side, it would be a fine stroke of fortune to me! What ho! Silverbell! what ho!"

"Here, your royal highness," replied Silverbell, who during Jack's reading of the letter had been pouring into Egbert's ear all the most improbable stories he could think of; "all here, may it please your royal highness."

"Send the page to me."

Silverbell at once departed, and in a few moments returned with the page.

"You did not tarry on your way hither?" queried Jack.

"Nay, worshipful sir."

"Nor tell anyone your business?"

"No, sir. Since I know not anything of what the message was, how could I have told anyone?"

"Well said, Sir Noble," cried Silverbell, delivering the page a mighty thwack on the back with his bauble. "You should have been a parrot, since you talk so well."

"And you were to return with a message?" said Jack.

"Who is with the duchess at the palace?"

"She is entirely alone, with the exception of her maids."

"Return to her ladyship at once, and say 'Louis Lemar will be with your grace at the time mentioned.'"

The page bowed, and Silverbell, taking him by the arm, led him away.

In less than ten minutes, he was well on the road to London.

Mark and Basil were now hastily summoned, and to them, as well as to Egbert and Silverbell—beyond question a wonderfully *wise* "fool," and an excellent councillor—he read this important document from the duchess.

All listened intently.

"What say you?" asked Jack, proudly replacing the letter.

"What say I?" cried Basil. "I say 'tis a splendid stroke of fortune."

"And what say you, Mark?"

"The same."

"And you, Silverbell?"

"I say 'tis a trap to catch Jack Straw!"

"Ha, ha, ha, ha!" laughed Jack. "A trap! On my soul! it must be a strange trap, indeed, that will catch Jack Straw."

"Nevertheless I believe that that letter is part of a trap to catch you. You know well enough that the Duchess of Lancaster has always been mixed up with State affairs. Both the duchess and her husband, the duke, are great favourites of the king, and do you imagine that she would try and forfeit his majesty's favours? I think not."

"You have frequently given me some wise advice, Silverbell," said Jack, "but on this occasion your ideas are undoubtedly wrong."

Silverbell bowed, but made no reply.

"I will keep the appointment" continued Jack. "I believe the writer of this letter to be sincere, and such a noble offer as is here made should not be despised."

"Then, if it is your intention to keep the appointment," said Silverbell, "let me advise you to go well disguised, and to take with you a strong escort."

"Again your ideas are wrong," replied Jack. "If I were to take with me a strong escort I should attract too much attention. I shall go well disguised, but my escort will consist of only three persons—yourself, Basil, and Egbert."

"Ha!" cried Mark, and will you expose Egbert to the dangers of London?"

"We are inseparable," answered Jack, gravely.

"Yet on this journey—"

"Say no more," interrupted Egbert. "For though I knew a dreadful death awaited me, I would not flinch did I know that I should breathe my last with Jack Straw!"

"A brave heart!" muttered Silverbell. "Pray heaven nothing occurs to divide them!"

*　　*　　*　　*

Three hours before midnight, Jack Straw, Egbert, Silverbell, and Basil Tremaine left the castle and took the road to London.

They were attired as well-to-do citizens, but under their disguises they carried their arms in convenient positions.

At his saddle-bow Egbert carried a small but powerful bow, and a small quiver of arrows with *silver points*, and upon each point were engraved the words—

"BY ORDER OF JACK STRAW!"

They had been manufactured at the castle by one of Jack's men, and were reserved for "illustrious personages."

Proceeding leisurely, and meeting with no interruption, the four reached the Strand just after midnight.

When within a few hundred yards of the palace, Jack paused.

"Await me here," he said. "In case I get into any danger you will hear me wind a loud blast on the horn I carry at my side. You do not still think this is a trap, Silverbell?"

"On my life, I do!"

"Cast your fears to the winds, then; I fear not."

Away rode Jack towards the residence of the duchess.

Upon his giving his name as Louis Lemar, an elderly and grave lacquey conducted him to the entrance to the palace.

The same name was given there, and he was at once admitted to the courtyard, and the massive gates closed upon him with a loud bang.

And now, for the first time, a strange feeling of danger crept over him.

As he dismounted, the moon's rays burst through a huge bank of black clouds, and looking up, Jack noticed the glitter of arms on one of the battlements.

"Pshaw!" he muttered, "'tis only the guard; and now for her Grace."

At this moment two tall yeoman appeared.

Behind them were at least twenty armed men, each carrying aloft a flaming link.

"Your name and business?" asked the leader of the men.

"My name is Louis Lemar, and my business to see her Grace the Duchess of Lancaster."

The man bowed, saying—

"Follow me."

As he said this, the men with the links turned and led the way through a long vaulted stone passage.

Several rooms, large, lofty, and furnished in a most princely fashion, were passed; then the party ascended a somewhat long staircase, and finally halted before a lofty doorway. A bell was then rung, and the curtains across the entrance were drawn aside.

The leader of the men stepped back, and Jack, with head erect, and firm tread, passed in. The curtains thereupon resumed their former position.

Jack found himself in an enormous and most sumptuously furnished apartment. The walls were covered with some splendid specimens of the painter's art, and on all sides were displayed more costly articles than could have been found in any of the king's palaces.

Before Jack had time to admire all this, a pair of dark curtains at the farther end of the room were drawn aside, and one of the loveliest women to be found in all England stepped forth.

It was the duchess.

Jack bowed, and the duchess gravely returned the salutation.

"In response to your letter, Your Grace," said Jack, "I am here to——"

"One moment," interrupted the duchess. "Pray allow me to speak first."

This she said in such a haughty tone, that for a moment Jack felt like one suddenly stricken dumb.

"The letter you received," said the duchess, speaking in low, deliberate tones, "was written at the instigation of two noble lords, and it was written on purpose to decoy you here——"

A wild cry left Jack's lips as the duchess said this.

Darting forward, he seized her by the wrist.

"You tell me this?" he cried. "*You, a woman,* dare to tell me that you had the heart to decoy me here, so that my enemies might kill me! I should never have dreamt that such a woman was allowed to live."

A loud cry left the duchess' lips, and ere it had died away the dark curtains were again hastily drawn aside, and two splendidly-dressed men, each having a drawn sword in his hand dashed into the room.

They were Lords Rochester and Walworth. Roused to a pitch of fury, and exerting all his enormous strength, Jack dragged the duchess towards him, and flung her with a crash to the floor.

"Surrender to us!" cried Rochester. "Surrender, Jack Straw, outlaw and murderer!"

The pair advanced.

But Jack, stepping back, snatched his heavy sword from its sheath.

"Hold!" he shouted fiercely, as he raised his sword over the fallen, and now terror-stricken, duchess.

"Advance but another step, cowards, and I will drive my blade through this woman's treacherous heart.

"Hold, I tell you! Listen! My life is not of much value, but I am always prepared to sell it dearly. The life of this woman, on the other hand, is, no doubt, held at considerable value, yet, if you advance, she dies!"

The last word had scarcely left his lips before the other curtains at the entrance were drawn aside, and a body of armed men made their appearance.

Before he could draw back, Jack received a terrible thrust in the chest by a burly fellow carrying a long pike.

Had he not been encased in chain armour, it is certain that his death would have followed.

But his disguise concealed his armour, and the ruffian expressed his wonder that his pike had not passed completely through his body.

He was not allowed much time for wonder, however, for like a flash Jack seized the pike staff with his left hand, and whirling his massive sword for a moment over his head, he brought it down with terrific force on the fellow's neck.

The keen blade instantly swept the man's head from his body, and his headless trunk fell over the prostrate duchess, deluging her with blood.

Springing quickly on one side, Jack was just in time to ward off a blow aimed at him by Rochester.

"You are fairly caught!" cried Walworth, also advancing to the attack. "Surrender, and your life shall be spared."

Liar!" replied Jack. "It is my life that is sought! Surrounded as I am, I have no doubt I shall fall; but ere I die I swear that you shall have something by which to remember Jack Straw."

Two or three cross-bow men now fitted their bolts, and endeavoured to get a shot at Jack, as he warded off the blows made at him by Rochester and Walworth; but he saw their movements, and by skilful manœuvring he contrived to keep himself covered by the two cowardly lords.

If either of the men had discharged his bolt it is a certainty that Rochester or Walworth would have been hit.

"Even if I could wind a blast upon my horn," thought Jack, "it would not be heard. Oh, that Basil and Silverbell were here!"

Suddenly his eyes fell upon the curtains through which the duchess and the two lords had entered.

Jack's spirits at once revived.

"If I could reach them," he thought, "I might yet escape. Sooner would I hurl myself from the highest battlement, than be slain by these cowardly lords."

Seeing that they had but little chance with Jack, whose sword seemed to be everywhere at the same moment, the two lords became desperate.

They called upon the men, who at once began to surround Jack.

Jack saw the danger he would be in if his opponents got him into the open, and he gradually worked his way to a massive oak sideboard, which was loaded with ornaments of the most magnificent and costly description.

But Jack paid no attention to either their value or their beauty.

Seizing the sideboard with his left hand he, with one pull, sent it over on its side.

The ornaments fell with a loud crash among the men.

This act elicited a shriek from the duchess, and brought up a numerous train of servants, who stood appalled at the sight.

"Dastard!" almost shrieked Rochester, making a swinging slash at our hero.

But ere his weapon could descend, Jack's sword fell upon the side of his head.

It just missed his skull, but it sliced off his left ear, and inflicted a deep wound in his shoulder.

With a loud howl the "noble" Rochester fell face downwards amid the heap of shattered ornaments.

There was now a pause, but it was a brief one.

Lord Walworth, his face running with perspiration, and his elaborate attire disordered with the exertions he had made, drew back, and snatching a dagger from one of the men at his side, prepared to renew the attack.

In the brief pause caused by Walworth snatching the dagger from the man-at-arms, Jack, too, got his opportunity.

Thrusting his hand beneath his jerkin, he drew out *his* dagger, and a long, terrible-looking weapon it was.

"Surrender, while yet there is time," said Walworth.

"Nay!" answered Jack. "Death a thousand times before surrender! Never yet was Jack Straw known to yield."

Once more Walworth advanced.

There was no doubt that he was an excellent swordsman, but though many years Jack's senior, he was not nearly so powerful as our hero.

The sword Jack wielded was three times the weight of Walworth's, yet he handled it as if it had been the lightest weapon ever made.

Once again Jack and Walworth became hotly engaged.

Most of the men drew back, as if inclined to witness the fight between these two; but one of them creeping up, managed, with his halbert, to strike Jack a severe blow on his left wrist

The consequence was that he was compelled to drop the dagger.

Nevertheless, despite the pain in his wrist, he fought on determinedly, and suddenly brought down his sword upon Walworth's head, causing the blood to gush forth in torrents, nearly blinding him.

Then making a sudden dash, and hurling to the ground some of the astonished men, Jack ran to the curtains.

He was about to dart through, when he found himself confronted by two men.

Their tall forms barred the way; but Jack, having got thus far, did not hesitate an instant what to do.

One of the men received a tremendous blow on the head, and the other was transfixed upon Jack's blade.

He fell to rise no more!

Passing through the curtains, Jack found himself in a dimly-lighted passage.

In front of him was a narrow flight of stone steps.

Where they led to he, of course, could not guess. But he was not allowed time to think.

Walworth had recovered from the semi-unconsciousness into which Jack's blow had thrown him, and our hero could hear his frantic cries to the men.

Up the stairs went Jack at a breakneck pace, and as he ran he heard the shouts below getting plainer and plainer.

On the first landing a link, stuck in a gold holder, was burning. Snatching this from its sconce, Jack again hurried onwards.

But though he continued to go at a swift pace, the shouts below became more and more distinct; and above the cries of the men, Jack heard Walworth's voice crying out that a large reward would be paid for his capture.

Arriving on the third landing, Jack perceived a doorway partially screened with heavy curtains.

Snatching at these with such force that he dragged them down, he rushed into the room.

Although he had never before seen it, he had heard of it scores of times, and he immediately recognised it from the description.

It was the room reserved as the sleeping apartment for the king when his majesty paid the Duke of Lancaster a visit.

Over the magnificent bedstead were the Royal arms.

The window was concealed by massive Oriental curtains.

Pulling these aside, Jack looked out and saw that the window overlooked the courtyard, standing quietly in which was his horse.

Sticking the link in a niche, and sheathing his sword, Jack caught hold of the Royal bedstead, and exerting all his strength, dragged it to the doorway, first bolting the door.

Only just in time, for in another moment the men, led on by Walworth, had reached the landing.

Horrible and ghastly in the extreme did Walworth look in the glare of the numerous links carried by the men.

His rich attire was almost completely covered with blood, and his matted hair hung over his forehead.

"Surrender!" he cried. "Surrender!"

But he got no answer.

Directly he had pulled the bedstead in front of the doorway, Jack seized the tapestry curtains hanging from the window and pulled them down.

Then he tore them into long strips, and knotted the ends of these securely together.

Having accomplished this, he secured one end of this hastily-manufactured rope firmly to an iron ring on the outside of the window, and flinging it out he looked over to see the distance the other end was from the ground.

He made out that it was between ten and twelve feet.

The shouts and cries outside the door increased, and presently some thundering blows told that hammers or axes were being freely used.

Undismayed by the terrible din, Jack took his horn from his girdle, and leaning out of the window, he wound upon the instrument such an ear-piercing blast, that, for a moment, the men outside paused to ask each other what it meant.

Again, and yet again did Jack wind his horn, and the third blast had barely died away ere he perceived a sight which gladdened his heart, and caused him to heave a great sigh of relief.

Three horsemen were riding at a breakneck pace towards the courtyard gates.

They were, of course, Basil, Egbert, and Silverbell.

Placing his sword between his teeth, Jack began the descent.

He had no fear for the strength of the rope, for he was well aware of what stuff this tapestry consisted.

"If I can but reach the end," he thought, "I may yet escape. My escape would be certain if my companions could but obtain admittance into the courtyard."

Before he had got a dozen feet, a tremendous crash was heard. The door had been battered down.

Rapidly down the rope went Jack, and ere Walworth, maddened with rage, could reach the window, our hero had nearly reached the second battlement.

For a moment we will return to Jack's three companions.

They waited where he had left them. Not an inch did they move from the spot.

But as the time passed they cast many an eager glance towards the lofty towers of the palace.

Then they became impatient; the horses also became impatient, and pawed the ground and champed their bits, as much as to ask, " When do we move ?"

Silverbell shook his head gravely, and repeatedly muttered that Jack was caught in a trap.

He and Basil conversed in whispers, and several times their hands wandered to their sword hilts.

As for Egbert, he spoke not a word. As the time passed, though, tears filled his beautiful eyes, and he heaved more than one sigh. At last he burst out—

"Let us to the gateway."

"Nay," replied Basil, "we dare not disobey his orders, since he is our acknowledged commander. We must not move unless we hear him wind a blast on his horn."

"My heart! my heart!" whispered Egbert, but the whisper reached the ears of Silverbell, who, taking Egbert's hand, said—

"Trust to heaven! I would have given ten years of my life rather than you should have accompanied us on this journey."

Turning to Basil, he said—

"Though 'tis midnight the Strand appears to me to be more than usually silent. See how dark and dismal everything is. Mistress Moon appears somewhat lazy to-night, and— Ha! now we see! Now we see!"

The moon had burst through the threatening black clouds, and had flooded the palace with its silvery rays, bringing out the outlines of this splendid structure with startling distinctness. The three now watched for some time in silence.

Suddenly the loud blast of a horn burst upon their ears; then another and another.

"Jack Straw is in danger, and my words have come true!" cried Silverbell, who, as he said this, plucked his flashing blade from its scabbard.

Basil did likewise.

"Forward ! " he cried. Let us rescue him or die in the attempt. Egbert, I implore you to await us here."

"No—no—no!" replied Egbert. "Go with you I will. His life is of more value to me than mine own. On, for the love of heaven—on!"

And without more words, away dashed the three.

We have already said that Jack saw them coming.

Arrived at the gate, Basil knocked loudly with the hilt of his sword.

But he got no reply, for the whole of the men were engaged upstairs.

"See!" shrieked Egbert, "Jack is escaping from yonder window! Ah, heaven! One false movement, and he will be dashed to pieces."

"The gate is barred," said Basil, "and no one in attendance."

"I know the palace and its surroundings well," said Silverbell, as he reined in his horse, "and I will scale the wall, and admit you. Look, look! Jack Straw is descending!"

Silverbell vaulted upon the saddle, and was on the top of the wall in an instant.

The height on the other side was, at least, a dozen feet, yet Silverbell did not hesitate.

He at once leaped to the ground, and running to the gate, undid the massive bars and chains, and swung it open.

Egbert was the first to enter. Basil followed, leading Silverbell's horse.

To return now to Jack.

"Surrender!" roared Walworth, who was the first to reach the window.

Again he received no answer.

Jack's thoughts were too much engaged for him to notice what was passing above.

His feet had just rested upon the battlement, when Walworth, with an oath, severed the rope with his sword.

The consequence of this was the whole of it fell into Jack's hands. And this was just the very thing he wanted, for now it would reach to the ground.

Taking the end of it, he tied it round the stonework.

This was several feet round, but still the rope was nearer the ground than before.

As he commenced to descend, the shouting above grew louder still, and Jack saw, to his dismay, that a long, stout rope, had dropped almost by his side.

Yet he did not hesitate, for at this moment Silverbell and Basil raised shouts of encouragement.

Jack, however, could not help being considerably more than surprised when he saw Lord Walworth, with his sword between his teeth, descending the rope.

Had Jack thought that there would have been no armed men to have interfered, he would have waited for Walworth on the battlement, and then— well, then it would have gone hard with Walworth!

Still, all things considered, it was well that Jack did not pause to meet the nobleman; for being weighted with his armour, he was now nearly exhausted.

Down, down went Jack. Walworth followed, and soon reached the battlement.

He was in the act of raising his sword to again sever Jack's rope, when suddenly he uttered a loud cry of agony.

The sword dropped from his grasp, and after staggering backwards and forwards for a few moments, and, con-vulsively beating the air with his clenched hands, he fell on his face upon the ground!

The men above were eagerly watching his movements.

When they saw him fall, they, with wild yells of dismay, slid down the rope on to the battlement, and turned him over.

He was not dead. But consciousness had almost deserted him.

A score of men surrounded him, and one, undoubtedly of superior rank among them, having a link in his hand, suddenly snatched at something which was deeply buried in Walworth's right shoulder.

It was an arrow.

The man plucked it forth, and he was struck by its appearance.

It had a silver head.

The men crowded round, and, for a moment, Jack Straw was forgotten.

"On my soul!" shouted the man, "did you ever see the like! Behold! see what is here written!"

The men crowded still closer, and looked at the words upon the point, which the leader indicated.

The majority of the men could not read, so they called out for their leader to read it for them.

"Here are five words," said the leader, "and they are—

'BY ORDER OF JACK STRAW!'"

The last word had hardly left his lips ere a bolt from Egbert's bow crashed through his helmet, and entered his brain.

He fell dead by the side of Walworth.

"Heaven's mercy on us!" cried one of the men, as he snatched the still burning link from the hand of the dead leader. "Let us, at least, try to avenge our captain's death! See! mounted men are in the courtyard, and, as I live, this bloodthirsty and daring outlaw has reached the bottom of the rope. Follow! We outnumber them by dozens. Let us throw ourselves upon them, and slay them!"

"Oh, that I had the power to lead you!" moaned Walworth, as, with difficulty, he raised himself on his side; "but take him dead or alive, and a large reward shall be yours!"

But by the time the men reached

the courtyard, Jack had mounted his horse.

"Run to the gates!" shouted one of the men, who, at once, set off in order to close the massive gates. But he was not allowed to proceed very far.

Silverbell, wheeling his horse round, dashed up to him, and ere he could move aside, he was a dead man.

"Keep close to me!" shouted Jack, who, spurring his powerful animal among the men, fought desperately.

Several times he was hit, and had it not been for his armour, he would have received more than one wound.

Basil and Silverbell did not fail to keep close. Both knew it was a matter of life or death.

Though Jack and his companions were fearfully outnumbered, they yet had a great advantage, being mounted on powerful steeds.

With such determination, and with such effect, did the adventurers fight, that Lancaster's men at last became disheartened, and shouted lustily for quarter.

The appeal for mercy was never made in vain to Jack Straw.

The clash of arms instantly ceased, and as Jack and his companions withdrew a short distance, they looked upon a horrible picture.

The courtyard was deluged with blood, and no less than twelve men lay dead or dying.

Jack lowered his aching arm, and in a loud voice said—

"Who is responsible for this? No one but Rochester, Walworth, and the Duchess of Lancaster, whose husband, I feel sure, knows naught of it. Well, Rochester and Walworth are well punished, and a time will come when I will well repay the Duchess of Lancaster for her treacherous conduct. That I swear! Though she, no doubt, was prevailed upon by those detestable lords, I, nevertheless, hold her guilty of entrapping me. Let her beware! Oh, that I had had a few hundred of my men with me! I swear that I would not have left the gates of this palace until every room had been utterly wrecked!"

Turning to his companions he gave the word, and the four of them departed, leaving the survivors of Lancaster's men gazing after them in stupid astonishment.

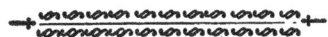

CHAPTER XIII

HOW JACK STRAW AVENGES HIMSELF ON THE DUCHESS OF LANCASTER— HOW HE IS STOPPED BY A GIPSY, AND WHAT THE GIPSY SHOWS HIM IN A MAGIC MIRROR.

THOUGH, as may be supposed, Jack and his companions were almost worn out, they, after a brief consultation, decided to set out for Blackfoot Castle.

Egbert rode by Jack's side, supremely happy in the knowledge that our hero was at least safe.

He (for "he" we will call Egbert a little while longer) tried hard to get Jack to converse with him, but the effort was useless.

Our hero, after a short time, became deeply buried in thought.

His companions guessed what was passing in his mind, but they considered it best not to disturb him.

Terribly weary, and covered with dust, the four reached Blackfoot Castle just as the first streak of dawn appeared in the sky.

*   *   *   *

On the following day Jack, having received information that the king was making spirited arrangements to capture him and the whole of his men, who now numbered close upon a thousand, held a consultation as to what was to be done.

It was eventually arranged that Silverbell was to go to the palace disguised as a pedlar.

Knowing the place so well, there was no doubt that he would gain admittance to the servants' apartments, and from the domestics he would, no doubt, be able to pick up a great deal of information as to what was passing at Court.

Accordingly, when evening came round, Silverbell, attired as a pedlar, set out for the palace.

He met with no opposition, either on his way, at the gates of the magnificent park, or at the gates of the long avenue leading to the steps of the terrace.

Pedlars in those days were regarded as inoffensive, harmless individuals more to be pitied than anything else, and they generally got more money by consenting to be made fools of for the time being, than they did from the sale of their wares.

Though, when he reached the terrace steps, Silverbell wandered along like a man totally unacquainted with the place, he yet knew every inch of the ground.

Walking slowly along the path leading to the principal kitchen, and pretending to admire and appear awe-stricken at everything he set eyes on, he at length came in sight of the lodge, through which everyone had to pass ere they were allowed to visit any part of the palace.

At the entrance to the lodge, two men-at-arms were stationed; but instead of walking up and down as were their directions, they were conversing with two fat female cooks.

Directly these individuals set eyes upon Silverbell, they indulged in a loud, hearty laugh.

"Well, Sir Snail," cried one of the men-at-arms, bringing his halberd with a thud to the ground, "and how do ye?"

"But badly, my masters, but badly," replied Silverbell, assuming to perfection the voice of a man of fourscore years. "And how fares it with ye all?"

"But badly, but badly," replied the man, endeavouring to imitate Silverbell's voice and manner. "We are not so *high* in the world as we should wish."

"Ho, ho!" replied Silverbell. "Not so *high*, eh? Well, well, my masters, you should thank heaven that you are so *low* in the world; for, on my soul, I have seen people *lower* than yourself suddenly *rise* to their disadvantage."

"How so, Sir Pedlar? How could they rise to their *dis*advantage?"

"Why, *they were hanged!*"

The other man-at-arms, and the two fat cooks, burst into a roar of laughter.

"You are a fool, sir," said the soldier who had hitherto spoken.

"*Yes* and *no*," replied Silverbell. "People say—always *have* said—that I am a fool, and yet—and mark this! —though I am, or people *say* I am, I actually know the difference between—"

He stopped.

"Between!" said the man-at-arms. "Go on, Sir Pedlar, you are interesting."

"Between a fool and a fool's money."

"What *is* the difference?"

"'Tis easy enough. The fool cannot easily be *parted*, but easily his money *can*."

"Ho, ho! where did you learn that? You must have been to school in England, Sir Pedlar."

Silverbell gravely shook his head.

"I was never at school, your worship," he said. "It was my father who taught me all I know."

"What, then, was the principal thing he taught you?"

"He said that, whenever I visited any of the king's palaces, the king's servants would purchase what I offered them."

"Your father was, indeed, a man of great perception," said one of the cooks. "Put your wallet upon the ground, that we may select such articles as we fancy."

Silverbell did so. He opened his wallet, and laid before the greedy eyes of the two cooks its contents.

"Are these articles of good gold?" asked one.

"They are," replied Silverbell.

"And expensive?"

"Some."

"Some?"

"Most of them."

"How comes it that you, being but a pedlar, can carry such expensive things?" asked one of the men-at-arms.

"How comes it, master?" retorted Silverbell. "Why, 'tis thus. You say I am a pedlar. Good! I am an old man, and have travelled the country many years of my life. What I earned I saved, and so—"

"Ay, ay, old man," interrupted one

of the cooks; "but if you *saved* what money you earned, how did you manage to *live* ?"

"Thus : I have ever offered my wares to honourable persons like yourself. Generally my wares have been bought, and the buyers, out of compassion for me, have invited me to their apartments, and have given me sufficient to eat."

"By the Virgin!" laughed one of the men-at-arms, "besides being a good salesman, you are also a most excellent beggar."

"And I will tell you a secret worth knowing," said his comrade. "If you have any spare crowns by you, his majesty will borrow them with pleasure."

"Ay, ay—and the interest ? "

"There would be little of that, Sir Pedlar ; but his majesty would reward you with one of his gracious smiles."

"'Tis a huge reward of a surety," replied Silverbell, in sarcastic tones ; "but I would not have his majesty so disturb himself on my account for worlds. My crowns are being well taken care of, Sir Soldier, but as you seem to be a poor man—"

"No poorer than thousands of my comrades, who, like me, are never paid the money due to them."

"Ho! ho! Well, as I said, since you are a poor man, and since your comrade is also a poor man, I will make each of you a present, which you shall keep in remembrance of me."

Saying which, Silverbell took out two small gold trinkets, and presented one to each of the men-at-arms, who were profuse in their thanks.

"And what will you present *us* with?" asked one of the cooks.

"I will make each of you one another time. At present I am hungry and athirst, and—"

"If the sentries will allow you to pass, you shall come to our kitchen, and shall partake of whatsoever you fancy."

"Truly, you are good Christians. If these, the king's brave soldiers, will allow me to pass——"

"Oh, by all means, Sir Pedlar!" cried one of the men. "Pass on, and don't forget to fill yourself right well. For though his majesty has not much money, he hath plenty of food of a surety."

Having thus cleverly obtained admittance, Silverbell accompanied the cooks to the chief kitchen, a spacious apartment, in which the spits before the huge wood fires were kept going night and day.

Many thousands of times had Silverbell been here during the preparing of feasts, and had amused the servants. There, by the centre fireplace, was the self-same curiously-carved oaken chair in which he had been in the habit of sitting.

Placing his wallet upon the ground, he was about to sit down in the chair, when one of the cooks cried—

"Hold ! "

"Wherefore ? " asked Silverbell.

"Sit not in that chair," said the cook, solemnly. "There is a history attaching to it. That is the chair in which Silverbell, the king's principal jester, used to sit. Have you ever heard of him ? "

"Yes. I have heard he is a merry fellow. I trust no harm has befallen him ? He is not dead ? "

"Nay, not that we know of. But harm *has* come to him. Notwithstanding the great attractions of the Court, and the favours heaped upon him by the king and his courtiers, Silverbell has deserted his majesty, and has become jester to the bloodthirsty outlaw who calls himself Jack Straw."

"The Lord save us ! He must have been mad ! " replied Silverbell.

"Mad, indeed, is hardly the word. But we were all mighty proud of him, Master Pedlar," replied the other cook, who seemed very much inclined to burst into tears, "and we sadly miss him. Though he was occasionally somewhat rude, and took it upon himself to kiss and embrace all the girls in the palace, he was a merry fellow in good truth. Not to have him with us on trying occasions, is like the flowers not having a gleam of sunshine. Now he has joined Jack Straw, he is lost! Have you ever visited Jack Straw, Sir Pedlar ? "

"Yes."

"More than once ? "

"Yes, on many occasions."

"We have heard much of him. What sort of a creature is he ? "

"Tall, and, to my thinking, somewhat thin, but possessed of muscles like iron. He is dark, with black wavy hair, and eyes like great brilliants, and with lungs which, for their power, would be enough for three ordinary men. He is as brave and fearless as a lion, and quick to forgive or avenge an injury."

"You must have taken much notice of him to have given him such a character," said one of the cooks.

"I have lived long enough in the world to be able to form a quick judgment," replied the supposed pedlar.

"But they say he comes of a lowborn family," said the other cook; "and if that be so, how is it reported that he is the only son of Sir Guibald le Manduit?"

"There is a mystery connected with the birth of the youth," replied Silverbell. "But let me have something to eat and drink; and while you are preparing it, I will select your presents."

The meal was now placed before him, and a fine meal it was.

There was a magnificent middle of a large salmon, the remains of a baron of beef, a venison pasty, a huge platter of fried trout, a pile of "king's loaves," and a "London cake," and on a silver tray several flagons containing Gascoigne, Rhenish, Gaillac, and Osey wines. Silverbell sighed as these were placed before him.

"Why do you sigh, Master Pedlar?" asked one of the cooks.

"I sigh because I see 'tis impossible that I can consume so great a meal at one sitting."

"Ha! ha! Why, that was exactly what Silverbell used to say whenever he sat to a merry meal."

"Then he was not much of a fool, for by the Virgin! 'twere far better to eat than waste a fine meal such as this," replied Silverbell, at once attacking the viands.

"Fear it not, Master Pedlar, 'twill not be wasted. What of this and the other joints in the larder that his majesty's servants do not want, will be eaten by the bloodhounds."

The conversation proceeded merrily enough, and at last, by a clever move, Silverbell shifted it to the current topic at the Court.

This was, of course of the trap into which Jack Straw had been led.

The cooks by this time had been joined by about a dozen menials, men and women, who being full of this affair, were glad to meet with someone into whose ears they could pour the "horrible tale."

Silverbell, who professed to know nothing of the matter, listened intently, and expressed the utmost astonisnment at all he heard.

"'Tis a very dreadful narrative," he said, when the story was concluded, "and what did his majesty think of it?"

"He now thinks the same as all think, which is that an attack should be made on Blackfoot Castle, that all the rebels—for they can scarcely be called by any other name, except it is robbers—should be scattered, and the castle razed to the ground."

"A wise plan—if it can be carried out. When is the attack to be made?"

"We are not certain. It will be done without warning, and probably Rochester, for whom the king has found a new name—"

"What is that?"

"'One Ear'd Rochester. Probably he will have control of the troops. It is feared that Jack Straw, as soon as he can get more men together, will attack the Savoy Palace. It is said that he has sworn to avenge himself on the Duchess of Lancaster. But ho, ho!"

"Why do you laugh?"

"The duchess will steal a march on him. By the king's order she will remove, for the time being, to this palace, where she will be under the immediate protection of his majesty. The Duke of Lancaster is already well on the road."

"But don't you think it likely that Jack Straw will get to know that the duchess is about to—"

"Nay, nay," interrupted a yeoman usher, "it has been arranged that her ladyship shall be provided with a small escort, that she shall travel in a poor-looking litter, which is not likely to attract attention, and that she travels this very night, and by Southwark, instead of the ordinary road. So you will see that by these arrangements, Sir Pedlar, all is sure to be well."

"'I SWEAR I WILL MAKE YOU MY WIFE!' CRIED JACK STRAW.'"

"True, true, a most excellent and wise plan. Whoever planned these arrangements is certainly clever."

"Why, 'twas planned by no less a person than his most gracious majesty."

"Ah, indeed!" replied Silverbell, indifferently, as he left the table. "Well, I will now return my thanks to ye for your kindness. I have had my fill, and feel twice as strong as I did a short time ago. And now I will depart."

"Farewell, Sir Pedlar, and a good journey to you, and when you come this way again forget not to give us a call."

"Especially if you have any more presents to spare," said one of the cooks.

Placing his wallet over his shoulders, Silverbell, with many a bow, and many a wish that his entertainers might always retain their good health, went his way.

Slowly he went at first, but directly he was out of the park, it was truly marvellous how he got over the ground.

He soon reached Jack Straw's Castle, and we need hardly say that his return had been most anxiously looked for.

At once throwing off his disguise, he hastened to Jack, whom he found in deep and earnest conversation with Mark, Basil, Egbert, and Simon Sampson, who now had command of some two hundred men.

"Well," Jack asked Silverbell, "did you gain much information?"

"Aye. Listen."

And Silverbell told him of how he had obtained admission to the kitchen of the Royal palace.

"The first news of importance I gleaned," he said, "is that it is now really the king's intention to attack this castle."

"I have heard so," said Jack, "and arrangements are now going on for its defence. You did not hear when the attack was to be made?"

"Nay; but 'tis to be done secretly."

"So I hear."

"And it is probable that Rochester will lead them."

"All the worse for the king's troops, then," replied Jack, grimly.

"Rochester has now a new name. He is called 'One Ear'd Rochester.'"

Jack and his companions burst into a roar of laughter.

"Truly," said Jack, "the name is most appropriate. If he leads the troops who attack us, it is probable he will lose the other ear. But the other news, good Silverbell? I doubt not it is of little importance compared with the news of the intended attack on our castle?"

"You are entirely wrong," replied Silverbell. "The other news is of the utmost importance."

Silverbell's announcement caused a look of surprise to overspread Jack Straw's features.

"The other news of the utmost importance," he ejaculated.

"Aye," replied Silverbell. "A splendid opportunity is open to you. You can avenge yourself on the Duchess of Lancaster, and deal the king and his nobles a blow they would not be likely to forget in a hurry."

"Ah, say you so? Quick, the news!"

Silverbell told him of the Duchess of Lancaster's intended journey, and by whom it was planned.

"Now, by all the saints!" cried Jack, "this is most fortunate. It seems like the act of Providence. By heaven! the duchess shall fall into my hands."

"'Tis not only the duchess who will fall into your hands," remarked Basil, "but also her treasure."

"An idea flashes across my mind!" cried Jack. "A small escort, say you, Silverbell?"

"Yes. So as to not attract attention."

"Ah! Then if that be really so, my idea is a brilliant one."

"What do you propose?"

"That we not only capture the duchess and her treasure, but also *the whole of the escort*, and convey them, by way of Dartford, to this castle."

"An excellent proposal, on my soul!" cried Mark and Basil.

"I long to see the duchess," said Egbert. "You have said that she is very beautiful, Jack."

"Yes, *very* beautiful, there can be no doubt of that. But her beauty will have no effect upon me."

"You do not intend to—to——"

"To kill her, you would say? No,

that is not my intention, though she deserves death."

" But her husband, the duke?"

" He took no part in the affair. Of that I feel certain."

" What, then, will happen to him?"

" Naught. He will not be with the duchess, Silverbell says."

" No," said Silverbell. " I heard he was already on the road to the palace."

" Even if he were with the escort," said Jack, " he should be treated well. Since, up to the present, he has done no injury to me, I would do no injury to him. Now away, and let us prepare to meet the duchess."

" How many men will you take with you?" asked Mark.

" Two hundred. Those under Sampson's command will do. Simon, prepare them."

Simon at once withdrew.

" Mark, you will stay here in command; let every man remain under arms in case of surprise, and let the drawbridges be raised."

" All shall be as you wish," replied Mark, hastening away.

" The hour is at hand, your grace," said Jack, fiercely, " though I thought the time was far distant, when I should be able to repay you for your treachery."

" Be merciful to her, Jack!" said Egbert, placing his hand upon Jack's shoulder, and looking pleadingly into his face.

" Silence!" replied Jack, in stern tones. " Though she deserves no mercy, I may show to her more than she showed to me."

* * * *

Shortly after sunset the weather became unsettled, and it was certain that ere long a storm would be the result.

When night had fairly set in, the wind, from fitful gusts, rose almost to a hurricane. It whistled, howled, and moaned through the branches, and hurled many a young tree from its position.

Upon this undesirable picture the Duchess of Lancaster looked.

She was standing at her bedroom window, watching the preparations for her departure going on below.

She was attired from head to foot in a furred cloak—evidently intended to conceal her features.

By her side stood one of her maids, also attired for travelling.

" Your grace looks somewhat pale," said the maid, after a moment of silence.

" Yes, Editha," replied the duchess. " The noise of arms seems to disturb me. I shudder to hear it; and look at the night. Ugh! I would to heaven we were not about to travel."

" Your grace will be perfectly safe. We shall be in the litter with closed doors, and the wild wind cannot reach us. Then we travel by a different and safer road, and we shall be accompanied by sixty brave and well-armed men."

" You do much to reassure me, Editha. But I have a foreboding that some harm is about to befall us."

" Try to shake off the feeling, your grace. All will be well. Yet I must admit it would be better were his grace, the duke, with you."

" He is dull company, Editha," sighed the beautiful duchess. " The last time I travelled to Greenwich, as you may remember, Lords Wakely, Roscommon, Stanley, and that very handsome young Stanmore were with us, and I am sure I never enjoyed a journey so much. Dear me, they really amused me immensely."

" His grace heard of it, I remember," replied the maid, gravely, " and he was very jealous."

" And wherefore? If he cannot amuse me, he must expect that I shall have some one to take his place."

" But," persisted the maid, " your grace must not forget that the duke is years your senior, and, besides, that he is always much troubled with State affairs."

" Truly so. I troubled myself with State affairs so far as to join with Rochester and Walworth in the attempted capture of the notorious Jack Straw—ha! how I shudder at the name!—and what was the result? Dreadful! And what did the duke say?"

" I have not heard, your grace."

" He was pleased to express this opinion—that all who had anything to do with the trooping of Jack Straw were worse than fools!"

" Indeed!"

"Yes, and he said that Rochester and Walworth received a well-merited punishment, and that—and mark this—I was responsible for the death of his men. He also said that Jack Straw, having sworn to avenge himself, would not fail to do so. That is, of course, the reason I am about to be put under the immediate protection of the king. What think ye of Jack Straw avenging himself on me, Editha?"

"I know not what to think, your grace."

"He openly threatened me—*me*, the Duchess of Lancaster!" cried the lady, drawing herself proudly erect; "but even if such be his intention, he will have no opportunity of carrying it out. I am, indeed, thankful that this road has been chosen for our journey. Hark! that is the bugle! All is ready! Pray heaven all the jewels are safely stored!"

In less than an hour the duchess and her escort left the palace.

The escort consisted of sixty heavily-armed men, commanded by a captain, from the Royal guard.

The party made their way to Old London Bridge, and thence across what was known as Southwark Fields.

A more wild and desolate place could not have been found in all London.

Though this, being almost a disused spot, had been selected for the better safety of the duchess, she did not like it by any means, and more than once she expressed her horror at the appearance of the place.

As the party proceeded, the storm, so long threatening, broke out in all its fury.

The rain poured in torrents, and occasionally a blinding flash of lightning illuminated the fields for miles around, and a deafening crash of thunder caused the horses to prance and neigh with terror.

Not the slightest shelter was to be found.

In vain did the duchess entreat the captain to lead them to an inn of some kind.

Any rambling, foul-smelling place would have been acceptable to her just then.

But the captain, much as he would have liked to gratify the wishes of the duchess, could do nothing.

For one thing, he was ignorant of the locality, and the men under him knew but little of it, and what they did know was by no means complimentary to the place.

The captain's directions to his men (as he had been minutely instructed by the duke) as to the ditches, was to constantly cry to those whose duty it was to lead the way—

"Keep the ditches on your left!"

But it was all very well to say—"Keep the ditches on your left!" The principal difficulty was to *see* the whereabouts of the ditches.

Except when the flashes of lightning lit up the path, all was exceedingly dark.

At last the captain gave the word to stop.

"Why do you tarry?" asked the duchess, now greatly alarmed, as she thrust her head from the litter.

"We must pause awhile, your grace," said the captain, "because from what I can see of it, we have entirely lost our way."

"But surely some of the men know where we are?"

"They would know, your grace, were it daylight, and the ground dry for them to proceed and find out."

"What is that very black-looking object close by me?" asked the duchess, pointing towards a huge oak by the roadside.

"I see naught, your grace," replied the captain. "Ah, pardon! I do now. That is only a malefactor's bones swinging in chains."

"Heaven!" almost shrieked the duchess, "and yet you stop here? Proceed at once, I command you!"

"We must turn back, your grace, and find another road. We cannot proceed farther along this."

"But why?"

"There is an immense pool in front of us, your grace. Be pleased to look."

The duchess again put out her head.

"Your eyes are, indeed, good if you can see a pool," she said. "On my soul *I* cannot, and it—"

At this moment a terrible flash of forked lightning burst through the heavens, cut off a mighty oak near its roots, and sent it flying into the pool the captain had spoken of.

A huge volume of water went up like a waterspout, and descended in a perfect torrent on the litter, and on those in front and behind it.

Hastily drawing in her head, the duchess sank trembling into her seat.

"Heaven have mercy upon us!" she moaned. "What will become of us?"

"We had better wait here until the storm has cleared off," suggested the captain. "Here, we are only in danger of the lightning (which, by the Blessed Virgin, is more awful than ever I saw it), whereas, even if we take another road, we are in danger of getting into some pool or ditch."

"I would give half the valuables with me if we could move on!" moaned the duchess.

"I should order the captain to find the other road," said the maid.

"You would, Editha?"

"Of a surety, your grace; do you not remember what the Archbishop told you?"

"At this moment I am unable to remember anything."

"He said that whenever you found yourself in danger, you were never to forget to pray to heaven to watch over you."

"When he said that, he could not have dreamed that I should ever be placed like this. In my own private chapel I never forget to pray—here I am forced to do so. But you propose that the captain should find another road?"

"Yes, at once."

"Pray direct him so to do."

The maid put out her head to give instructions to the captain, when the latter's voice suddenly rang out—

"Hold!" he shouted. "Let not one of you stir until we find out what this is. Heaven's mercy on us! I believe the place is haunted!"

The duchess started up, and clutching her maid, pulled her back.

Stepping from the litter, she cried—

"What mean you? Speak!"

The captain pointed ahead beyond the pool.

"I see naught but a long black line of trees," said the duchess.

"They are not trees, your grace," replied the captain. "If they are, they are strange trees, indeed. If you will watch intently, you will observe that that long dark line is slowly moving."

"Ah, 'tis so!" said the duchess, in a low whisper.

The whole of the escort crowded round the litter, and watched in silence this extraordinary phenomenon.

Nearer and nearer came the line, then it suddenly stopped, and like a flash of lightning, a light appeared at one end.

It was a link

That was plain enough.

Before any one could express any astonishment, lights spread along the entire length of the line, and were held aloft.

Then it was that a loud cry escaped the duchess and her attendants.

"We are lost!" cried the captain.

"Lost?" replied the duchess. "How? What means this strange exhibition? Ha, as I live, this long line is nothing more nor less than armed and mounted men. I see the steel breastplates glistening in the glare of the torches. We are not lost, but saved; for these men are, no doubt, sent by the duke to meet us."

The captain smiled grimly.

"Your grace is mistaking," he said. "Observe the centre of the line."

The duchess watched closely.

A word of command was given by a loud voice, and instantly the flashing of swords, as they were plucked from the scabbards, ran along the line, then from its centre three horsemen advanced.

The glare of the torches brought out their outlines most distinctly.

The horsemen, on each side, held aloft a torch, but the centre one carried nothing but a formidable-looking battle-axe.

He was encased in chain armour, and in the helmet upon his head there flashed a splendid brilliant.

Advancing to the edge of the pool, so that their figures were reflected in the dark, slimy water, the centre horseman raised his hand.

"See you now who it is?" asked the captain.

"Who?—who?" cried the duchess.

"*Jack Straw*, your grace, and from what I can see of it, there is no telling what force he has."

"Jack Straw!" almost screamed the duchess. "Then we are, indeed, lost!"

The maid, who had become almost frantic, said, as she burst into tears—

"'Tis not *all* who are lost, your grace. You will remember that this Jack Straw swore to revenge himself on *you.* What have *I* done that I should suffer?"

But the duchess was too much occupied with herself to pay any attention to what her maid said.

"Captain," she whispered.

"Hist!" said the captain. "This daring outlaw is about to speak."

In loud, clear tones these words rolled over the pool—

"*Death to tyrants!*"

They were echoed by Jack Straw's men. The shout burst upon the air like the roll of thunder.

"*Death to tyrants!*"

And as the men shouted it out, they raised their flaming links still higher, and waved them to and fro.

"Mark you," cried Jack, rising in his stirrups, "we know this is the train of her Grace the Duchess of Lancaster. Let the leader of it come forward."

After a slight hesitation the captain moved forward a few paces.

"Are you the leader?" asked Jack.

"I am," replied the captain.

"How many men have you?"

"That I decline to answer."

"I will not press you since it is a matter of but little importance. Are you aware who I am?"

"Yes; you are the notorious robber, Jack Straw."

"Let me fly a bolt at the fellow for his insolence!" growled Simon Sampson.

"Nay, nay," said Silverbell, "let us wait awhile."

"List ye, captain!" cried Jack. "We are here to capture the Duchess of Lancaster, and the whole of her property and escort."

At the word "escort" the captain uttered a stifled cry, and his men muttered their determination to fight to the death, rather than be taken.

"We may just as well fight for it," said one. "This Jack Straw owes a debt to the duchess which he has sworn to pay, and since we are found in her train, the rope will be our portion. May the foul fiend take the duchess! Here have I six children at my cottage, and not one of them will ever see me more!"

"Captain!" moaned the duchess, who had fallen upon her knees in the litter. "Don't let me be captured. If I am taken by Jack Straw I shall be put to death! Oh, mercy! mercy!"

"Your grace," said the maid, "you must remember that you showed *him* no mercy."

"Oh, Editha, Editha! are you, too, turning against me?"

"Heaven forbid! But you must now remember what you did to him. 'Twas you who led him into the trap, that Rochester and Walworth might fall upon him. And now we may all suffer for your act."

"Ah!" suddenly cried the duchess. "I see a way out of the difficulty. Captain—captain! offer him my jewels—my—"

"One moment, your grace," interrupted the captain, raising his hand, "this outlaw speaks again. Yet 'tis not he who comes forward this time— 'tis a taller man. Hark!"

It was Silverbell.

"Hark ye!" he cried, in stentorian tones. "Jack Straw has no wish to fall upon you without warning. Are you prepared to surrender the duchess and yourselves?"

"No!" shouted the captain, snatching his sword from its scabbard. "We will fight to the death!"

"On your head be the consequences," replied Silverbell. "We know not how many men you have, though we see the glitter of your arms; but before we fall upon you, we will give you a short time for reflection, We should advise you, as you value your lives, to surrender peacefully. Look around you, and you will see that you are powerless to fight with Jack Straw."

Jack issued another command, and instantly another line of torches sprang, as if by magic, into existence. Then another and another.

Uttering a deep groan, the captain lowered his sword.

His men did likewise, and gazed— speechless with wonder—on the strange sight before them.

What struck them most was that the horses and the men seemed as motionless as statues.

"Save me! save me!" cried the duchess.

"I cannot save myself," replied the captain. "Alas! that I should have undertaken the command of your escort."

"Your answer!" cried Silverbell.

"We are forced to surrender," replied the captain; "but what have we done that *our* lives should be forfeited?"

"Your life, and the life of every man under you, shall be held sacred," replied Jack. "On this cross I swear it."

And raising a small silver cross to his lips, he kissed it.

"Enough," answered the captain. "I trust in your mercy."

"Forward!" cried Simon.

In one long, unbroken line the men advanced, passed across the pool—the actual depth of which was not more than three feet—and the litter and the escort were completely surrounded.

Simon and Silverbell collected the arms belonging to the men of the escort, and then Jack advanced to the litter.

He found the duchess on her knees, her face buried in her hands.

For a few moments he looked at her sternly.

The duchess raised her head.

"Mercy!" she cried.

"Rise, madam," replied Jack. "I wonder that such a word as *mercy* can pass your lips."

"Let me proceed on my journey, and I will place in your hands the whole of the jewellery in my possession, the value of which is enormous."

Jack smiled scornfully.

"You mistake me, your grace," he said. "You, like others, are under the impression that I am a common robber. It is not so; yet I may tell you that your jewellery and plate, or whatever of value you may have with you, will be serviceable. All of it will be sold, and the proceeds distributed among the poorer classes."

"You seek my life!" sobbed the duchess.

"I have no answer to that at present," replied Jack. "You are my prisoner, and, as such, you will be conveyed to my stronghold."

"May Heaven pardon you for the crime you are about to commit," said the duchess.

"Ask pardon of Heaven for the crime you *have* committed," answered Jack. "Not even the basest born serf would have stooped to such a treacherous action as you have been guilty of."

During this conversation, Egbert had approached the litter.

"See," he whispered, "another lady is present."

"Ha, so there is," replied Jack. "I had not noticed her. Come forth, fair lady," he added, "and let us see your face."

Editha crept out, and stood tremblingly before him.

"Mercy!" she gasped.

Jack smiled.

"Fear not," he said. "Neither my followers, nor myself, will offer you harm or insult. What is thy name?"

"Editha Wellcombe."

"And your business with her grace?"

"I am one of her ladies-in-waiting."

"Well, had I anyone to wait upon her grace, I would place this litter at your disposal, and you should return, properly escorted, to your home; but as I have not, you must accompany her."

"I am to meet with no harm?" asked the maid, imploringly.

"I have already said so. Return to the litter, for I fear the duchess is fast losing consciousness."

This was found to be the case.

Jack untied a flask, which was affixed to his saddle bow, and handed it to the maid.

"Use this freely," he said, "and she will soon recover."

The doors of the litter were now closed, the torches were extinguished, and Simon Sampson, who knew every inch of the ground, placing himself at the head of the now long train, Jack gave the word, and the whole party moved off.

The cavalcade proceeded along narrow and seldom-used paths on purpose to avoid meeting with anyone likely to convey the information to the palace.

But, despite Jack's caution, the party was seen by one of the guards, who, concealing himself behind a hedge, watched the procession go by.

Never was man more startled than this soldier.

As soon as the procession vanished, the man started off towards the palace at a breakneck pace.

When within sight of Blackfoot Castle, the cavalcade proceeded yet more cautiously.

Jack was about to issue some command, when a harsh voice croaked—

"Halt, Jack Straw!"

"Who cries halt?" asked Jack.

"I do," was the reply.

Jack saw before him a withered old gipsy woman, dressed in a mass of rags; she looked frightfully hideous with her long, grey locks flying about her shoulders.

In her right hand she carried a long staff, evidently to assist her in walking.

Her left hand was concealed under her ragged cloak.

"Well, mother, what would you?" asked Jack, kindly.

The old hag laughed wildly. Her laugh sounded like the croak of a raven.

"Mother!" she said. "Mother! Ho, ho! Ay, but 'tis like her son— like her son."

"Your mind wanders, mother?" said Jack. "What do you want? I have but little money with me; but if a few crowns will be of any service to you, you shall have them."

"I want no money."

"Then get you hence, you harbinger of evil," said Silverbell, in stern tones.

"I am no harbinger of evil," croaked the old woman, shaking her head gravely, "and he who was the king's jester should know it."

Silverbell started.

"How is it that you know me?" he asked.

"No matter how,'" replied the old woman. "'Tis sufficient for you to know that I *do* know who you are. But depart, and leave me with Jack Straw."

During this brief conversation, the cavalcade had continued on its way, and was now some distance ahead.

Something in the old woman's manner caused Jack to think she was the bearer of some message, though from whom he could not imagine.

"Join the train," said Jack to Silver-bell and Egbert. "I will follow you in a few moments. Now, mother," he said to the old woman, when Egbert and Silverbell had galloped off, "be quick, and tell me what you want."

"Ay, ay, I will not long detain you. Listen! When did you last see Sir Guibald le Manduit?"

Jack started in astonishment. He was about to question the woman as to how she became possessed of the knowledge that he was anything to do with Sir Guibald, but she said, sharply—

"Ask *me* no questions, but answer *mine*."

"'Tis so long ago that I cannot call it to mind," was Jack's cautious answer.

"'Twas when you returned from Rome?"

"It was."

"And when you saw him did he say anything about your *mother?*"

"My mother! Ah, heaven, what mean you, woman? Quick—"

"He disowned you, did he not?"

"He did. But he did not mention anything of my mother. But if you have anything to tell me—if, in the years long past, you knew my dead mother—"

"Hist, hist! She did not die— nay, at this moment she *lives!*"

"Lives!" cried Jack, leaping from his saddle.

"Silence! lest we are overheard. I am not here to tell you anything. I am here to deliver to you this roll of parchment, and to show you one picture in this."

And from under her cloak she produced what looked like a small hand-glass.

"That parchment contains the solution of the mystery which, for so many years, has surrounded you. *This glass will show you your mother as she is at this moment!* It will be your duty to rescue her from the power of one of the most horrible wretches who ever walked the earth. What do you see?"

"A large mansion."

"Would you know that mansion again?"

"I would."

"Proceed."

"The castle has vanished, and in its

place I see the door of what looks like a cell and—ah! the Virgin guard me! What is this? I see a woman almost naked—she is holding forth her hands towards me, and she has a chain fastened to her waist. She turns—she is frightened—a man enters; he has a whip in his hand; he raises it, and is thrashing the woman. I see his face now. Oh, heaven!" almost shrieked Jack, starting back with clenched hands. "It is Sir Guibaid le Manduit!"

These words had barely left his lips ere a blinding flash of lightning burst forth, and before the sound of the thunder which followed it had died away, the woman had vanished.

Placing his hands across his eyes, Jack leaned upon his saddle for some few moments.

"'Twas no dream," he cried, starting up. "Nay, here is the roll of parchment. My *mother!* Can this be so? Oh, that I could now tear this parchment open and read its contents."

At this moment the distant sound of a bugle broke upon his ears.

Giving a last look round as if to be sure that the old woman had vanished, Jack sprang into the saddle.

As he did so the sound of several bugles, which seemed to proceed from the king's palace, was heard.

"On, good horse!" cried Jack, and the next moment, he was dashing madly forward.

CHAPTER XIV.

THE ATTACK BY THE KING'S TROOPS ON BLACKFOOT CASTLE—THE GREAT BATTLE FOUGHT UNDER JACK STRAW'S LEADERSHIP—THE DEATH OF WALWORTH—HOW JACK STAYED THE BATTLE.

JUST as Jack reached the drawbridge, the last man of the cavalcade had passed into the stronghold amid the loud blasts of horns, the rattle of arms, and words of command.

"What means this commotion?" asked Jack of Mark Trevor.

"Thank Heaven you have returned," replied Mark. "Hie to the first battlement; look towards the palace, and you will see the reason of the commotion. Information has reached the palace that you have captured the Duchess of Lancaster and her train. The whole of the troops from Woolwich and from the palace are now being gathered together, and an immediate attack will be made on us. Lords Rochester and Walworth, from what I can gather, are at the palace, so it is evident that they will take the command."

"It may be so much the worse for them," replied Jack, grimly. "How many men do you think the king can muster?"

"I should say about three thousand. In a few hours, of course, the number could be increased to ten thousand."

"No doubt. Three thousand! 'Tis a large number compared with the men we have. How many can we muster?"

"About a thousand. But if you will allow me to suggest—"

He stopped abruptly.

"No time is to be lost," said Jack. "What do you suggest?"

"That we abandon the castle, and—"

"Never!" cried Jack. "I wonder, Mark, that you can propose such a thing. 'Tis not like you."

"I merely—"

"We will fight, Mark—fight! Ay, if the king's troops come in their *tens* of thousands, we will fight. If we are outnumbered and our own men waver, we can make good our escape by means of the subterranean passage. But we must not show the white feather before the king's troops reach the castle. Where has the duchess been placed?"

"We thought it best to confine her in the Stone Chamber."

"Right. We must not treat her with too much consideration."

They were now joined by Basil, Silverbell, Simon Sampson, Egbert, and several men, who each had the command of fifty or sixty troops.

"Do not look so grave," said Jack. "All will yet be well—what say you, Silverbell?"

"I know not what to say," replied Silverbell, gravely.

"You advise me to order a retreat?"

"*I* advise a retreat? Heaven forbid! We may, of course, be forced to retire—but do so without striking a blow? Never! Yet hark! the sound of the bugles grows nearer. Look! look! I see the glare of torches. Yes, the king's troops are advancing."

"'Tis indeed, true," said Jack. "The torches make everything distinct. I can see the banners waving in the wind. To arms! to arms!" he shouted, drawing his sword, and brandishing it aloft.

The whole of the men gathered round, and followed the action of their leader.

"Death to tyrants!" cried Jack.

"Death to tyrants!" was the response.

"My men," said Jack, "we are at last to be attacked by the king's troop. But fear not, they shall have a good account of us to take back to his majesty.

"Let the archers be placed on the second battlement, and let the rest stay with me on the first.

"It is probable that the troops will endeavour to enter the castle. If we allowed them to do so, we should be taken like rats in a trap. Silverbell, and you, Mark, direct a guard to be placed over the duchess, and see that the litter is ready for immediate departure. You, Basil, collect all our valuable property, and place it upon some of the horses in the subterranean passage.

"Then gather together all the faggots you can find; place a pile in each room, and let a man stand at each door with a lighted torch. If we are beaten we will fire the castle, and let the king have only the bare walls. Courage, my men! Fight for life and liberty!"

"Three cheers for Jack Straw," cried Basil.

A tremendous roar thrice rang out—much to the wonder of the king's troops, who were steadily advancing—and then every man stood at his post.

By this time the storm had ceased, and the moon was peeping through the clouds.

It shone upon the castle, and upon the glittering arms, and reflected itself in the moat.

Nearer and nearer came the king's troops.

They halted twenty yards from the moat, and the leaders rode forth.

Jack recognised them at once.

They were Rochester and Walworth.

"Jack Straw!" cried Rochester, "we are here by order of the king, to call upon you, and those under you—firstly, to deliver up to us for safe conveyance to the king, the person of Margaret, Duchess of Lancaster; secondly, to surrender yourselves to his majesty, that justice may be done upon you."

"Do you require an answer to your insolent demands?" asked Jack.

"At once."

"You shall have it."

Jack waved his hand, and his men let fly a shower of arrows at the king's troops.

Many men were struck, and they rolled from their saddles to rise no more.

This was entirely unexpected, and for some moments the king's men seemed thunderstricken.

But they quickly responded to the cries of Rochester and Walworth.

The mounted men gave place to the archers, who, to the number of at least a thousand, came forward, and discharged flight after flight at Jack's men.

They were answered quickly enough.

For some minutes this arrow fight raged furiously.

Jack met with severe loss; but when the shooting slackened, it was seen that the ground was thickly strewn with the bodies of the king's men.

Rochester now ordered up the men with scaling ladders.

Jack bade his men place ladders on the inside of the walls, and prepare to meet those of the king's troops who managed to mount.

Rochester's men found it extremely difficult to swim the moat.

It was deep and slimy.

Several of the men neglecting to take off their breastplates, were drowned.

At last, however, a long ladder was placed right across the moat, and half-a-dozen men, by Rochester's directions, sliding into the water, endeavoured, by holding the sides of the ladder, to get across to the other bank, where with ropes, they could easily pull over the other ladders.

Jack was immediately above them, and, assisted by half-a-dozen of his men, he carried a huge stone to the top of the wall, and rolled it over.

Down it went, and crashed on to the middle of the ladder, destroying it and hurling the men into the water.

A loud roar from Jack's followers greeted this; but several of those who shouted were struck dead by a flight of arrows, which was discharged at them as they incautiously exposed themselves by looking over.

Walworth having, in loud, impassioned tones, called upon the men to avenge their fallen comrades, they responded with loud shouts of vengeance.

A rush was made to the moat by some five hundred men, under Rochester, while Walworth, with about the same number, advanced towards the drawbridge.

The archers on both sides resumed their arrow shooting.

By Rochester's orders a ladder was again thrown across the moat, and a number of men instantly sprang into the filthy water.

Jack's followers greeted them with a flight of arrows, and howls of derision.

But this time more than half-a-dozen of them had managed to get across, and creep under the walls, where they were comparatively out of harm's way.

Ropes were thrown to them, and the ends having been secured to several scaling ladders, the latter were rapidly drawn across.

At this moment a loud shout arose, and looking towards the drawbridge, Jack saw that a fierce fight was in progress there.

Knowing that if possession was obtained of the drawbridge, the castle was as good as taken, Jack, calling upon his men to resist Rochester's attack, hastened towards the bridge.

He saw that, by some means or other, a vast number of Walworth's men had got across the moat, and that a fierce fight was being waged for possession of the drawbridge.

Jack called upon his men to "hurl back the king's bloodhounds into the moat."

This command his followers, now thoroughly aroused, proceeded to carry out.

By Jack's orders, the gate, which had been partially forced, was suddenly thrown open, and in a moment, the men on both sides were engaged in a desperate conflict.

Of course, neither cross nor long bows could now be used.

Short and double-handed swords were the weapons, and used they were, with an energy horrible to behold.

Quarter was neither asked for nor given.

Jack's men fought bravely and unflinchingly.

Suddenly, with a loud crash, the drawbridge fell across the moat.

Whether this was accomplished by Walworth's men, or whether it was accidentally done by Jack's, was never known.

Walworth, who was mounted on a splendid horse, calling upon the men in reserve to follow him, at once dashed across the bridge, and the fight now became a general slaughter.

Jack, with Silverbell, Basil, and Simon close beside him, made his way through the struggling mass of humanity, and at last reached Walworth.

That "noble lord" immediately recognised him, and digging his spurs deep into his horse's flanks, he endeavoured to ride him down.

He would have succeeded but for Jack's wonderful agility.

Stepping quickly back, our hero raised his battle-axe, and the next instant it had crashed into the skull of the noble steed.

The animal fell, bringing its rider heavily to the ground.

Walworth was now completely at Jack's mercy; but our hero did not take advantage of him.

"Rise quickly!" he cried.

Walworth was speedily on his feet, and, with a bitter imprecation, he attacked our hero with great fury.

The men on both sides paused to watch the conflict between the two leaders.

Jack's superior strength soon began to tell upon his enemy.

Our hero's ponderous battle-axe descended again and again upon him, and, at last, Jack making a sudden dash, seized him by the throat, and then getting him on the edge of the drawbridge, he plunged his dagger into his breast, and hurled him into the moat.

It must not be imagined that Jack Straw escaped without a scratch.

Nothing of the kind.

He was severely injured, more especially in the neck, from which the blood slowly trickled and ran down his armour.

In the meantime, Rochester had been vainly attempting to get his men over the walls.

As soon as the scaling ladders were placed against them, and had been filled with men, they were hurled back into the muddy moat.

Jack Straw fought his way back to the courtyard.

"Follow me, Simon!" he cried.

"I am at your side," replied Simon, as he joined him.

The words had scarcely left his lips ere an arrow, shot at random, struck him in the throat.

Simon, with a wild gasp, fell to the ground.

Jack dropped upon his knees by his side, saying—

"Alas! that you should fall when victory seems so near!"

"I fear not death!" replied Simon, in faint tones; "but I should like to live until I saw you conqueror. That, however, is not possible. Give me the cross you have at your girdle. 'Tis all I ask."

Jack at once unbuckled it, and placed it in Simon's hands.

When the battle was over, Simon Sampson was found quite dead with the cross pressed to his lips.

On Jack reaching that part where the scaling ladders were being so freely used, he found that a desperate battle was being waged on the walls, and he saw that the courtyard was strewn with the dead bodies of many of his men.

"Mark! Mark!" he cried, as he leapt over them, "join me—even now 'tis not too late!"

"Alas!" said a man near him, "Mark Trevor was shot down directly you left us to attack Walworth."

"Dead?" gasped Jack.

"Ay, the arrow struck him in the breast, and buried itself in his heart!"

"Heaven have mercy upon his soul!" ejaculated Jack, doffing his helmet.

"Amen!" replied the man, "but let us be thankful he is avenged. I made a mark of the man who discharged the arrow, and when he reached the top of one of the scaling ladders, I struck his head from his body!"

"You did well," replied Jack; "and if you and I are spared, I will reward you. There is now— Ha! what is that?"

A shout, far louder than any previously heard, rent the air at this moment, and simultaneously the sounds of deadly strife ceased as if by magic.

"By heaven!" cried Jack, "*the castle is on fire!*"

Ay, this was so. Dense volumes of smoke were rolling from the windows, and, high up on the roof, long tongues of flame were leaping upwards with an angry roar.

Rochester looked at this for some moments like a man in a dream.

But recovering himself, he shouted to his men to follow him to the drawbridge.

Jack noticed the movement, and seeing that it was useless to attempt to check the mad rush, he called to those of his men who were fighting on the drawbridge to enter the castle.

They proceeded to obey, and before the king's troops could understand what was about to be done, they had entered the burning castle, and closed the great gate.

And now we will return to the duchess.

She had been placed in the "Stone Chamber," a small, but well-furnished apartment, and a couple of guards left over her.

Within easy distance, Egbert waited and watched.

He looked from one of the windows, and gave to the anxious guards a faithful account of all that was passing below.

One by one his arrows were discharged with unerring accuracy.

During his struggle to reach Walworth, Jack was more than once in danger of losing his life ; but Egbert's loving eyes watched his movements, and his arrows always found a mark at the right moment.

As the battle progressed, the guards became uneasy.

The sounds of fighting reached their ears, and they longed to join in the fray.

And if the men were anxious, what of the duchess ?

She thought every moment would be her last.

The doors of the Stone Chamber being left open, the duchess' maid crept forth ever and anon to implore the men to tell her how the battle was proceeding.

But not one word of information did she get from them.

They were too busy with their own thoughts to heed her entreaties.

The Duchess of Lancaster was familiar with martial sounds ; but this was the first time she had ever been within hearing distance of a battle.

As the din grew louder and louder, she slid from her seat on to her knees, and in that attitude she remained. She would have prayed, but she felt she dare not do so.

When Egbert reported that Walworth had been slain, the guards set up a yell of triumph ; but when they were told that the king's troops were gaining ground, they began to lose all command of themselves, and threats were uttered against the duchess.

At last Egbert, who had continually watched the movements of the troops, cried out, in startling tones—

"All is lost ! The walls have been scaled ; the king's troops are crowding across the drawbridge."

Rushing into the Stone Chamber, he shouted, in frantic tones, as he snatched his dagger from its sheath—

"Rise, woman, rise ! Do you hear me ? Rise, I tell you !"

And rushing forward, he seized the duchess by the wrist, and dragged her to her feet.

"Mercy ! " gasped the duchess. "Have mercy upon me !"

"Mercy !" cried Egbert, fiercely. "Do you deserve one spark of mercy ? No ! you deserve naught but death."

"Kill her !" shouted the guards.

"No, no, no !" implored the maid, rushing between Egbert and her mistress. "Spare her—oh, spare her ! She has never harmed you."

"What !" replied Egbert, starting back, his eyes flashing dangerously. "Not harmed *me* ? She harmed Jack Straw, and through *him* she harmed *me* ! Know that I am not a boy, as you think me, but a woman—ay, a woman, with a woman's loving heart beating within my bosom ! Know that Jack Straw is my affianced husband. *I* would deal with you, madam, were I allowed ; but that task I must leave to Jack. Yet mark this— Ha ! those shouts. Listen ! Yes, Jack has been beaten back.

"Take your burning brands, guards, and fire the castle. On me let the responsibility rest. Come with me !" she (for we will now speak of Egbert as a female) almost shrieked as she again seized the duchess ; "and mark it well : if Jack Straw falls, by me shall his death be avenged ! I will drive this dagger into thy treacherous heart. Come, and pause not, or I will leave you to be consumed by the flames !"

Saying which, Egbert half led, half dragged the terror-stricken duchess towards the subterranean passage.

The men, knowing the influence Egbert had with Jack, at once proceeded to carry out her instructions, and they fired the piles of faggots in every room.

The flames took a firm hold of the ancient pile, and soon made an appearance through the roof.

Just as Egbert, dragging the duchess after her, was descending the stone steps leading to the passage, Jack Straw appeared like an apparition in front of them.

He presented a terrible appearance.

His helmet had gone, and his long, curly hair was matted in several places with blood, some of which had flowed down his face.

His armour was broken in more than one place, and the dents in his sword-blade showed to what use the weapon had been put.

"Who fired the castle?" cried Jack.

"The men, by my orders," replied Egbert.

"You have acted rightly, Egbert," said Jack; "but where are you now going with the duchess—the woman who was the real cause of all this?"

"To the subterranean passage."

"Not so. See, the remainder of the men are going there. The treasure, is it ready?"

"It is. The horses are ready for departure, and your own is in front."

"Good. Go and see to the men, while I stay any further attack."

"What mean you?"

"Do my bidding, and question me not. Take the maid with you. Now, your grace," he added, turning fiercely to the duchess, "come with me."

And taking her wrist, he proceeded to drag her up the narrow stairs leading to the highest battlement.

He was followed by Silverbell, Basil, and a number of men, who, despite the terrible position in which they now stood, had no thought of deserting their leader. As they proceeded, they could hear the roaring of the flames, and occasionally a dense volume of smoke rolled over them.

More than once the duchess hesitated, and gasped for breath.

"Pause not," cried Jack; "if you give way and faint, you are lost, for I swear I will leave you to your fate!"

As they reached the top of the stairs, the flames lit up the scene with startling distinctness, and a great sob escaped our hero's breast as he looked down into the courtyard.

It was strewn with the bodies of the dead, and ghastly in the extreme did they look in the glare caused by the flames.

Rochester's men were standing at the massive gates.

They had been constructed for resistance, it is true, but they could not long withstand the onslaught now being made upon them.

"Hold!" shouted Jack; "hold!"

And he raised a white flag.

Rochester saw it, and at once ordered the bugle to be sounded.

The terrible din the men were making instantly ceased.

"He surrenders!" laughed Rochester.

"He shall have any terms he may name—that is, if he be spared by the flames; but when we have him, we will hang the traitor from the highest church spire that can be found. But, by the Blessed Virgin, what can have become of the duchess? Sacrificed, no doubt; but it concerns me not. Ho, ho! Do you surrender?" he shouted to Jack.

"No!" was the answer, clearly and distinctly given.

"Then why do you wave the white flag?"

"Hark ye, my Lord Rochester. I call upon you to withdraw your troops. If you do not, a heavy charge will be laid at your doors!"

"How so?"

"Look!"

And Jack pressed forward the duchess.

A great shout rent the air as the men beheld her.

"What is to be done, my lord?" asked one. "If you do not make terms with him, he—"

"Well, well? Go on!"

"Well, my lord, it is possible that he may order the duchess to be slain before our eyes."

"Ay," replied a captain, "and the king would hold us all responsible for it. My lord—quick! see the flames are fast working round to where they are standing."

At this moment the duchess raised her hands.

"Save me, Rochester!" she cried. "Save me!"

"On what terms will you deliver the Duchess of Lancaster into my hands?" asked Rochester.

"That," replied Jack, "you shall withdraw your men to a distance of five hundred yards, and you shall not move until one hour has elapsed. At the expiration of an hour the duchess shall be safely placed in your hands."

"Caitiff!" roared Rochester, "think you I will agree to such terms?"

"If you will not, then I, my comrades, and the Duchess of Lancaster will perish in the flames. *We* are not afraid to die; but *you* are, my Lord Rochester. Coward, robber, and *murderer* that your are! you shrink at *death!* Yet, if you refuse my terms, the duchess will surely die, and then what will be *your* fate? The king sent you to rescue her. *Are you attempting to do so?* My lord, if you fail to deliver the duchess to his majesty, your head will answer for it! The time grows short—decide—quick!"

Rochester muttered a terrible oath. He had considered that he had at last got Jack safely trapped. He, however, saw the force of our hero's argument, and said—

"I agree."

Jack disappeared with the duchess, while Rochester, ere ten minutes had passed, had the whole of his men massed at a distance of five hundred yards from the castle.

The time passed slowly, the fire raged fiercer and fiercer, the flames roared and hissed, and split the massive walls in all directions.

Rochester and his men watched this in silence ; a spell seemed cast over them.

At last, when nearly an hour had passed, Rochester cried—

"By the Blessed Virgin! I verily believe Jack Straw, the duchess, and every one that was in the castle, have been burned alive!"

"Why so, my lord?" asked a captain.

"Why so? Why, if such is not the case, where are they?"

"My lord, you are aware that this accursed outlaw is gifted with the power of appearing and disappearing at his own will."

"Pshaw! that is but childish prattle. In the name of Heaven, how could he vanish from a burning castle?"

"I know not, my lord."

"Have you sought the body of Lord Walworth?"

"We have, my lord. It is in the moat, and we cannot at present recover it. The moat is full of the bodies of our comrades."

"Ha!" replied Rochester, fiercely. "A time will yet come when I will avenge both Walworth's death, and the blows Jack Straw has dealt me. Who knows?" he muttered; "I may yet get Dorothy Leighton safely within my clutches. It would be a glorious revenge! and the possession of the miser's gold would repay me for all I have lost and suffered."

In a few minutes more three dark figures emerged through the gloom.

"Who goes there?" cried Rochester.

"The Duchess of Lancaster," was the answer, and the duchess and her maid were ushered into Rochester's presence, by Basil.

The silence of the grave reigned for some few moments. At last Rochester, by a great effort, managed to find his tongue.

"Welcome, your grace," he said. "I trust the events of this night have not greatly disturbed you?"

This was said in such sarcastic tones, that the duchess, half-distracted though she was, instantly detected it.

"Your observation is an unwarranted one, my lord," she said, in reproachful tones. "The answer for all that has occurred will be required from *you*."

"I fail to see that, your grace."

"The king shall be informed of all that has occurred between us," she said, in an undertone.

Rochester smiled.

"Your grace has too much sense to inform the king of anything that has occurred between us," he returned. "I have always considered the Duchess of Lancaster to be a lady in possession of more than the *ordinary* amount of common sense, and I should be very sorry to be forced to alter my opinion."

Turning to Basil, he added, in fierce tones—

"Where is the litter belonging to the duchess, vile follower of an accursed outlaw?"

"'Tis ere now but a pile of ashes!"

"Ha! and your valuable property, your grace?"

"Is all in the possession of Jack Straw."

"*All?*" said Rochester, aghast at this astounding intelligence.

"Yes, all! He has taken *everything*, even to the bracelets from my wrists, and the rings from my fingers."

"Where is Jack Straw now, sirrah?" he asked Basil.

"That I may not tell you," replied Basil boldly.

"How did he escape from that burning castle?"

"That also I may not tell you."

"We will see whether you will not tell us. But no doubt your grace can inform me how this daring villain escaped?"

"'WELL, SIR SNAIL!' CRIED ONE OF THE MEN-AT-ARMS, 'AND HOW DO YE?'"

"Nay, I am powerless to tell you. I only know that we were taken through a long subterranean passage, and that eventually we emerged amid a mass of trees and foliage."

"You cannot tell where that was?"

"Nay. If I could tell you the exact spot I dare not."

"*Dare* not, your grace? And why?"

"Because, previous to my leaving him, Jack Straw made me swear upon the cross that I would not reveal it."

"What is an oath taken upon the cross to you, your grace?"

"Rochester! how dare you insult me?"

"Well, well, your grace, it matters not, I shall meet with him ere long. But since we have one of his confederates here, we will make an example of him."

"Stay!" interrupted the duchess, "I have also sworn that this youth should peacefully depart."

"Indeed!" sneered Rochester. "Your grace has sworn too much."

"It was to save my life," cried the duchess, stamping her foot; "and though my life may be of little value, it is not so worthless as is yours."

"Your grace is complimentary; but I am not easily provoked, and so I can well pass it over. Look you," he added, to Basil, "go back to Jack Straw, and tell him that the next time we meet I will assuredly pay him the debt I owe him."

"I will not fail to do so, my lord," replied Basil; "but your lordship will let me remind you that Jack Straw owes *you* a debt. Perhaps, when next he comes face to face with you, he may pay it—with interest."

And before the maddened Rochester could reply, Basil wheeled his horse round, and was soon lost to view in the darkness.

Rochester ordered horses for the duchess and her maid, and when all was ready, the command was given, and the shattered remainder of the king's troops left the scene.

CHAPTER XV.

OF HOW JACK DISBANDED HIS MEN, AND OF HOW HE AND HIS COMPANIONS WENT OFF TO LONDON—WHAT WAS WRITTEN ON THE PARCHMENT.

WHEN Jack and his comrades had reached the end of the subterranean passage, and had despatched Basil with the duchess and her maid, he produced a large roll of parchment, and proceeded to call over the names of the men.

It was a sad roll-call!

Out of all the men he had had before the battle commenced, only about one hundred now answered to their names.

"Let us not forget," said one elderly man, "that those of our comrades who died, did so in a good cause. May their souls rest in peace!"

"Amen!" was the fervent response.

"What has become of the train of the Duchess of Lancaster?" asked Jack.

"All slain!" replied Silverbell.

"Slain?"

"Yes. They would neither fight nor retire, so they were slain by the arrows of the king's troops where they stood."

"And we have here all the treasure?"

"All of it, and the value of it must be enormous."

"No doubt of that. How many horses have we?"

"Nearly two hundred."

"And here is my own tried steed. Thank heaven he is spared to me. Now let us begone, for the time is flying. and our hour of grace will soon have expired. Mount!"

Every man was at once in the saddle. Then they took the bridles of those horses which carried the treasure, and the word being given, the whole party moved off at a quick trot.

"Will Basil find us?" asked Egbert.

"Yes, he is well aware of the road I shall take," replied Jack. "We shall stop at the ruined abbey."

Without pausing the party rode to

the abbey, which our readers will remember was the place where Jack Straw first rescued Dorothy Leighton from the clutches of Rochester.

"Why are we here?" asked Silverbell.

"You will see directly, and I think that you and everyone else will agree with what I am about to say. First, have we any links?"

"I have three," said one of the men.

"Dismount all of you, then," said Jack. "Let the torches be lit, and the whole of the treasure brought in."

This order was carried out. All knew that something entirely out of the common was about to happen.

For some little time Jack conversed in whispers with Egbert, but when Basil galloped up and entered, our hero mounted the ruined pulpit, and addressed the assembled men.

"Friends," he commenced—"nay, let me say, brothers and companions-in-arms, allow me to address a few last words to you."

A low murmur ran round the abbey.

"Ha!" continued Jack, "last words they must be ; for here, on this spot, we part, probably never to meet again in this world. Mark it well, I have not hastily arrived at this conclusion. I have been thinking of it during the progress of the battle and since. It is certain that the time has not arrived for the people to rise, draw the sword of freedom, and proclaim their independence. Were they ready to do so, how willingly would I assume the command!

"At present I see it is useless to further defy the king and his dastardly peers. Now that so many of our comrades are slain ; now that the king knows we can offer no further effectual resistance, it is certain that he will send his troops to hunt us down. Could I at this moment gather together a thousand trustworthy men, I would still defy him. But since that is impossible, we must disperse.

"But we will still remain comrades in heart. We have here an enormous amount of treasure, and it shall now be equally divided, and not one among you will want during his life, if he take good care of his share. Silverbell, do you approve of my determination?"

"Yes," replied Silverbell. "You have spoken only what is right and proper."

"And you, Basil?"

"You have said only what I should have said myself," replied Basil, sorrowfully.

"I would that Mark were here," added Jack, sadly. "Poor Mark! would that we could have had the satisfaction of carrying away his body. Well, well, 'tis the fortune of war. Now, my men, what say you to my determination?"

A deep silence reigned for some few moments.

It was broken by the oldest man among the lot coming forward.

Snatching off his helmet, he said, in husky tones—

"I think I shall be speaking the sentiments of my comrades, if I say that your words are true, and that, under all the circumstances, you are acting wisely. But the principal thing that we shall be sorry about is, that we shall be entirely parted from you, from brave Basil Tremayne, from merry Silverbell, and last, but not least, from—"

He paused abruptly, and pointed to Egbert.

"From the one I value more than my own life," said Jack. "Well, you have all along known that Egbert was a woman—ay, a woman with a true and faithful heart ; but know her now as the one with whom I hope to pass my life. Her real name is Nell Bartlott. There is a mystery connected with her, it is true ; but it is known only to me. And now for sharing the treasure."

With a will every man set to work, and soon all the treasure was laid in the centre of the abbey, and then divided among the men.

Jack took the same amount as the others, despite their entreaties that he should take more.

Each man became possessed of more than sufficient to keep himself and a family for the remainder of his life.

"And now," said Jack, "as to the horses. They are of no value to me. I only want my own steed. Egbert, Silverbell, and Basil, who come with me, will want theirs. The others had better be divided among you, and you may dispose of, or keep them, as you see fit."

This being agreed to, the animals were divided among the men.

All was now finished.

The men ranged themselves in a sort of circle, while Silverbell, Basil, and Egbert bade each of them farewell.

It was Jack's turn next, and as he grasped the horny hands of his brave followers, more than one tear rolled down his cheeks.

At last every man was mounted, and with a last farewell, and a loud cheer, they set off, some in one direction, some in another.

Jack Straw and his companions stood looking after the men for some time in silence.

"Whither are we bound?" Basil presently asked.

"For London. You will go with me, Basil?"

"With all my heart."

"And you, Silverbell?"

"I will never desert you."

"Thanks. In London we will disguise ourselves as well-to-do citizens, and by that means no doubt we shall escape detection."

"How shall I disguise myself?" asked Egbert.

"There will be no reason for you to don a disguise. You will attire yourself as a lady—your proper dress."

"I shall feel somewhat awkward in it," smiled Egbert.

"And henceforth you will be called Nell."

"Good. A change will be most acceptable."

"And no doubt you will soon be Mistress Straw," said Silverbell.

"I trust she will," said Jack; "but she cannot be my wife until the mystery of my birth is solved. I have not yet told you of what the gipsy said, nor of what I saw in a magic glass she carried. Neither have I told you that, under my saddle, I have a roll of parchment which gives me every particular."

Basil shook his head, and Silverbell did likewise.

"I don't think it likely that what that old hag said will turn out true," said Silverbell.

"And why?"

"No doubt she is like the rest of her class. What she says and does is done only with the intention of obtaining money."

"That I offered her, and she refused it."

"Well, let us hope that the parchment will reveal something startling."

"Let us now set out. Is our share of the treasure properly secured?"

"Yes."

"Mount, then."

The links were extinguished, and the four mounted their steeds.

"Farewell, old abbey," said Jack. "Heaven only knows whether I shall ever behold you again. Now let us on as rapidly as possible."

* * * *

The morning was far advanced when the four reached Westminster, where Jack proposed to halt and rest at the house of a Jew of the name of Morris Scharf.

"I don't exactly know the whereabouts of the house," said Jack; "but we must see about discovering it at once, for we are attracting attention."

This was true enough, and was it to be wondered at?

What could be more calculated to attract attention than four mounted persons, not only covered with dust, but whose attire bore distinct traces of blood?

"I know of one Morris Scharf," said Silverbell; "he is a lender of clothes. He has supplied me on many occasions when I wanted to disguise myself."

"There can be no doubt that he is the same person. It is to him that I am going to purchase disguises as well as rest."

"Follow me, then, and I will take you to his house."

Across several muddy fields went Silverbell, and at last he halted in front of a low, tumble-down wooden house on the bank of the river.

Silverbell knocked on the door, and in a few moments a most hideous head was cautiously thrust out of one of the holes which did duty for windows, and a cracked voice asked, in whining tones—

"What want ye, my masters?"

"Admittance first," commenced Jack, "and after that—"

"The lord have mercy on us!" interrupted the Jew, who had caught sight of the blood upon his visitors' clothes. "What are ye—murderers?"

"Nay," replied Basil. "We are simply peaceful citizens."

"Bah! ye cannot deceive me. I have been too many years in the world, young sir, to be deceived. I like not the appearance of either of ye, except it be yonder pretty boy, whose cheeks are—"

"Silence!" interrupted Jack. "Come down instantly, and unbar the door, or we will bring the whole house down about your ears."

"Have mercy upon me, sirs! I assure you I am but a poor, lonely old man, whose only desire is for—"

"All the crowns you can get, no doubt," laughed Jack. "Well, we are not here to rob you, but to put money in your purse."

"What guarantee have I for that?" whined the Jew.

"My word of honour," said Silverbell, as he took off his cap. "Do you recognise me?"

"I think I can recall to mind your features, but I don't know your name."

"My name is Silverbell, the king's jester."

"Ha! to think I should be so foolish as not to recognise you at once. And who are your companions? Who is yonder fierce-looking youth, with the battered and blood-stained armour?"

"JACK STRAW!"

The Jew's eyes opened to their fullest extent, his lower jaw fell, and he uttered a cry of wonder.

"Jack Straw!" he ejaculated.

"Yes," replied Silverbell; "so come down at once."

The Jew did not again require to be told.

Throwing the door back, he said—

"Enter, my masters, you are right welcome to my humble roof. Stephen! Stephen!" he cried, "come hither, and take these noble gentlemen's horses to the back."

Thereupon a withered-up old man crawled through what looked like a huge rat-hole, and proceeded to carry out the order.

"I have no stable," said the Jew, "but there is a large shed at the back, and lots of straw, and plenty of fodder can be had if—"

"We pay for it, you would say," said Jack. "Well, we have plenty of money to pay for what we have, so order fodder to be given to the horses, and, mark you, *plenty* of it."

"It shall be done, honourable sir. Pray enter."

Having whispered to his man, the Jew carefully closed the door, and then led the way through a narrow shop, which was filled with attire of almost every description.

Halting at the end of the shop, the Jew took down a lighted lamp, then stooping, he took hold of an iron ring, and exerting all his strength, raised a heavy, iron-bound flap.

This he held back, and handing the lamp to Silverbell, said—

"Lead the way, noble sir; but don't jest, for the stairs are somewhat rotten by reason of the water from the river, which penetrates into the house, no matter what I do to keep it out."

Silverbell took the lamp and descended a ladder. He was followed by Jack, Basil, Nell and the Jew.

They found themselves in a small and foul-smelling cellar.

"This way," said the Jew. "This is only a place for Stephen. I have a better place for gentlemen—ah, much better."

Thereupon he took the lamp, went along a passage, and finally stopped before an iron door.

Producing a bunch of keys he opened it, saying—

"Pray enter."

Our four friends did so, and found themselves in a small, though richly furnished, apartment.

"This is only reserved for illustrious visitors," said the Jew, with a chuckle, "and by the side of this are two more."

"My intention is, if you can accommodate us," said Jack, "to stay here for a short time."

"I understand," replied the Jew; "and you desire to remain out of sight?"

"Precisely."

"Then you could have nothing better than this, noble sir, and the outlay for such princely accommodation is but small."

"No doubt your terms will suit us," said Jack.

"In the first place," said Silverbell, "I propose that the treasure be at once unpacked and brought here."

"I will do it," said Basil.

"And I will help you," said the Jew. "Treasure, eh!"

"If you help," said Silverbell, "you will be pleased to take off that coat."

"Eh?"

"Take off that coat. There are many articles of jewellery among our treasure, and some might *accidentally* drop into your capacious pockets."

"I am as honest as the king himself," retorted the Jew.

"Then," replied Silverbell, if you are as honest *as the king*, it behoves us to keep an eye upon all that comes within your grasp. But depart at once."

The Jew shuffled off, followed by Basil, who was also to bring the parchment from beneath Jack's saddle.

It was not long ere they returned with the treasure.

As it was laid upon the floor the Jew's eyes sparkled, and his mouth watered.

The restless motions of his hands and feet were sufficient to tell how enraptured he was.

"Now, Jew," Jack said, "kneel down there, look at those articles, and tell me their value."

The Jew knelt down, and carefully sorted over the precious pile.

At last he said—

"These are worth much money, noble sir."

"I am perfectly aware of it," answered Jack. "What is the value?"

"To the owner or the buyer?"

"Dolt! to the buyer."

"They are worth, to the buyer, no less a sum than forty thousand crowns."

"Fool!" cried Jack; "worth forty thousand crowns? By the soul of the Virgin! a *hundred* thousand crowns is not the value to the buyer."

"And he is well aware of the fact," said Silverbell. "Mark well the greedy glitter in his little eyes."

"Well, we do not want *you* to buy them," said Jack; "for we have plenty of money without disposing of all this."

The Jew now looked very black indeed.

"I thought you wanted *me* to buy them," he said.

"Of course you did," said Basil, "and that was the reason you put your own value on it."

"If you say the value to the buyer is a hundred thousand crowns, noble sir," said the Jew, in wheedling tones, "it must be so, though I should not have thought it."

Jack and the others laughed outright at this monstrous lie.

"I have not so much money in the world," said the Jew, shaking his head.

"What will you give me?" asked Jack.

"Sixty thousand."

"No."

"Sixty-five thousand?"

"No."

"Seventy thousand?"

"No. You shall give me eighty thousand crowns, provide each of us with such disguises as we may select, and give us food and lodging here for a few days."

"Agreed!" cried the Jew, after the manner of a hungry dog snapping at a meaty bone. "Agreed!"

And forthwith he was about to pounce upon the treasure.

"Hold!" shouted Jack. "Keep away thy vulture-like claws until you have placed the money by the side of it."

The Jew rose.

"It will take me a long time to count such a vast sum," he said.

"No matter for that," said Basil. "The jewels can wait, and we will give you our word that we will take nothing from the pile."

"And now," said Jack, rising, "be good enough to place the other rooms at our disposal. One room is for this lady," pointing to Nell.

"Lady?" cried the Jew, staring hard at Egbert. "Ah, fool that I was not to have guessed as much! That I did not guess such a beautiful— Your pardon, gracious lady," he said, as he tried hard to make a bow, which was a most dismal failure—"ten thousand pardons."

"Eighty thousand, if you like," said Silverbell, "and they are granted. Show the lady the entrance to your principal room."

Nell rose and followed the Jew.

When he returned he showed the other room.

"Now send us plenty of food and wine, good Jew," said Jack, "and then you may leave us for five hours. All of us are weary, and require rest."

"Five *hours*, honourable sir."

"Yes."

"During that time then I shall be able to count the money."

"Very well, do so. Let it be tied in three bags. Two are to contain twenty thousand crowns each, and one forty thousand."

"Your order shall be faithfully carried out, noble sir. But what of the disguises?"

"As to them I will speak to you later on."

The Jew bowed, though his eyes were not directed upon those to whom he made the bow; they were riveted upon the pile of dazzling brilliants and the gold upon the floor.

Even on the threshold his eyes were not taken off the precious heap.

As the door closed upon him, Jack said, gravely—

"There is a man who would be content to live upon the filth of the land, and would even sell his soul into the bargain, providing his hands could meddle with such trash as lies there."

"He is not the only one in the world," said Basil.

"Nay, not by many thousands," said Silverbell.

The Jew soon returned, bringing a large quantity of food, while his man Stephen carried a huge pitcher of wine and two more lamps.

Having placed these articles down, the Jew and his man were instructed to withdraw, and the former was told to return in five hours.

*   *   *   *

The Jew aroused Jack and his companions punctually at the time stated, and they awoke thoroughly refreshed.

When they had washed themselves, Jack gave the Jew the instructions as to the attire he was to procure for them; and, to tell the truth, he provided Jack,

Basil, and Silverbell with very respectable disguises. When they had donned them, they found themselves transformed into wealthy-looking citizens.

Barely were they attired in their disguises, ere the door of Nell's room opened, and the maiden appeared.

It was like a gleam of sunshine suddenly bursting into a dark room.

She was attired in a becoming dress of grey satin open at the throat, and about her waist was a splendid girdle, to which was affixed a mother-o'-pearl cross.

On her wrists were diamond bracelets, which on many occasions had adorned those of the proud Duchess of Lancaster.

These were Jack's presents, as were also a diamond star in her hair, and a string of pearls she wore round her neck.

"You look lovely!" cried Jack.

"Surpassingly beautiful, on my soul!" said Silverbell. "Had you been at Court you would have been the envy of all the ladies."

At this moment the Jew and his man once more made their appearance.

They carried the bags of money.

"Here are the three bags," the Jew said. "Two contain twenty thousand each, and this large one forty thousand, and I need hardly tell you that it has nearly broken our backs to bring them."

"You are quite certain the amount agreed upon is there?" asked Jack.

"Yes, quite sure. Will you count it, noble sir?"

"No. I will trust to your word at present; but if I eventually find anything short, look to yourself. There is your pile of jewels—take it away."

The Jew opened his coat, and produced a bag.

In a few moments he had clawed up the whole lot, and had put them into the bag.

"When you want anything—"

"We want something now, Jew. We are hungry and would eat."

The Jew opened his eyes in wonder.

"Hungry!" he whined. "Why, on my soul, it was but five hours ago that I brought you sufficient food and wine to have fed a round dozen of his majesty's troops for a month."

"Your acquaintance with his majesty's

troopers is very limited," said Silverbell. "Now *my* acquaintance with them has been of an extensive character, and I have known a round dozen of his majesty's troopers to eat at one sitting two Royal bucks, two sheep, a huge dish of trout, as many loaves as two cooks could carry, and, after that, being still hungry, they swallowed the handles of their pikes."

"May Heaven forgive you!" cried the Jew; "but jesters are professed perverters of the truth; yet from what you have just said, it is no wonder that you are called the principal jester. Well, since you are hungry, my masters, I will bring you food."

"It is part of the bargain," said Jack; "nothing more. And look you, Sir Jew, this lady requires something more delicate than do we."

"I have nothing delicate in the house, may it please you, noble sir—that is, nothing delicate but my own poor body, and—"

"It doesn't please us!" cried Silverbell; "and, besides, do you think the lady could eat your body?"

"Ah, Sir Jester, it is a pity to waste your wit over a poor man like me."

"Poor?" exclaimed Jack, in disgust. "How can you call yourself poor when you can afford to pay at one time as much as eighty thousand crowns?"

"I mean—"

"No matter what you mean. Be off at once and bring what is required."

The Jew shuffled off, being followed by his man, who whined in piteous tones—

"'Tis I who am hungry! I am dying of starvation!"

"It is false!" said the jew, shaking his fist in the old man's face. "You have had no less than two loaves in twenty-four hours. Come on, and if you lie to me like that again, and within hearing distance of noble gentlemen, I'll—I'll stop *all* your food."

When the food had been brought and partaken of, Jack took up the roll of parchment.

With trembling hands he broke the seal.

"How I have longed for this moment!" he said, as he spread out the parchment.

"Let us hope that it is something more than a pack of nonsense, dear Jack," said Nell.

"What strange writing," cried Basil.

"Ay, it is strange, indeed," said Silverbell.

"Nevertheless," said Jack, "I shall be well able to read it. I will do so aloud. Listen:

"'After many years!

"'And the son shall find the mother, and the mother shall behold the son, for which glory should be given unto the One Being who continually watches over us. It is He who is the worker of all great wonders, and who, after a woman has been for years the victim of a great wrong, will, at last, set right the wrong.'"

Jack paused, and looked at his companions.

They returned his glance in silence.

Silverbell, shifting uneasily in his seat, said—

"By all the saints, if that is not the writing of a witch, then I am not called Silverbell."

"If the woman be not a witch," said Nell, "I should say she is a religious fanatic, and, unfortunately, England is crowded with such persons!"

Jack made no reply to this.

He read on—

"'The writer of this is, and has been for years, a wanderer on the face of the earth. But such was not always the case. There was a time when I was courted and flattered by the highest in the land. Not, it is true, for my beauty, for I had but little of that, but for my great influence. I was in the confidence of nobles—ay, and of Royalty, because I was a great scholar. I spoke the languages of many distant lands. My fall was sudden, but how that came about need not here be said.

"'Among my principal friends, in my better days, was one Lady Amelia, only daughter of the Duke of Exeter. She was a very lovely woman, and for that reason, no doubt, she was flattered and petted by all, including the king, who, on more than one occasion, was heard to declare that, were it permissible, he would make her his queen.

"'However, after a brief stay at Court, Sir Lyon Steel fell in love with her, and she returned his affection. The result was, they were married.

"'Time passed on, and the pair were very happy. At the expiration of two years Lady Amelia gave birth to a girl. That the child was not a boy grieved Sir Lyon ; but his wife's death, which took place within twenty-four hours after the birth of the child, grieved him more ; indeed, from the time his wife was lowered to her last resting-place, he became a changed man, and lived almost in absolute seclusion at his mansion in Finsbury. He devoted the whole of his time to the study of the future welfare of his child.

"'The girl grew up, tall, graceful, beautiful, the exact counterpart of her mother. Sir Lyon wished to keep her all to himself. He could never bear her out of his sight. But, at last, the girl (who was christened Maud), though devotedly attached to her father, grew weary of constant confinement. She longed to be presented at Court, for her maids told her that, with her beauty, she would be welcomed with open arms.

"'At last she prevailed upon her father to let her go, and she was presented at Court by a lady, whose name I forget. Edward II. took a great deal of notice of her, and informed Sir Lyon that if he did not allow his daughter to be constantly at Court, he would incur his great displeasure.

"'The consequence of this was that Maud was almost always at Court. It was not long before she had an offer of marriage. It came from Lord Linsay, a young, handsome, and brave man.

"'He asked Sir Lyon's consent to the union. It was indignantly refused ; the reason being that Lord Linsay's father and Sir Lyon had been for many years deadly enemies.

"'This refusal was a great blow to both Lord Linsay and Maud, who loved his lordship with all her heart.

"'Suddenly Lord Linsay was given the command of a number of troops, who were told off to put down the rebellion which had broken out in Manchester. A battle was fought, and it soon became known that Lord Linsay, with many more officers, had been killed.

"'This news was almost the death of the beautiful Maud. The phy- sicians were hastily summoned. In the presence of Sir Lyon they examined her. But they asked her no questions. Turning, they consulted each other, and then shook their heads very gravely. Sir Lyon was frantic. He implored them to tell him whether there was any immediate danger, and the reply was : "In a few hours your daughter will give birth to a child, and if you will be advised by us, you will depart and leave her in peace."

"'This Sir Lyon would not do. Uttering loud and bitter lamentations, he cast himself by the bedside, and implored his daughter to tell him the name of the father. Then Maud told her father of how, months before, she had been secretly married to Lord Linsay.

"'Sir Lyon cursed and raved ; but though the blow to him was severe, he thanked Heaven that at least his daughter had been married.

"'The child, a fine boy, was born, and it was at once taken away from its mother, and placed in charge of a nurse.

"'That the daughter of Sir Lyon Steel had been privately married, or that she had a child was kept a profound secret.

"'Now there was one who, for a long time, had endeavoured to make an impression upon Maud, and that was Sir Guibald le Manduit, a descendant of a French family. He was somewhat poor, but when he, only a month after the birth of the child, asked Sir Lyon whether he would be allowed to pay court to his daughter, he received a reply in the affirmative.

"'After some consideration, Sir Lyon determined to tell Sir Guibald all. He did so, and added that if that would make no difference, he should, on his marriage, receive the sum of one hundred thousand crowns. This money was left to Maud by her mother.

"'Sir Guibald, as may be supposed, jumped at the offer. The marriage took place, and the pair removed to Dartford. After a lapse of time, it was given out that a son was born, after that, that Maud had died. No one knew the rights of it—every one believed, and must still believe, that Maud died, for the funeral took place in her name. Then the son was again placed out to nurse.

"'The one into whose hands I shall place this is that son. Yes, your name is not Guibald le Manduit, it is not Jack Straw. You are the son of Lord Linsay, and his wife Maud, and both of your parents are alive, but in the power of that scoundrel, Sir Guibald le Manduit!'"

Jack started up, and his companions did likewise.

"This must be true!" exclaimed our hero in a voice of emotion.

"Ay," said Silverbell, "only too true. The latter part of that narrative I can vouch for, as I heard a great deal of it at Court. It was whispered that Sir Guibald had murdered his wife; but it was never believed. I pray you calm yourself, and continue the reading. I am deeply interested."

Jack went on—

"'And now comes the secret. A few months ago I returned from abroad; but it was for no other reason than that I wished to die in my native country, for the years I have lived now number close upon four score. I went straight to London, for there I have a few friends, they being the sons and daughters of those who knew me in my younger days. The one on whom I called was Elias Leighton, who, at one time, was known as the "Strand Miser"—'"

Again Jack paused.

"Mystery upon mystery!" muttered Basil.

Jack continued—

"'And it appeared that I had called at the proper moment, for it seemed that on the previous night two men had fought in the Strand, and one had been almost killed. The fight had been watched by the miser's daughter, who, when one lay stretched upon the ground, begged her father to have him removed to the house.

"'This was done, and it was then found that he was a Frenchman, and could not speak English. I went to him, and he told me that he was, and had been for many long years, a servant of Sir Guibald le Manduit. He said he had a great secret upon his mind, and feeling that he was about to die, he wished to reveal it. I implored him to tell it me, and, after a little while, he consented.

"'He said that he was one of three servants—two men and one woman—kept by Sir Guibald at his mansion (once the property of Sir Lyon Steel) at Finsbury. He asked me if I had heard of Sir Lyon Steel. I replied that I knew him, his wife, his daughter —all of them. Then he startled me by saying that neither your mother nor your father was dead.

"'It seems that Lord Linsay was not killed at the battle in Manchester. He was, however, grievously wounded, and he was kept a prisoner for some months. When he recovered he heard of his wife's marriage with Sir Guibald.

"'Disguised, he sought out his wife at the mansion at Dartford. Having made inquiries, and being informed that Sir Guibald was absent, he, by bribing one of the servants, gained admittance to his wife's room. What followed is not known. It is certain, however, that the servant had made a mistake, for Sir Guibald came suddenly upon the pair.

"'He found them locked in each other's arms. He instantly fastened the door, and summoned all his men. These he armed, and proceeding to the apartment, unlocked the door, and called upon Lord Linsay to surrender.

"'Finding it useless to resist, his lordship allowed himself to be secured. He was then taken to a vault.

"'In that vault he was kept until after the death of Sir Lyon, which took place soon after this, and the beautiful Lady Maud, your mother, was locked in a vault opposite him.

"'When Sir Lyon was buried, all his servants were dismissed. The whole of the furniture, valuables and decorations were taken away, and Lord Linsay and Maud were, in the dead of the night, secretly conveyed to Finsbury.

"'The stone vaults, under the moat of this mansion, are of the most horrible description. Sir Guibald picked out the worst, and had Lord Linsay and Maud chained to the walls. They were placed so that they could see and speak to each other, and that was all, and there for over fifteen years they have been.'

"Terrible!" cried Jack. "Can anything be more horrible! The dastardly wretch! Oh heaven!" he cried, raising his hands aloft, "spare him! Spare him until I come face to face with him!"

Basil and Silverbell sat as if petrified with horror.

Nell had covered her face with her hands, and was sobbing bitterly.

Jack continued, though not in so clear a voice. It was husky now and trembling—

"'The three servants of Sir Guibald had been sworn to secrecy.

"'Lord Linsay and his wife receive no more food than is sufficient to sustain life.

"'And now I come to the worst. At midnight, on the first of every month, Sir Guibald visits them. He tortures them with his tongue as long as he pleases, and then he thrashes them with a heavy whip. This he has done every month for fifteen years.'"

Jack again paused, and a deep groan escaped his lips.

"What a monster!" cried Silverbell. "Why, the State never yet thought of such a punishment for its worst prisoners."

Jack went on reading—

"'When the man had made this confession he died. I at once communicated what he had said to Elias Leighton, and, after due reflection, he suggested that you should be informed.

"'And now, Jack Straw, arise! Release your parents, and avenge their wrongs. Yet be careful. Unless you are cautious all may be lost. The first thing you must do is to seek out Elias Leighton.

"'And now farewell!'"

Thus ended the manuscript.

"I must go to work at once," said Jack.

"Take the advice given by this strange woman," said Silverbell, "and be not too hasty. Let us talk the matter over together."

"In the meantime my parents are suffering," said Jack.

"They must wait yet a little longer. A rescue cannot be thought of at a moment's notice."

"I would I had not dispersed my men. With them at my back I would have stormed and taken the mansion ere two hours had passed over my head."

"Well, let us thank Heaven you are in possession of plenty of money. That will do a great deal."

"It will. Well, let us consult together. You are older than I am, Silverbell."

"True; but not wiser."

CHAPTER XVI.

IS OF THE VISIT TO ELIAS LEIGHTON—HOW JACK IS SUDDENLY SET UPON BY ROCHESTER, AND OF THE RESULT.

WHEN night came on, Jack prepared to set out on a visit to Elias Leighton.

For many hours he and his friends had been in consultation as to the best way to set about effecting the release of his unfortunate parents, and at last they had hit the right nail on the head.

"But will you not allow either Basil or Silverbell to accompany you?" asked Nell.

"Nay, that would be folly," replied Jack. "One may pass through the streets at night without attracting attention, but not two or three. And you must remember what the Jew told us only an hour ago, which was that the king's troops are searching for us, under the command of Lord Roch—"

"One Ear'd Rochester," interrupted Silverbell, with a laugh.

"Well, One Ear'd Rochester."

"It is not very likely that he would recognise us, dressed as we are now," said Basil.

"I'm not so sure of that," Jack returned. "No doubt he will think that I am somewhere in London. No, 'twill be better that I go alone, and also on foot."

"Supposing you should meet with Lord Rochester?" asked Nell.

"On this occasion he would avoid him," said Basil.

"You are in error," replied Jack, emphatically. "I would *not* avoid him if I met him alone. No. I would endeavour to wipe out the murder of Dorothy's lover, and the debt I owe him."

"Then I trust you will not meet him," said Nell.

"And I," said Silverbell, seriously; "for although it might appear that Rochester was alone, he seldom moves without a few of his followers at his call."

Little more was said upon the subject, and just before midnight, Jack left the house of the Jew, and proceeded leisurely towards the Strand.

As we have said, he was attired as a well-to-do citizen; yet his clothes were not of such a remarkably rich material as to attract attention.

But though his attire did not attract attention, he himself did.

His soldierly bearing caused more than one pair of eyes to be directed upon him.

He, however, was not interrupted on the journey, and for this he was very thankful, for he was exceedingly anxious to reach the house of Elias Leighton.

Since we last saw Elias Leighton, a great change had taken place in him.

Some people said that since the murder of his apprentice, the house had been haunted.

This was, no doubt, idle talk; but people spoke of the white face and the far-away look of Dorothy Leighton. They pointed to her as she sat on the balcony of the house—often at midnight—looking at the bright sky, reading, as it were, the stars.

The principal change in the miser was this: that whereas he had never before been known to give away a penny, he now distributed plenty.

He, in fact, seemed to be trying to make the last years of his life useful to his fellow-men.

Who was the real cause of all this change?

Sweet Dorothy Leighton.

All was very silent when Jack reached the gloomy-looking house in the Strand.

"I wonder whether anyone is at home?" he thought. "I don't see a light anywhere—I don't hear a sound. Ah, what is that? A woman's voice—perhaps Dorothy's."

He had guessed aright.

A soft, sweet voice commenced to sing a ballad—a sad one.

Stepping back, Jack glanced upward, and saw, upon the balcony, a white figure.

He at once recognised it. It was Dorothy Leighton.

He knocked at the door.

"Who knocks?" asked Dorothy. "Does anyone summon me to attend the bedside of a dying sister? Father, approach and question the one who seeks admittance."

Thereupon Elias joined his daughter.

Leaning over the balcony, he said—

"Who knocks?"

"'Tis I," replied Jack.

"What is your name?"

"I will whisper it in your ear."

"That may not be. It is good to guard against surprises. Whence come you?"

"From Blackfoot Castle," whispered Jack.

"Ha!" said Dorothy. "I now recognise the voice."

Then placing her lips to her father's ear, she whispered—

"It is Jack Straw!"

"Ah," replied Elias, "I thought the voice sounded familiar."

Hastening down, he unbolted and unbarred the door.

"Welcome, brave youth," he said. "Pray enter my humble dwelling and issue your commands. They shall be obeyed, fear it not."

"I have no commands to give," replied Jack, passing into the principal room.

As he crossed the threshold, Dorothy entered through an opposite doorway.

Advancing, she placed her little hand in Jack's, and with tears in her eyes, said—

"My preserver—my *father's* preserver—welcome!"

"Thanks," replied Jack. "How happy am I to meet you once again! But how changed you are!"

"Sorrow has changed me," replied Dorothy, sadly, as she cast her eyes upon the ground.

"Aye, sorrow has changed her," said Elias Leighton, who now joined them. "I would I had given my consent to her marriage. All would then have been well. They would, I am sure, have been happy, for I had enough for them. I was selfish. I craved for a title for her—and the result? Her lover murdered by the bloodthirsty Rochester—her heart broken!"

And sinking into a seat, the white-haired old man burst into tears.

"Do not say that her heart is broken," said Jack. "She is young—time may heal the wound."

"Oh, that I could see her happy—that I could see her married to one who would guard and protect her with his life! Then I could die happy indeed. But you are here to speak of your own affairs."

"You have heard that I have dispersed my men?"

"I have. Though I was startled at first, I, after some little consideration, came to the conclusion that you acted rightly. My firm impression is that the people will not move unless they are led by a few nobles. And at present it seems to be to the advantage of the nobility to stick close to the king."

"He is indebted to you?" said Jack, inquiringly.

"Yes, to a large amount," replied Elias.

"And have you no hope of recovering any of the money?"

"None. The king borrows here, there, everywhere, but he invariably *forgets* to repay it. Did the lender press for payment, it would be to his disadvatage."

"I think I can understand."

"There can be no difficulty in understanding, my son. He who had the courage—the king would call it the audacity—to press for payment would be thrown into prison, and without a prospect of being released."

"Monstrous!" cried Jack.

"Yes, 'tis monstrous, indeed! But proceed, my son. I can tell that you have received a parchment from a certain gipsy, who—"

"Can you tell me her name?" interrupted Jack, eagerly.

"I can," replied Elias, gravely; "but I would rather not."

"I will not press you."

"Nay, a secret is a secret. You have received a parchment from the gipsy, and you have read it?"

"I have—with surprise and horror."

"No doubt. It is a strange and dreadful story. You are here to ask my advice?"

"I am—as directed."

"You shall have it. I have taken a great interest in the matter. I was personally acquainted with Lord Linsay."

"You were?" cried Jack, excitedly.

"Yes."

"What sort of man was my father?"

"One of the best of men in all respects. A more generous, or a more true-hearted and brave man never existed."

"The gipsy spoke of him with much warmth," said Dorothy. "He must have been a man that any woman would be proud to own as husband. Alas! what must he be now?"

"Hist! my child," said Elias; "it may be that Providence has sustained him and his unfortunate wife more than we can think or hope for."

"Your advice," said Jack, impatiently, "what is it?"

"This. The day after to-morrow is the first of the new month. That, then, is the time for you to meet with Sir Guibald le Manduit—that is, if such be your intention."

"It is, and by heaven—" began Jack, excitedly.

"Stop!" interrupted Elias. "Do not excite yourself, or all may be lost There is no doubt that Sir Guibald has been informed of the disappearance of his servant, and he may fancy that the man has deserted him, and that he will inform upon him. Do you understand?"

"I do."

"Very well. And he may have taken precautions against surprise. On the other hand, he may know nothing of the man's absence. My advice to you is to obtain admittance before midnight on the first of the month to this accursed mansion at Finsbury. How such a thing is to be done I know not—I am powerless to advise you. You are more versed in the art of stratagem than I am."

"As to effecting an entrance, leave that to me," said Jack. "I will obtain admittance, and I will rescue my parents, and avenge their cruel wrongs, or I will sacrifice my own life in the attempt."

"Nobly said."

"What became of the man who died?" asked Jack.

"I buried him," replied Elias.

"Where?"

"Is that a matter of any importance, my son?"

"Nay, it was simply curiosity that prompted me to ask the question."

"Your curiosity shall be gratified. I put his body in a sack. At each end of the sack I placed a heavy stone. Then one dark night—the third after his death—my man and I placed him in a boat. We then rowed into the middle of the Thames, and dropped him into the water. It was a fitting burial for such a rascal."

"In good truth it was. It may be that his master will not get such a decent burial, and—"

"Hark!" interrupted Dorothy, as she started wildly forward.

"What is it?" asked Jack.

"'Tis naught, my child; calm yourself," said Elias, looking nervously about him.

"I thought I heard voices without," said Dorothy.

"The voices of enemies?" asked Jack.

"Yes, my son, of enemies," replied Elias; "but she is mistaken."

"Has such a sweet creature enemies?"

"One only—and you know him well, for more than once you have rescued her from his clutches."

"Do you mean to tell me," cried Jack, "that she is still persecuted by Lord Rochester?"

"She is. She is closely watched by his spies, and he himself was seen near this house last night."

"Fear not, Dorothy," said Jack. "A time will come when I shall settle accounts with Rochester."

"I trust if ever the time come that you and Rochester again meet, you will not risk your life on my account," responded the maiden. "Sooner or later, I feel that I am doomed to get in the clutches of Rochester."

"Never!" replied Jack. "To-morrow I will send you a long-tried friend."

"May I ask who that is?" asked Dorothy.

"You remember the youth who rode by your side after you were rescued by Silverbell, and who watched over you so carefully."

"Egbert, I think he was called."

"Ay."

"Yes, yes," cried Dorothy. "Oh, that I had her in my company. How I would prize her!"

"*Her*, you say. How did you know that Egbert was a woman?"

"Am I not a woman myself?" said Dorothy.

"I trust she has now assumed her proper attire," said Elias.

"She has."

"You are not married to her yet?"

"Nay, not yet. But I hope to be in a very short time."

Dorothy had cast her eyes upon the ground. A sorrowful look rested upon her face.

What were her thoughts at this moment? Were they jealous ones?

We cannot say.

It was long past midnight when Jack emerged from the house of Elias Leighton and hurried away.

He met with no interruption in the Strand.

Indeed, not a single human being crossed his path.

But on turning into Whitehall, he saw three dark figures approaching.

He was too deeply buried in thought to notice them particularly, or to try to avoid them in case they might be midnight revellers.

Walking briskly, he endeavoured to pass them.

He reached the side of the one nearest the wall, when the centre man shouted—

"How now, knave! Is that the way you endeavour to pass gentlemen? Go back and give place to us. Know that we are nobles."

And seizing Jack by the arm, he endeavoured to turn him off the path.

But he had miscalculated his strength.

Jack shook him off as a dog would a rat, and again attempted to pass on.

He had recognised his assailant.

It was Rochester!

Who the others were he knew not; but though he longed to square accounts with Rochester, he knew it would be foolish to attack him when he had a couple of friends to assist him.

Rochester staggered slightly, but instantly recovering himself, he pushed Jack against the wall.

"Dastard!" he yelled. "Do you thus resist your superiors? Let us look at your face."

Saying which he snatched off the cap Jack was wearing.

Rochester started back with a loud cry.

"As I live!" he shouted, snatching his sword from its scabbard, "it is the robber, Jack Straw! Draw, companions, and cut him down! The king has offered ten thousand crowns for him, dead or alive!"

Drawing his sword, and throwing back his cloak, Jack placed his back against the wall.

The two companions of Rochester had drawn their weapons, and placed themselves in an attitude of attack; but it was a very careful position nevertheless, for they were very well acquainted with the fact that Jack was a brilliant swordsman.

Rochester fairly chuckled with glee.

"There is no escape for you this time, Jack Straw," he said.

"You are cowardly, as usual," sneered Jack. "Let your companions stand aside, and we will see who will get the better of this encounter."

"Dastard! Robber!" shrieked Rochester, dashing madly at Jack. "Die!"

At the same moment Rochester's companions advanced nearer, and they were treated to a remarkable display of swordsmanship.

Presently one of Rochester's friends —a young and powerful fellow— becoming greatly excited, advanced nearer, and, drawing back his arm, made a plunge at Jack's breast.

Our hero detected the movement; with a rapid upward stroke he disarmed him, and then with a powerful down stroke clove his skull in twain.

He fell between his companions a corpse!.

Rochester and his surviving comrade uttered a cry of rage and attacked Jack with increased fury.

At the same moment loud voices were heard, then the rush of feet, and three men, with drawn swords, suddenly appeared upon the scene.

"How now?" cried the foremost, a big, burly fellow, "a battle waged in the streets! And," he added, as he went over to the one who had fallen, "one here has received his death-blow, and a mighty blow it must have been, on my soul!"

"Serves him right!" growled another; "for see—three to one."

"So there were. That is cowardly!"

Of course the sudden appearance of these men had put a stop to the unequal fight.

"Look you, my men," said Rochester, lowering his blade, and drawing himself proudly erect. "I will give you each a hundred crowns if you will assist me in capturing this youth."

"You will?" cried the burly one. "Well, first, tell us who you and your companion are?"

"I am Lord Rochester; this is my friend."

"Lord Rochester, eh? I have heard of you, your lordship. And your name is quite enough. We can't oblige him, can we, comrades?"

The other two men shook their heads.

"But when I tell you that this youth *is no other than Jack Straw*, on whose head such a large reward is set, you will?"

The three men started forward.

"Jack Straw?" they cried.

"Yes, my men, it is Jack Straw," replied our hero, "and I trust your good sense will not allow you to interfere with me."

"No," said the burly one, emphatically. "All our interference will be to see fair play."

This announcement was received with approval by the other two.

"Either let him go," said the burly one, "or fight one at a time."

Jack again raised his sword, and Rochester and his companion did likewise.

But this did not suit either the burly one or his comrades.

"IF YOUR GRACE WILL WATCH INTENTLY, YOU WILL OBSERVE THAT THAT LONG, DARK LINE IS SLOWLY MOVING."

"If you both attack him," he cried, in tones which showed he meant what he said, "I and my companions will attack you. Fair's fair. One at a time. Pray fight first, your lordship, and look after the other *ear*. Ha, ha!"

"Since you have taken the part of this notorious robber and traitor," said Rochester, "it would be useless for me to attempt to fight."

"Well, then, let him go away."

"I do not wish to do so, my friends," cried Jack. "My sole desire is to cross swords with this dastard lord."

"Dastard lord! Well said — well said. Ho, ho!" laughed the burly one. "Well, his one-ear'd lordship can't refuse to fight. If he does, as I live, I will brand him as a coward all over the country. Dastard lord! Ha, ha! We have heard of him as 'his abducting lordship,' have we not, comrades?"

"Ay, and the name is good," they replied, with a laugh. "But 'his dastard lordship' is better. Ha, ha!"

This bantering had the effect of rousing Rochester to fury.

"I am not fearful of engaging with Jack Straw, or any one else in fair fight," he said; "but not when armed men, by whom I may be treacherously stricken down, are present."

"We will soon get over that difficulty," said the burly one. "Your friend and we three will stand on one side, and your friend shall have our swords in his possession—that is, he shall stand over them."

This proposal could not possibly have been declined.

Lord Rochester saw that he was in a fix, and that the only way of trying to get out of it was to fight.

He was well acquainted with Jack's powerful arm, and his extraordinary dexterity with the sword.

However, he saw there was no help for it. Fight he must.

"I agree to that," he said.

The burly one motioned to his two companions to place their swords against the wall.

They did so.

Then he asked Rochester's friend to do likewise. After a little hesitation the latter placed his weapon by the side of the others, and the burly one placed his by the side of that, saying —

"Now, my lord, the fight can commence. We will not interfere. We will not move a peg. But if your friend attempts to pick up his weapon, we will strangle him!"

Having delivered himself thus, he folded his arms, and placed his back against the wall, his companions doing likewise.

"I am perfectly satisfied with the arrangement," said Jack. "And now, my Lord Rochester, we meet, as I have prayed we would meet scores of times. On this spot I will answer the last cry of him you so foully murdered. I mean the apprentice to Elias Leighton. On this spot I will avenge your many insults to Dorothy Leighton, as well as wipe out the debt I owe you."

"And I," replied Rochester, fiercely, "will pay you the debt I owe *you!* It was you who disfigured me for life!"

"You both waste your breath in talking thus," growled the burly one, who was impatient for the fight to commence.

And commence it did by Jack boldly advancing, and assuming the offensive.

Gradually the fight became fiercer and fiercer, and as it proceeded the bloated one and his two companions, as well as Rochester's friend, became greatly excited.

Every movement of the glittering blades was watched with the keenness of a tiger watching its prey.

Before the fight had been in progress twenty minutes, Rochester showed distinct signs of distress.

His breath came in short gasps, and he became somewhat dazed.

Had his pride allowed him, he would have craved a rest.

His companion noticed his distressed condition, however, and said to the burly one—

"Would it not be as well for both to take a rest? Observe, not even a wound has been given on either side. Skilled swordsmen require rest in an affair like this."

The burly one and his companions burst into a roar of laughter.

"You speak for Rochester," said the former. "Jack Straw requires no rest. And," he whispered in his ear, "Rochester will soon take a rest by the look of it—*under the earth!*"

At this moment a sharp cry left Rochester's lips.

His left arm hung powerless at his side, and from his shoulder trickled a little stream of blood.

This wound, however, had the effect of rousing him to renewed exertion.

Uttering a horrible imprecation, he cut and thrust furiously at our hero.

He was very calmly received.

Jack knew that coolness and determination alone would give him the victory.

Not one of Rochester's cuts or thrusts took effect.

As he fought, he raved and swore fearfully ; but no word escaped Jack's lips.

Working gradually round, watching his opportunity as a cat watches a mouse, he at last found it.

He fixed his sword's point in the hilt of Rochester's weapon, and by a quick movement, wrenched the sword from his lordship's grasp.

The blade went flying over the heads of the burly one and his companions.

Uttering a bitter imprecation, Rochester staggered back, foaming with rage.

Ere another sound could leave his lips, Jack had dashed upon him.

"Die!" he cried. "Die, accursed of all England's nobles."

And his sword passed through Rochester's neck.

Wildly throwing up his arms, and for a few seconds staggering backward and forward, Rochester at last fell with a hollow thud upon the ground.

His companion rushed to him, and raised his head.

With eyes which seemed starting from their sockets, Rochester gazed at him.

His lips opened ; but only to allow of the rush of a volume of blood.

Violent, indeed, were his struggles to speak.

But they were in vain.

He raised his clenched hand towards Jack, and shook it several times ; then it dropped to his side.

"To your feet—quick!" cried the burly one to Rochester's companion, as he handed him his sword. "No doubt Jack Straw would wish to cross swords with you now."

Rochester's companion took the weapon, but he said—

"I decline to fight Jack Straw."

"Decline, eh?" sneered the burly one. "You did not decline to fight him when your two companions were by your side."

"No matter," said Jack. "I would rather not fight another coward. Go, whoever you are, and quickly."

Rochester's companion was about to turn when the burly one seized him by the shoulder.

"Look you," he said, pointing to Rochester and his dead companion, "is that the way you would leave them?"

No reply.

"No matter," continued the burly one; "we will see them decently buried—in the water yonder. Before you go, your sword—quick!"

Rochester's companion handed it over, and the burly one gave it to one of his friends. Then he said—

"Now your purse, the chain from your neck, the rings from your fingers, and your scabbard and belt."

"I *thought* you were robbers!" sneered Rochester's companion.

"Keep your tongue still, and do as you are bidden," growled the burly one, "or you shall soon lie by the side of your cowardly friends."

The young man having handed over to the burly one the articles demanded, the latter said—

"Now you may go."

As he spoke, he delivered upon his back a tremendous thwack with the flat of his sword, and with a howl of mingled rage and pain, the recipient of the blow took to his heels, not ceasing to run until well out of sight of his enemies.

Turning to Jack Straw, the burly one made a profound bow.

"Noble master," he said, "have you any commands for us? Fear it not, whatever they may be, we will carry them out, if it is possible."

"We will," said the other two. "We swear it."

"Nay," replied Jack, "I have no commands for you, my friends. I, however, must not leave this spot without returning you my thanks for your timely interference."

"It was only our duty to do so, noble sir," said the burly one. "We are not very particular individuals, but, by Heaven! we like to see fair play. Is that not so, companions?"

"It is—it is," they replied.

"The only favour I ask of you is, that you will see that these two corpses are placed out of sight," said Jack.

"Fear not, noble sir; we will see to that. We will throw them into the Thames."

"As you please."

"Much the best place, noble sir. But it would be better did we search them, and relieve them of what valuables they may have before we throw them into the river."

The burly one and his companions then proceeded to take away from Rochester and his friend whatever of value they had about them.

"I bid you a good-night—or, rather, morning," said Jack.

"Good-morning to you, noble sir, and good fortune attend you. If ever you should require any assistance, noble sir, don't forget to come to Strand Lane and ask for Abel Harkwell."

Jack nodded, and, with a last look at Rochester, he proceeded on his way to Westminster, where he arrived without further molestation.

CHAPTER XVII.

IS OF THE DEPARTURE FOR FINSBURY—OF THE ARRIVAL, AND OF WHAT OCCURRED.

WHEN Jack reached the Jew's house, he found Nell, Basil, and Silverbell in great anxiety about him.

Nell, indeed, was almost beside herself. She would have it that some dire calamity had befallen her lover.

Even the Jew was anxious; but his anxiety was of a different nature from that of the others. He was under the impression that if Jack was captured, he might give some information about where his friends were concealed, and by that means bring the king's troops about his (the Jew's) ears, and that would not have suited him by any manner of means.

Directly Jack entered the cellar, Nell threw herself upon his breast.

"Thank Heaven, you have returned, dear Jack!" she cried.

"Were you fearful for my safety, Nell?"

"Oh, yes, yes! We imagined that something dreadful had happened to you."

"We thought it possible you had been captured," said Basil.

"I am certain, now that I look at you," said Silverbell, "that something *has* happened."

"Ah, yes," cried Nell. "See here, your attire is all in a state of great disorder. Tell me, Jack, what has happened?"

"I trust the noble youth has not received any wounds," whined the Jew; "but, if he has, I possess a splendid healing salve—it never fails to cure a wound, however severe."

"Thank Heaven, I am not wounded," said Jack, "though I must admit Silverbell is right. Something has indeed happened. Bring me a flagon of your best wine, Jew, and I will then relate my adventures."

The wine having been brought, Jack related all that had occurred.

"Thank Heaven, the villain has at last ceased to exist," cried Silverbell. "It is a question whether such another scoundrel ever walked the earth."

"There *is* a greater scoundrel still walking the earth," said Jack, "and that is Sir Guibald le Manduit."

"True," replied Silverbell, "I had forgotten him for the moment."

"And you propose to do as Elias Leighton says?" asked Basil.

"Exactly."

"Nothing could be better," said Silverbell; "and if you meet with the villain—kill him! It will not be a crime."

"Fear not," replied Jack. "If I once come face to face with him, he shall not escape my vengeance."

* * * *

On the following day, a few hours before midnight, Jack and his companions set out.

It had been fine all day; but suddenly the sky became overcast, and when the shades of evening were gathering, it seemed as if a storm of unusual severity was about to burst.

The horses having been brought round, the whole of the money was placed in two sacks, and thrown over the back of the horse Nell had ridden.

"I will take it to Elias Leighton," said Jack; "it will be safe enough with him."

All being ready, the four set off, Nell riding behind Jack.

The Jew was profuse in his good wishes, and said he sincerely regretted they would not stay another few days. When they were out of sight he danced with joy.

"Safe enough now," he chuckled. "The king's troops, if they came here and found they had gone, would not hurt a poor, inoffensive old Jew like me."

Without any mishap, our four friends reached the house of Elias Leighton.

Dorothy was on the balcony, and directly she caught sight of Jack, with Nell behind him, she darted to the door.

In a moment she and Nell were in each other's arms.

"Welcome—a thousand welcomes!" cried Dorothy. "How long have I prayed Heaven to raise me up a friend such as I feel sure you will be?"

"If you will let me," said Nell, in a voice full of emotion, "I will be as a sister to you."

"Ay, ay," cried Elias. "One look into that beautiful face is enough to assure one that a kind and true heart beats within her bosom. Enter, enter, and Heaven bless you! Master Straw, you are on your journey?"

"I am."

"May success attend you. But will not you and your companions enter my humble dwelling and partake of some repast?"

"Nay, thanks."

"Have you no request to make to me? If a sum of money——"

"No" smiled Jack. "I thank you heartily; but we do not require money.

On the contrary, I wish you would do me the favour to mind what we have with us. Will you do this?"

"With pleasure."

The three friends dismounted, and took the bags from off the horse.

"Pray convey them to my vault," said Elias. "Whatever the bags contain will be safe there."

The bags were forthwith conveyed to the vault.

Dorothy and Nell followed, and as Elias raised his link to show the way back, a bitter sob was heard.

It was from Dorothy's lips. She had laid her head on Nell's shoulder, and was crying bitterly.

Jack was about to ask, in some alarm, what had occurred, when Elias Leighton pointed to the passage.

"Here," he said, in hollow tones, "Edmund Gerston was murdered. Here he traced, in letters of blood, an appeal to you, Jack Straw, to avenge him. It is the sight of this spot which causes my daughter to weep."

"His appeal was not in vain!" replied Jack. "He is avenged. Lord Rochester is no more!"

"What?" almost shrieked Elias, as he nearly let the link fall to the ground. "Rochester no more! The news seems too good to be true."

"Dead!" cried Dorothy, sinking upon her knees, and raising her clasped hands on high.

"Oh, can this be true? Am I at last released from the persecutions of that man?"

"He is dead!" said Jack. "With my own hand I slew him, and in fair fight."

"When—in heaven's name—when was this?" asked Elias.

"Soon after I left your house," replied Jack. "Listen, and I will tell you all."

When Jack concluded, the old man fairly trembled with excitement; but it was excitement of a joyous description.

He seized Jack by the hand, and wrung it warmly.

"Brave and fearless youth!" he cried. "You have indeed done me a great service—a service which I can never repay."

"I require no payment," smiled Jack.

"The knowledge that I have rid the earth of such a dastardly villain is sufficient reward. Come, comrades, let us depart."

Taking Nell in his arms, he pressed a kiss upon her willing lips, and then he, Basil and Silverbell bade Elias and Dorothy good-bye.

Soon they were in the saddle again, and on their way to Finsbury.

Before they had proceeded far, the storm, which for so long had been threatening, burst forth in all its fury.

The flashing of the lightning was fearful, and the peals of thunder were terrific. But still the three rode on.

Ever and anon the lightning revealed their figures to persons, who, in great terror, watched the storm from their windows, and it is not too much to say that, by them they were regarded as lunatics tempting Providence.

The streets were soon transformed into rivers of mud and filth, and holes (treacherous in the extreme for horses) were soon made, so that it behoved our three friends to proceed at a cautious pace.

Never had Jack or his friends passed through such a storm as this, nor indeed had the horses.

Used, as the noble creatures were, to the din of battle, they became nervous as flash after flash of forked lightning danced before their eyes, and they trembled violently as peal after peal of thunder, which seemed to shake the very earth, broke over them.

But, fortunately, as they neared Finsbury Fields—in those days a wide waste of marsh land—the storm began to clear off.

The heavy peals of thunder gave way to low, angry mutterings; the forked lightning, to feeble flashes of sheet, and, at last, the storm rolled right away.

At the period of which we write there stood, at the extreme left corner of the "fields," an hostelry called "The Mug o' Malt."

It was a small tumble-down hovel.

The proprietor of this so-called hostelry was a man of the name of Clinch, who was fat, careless, lazy, and saucy, as also was his wife.

It was at this place Jack and his companions halted.

Dismounting, Jack walked up the two steps leading to the doorway, and looked in.

There, in the centre of numerous barrels, large and small, sat the full-bellied host.

In his right hand he held an empty flagon, in his left a few coins, over which he was chuckling.

No doubt he had swindled some belated traveller.

"What ho!" shouted Jack.

"What ho!" returned Clinch, simply raising his eyes, but not stirring. "By all the saints! ye bawl loud enough."

"Are you host here?" asked Jack.

"Host, yes, and a good host too. I charge nothing but a fair price for what people have."

"Then you certainly are a paragon of virtue," sneered Silverbell; "but there is something else which, if you don't care to *give* away, you may sell at a fair price."

"What's that?"

"Good manners!"

"Manners!" cried a shrill voice, and Clinch's wife, who could hardly waddle, made her appearance. "Did anyone ever hear of Clinch having good manners? Ah, ah, ho, ho!"

"As a host, he *should* have them, dame," said Basil.

"Yes, that I will not deny. I have often told him so. But you see, Clinch, before I knew him, was kitchen servant to Lord Calford; then he *had* good manners; but since I married him, I can't get it out of his head but that he's as good as other people. Ha, ha!"

"If he looks at his reflection in a pail of water," said Silverbell, "he will soon see that there is a vast deal of difference between himself and the majority of people."

"You are right there, noble sir," said Mistress Clinch. "I frequently tell him so."

"With what result?" growled Clinch.

"A bottle or a flagon at my head," replied Mistress Clinch.

"And a good thing too," said Clinch, rising. "A woman with too much to say should be checked. Generally speaking, women are born with one tongue—*you* were born with many. Go to your room, madam, and stop there until it pleases me to call you. And mark you! if I hear you prattle again to-night, I'll—I'll—"

And seizing a small, empty barrel, Clinch raised it above his head.

No doubt he would have thrown it at his wife, had not Silverbell delivered a tremendous kick on the lower part of his body, thereby compelling him to fall with a crash.

"Have done with this fooling," said Jack. "Get on your legs, host, and get us a couple of flagons of your best, and here is double payment if you hurry."

The double payment instantly calmed the host.

"Two flagons," he said, as he grabbed up the money. "They shall be instantly supplied. Are there any further orders, your worships? Cold fowl—some rare speckled trout, some—"

"Silence!" shouted Basil, "and listen to what is said to you!"

"Outside," resumed Jack, "are four horses which I want you to take charge of for a few hours."

"Certainly, noble sir. And the charge will be very—"

"Silence!" again shouted Basil.

"Have you a stable at the back of your house?" continued Jack.

"Yes, and it is full of straw."

"Very good. Take the horses there; and remember—don't take off either saddles or bridles."

The host bowed.

It was just the very thing for the lazy fellow. Had he received orders to have had the saddles removed, his wife would have had to do the work, for Clinch would not have thought of exerting himself to that extent.

"All your orders shall be faithfully and conscientiously carried out," he said. "Payment for that will, no doubt, be made—"

"When we think proper, ass!" cried Silverbell, who was disgusted with the man.

"Thank you—thank you!" responded Clinch, by no means taken aback by this. "I hope always to remain your humble servant."

"That is more than we hope," replied Silverbell; "but take charge of the horses, and if any one asks you whether three horsemen, with a spare horse, have passed this way, you are to say, no."

Having partaken of the wine with which Clinch supplied them, Jack, Basil, and Silverbell departed.

The host watched them until they disappeared in the darkness.

Then he muttered—

"Ha! Now I wonder who they are? And as I live, they are gone off in the direction of the mysterious house! And I wonder who that tall, determined looking youth is? He answers to the description of Jack Straw; but he cannot be Jack Straw. If I thought he was, I would soon inform upon him, ho, ho!"

Across the dark and muddy fields went the three.

They had to proceed with extreme caution; for there were many places where a false step meant certain death.

"It would have been much better had we asked the direction of the host," said Basil.

"Nay," replied Jack. "A still tongue makes a wise head."

"Let us pause a few moments," said Silverbell. "From what I can see of it, we are floundering about and making no progress."

"No progress?" cried Jack, in astonishment. "We are moving across the fields."

"I think not," replied Silverbell, in decided tones.

"What makes you think not?"

"Look on our right."

"Yes."

"What do you see?"

"Three trees."

"If you look close you will see only two and a half, for the centre one, by the whiteness of its trunk, has only recently been struck by lightning. By the side of it lies its shattered branches. Is it not so?"

"It is," replied Jack, thoughtfully.

"Then was not that the first thing which attracted your attention as we entered the Fields?"

"Indeed it was! I remember now. Then how on earth have we travelled?"

"We have evidently been going round," said Basil.

"Yes, that must be so," cried Silverbell; "there can be no doubt of it."

"The darkness is so profound," said Jack, "that no wonder we have been travelling in a wrong direction. Ha! look, look! at last we have it. By heaven, the picture I saw in the gipsy's magic glass!"

The moon had suddenly burst through the clouds, and had cast its silvery rays over the black, marshy ground; and, as the three stood, they could see the outline of the mansion they sought.

"You recognise it from the picture you saw?" said Silverbell.

"I do—I do! Forward—forward! for no time is to be lost."

"Yet let us be careful," said Basil. "These little pools hide treacherous pitfalls, and the rain has made the ground everywhere soft."

But Jack was so impatient, that instead of going round the pools, he bounded over them.

At length they stood before the mansion.

Gloomy and deserted in the extreme it looked, and yet picturesque.

The moat was nothing but a mass of slimy mud of uncertain depth. The wall in front of this, broken in many places, was completely covered with thick clusters of ivy, which sturdy evergreen clung to the walls of the mansion itself.

Not a light was anywhere visible, and not a sound could be heard.

"See here," said Jack, pointing to what looked like a mass of brushwood on the moat; "here is another tree which has been struck by lightning, and, fortunately for us, it has toppled over into the right place.

"This is, indeed, most fortunate," said Basil, "and I will make the first attempt at crossing."

There was no difficulty in this, for the trunk of the tree, being of great breadth, afforded a firm foothold.

The three were soon across.

"And now," said Jack, "since there are so many openings in this wall, we will avail ourselves of one. Follow me —make as little noise as possible—keep your weapons ready, and if there is any necessity—*strike hard!*"

"Fear not," replied Silverbell, grimly. "If there is any necessity for striking, by heaven! I will strike hard enough."

"And I," said Basil, placing his hand on the hilt of his sword.

Jack led the way through one of the many openings in the wall, and the three entered the courtyard.

The latter was full of weeds of every description, and of such a height, that they were almost impassable.

Among them were huge pieces of stone, and immense beams of wood, so that it really looked as if a kind of barrier had been formed.

"Heaven's mercy!" ejaculated Silverbell, "'tis certain we can never penetrate through this mass of weeds. They must have been here for years and years to attain such strength."

"As long as my poor parents have been here, Silverbell," replied Jack, in a voice which quivered with emotion.

"No doubt—no doubt," replied Silverbell.

"We *must* penetrate through it," said Jack.

"But how?"

"I will show you."

Drawing his sword, Jack commenced to slash vigorously at the weeds before him.

They fell like grass before the scythe.

"I had not thought of that," laughed Silverbell.

"Nor I," said Basil; "though it is simple enough."

They, too, went to work with their blades, and soon a passage up to the walls of the mansion was cleared.

"And now," said Jack, "we must proceed swiftly and cautiously, for it cannot want more than an hour to midnight."

Creeping round, Jack, at last, came to the principal door.

Placing his ear to the grating, he listened.

"I hear a sound as of the rattling of keys," he whispered.

"Or of chains?" asked Silverbell.

"Nay, of keys, and— Ah! I hear a man's voice."

"What is he saying?"

"That I cannot distinguish."

"Listen."

"I now hear the voice of a woman. It appears as if the man and woman are in angry conversation."

"Most likely—most women enjoy angry conversation," said Silverbell.

"Hist! the sound grows more and more distinct. Now can you hear?"

"I can," replied Silverbell.

"And I," said Basil.

"They are coming to open the door," whispered Jack. "Draw your swords, for there may be more here than we think for. Understand, if the man offers the least resistance, he is to be cut down."

"Fear not," replied Silverbell. "I shall have no hesitation."

"Nor I," said Basil.

Nearer and nearer came the sound of voices, and louder became the rattling of keys.

At last a flood of light burst through the grating.

A key was inserted in the lock, and the next moment the massive door was thrown back, and a man appeared on the threshold.

He was somewhat powerful looking, and of about forty.

He was attired as a retainer, and carried at his side a heavy sword. Behind him came a woman, whose age might have been forty-five.

A withered, fierce-looking wretch she was, with a voice which bore a strong resemblance to the screech of the owl.

"There," cried the man, raising aloft a flaming link, "what did I tell you, eh? Now where is your storm?"

"Ha, ha!" growled the woman; "there *has* been a storm. Did I not hear the roaring of the thunder?"

"Well, there's no storm now. That is what I said. See, the moon is at the full. But it would not have mattered to *him* had it continued to thunder and lighten for hours and hours. He would come—ay, he would come. Think you he would deny himself his greatest pleasure? No—oh, no!"

"Well," croaked the woman, "she deserves it this time. For the last week she had been crying and crying, so that—"

"Look here," said the man; "so far as the woman is concerned—"

Jack dashed forward at this moment, and seizing the fellow by the neck with his left hand, he raised his sword on a level with his throat.

At the same moment Silverbell jerked the man's sword from its scabbard, threw it away, and then snatched the link from him.

Basil seized the woman.

As may be supposed, both were petrified with astonishment.

"Attempt any resistance," cried Jack, "and as sure as yon moon is shining, I will kill you!"

"Release me, villain!" screeched the woman. "What have I done that I should be thus set upon? Away, or I will—"

"Silence!" cried Basil, shaking her somewhat roughly; "we will tell you what you have done anon. It is at present sufficient for both of you to know that you are our prisoners."

Jack took a long piece of stout cord from his pocket, cut it in two, and with one piece, tied the man's hands behind his back; and with the other piece the woman's.

Then he took from the fellow's girdle the bunch of keys.

"Now, march on!" said Jack, sternly. "Lead us to your principal room; and mark! if either of you should attempt to pause, the points of our swords shall instantly be used on your carcases."

"Villains!" screeched the hag.

"Silence, woman!" cried Basil.

"*Woman!*" again screeched the withered-up wretch.

"I crave your pardon," sneered Basil. "I quite forgot for the moment that you were *not* a woman, but a *fiend* in the *shape* of one. If such were not the case, you would not be here."

"Oh, that I should have lived to see this day!" groaned the wretch, as she pretended to weep. "Holy Virgin! have pity upon—"

"Silence, I tell you!" shouted Basil.

Silverbell having slammed the door to, the party proceeded.

The man was placed first, and he led the way very slowly.

He had not been able to find his tongue yet.

Through many long, low-roofed, slimy passages they went, and at last the man turned into a large and lofty apartment.

The walls and the ceiling of this place bore traces of having been, at one time, most beautifully decorated.

It was a room which required some splendid furniture.

But of splendid furniture there was not a vestige.

The only furniture was a table, a low bedstead, and two or three stools, all made of rough oak.

"Now," said Jack "listen to what I am about to say. Of course, you have never before seen me?"

The man shook his head.

"Can't you speak, villain?" roared Silverbell, catching hold of and shaking him as a terrier does a rat.

"Wine," gasped the man.

"Wine!" cried Silberbell. "*Wine!* Hear the villain! If he is thirsty this will do for him."

And he seized a pitcher.

The man instantly found his tongue.

"I can't drink it," he said; "it is—it is—"

"Go on," said Jack.

"Too dirty. It is for—for—"

"Go on, or it will be the worse for you," shouted Basil, who was almost beside himself with rage.

"For those we are taking care of."

"*Those you are taking care of,*" said Silverbell.

"Drink of this, scoundrel, or I will pour it over you."

But the man shrank from doing so.

Without another word, Silverbell raised the pitcher, and dashed the contents over him.

Simultaneously a great cry escaped Jack's and Basil's lips.

From the pitcher dropped—a dead rat!

"Oh, heaven!" moaned Jack. "How horrible!"

"I didn't know it was there," cried the man. "On my soul, I did not."

"It is false!" cried Jack, as he laid his hand upon his sword. "I have a mind to kill you—but wait. Hark ye. When do you expect Sir Guibald le Manduit?"

Both the man and woman started.

They looked hard at each other.

To tell the truth, they had taken Jack and his companions to be nothing more nor less than three robbers.

"Answer me!" shouted Jack.

"In one hour," replied the man, in sulky tones.

"Then heaven be thanked, we have plenty of time. Listen to me, villain!" he said, to the now terror-stricken retainer, 'this night your master, Sir Guibald le Manduit, dies! Ay, and

dies by my hand. You have heard of Jack Straw?"

"I have, honoured sir," replied the man, now assuming a whining tone of voice.

"Know, then, that I am he, and know also that the persons in confinement here are my parents."

"I know it, honourable sir. I know it."

"*You* know it? How do *you* know it?"

"Sir Guibald told me. But I was powerless to do anything in the matter. He bound me to secrecy."

"What did he bind you with?"

No answer.

"With money, no doubt," said Silverbell. "Look at the villain—look how he trembles! He knows that his last hour has arrived."

"Look you," said Jack, after a moment's thought. "Your life will be spared only on condition that you do my bidding. Will you do it?"

"I will."

"Swear it on this cross."

And Jack produced a small silver cross, and held it to the man's lips.

He hesitated.

"Swear!" shouted Jack, "or you are a dead man."

The man kissed the cross, saying—

"I swear it!"

"With Sir Guibald dead, what would you gain?" asked Jack.

"Naught," replied the man.

"Very well. It will pay you far better to serve us, will it not?"

"It will, honourable sir."

"And you *will* serve us?"

"Willingly."

"Release his hands, Silverbell," said Jack; "he is now *our* servant, not Sir Guibald's."

Silverbell soon cut the cord from his wrists, though, to tell the truth, he did not care about doing so.

"Let the woman remain here, and lock the door upon her," said Jack. "Come now, my man, and lead us to this accursed vault, which holds— But go on, I cannot say it."

Jack, Silverbell, and Basil, with the man before them, left the room, and the latter locked it.

"Don't hesitate," said Jack, as he saw the retainer looking anxiously about him.

"I am only awaiting your commands, noble sir," replied the man.

"Lead the way, and pause not."

"Hold the sides of the walls carefully and firmly," said the man. "The steps are slimy, and—"

"Go on," cried Silverbell, impatiently. "We will take particular notice as to where we are going."

Down, down, deep into the earth went the man.

Down, deep down into a place reeking with slime.

And as they went, the loud, shrill cries of the rats, disturbed from their haunts, could plainly be heard.

"Oh, heaven!" cried Jack, "and in such a place as this my parents are confined."

"Hist!" said the man. "The lady and gentleman may be sleeping."

At last the retainer paused before a small, low-roofed passage.

"Go on," said Basil.

"This is the place, noble sir," said the man, addressing Jack.

"Where?"

"Here, on your right."

"Lead the way, then."

Opening a small door on the right of the passage, the man entered, and he was followed by Jack and his companions.

"Is this the place?" asked Jack.

"It is."

"I see nothing but damp walls."

"Nay, honourable sir," whined the man, "not yet, but— Ha—hist!"

A low, plaintive cry was heard.

"It is a woman's voice!" cried Jack, and snatching the link from the fellow's hand, he darted forward.

"Torture us no more," said a low, deep voice; "we are dying! We know the time is at hand for our torture, but for once leave us in peace! Both of us are dying—Heaven has at last taken pity upon us. Sir Guibald, leave us—let us die in peace!"

Jack dashed forward.

He raised his link on high, and a cry of horror left his lips.

He found himself in a kind of cell, with a division between it—a division about three feet high.

On one side was a woman—a wild-looking creature, chained to the wall; on the opposite side a man—a man who evidently had been at one time a tall, handsome fellow, but who now was a terrible-looking object. His beard reached almost to his feet. He also was chained to the wall.

Both were nearly nude.

The gipsy's picture was a faithful copy of this terrible scene.

Raising his link on high, and snatching his sword from its scabbard—an action followed by Basil — Jack shouted—

"At last!"

"Are you sent by Sir Guibald le Manduit to put an end to our misery?" asked Lord Linsay.

"Ah! surely—surely this is too good to be true!" moaned the unfortunate lady; "but if Sir Guibald has granted such a boon, let me die first. Strike here!" she cried, beating her breast—"slay me quick, or Sir Guibald may withdraw his orders."

"Nay," said Lord Linsay, "rather let *me* be the first to die, for," glancing at his wife, "I would rather have you hear how, with my last breath, I still love you."

"Heaven! what devotion," cried Silverbell.

Giving his torch to the jester, Jack started forward.

"I am not here to slay you, but to save you, and to kill him who for so many years has tortured you. Hear me—hear me, both of you," Jack cried, wildly. "If your reason has not left you, hear me! I am come to save you—I am *your son!*"

"My son!" shrieked Lady Linsay—"my son! Ah, you mock me! Sir Guibald said he was dead—dead!"

"He lied! I am your son, I swear it! And ere long you shall hear it from the very lips of this monster. Silverbell—quick! Ah, Heaven, she has fainted! Quick!—wine!—wine! and let that villain bring hammer and chisel to break these chains!"

"I have the keys, noble sir," whined the man.

"Bring them, then—quick—quick!"

The fellow obeyed, and in a few moments Lord and Lady Linsay were released from their chains.

Lord Linsay commenced to dance, caper, and howl like a madman; but at last, with a long, heartrending cry, he fell senseless upon the stone flags.

"Carry them upstairs," cried Jack. "Let my mother be placed in the care of the woman. I will attend to my father—he will be all right in a few minutes."

But neither were all right in a few minutes.

Wine and food were given them when they were restored to consciousness, and they ate ravenously.

As they ate, Jack told them all that we have recorded in this history.

Barely had he finished ere a loud "What ho, within!" coming from outside the mansion, reached their ears.

"It is Sir Guibald," said the retainer.

"Admit him instantly," said Jack; "and, mark you, say that your charges have been crying for hours. The effect of that, you told me, will be that Sir Guibald will at once proceed to the vault."

"Ha! that he will!"

"With the whip?"

"Yes! that he always carries."

"He does, eh? By heaven! he shall *feel* it to-night! Do all I have said, and you and the woman shall eventually go free, and with plenty of money in your pockets."

In another minute Sir Guibald was admitted.

The man told him what Jack had directed him to say.

Sir Guibald at once burst into a fearful rage. He raved in a manner that was awful.

In his hand he carried a heavy whip.

"Bring the link," he hissed, "and I will quiet them. Bring it—quick!"

The man went for the link, and, while he was getting it, Jack, Basil, and Silverbell crept into the vault.

In a few seconds Sir Guibald came down.

Ere he had taken two strides into the vault, he was seized by six powerful arms, the whip was snatched from his grasp, and his sword and dagger from their sheaths.

"Treachery!" he yelled; "help—help!"

"There is no help here for you," said Jack, as Silverbell tied Sir Guibald's hands behind his back; "not a soul is here to aid you. Do you know me?"

"Yes, yes; I do. You are—you are—"

"Jack Straw, or, rather, the son of the parents you have so disgraced. Monster! prepare for your doom! Where are your victims now? Are they confined to the walls by chains? No! I have released them—I have stepped in ere the hand of death which was over them could reach them! I have sworn to slay you, accursed monster, and I will! But not yet—not yet!"

"Mercy!" howled the wretch, "Mercy!"

"*Mercy?* None—not an *atom* shall be shown you! Silverbell—Basil, commence."

Before Sir Guibald had time to think of what was about to be done to him, he was stripped to the waist.

Then he was hurled up against the wall, and one of the chains passed round him and locked.

His howls were frightful.

But neither Jack nor his companions heeded them.

While the retainer held aloft the link, Jack seized the whip, and bared his arm.

Sir Guibald's howls now rose to shrieks—shrieks which were now heard above by Lord Linsay and his wife.

"Mercy!" shrieked Sir Guibald.

"No, I tell you—no! Not a spark of mercy will I show you! For fifteen long years, monster, you have tortured my parents, and thus I torture you!"

On Sir Guibald's naked body the whip descended.

His howls—his agony, cannot possibly be described.

When Jack's arm became tired, Silverbell took the whip, and, when *he* was tired, Basil took it.

By the time the three had finished, Sir Guibald lay on the stone floor, his back a mass of frightfully lacerated flesh.

"Now," said Jack, to the retainer, "fill that pitcher with water, put the dead rat in it, and bring it here. This is all he shall have. Not an atom of food shall pass his lips. There he shall lie, and starve, and die!"

The pitcher was brought, and placed by the side of the now senseless Sir Guibald, and then Lord Linsay and his wife, both of whom had been provided by the woman with some clothes, were brought down to look on their persecutor.

But both averted their eyes, and fled from the vault.

In little more than half-an-hour the horses were procured from Clinch, and the one Sir Guibald had ridden was also used. The whole party were thus accommodated.

"Walk by our side," said Jack to the retainer and the woman ; "at present we do not wish to lose sight of you."

Thus, with the gates of the mansion securely locked ; in chains ; without food, and without a prospect of any, Sir Guibald was left to starve—to feel for a short time the torture he had inflicted upon Lord and Lady Linsay for fifteen years !

CHAPTER XVIII.

OF HOW ROCHESTER WAS TAKEN INTO THE HOUSE OF MASTER ESTRANGE AND CHAINED TO THE WALL—OF HOW HE WAS RESCUED BY A SERVANT, AND WHAT HAPPENED NEAR THE OXFORD ROAD.

THE reader will remember that it was the intention of the man who had given the name of Harkwell, and his companions, to throw the bodies of Rochester and his companion into the Thames, which was close handy.

The first they caught hold of was Rochester's friend.

"Remain here, Dick," said Harkwell, "while we two take this body— But, no—that won't do. The watch may drop on us. Go on a short way in advance, Dick, and see that the road is clear. Then, when we have flung this body into the river, we'll return for the other."

"Ay, ay ! But suppose, during our absence, the watch comes this way ? "

"In that case they will save us the trouble of removing it, because they will remove it themselves. So now— take hold."

Dick went on in advance, while Harkwell and the other man, taking hold of the body, lifted it and followed Dick, who made his way rapidly in the direction of the river.

The sound of their footsteps had scarcely died away, when the door of the house close to where Rochester had fallen was cautiously opened, and an old man of diminutive stature, and wearing a white beard of extraordinary length, appeared.

He was seventy years of age, if a day.

Behind him was a woman of about his own age.

Her height, however, was very different, for she was head and shoulders taller than the man.

The name of this couple, who were man and wife, was Estrange.

The name was very well known in London, for Estrange had long carried on the business of a " money-lender."

"All's well," he chuckled. "They've taken the other body away to bath it in the Thames. Ah ! a nice idea, truly—but just like Harkwell."

"Listen," said the woman, hurriedly. "Are you sure this is really Rochester ? "

"Have I not said so a dozen times ? "

"You have ; but then—"

"I tell you I heard his name uttered. Besides, I recognise him."

Down upon his knees he dropped, and tearing open Rochester's doublet, placed his hand upon his heart.

"He still lives," he cried, excitedly. "Quick—let us carry him within ! You see, the blade passed through his neck ; but many a man, with skilful treatment, lives after that."

The pair, who had watched the fight from beginning to end, seized Rochester and carried him inside the house, the door of which they bolted and barred.

In another five minutes, Harkwell and his companions reappeared.

"Hillo !" said the former, "so it seems as if the watch have been here. At any rate, the body's gone."

"Well," said Dick, with a grin, "it is more than likely that the Evil One's been here and claimed his own."

"Not he. The watch has had the body. Look here ; this is old

Estrange's house. Let us inquire if he heard anything."

"If he did not hear the ring of the steel and the shouts, it is scarcely likely that he heard the watch. However, we'll see."

Thereupon they knocked at Estrange's door.

But they had to knock again and again before they were answered.

At last Estrange, who had thrust a nightcap upon his head, appeared at an upper window.

"What seek you, good people?" he asked. "Why arouse a peaceful citizen, unless the city is on fire?"

"A *rare* citizen are you, Master Estrange!" sneered Harkwell.

"What?" said Estrange, "is that Abel—Abel Harkwell?"

"It is; and I want to know whether you saw anything of a dead body outside your door?"

Estrange appeared to be horrified.

"A dead body!" he gasped, "the saints forbid! You don't mean to say there *was* a dead body outside?"

"There was, but a short time ago. There was a fight here; did you hear ought of it?"

"Not I—I was asleep; but what was the fight about, good Abel?"

"Between two or three men, as to who should go to heaven first. Well, a good-night to you, Father Graball."

The three men, with a loud laugh, departed, while Estrange, with a chuckle, closed his window.

"Ah, ah!" he said, as he rubbed his withered hands—the nails of which were like the claws of a vulture—"how witty he is to be sure! What an excellent jester he would make. He might be *so* useful to many a noble lord, for he could jest with a man one moment and kill him the next!

"Truly he is a right merry fellow— ho! ho! I like Abel— *very* much!— at a distance—yes, a very *long* distance!"

Thus chuckling, he descended the stairs, and entered a small parlour at the back, where he found his wife busy attending to Rochester.

She had a box beside her containing a number of bottles, each filled or half filled with some preparation.

"Well?" asked Estrange, eagerly.

The old woman shook her head.

"Nay," she said, "it is *not* well as yet. I have tried everything, but in vain."

"Patience — patience, Catherine! This is not the only case you have attended, and which was eventually successful. What of the wound, which I see you have bound up?"

"He has lost a large quantity of blood, and unconsciousness is the result of exhaustion."

"Let us wait, and see what the result will be."

"I have applied Doctor Wallack's elixir. The effect of that should soon be seen. If he stirs not in half-an-hour, the case is hopeless."

"We will wait patiently and see. If there is really no hope, we will carry him out and put him in the street a few doors down."

"But why not tell his friends?"

"No, no! That would never do. You well know what they are. They might accuse us of being concerned in the matter."

Little did they dream as they spoke that Rochester overheard every word.

But he did.

Under Mother Estrange's decidedly skilful treatment, he had recovered consciousness.

At the same instant what had happened occurred to him.

Not knowing where he had been taken, he considered it advisable to remain as he was until he could obtain some information.

"If," continued Estrange, "we find that he is certain to recover, we will take him below and put him where he cannot escape. Then we will communicate with Mistress Dennison."

Rochester shuddered as this name was uttered, and so visibly that Estrange noticed it.

"A quiver ran through him then, Catherine," he said. "I would almost swear that he will recover."

"Go on," said Catherine, closely watching Rochester. "You said that you would communicate with Mistress Dennison."

"Yes; she, I am sure, will pay me what I demand for an interview with Rochester. Of course, she will require me to see that he is chained up—just like a wild beast. Not that he could do much without his arms."

"You will do well to inform Mistress Dennison," said Mother Estrange. "And, as you say, she will pay you anything for an interview, so that she can have the revenge she has so long waited for."

"She is a woman who well knows how to pay a debt. But see—he moves again."

Yes. Rochester, for an instant, had forgotten his wound, and had attempted to rise.

He found that all his strength had left him.

He was utterly powerless.

They could do with him exactly as they liked.

As Mother Estrange ran to his side, he slowly opened his eyes.

"Where am I?" he asked.

"In a house," replied Mother Estrange, coldly; "in a house where you will be well looked after."

"What is your name?"

"Trouble not about that," said Master Estrange, "you will know all anon."

"Listen to me. I am the great Rochester!"

"We know it."

"And, if you will communicate with my friends, you can name your own reward. You may—"

He paused, for the pain in his throat was terrible.

"Take my advice and don't speak again," said Master Estrange; "we will attend to what you say presently."

Rochester paid no heed to the advice.

Again and again he tried to speak, but it was a failure, and, at last, when attempting to rise, he fell back and again became unconscious.

"He will recover," said Mother Estrange, "but it will be weeks before he is strong enough to stand."

"While he is weak is the time to secure him," said Master Estrange, "and we will now take him below."

No time was lost.

Between them, they half carried, half dragged Rochester below, and placed him where, at one period, had been a wine cellar, and then a place of confinement for more than one prisoner of importance; for, at one time, the house was the residence of a prominent Court leader, and a man whose habit it was to use considerably more force than argument.

It was a most dismal hole, there being but little ventilation and no daylight.

Moreover, with the exception of a table and a block of wood, there was no furniture.

On one side hung a ponderous iron chain with a "waist-grip," or iron ring, opening in the centre, and which went round a prisoner's waist and was locked.

The prisoners upon whose bodies this chain had been placed, could not have had much exercise, for it was of enormous weight.

Rochester was laid on the ground, and the ring was placed about him, and fastened.

Then Mother Estrange procured three or four armfuls of straw from an adjoining vault, and this was placed around him.

"Let us leave the lamp," said Master Estrange. "We shall have to pay him close attention."

"Yes—for three or four weeks."

"It will be as well not to inform Mistress Dennison for the present, or she will not rest. Ho! ho! my Lord Rochester, you are in the toils now, sure enough. Presently you will say that it would have been better had you been pierced through the heart by your enemy's sword.

*   *   *   *

On the opposite side of the Thames, and almost facing Westminster Abbey, stood what, at one time, had been a splendid house.

Since a great part of the material used, when it was first constructed, was a kind of white stone, it was called the "White Tower."

But the hand of Time appeared to have dealt hardly with it, for the white stones had changed to black, while many a terrible storm had played havoc with the upper part, until, at last, a more gloomy-looking building could not have been found in all England.

Nevertheless, here resided a lady who, at one time, had been one of the most beautiful and powerful women at Court; and this woman was Rochester's most deadly enemy.

"RUSHING FORWARD EGBERT SEIZED THE DUCHESS BY THE WRIST AND DRAGGED HER TO HER FEET."

The occupant of the White Tower was Mistress Margaret Dennison.

She married, when but eighteen years of age, a wealthy Devonshire gentleman.

His wealth, as a matter of course, was a key to one of the highest positions, which he soon obtained.

In consequence of repeated advances made to the king, he could have had a title, but this he placed at no value.

Among those who were Mistress Dennison's admirers previous to her marriage, was Rochester.

By him she was terribly annoyed; but she always treated him with the scornful contempt he deserved.

Rochester tried every means in his power to prevent the marriage, but without result.

However, determined to be revenged, he took the first opportunity of publicly insulting Mistress Dennison.

The result was a duel, between Master Dennison and Rochester, in which the latter was completely beaten; indeed, but for the intercession of a friend, he must have been killed.

A few months after this, Master Dennison mysteriously disappeared.

The hue-and-cry was raised, and the country was scoured from end to end.

But with no success.

Had the earth suddenly opened and swallowed up the unfortunate gentleman, he could not have disappeared more completely.

One night, however, three watermen found a body in the Thames, and took it ashore.

It was recognised as the body of Master Dennison.

The state into which the unfortunate lady was thrown, can be imagined.

The very first thing she did, was to go to the king and accuse Rochester of the murder of her husband.

The king sent for Rochester, who boldly declared that he knew nothing of the circumstances surrounding Master Dennison's death.

The king said he was satisfied—probably because he was aware of Rochester's influence — but Mistress Dennison was not.

She firmly believed that Rochester, or his myrmidons, had murdered him.

As to this she was soon satisfied, for one day a man called upon her, and confessed that he had been engaged—with others—by Rochester to murder Master Dennison.

They had intercepted him on the Thames, when crossing from Westminster to his own house; had seized him, and held him beneath the water until life was extinct.

The man added that he made the confession because, on his complaining of the sum of money he had received for his share in the horrible crime, Rochester had thrashed him.

Then and there Mistress Dennison vowed to have a terrible revenge; but, though she tried hard enough, she was not successful, principally owing to the many spies Rochester kept about him.

But Rochester knew then what sort of woman Mistress Dennison was—or, rather, what she had become; and he trembled to think what would happen to him if he fell into her clutches.

Since her husband's murder, Mistress Dennison had seldom quitted her mansion, and never, by any chance, attended Court.

The result was that her friends gradually deserted her, until at last it was a rare thing for anyone to call at the White Tower.

There were, however, two persons who stuck to her, and they were Master Estrange and his wife, who had been benefited to no small extent by Mistress Dennison.

One night—a month after the fight between Jack Straw and Rochester—Master Estrange called at the White Tower, and, as was the custom, he was at once conducted to Mistress Dennison by one of the two men-servants.

Despite the fact that her husband's murder still pressed heavily upon her heart—that she had, as it were, shut herself out from the world, and that not a day or a night passed but what she brooded over the crime, and the revenge she had promised herself—she still remained a woman of remarkable beauty.

Had she again gone forth into the world, there was many a man who would have been proud and happy to offer her his hand and fortune.

Mistress Dennison was tall and slender, but exceedingly graceful.

She was as dark as night, her hair, which she invariably wore in the Italian style, being magnificent ; and so were her large, expressive eyes.

A single glance would have convinced anyone that she was a woman of iron nerve, and of unflinching determination.

She received Master Estrange most kindly.

"I do not ask the reason of this visit, Master Estrange," said Mistress Dennison, with a somewhat sad smile, "because you are always welcome. And I have so few friends now."

"True, true. But my visit this time is of the greatest importance."

"You seem agitated," said Mistress Dennison.

"I *am* agitated. The news I bring you, madam, will throw *you* into a state of agitation. You will remember that, on many occasions, I have said that, if ever the time came, I would repay your kindnesses ? "

Mistress Dennison nodded.

"Well," continued Estrange, "a month ago the opportunity came, for the villain—the atrocious murderer, Rochester, fell into my hands."

"Ha !" cried Mistress Dennison, "into *your* hands ? "

"Yes. You must be aware—though you remain here in a state of seclusion —that Rochester has been missing for a month ? "

"Yes, yes. I have heard that."

"A month ago my wife and I were alarmed by the clashing of steel, and, looking out of one of the windows, we saw that a fight was in progress.

"We soon learned that the combatants were Rochester, two of his friends, and that brave and daring young fellow, whose name for so long has been on everyone's lips—I mean, Jack Straw ! "

"Ha ! Rochester's deadly enemy ? "

"Yes. Well, Jack Straw quickly slew one, and then engaged with Rochester.

"It is possible that Straw might have been worsted, but for a man of the name of Abel Harkwell and two of his comrades, who saw fair play. Rochester fell at last, Jack Straw's blade having passed clean through his neck.

"It was thought that he was dead. Harkwell told Jack Straw that he would throw the two bodies into the Thames; but, while he and his comrades went off with the one, we took Rochester into our house and attended to him.

"My wife, as you know, is skilful, and success attended her treatment, for Rochester soon recovered consciousness.

"We took him down into a vault, and chained him up like a wild beast.

"There, ever since, he has been. His wound slowly healed, and, once again, if free, he is ready for any villainy.

"I need not tell you what his conduct has been since he recognised the fact that he was chained up like a common felon.

"Neither of us dare approach him, and, each time he sees us, he, with terrible oaths, swears what he will do to us, if by any chance he can get free.

"It is for you, madam, that we have kept him here—for you ! Now is the time for vengeance on the monster. Take it therefore, without hesitation ! "

This recital, as may be supposed, threw Mistress Dennison into a state of the greatest excitement.

She could not keep still.

Her feelings compelled her to pace the floor with rapid steps.

But, when Estrange had fiinished, she paused, and said in low, earnest tones—

"You have, indeed, well repaid any kindnesses I may have shown you. You have acted wisely and well, and, do not think I am likely to forget the great service rendered. But, you have run a great risk."

"Risk ? "

"Yes ; for, if Rochester's friends had discovered what had been done, your life would have been forfeited."

"No doubt. But we have taken care to guard well the secret. And now, madam, what will be the nature of your revenge ? "

"Can you ask ? His body shall be found in the Thames in precisely the same way as my husband's was found."

"Well, after all, you see, had Harkwell thrown him into the river, it would have amounted to the same thing."

"But I should not have had the opportunity of standing face to face with him. Listen! I shall be at your house in two hours. In the meantime send your wife to me, for I would converse with her."

"She shall come—at once."

Estrange bade Mistress Dennison adieu, and departed, making his way to the river, where a boat awaited him.

Not the faintest idea had either of the two that their conversation had been overheard.

But it had.

Every word that had been uttered had been listened to by the man who had shown Estrange into Mistress Dennison's presence. He had caught the words—"my visit is of the greatest importance," and this had attracted his attention.

This man—Marville by name—was by no means a favourite with Mistress Dennison, who judged him to be one who was on no account to be trusted.

Many times she had received information from the other servants, which caused her to think about dismissing him from her service, and, as events will show, it was a pity that she did not get rid of him.

Marville—who was a short, evil-looking fellow of about fifty—darted away from the door as soon as the conversation had come to an end, and descended to the servants' quarters, pretending that he was feeling very ill.

He was advised to retire, and he promptly did so.

That is, he retired to his chamber, but not to rest.

From a box he took a coil of rope, and this he secured to the window, which looked upon the back of the premises.

Having secreted a couple of daggers about his person, he descended the rope, and was quickly outside the grounds.

With all speed he made towards the river.

He desired to get a boat to take him across, but not a single one did he see, nor did his cries of "Waterman," have any effect.

Thereupon he plunged into the river,

and swam across, though it was not without considerable difficulty.

Having shaken as much of the water out of his clothing as possible, he went on to Whitehall.

In a quarter of an hour, he had reached Master Estrange's residence.

Not a soul had he met the whole distance.

The quarter in which Estrange lived was in darkness.

Not a light was visible in any of the houses.

Marville, however, knew that Estrange was up, and he went boldly up to the door and knocked.

For some little time there was no response, but at last Estrange looked from the window.

"Who is it?" he asked.

"Marville," was the reply. "I have come direct from the White Tower with a message."

Estrange at once recognised the voice.

"Has Mistress Estrange arrived there?" he asked, entirely unsuspecting danger.

"Yes, just as I left," was the quick reply.

Another couple of minutes, and Estrange was at the door.

"Tell me what your message is, my good friend," he said.

"*This!*" replied Marville.

And, suddenly raising his clenched hand, he brought it down with such terrific force in the old man's face, that he fell like a log on the threshold.

Swiftly the wretch entered the house, and pulled the old man into the passage.

Then, seizing the lamp, which was burning on the stairs, he bolted the door.

Next he examined Estrange.

The old man's snow-white beard was saturated with blood, which flowed from a gash in his face.

Satisfying himself that it was not likely he would recover consciousness for some considerable time, he went into every room in the house.

His object was to ascertain whether any other person was present.

Fortunately for his purpose, there was not.

Had anyone suddenly appeared, Marville would have used one of the daggers he carried.

Returning to the old man he searched him, and found a bunch of keys.

With these he descended to the vaults.

Here all was darkness and silence.

Door after door he examined, but there was nothing to show in which vault Rochester had been placed.

So, raising his voice, he shouted.

"What ho, Rochester! What ho, my lord!"

Instantly an answer was returned—

"Who speaks?"

Guided by the voice, Marville found Rochester's prison, the door of which was fastened by two ponderous bolts.

These he at once shot from their sockets and pulled the door open.

Marville darted back in amazement.

More than once he had seen Rochester clad in the finest of raiment, and surrounded by gorgeously attired servants, but here was a contrast!

He now presented more the appearance of a furious lunatic than anything else.

Never since he had been in the vault had he attempted to arrange his hair, and so it hung over his face and neck in terrible disorder.

His eyes were bloodshot and sunken; his cheeks were hollow, while his whole body had wasted considerably.

But this was not all.

In his ungovernable rage he had torn his clothes nearly to rags.

"Who are you?" he demanded, eyeing Marville from head to foot.

"Do not distress yourself, my lord," replied Marville; "I am a friend."

"A friend! 'Tis false. I know you are here to—"

"Stay," interrupted Marville; "you, I see, fancy I am a friend of the money-lender; you are wrong. I am here to be *your* friend—in proof of which, take this dagger."

And he handed one of the two weapons to Rochester, who snatched it from him.

"A friend!" he repeated— "a friend—here in this house—in this accursed vault! Who are you?"

"My name is Marville, and, until a short time ago, I was in the employ of Mistress Dennison."

A sharp cry left Rochester's lips.

Marville quickly repeated the conversation he had overheard.

He thus concluded—

"I felt certain, my lord, that if, through me, you escaped from here, you would give me whatever reward I might name."

"Yes," cried Rochester, "you shall have everything you want, provided I can give it you."

"I believe you," continued Marville. "And it will be no more than I deserve, for, in but a short time, Mistress Dennison will be here to take her revenge."

"How did you enter this house?"

"Through the door," grinned Marville. "I summoned Master Estrange, and, as soon as he appeared I felled him. At this moment he is insensible in the passage."

"Good! By all the fiends, I will have my revenge on *him!* But release me from this chain—quick! Not a moment must be lost!"

"Is it locked upon you?"

"Yes. What is that bunch of keys you hold?"

"I took it from the old man."

"One of the keys will unfasten this belt of iron. Try—quick!"

Marville soon found the key, and in a moment the ponderous chain dropped from Rochester's waist.

The villain was so frantic with joy, that he capered like a madman.

Then he told Marville to lead the way to the passage.

They found Estrange just recovering consciousness.

Rochester seized him, and carried him down the stairs to the vault.

The old man was quickly secured by the chain.

"Hound!" hissed Rochester, "your turn has come. You thought to see me die by the hand of that woman, but you are foiled. Do you hear what I say?—foiled! They shall see *you* here; but their questions will remain unanswered. Die, caitiff!"

Suddenly springing forward, he buried the dagger deep in the poor old man's heart.

But this was not all.

Uttering the most appalling oaths, he again and again trampled upon the body.

Then, Marville showing the way, he once more ascended the stairs.

"A money-lender's house," he said, "should contain gold. Let us search for it."

Search they did, and at last, in an upstairs room, they came upon a cabinet.

It was locked, but Rochester, seizing a heavy stool, quickly smashed the doors.

So great was the exertion, that the wound in his throat, which had by no means entirely healed, burst open afresh, and blood trickled down his neck.

He, however, took little notice of it.

The cabinet was found to contain several small bags of gold, together with some valuable jewellery.

After a short search, a box filled with papers was found.

Rochester threw them out, and filled the box with the gold.

Then placing it upon Marville's shoulder, he descended.

In one of the downstairs rooms, he found an old cloak and hat, as well as a sword, and securing these, he left the house, followed by Marville, and took his way in a northerly direction, for he knew he would thus avoid Mistress Dennison—not that it was likely she would have known him.

He was utterly changed.

He himself was well aware of this.

"We may be stopped," he said, "but if so, leave all to me. I am sure the sword I carry is a strong one. Free once more! Free—free! The air revives me. I drink it in as I would the choicest wine."

"Your pardon, my lord," whispered Marville, alarmed at Rochester's appearance and wild gesticulations, "I implore you to preserve silence. Presently we shall be where you can obtain all you desire. But even then be prudent, or you may lose your life, after all. Blood is still streaming from your neck."

"True; but it does not flow as fast as that of my enemies shall flow. Revenge! revenge!"

* * * *

Had the villainous pair remained in the house but a very short time longer, they must have come face to face with Mistress Dennison and Estrange's wife, who arrived before they had got many hundred yards away.

Mistress Estrange knocked upon the door again and again.

Getting no answer, she became alarmed.

"It is astounding!" she said. "Never before have I had to knock more than once."

Again, and yet again did she knock, and at last the repeated summonses had the effect of rousing a youth in an opposite house.

"Hillo!" he cried; "who is it? By St. George, you will rouse the whole city. Go away! Master Estrange transacts no business after nightfall."

"It is me, little George," said Mistress Estrange.

"What! Mother Estrange?"

"Yes. I have been on an errand, and I left my husband here."

"Maybe he has dropped off to sleep?"

"Not he. I fear something has happened. Have you heard anything?"

"Nay, for I have not long returned."

"What is that in your hand?"

"A pitcher."

"Then hurl it through my window."

The lad did not hesitate.

With all his force he hurled the pitcher through the window.

The crash was tremendous, framework as well as glass being wrecked.

Still there were no signs of life.

"It is certain now something has happened," cried Mother Estrange, as she wrung her hands.

"Or your husband has gone out," said Mistress Dennison.

"Nay, he would not do that."

The lad, by this time, was also alarmed.

"If I had a ladder," he said, "I could get in at the window. But wait a moment, I will get the pole."

The pole he referred to was about fourteen feet in length, and was used in an upstairs room by his master, a ropemaker.

By exerting all his strength, he contrived to get it down and push it out of the window.

His idea was that, by resting it on the sill of the opposite window, and on that of his own, he could get across to the money-lender's house.

But he found it several feet too short.

"Throw the pole down and use it as a ram," said Mistress Dennison.

The lad did so, and descending, used it, with Mistress Dennison's assistance, in forcing the door.

This was soon accomplished, and the house was entered.

In a couple of minutes Mother Estrange had procured a light, and loudly did she shout out her husband's name.

Into every room she went, eagerly followed by Mistress Dennison and the lad.

At last they reached the one from which Rochester had taken the gold.

A wild cry left Mother Estrange's lips as her eyes rested upon the battered doors of the cabinet.

"Look!" she said, "robbers have been here! Oh, heaven! what have they done with my husband? Quick! let us go below!"

Mistress Dennison followed without remark; but her pale face showed clearly enough that she feared the worst.

So did the lad.

The little fellow fairly trembled as he followed.

The open door of the vault was seen at once.

"Rochester has escaped!" cried Mistress Dennison.

"Yes," said Mother Estrange, bursting into tears; "and my husband has been murdered. See!—Rochester has got away and has put him in his place. Look—look at the dagger buried in his body!"

So deeply affected was Mistress Dennison, that it was some time before she could utter a word.

At last she said—

"He shall be avenged, I swear it. No stone shall be left unturned to bring the monster to justice. But, in the name of all that is marvellous and mysterious, how did Rochester contrive to get away? Think you, it was likely that your husband approached too closely, and that Rochester—but wait."

As she spoke she took the lantern, and, stooping, pulled the dagger from Estrange's body and examined it.

"The mystery is solved!" she said; "this dagger, at one time, used to hang on the walls of my house!"

"Impossible!"

"Nay, it is as I say. I recognise it by these letters on the blade—'H. R.' For some time various weapons—and among them this dagger—have been missing, and I have frequently inquired about them. I have suspected that my servant Marville was the thief, and now I am certain of it."

"In heaven's name, tell me—do you think he has had a hand in this?"

"Yes. Do you not remember that, ere we left the house, I sent for him, and it was said that he had retired to his room?"

"Yes, yes; I remember."

"Depend upon it he was not there at all. He, no doubt, contrived to overhear what passed between me and your husband, and, thinking it probable that if he succeeded in freeing him, Rochester would give him a large reward, he made his way here. But return with me, and let us see how far I am correct. This lad will take charge of the house if I well pay him."

"I will," said the lad, who was so horrified with what he had seen that he had remained perfectly mute, "I will remain above."

Weeping bitterly, Mother Estrange left the house with Mistress Dennison.

They returned direct to the White Tower, and the reader knows what followed on examination of Marville's bedroom.

But that traitor servant was speedily to meet with his deserts.

He had heard a great deal of Rochester, it is true, yet he had not the faintest idea of his real character.

Rochester calmed down considerably before they had proceeded far, and for some time seemed to be lost in thought.

Had Marville known what those thoughts were, he would have fled in terror.

"Wine I want, and wine I must have," said Rochester, at last. "And, as I know where I can obtain it, thither will we go."

"But would it not be as well to proceed direct to your residence, my lord?" asked Marville.

"In this guise? Nay, it would be

madness. I must appear in my true character. More, I must appear suddenly; for, no doubt, the servants, thinking that I am dead, have made ducks and drakes of what is mine. If they have, my punishment will be swift enough."

"All the hostelries are fast closed," persisted Marville.

"True; but there is many a host who would open his house quickly enough did he know that Rochester was waiting for admittance. But we will not proceed to a hostelry. I have it. We will go direct to the house of one of my friends."

On, at an increased pace, went Rochester, and at last he paused before a small house beside Oxford Fields, and distant about half-a-mile from the Oxford road.

He knocked upon the door; then he gave a peculiar whistle.

His signal was almost at once responded to.

The door was opened, and a little grey-bearded man, clad in a long, black gown, appeared holding a lantern.

On coming face to face with Rochester he started back.

"Nay, nay," said Rochester, "it *is* I. Everyone thinks I am dead, eh?"

"Yes, and you look like a man suddenly restored to life by the necromancer."

"Pah! that is witches' talk, and the idle prattle of lazy women. But I am altered, I know."

"Enter, my lord. I long to hear all that has befallen you."

"No doubt—no doubt. Master Vallance, this is a friend of mine—a nobleman whose name we will not now mention. He is at present disguised as a servant. When he is attired in his proper garments, I will tell you who he is."

This flattered Marville to no small extent.

They entered the house, Vallance conducting them to a chamber on the ground floor.

"My friend Vallance," said Rochester to Marville, "though a Frenchman, is one of the best-hearted men in England. He will procure good wine for us, and then we will retire, for, by heaven! I long for a good bed."

Vallance was no Frenchman.

He was as much an Englishman as Rochester.

But Marville had no doubt that what his lordship said was true.

Rochester told Vallance of his imprisonment. He, however, did not say that Marville was one of Mistress Dennison's servants.

When a considerable quantity of wine had been consumed, Rochester suggested they should retire.

"In the morning," he said, "we will get into our proper clothes. You will have no difficulty in procuring them, Vallance?"

"Not the least. As soon as morning dawns, I will go in search of what you require."

Marville was shown into an upstairs chamber, and he soon prepared to retire.

Not the faintest idea had he that foul play was intended.

"Now," said Vallance, when he rejoined his lordship, "let me know your wishes."

"You have guessed that this is no noble gentleman?"

"Assuredly. Who is he?"

"Listen, and I will tell you all."

When he had concluded, Vallance said—

"And in that box?"

"Is the money taken from Estrange's house."

"I see."

"What else do you see?"

"That if this man lives, he will be a burden to you."

"You are right. He must be *removed*, and I leave that to you."

"I have but to obey your commands."

"And I have but to pay you for the trouble. Here I have the money."

"Had you spoken in time, I might have been able to drug his wine."

"That is of little importance. You have put him in the chamber I spoke of?"

"I have."

"Good! He will be sound asleep in an hour. When you have devoted a little *attention* to him, I will assist you in carrying him below. His burial I leave to you."

Rochester then put the box upon the table, and, having counted out part of its contents, handed it to Vallance.

When more than an hour had passed away, Vallance drew his hood over his head, and opening a drawer, took out a long, sharp dagger.

Then leaving the chamber, he entered the narrow passage.

At the end, close beside the stairs, he paused and placed his hand upon a certain part of the panelling.

A portion of it at once went inwards, and Vallance entered the aperture.

Just within was the commencement of a flight of stairs, and these led to the roof, though not in a direct manner, for they wound round and round much after the fashion of a corkscrew.

Several of the chambers in the house could be entered by means of this staircase, and in one Marville had been placed.

Vallance quickly reached it, and, for a few moments, he placed his ear against the woodwork.

Satisfied that Marville slept, he opened the panel in precisely the same way as the one below.

Then, like a shadow, he entered the chamber, and crossed to the window noiselessly.

Pulling the heavy curtains aside, sufficient light was admitted for him to see the sleeper.

Marville's sleep was most profound.

Probably the wine of which he had partaken, and to which he was not accustomed, caused him to slumber so heavily.

There was not the faintest doubt that Vallance was a most accomplished assassin.

His every movement—so cat-like and stealthy—showed that plainly enough.

Creeping to the bedside, he drew his dagger, and the next instant he plunged it deep into Marville's body.

A wild, terrible cry awoke the stillness of the night—a cry which reached Rochester's ears.

Then there was silence—the cry was not repeated ; Marville was dead.

Within three hours after leaving the White Tower, he had lost his life.

Truly his punishment had been swift.

Vallance coolly replaced the dagger and descended.

Lighting a lantern, he beckoned to Rochester to follow him, and both ascended the stairs.

Placing Marville in a sheet, they carried him down to the cellars.

"He will there remain," said Vallance, "until I have time to dispose of him. And now, my lord, to bed."

"Ay, and remember—wake me not. If I can but sleep for a number of hours, it will be of the greatest benefit."

"I trust you will have work for me soon ? "

"Ay, as much in the future as the past."

"Listen to this, my lord. Suppose I *interest* myself in Mistress Dennison ? "

Rochester started.

"You know what I mean," continued Vallance, "and you are aware that I am a good hand at forming a plot."

"True, true."

"If I removed her ? "

Rochester slowly shook his head.

"I fear me it would be impossible," he said.

"Impossible ! And why ? "

"She is too cunning."

"I do not fancy she could place her cunning beside mine."

"Then again, I have heard that she has many spies about—men who are devoted to her. Well do we know that she is quite capable of paying them well."

"What care I for spies ? "

"They might suddenly fall upon you and kill you. If that happened, I should be sorry indeed, for you have been, and would still be, very useful to me."

"What would you *pay* for her death ? "

"Any sum you choose to ask."

"Any sum ? Good."

"I mean in reason."

"Exactly. But I should prefer a *stated* sum."

"Say, then, five thousand nobles."

"You mean that ? "

"Mean it ! Assuredly."

"It is agreed upon."

"Then you will attempt it ? "

"I will. And if I do not carry it to a successful issue, my name is not—"

"Vallance," said Rochester, quickly.

"Ay, Vallance. So now, my lord, to your chamber. When you have had a long rest we will talk more fully of the matter ; and, in the meantime, I may have arranged a plan."

CHAPTER XIX.

OF THE PLOT HATCHED BY LORD PETERSHAM AND HIS CONFEDERATES, AND HOW THE KING'S LIFE WAS SAVED BY JACK STRAW.

ON the night following Rochester's escape from the residence of Master Estrange, our hero left the Strand, on a visit to the Duke of Gloucester, who, years before, was his father's chief friend.

Lord Linsay had dictated a letter, and Jack had it safely placed in his wallet.

With him was Silverbell.

Both were attired in handsome costumes and cloaks, and it is scarcely necessary to say that they were well armed.

Nothing whatever occurred until they were close to St. James'.

Then, suddenly they were confronted by a man.

So startled was Jack, that he half drew his blade.

The man laughed.

" That is not required, noble sir," he said, " keep it for a better purpose."

" Methinks I know you," said Jack.

" Ay, you have seen me before."

" Where, and when ? "

" More than a month ago, at White-hall. There was a fight—"

" I remember," interrupted Jack, as he extended his hand ; " your name is Abel Harkwell."

" It is," replied the man, who seemed delighted to shake Jack's hand, " and sorry am I that matters have turned out as they have."

" I fail to understand you. What matters do you refer to ? "

" Rochester."

" Has his body not been found ? "

" Found ? "

" Ay ; you and your companions threw it into the Thames."

" That is just what we did *not* do."

" Not ? " said Jack in astonishment.

" Nay, we did not. But where have you been for the past day or two ? "

" At home. We have not been outside the house."

" Then that accounts for it. Yet London is ringing with the news that Rochester has returned to life."

" What ? " thundered Jack, " returned to life ? Impossible ! "

" I assure you it is the truth. You see, we took the body of the first man to the river, and threw it in. When we returned—lo! the body of Rochester was gone. We took but little trouble about it, for we thought that the watch had taken possession of it."

" You had no doubt that Rochester was dead ? "

" By the Virgin ! we closely examined him, and were satisfied that he *was* dead."

" And I, for I passed my blade through his neck."

" Well, he was not dead nor anything near it. From what I have since learned, the fight was watched by a money-lender named Estrange, and his wife, and, when we had gone with the first body, they opened the door and dragged Rochester into their house.

" But a few hours ago, I had an interview with the wife, who knows me well, and she added what I did not learn."

And Harkwell narrated the story known to the reader.

He concluded thus—

" But a single hour ago, I saw Rochester at the head of a number of his retainers, proceeding in the direction of Whitehall. He is strangely altered, it is true, but there is no mistaking him.

" He was dressed with unusual magnificence, and I was told that he was about to have an audience of the king, who, as you are no doubt aware, is in London ; and here, considering the state of the country, he is likely to remain for some time."

" Alive ! " said Jack, " the villian whose body I thought had long since been claimed by the fishes. I shall never rest while he lives—never! The fact that Rochester is alive, will have the effect of altering many of my plans."

" Fear not," said Silverbell, " a man does not *always* recover."

" I am glad it was my good fortune

to be the first to convey this information to you," said Harkwell; "but it was not this which caused me to intercept you."

"It was not?"

"No; the fact is, it was my intention to pace up and down the streets in the hopes of meeting you; but good fortune threw me in your way without difficulty, and so I am able to place in your hands this letter."

"A letter! Who is it from?"

"Read it first."

Jack opened it, and, by the light of the moon, read as follows—

"To JACK STRAW, the people's firm friend. Greeting.

"I am aware that you are in London. Whatever you may be doing, I pray you abandon it, and come with all speed to me. A plot is afoot, and I am most eager to communicate to you the particulars.

"Your friend,

"ALLISON LATIMER."

"Latimer!" said Jack; "who is he?"

"I know him," said Silverbell; "he was at one time in the king's train."

"He is an honest man," said Harkwell, "and you can rely upon him."

"What say you, Silverbell? Shall we go to him?"

"By all means. I well remember him. He is a man who can be trusted."

"Where does he reside?"

"Within a stone's throw of this spot," said Harkwell. "Follow me, and I will take you there."

"A moment," said Silverbell. "Methinks I recognise you."

"It is possible. Certain it is that I recognise *you*."

"Indeed! Who am I?"

"Silverbell—once the king's jester."

"It is true."

"You recognise me as the son of the once rich landowner, Thomas Manby, of Chester."

"I do now. But you are sadly altered."

"I am; and the mirror tells me it is not for the best."

"Whence comes this alteration? And how is it that you have changed your name?"

"You must well remember, Sir Jester, that my father devoted a considerable portion of his wealth to bettering the condition of the working classes?"

"I do."

"This preyed upon the minds of the nobles to such an extent that, at last, they hatched a plot against him; and they succeeded in persuading the king that he was a traitor. The result was as they desired—my father was hanged, his estates were confiscated, and I was cast forth a beggar.

"By way of revenge I joined the men who infest Strand Lane—"

"What! The Red Masks?"

"The same. Soon after I joined them, the leader died, and I was appointed in his place. From those who took what was mine, and their friends, I levy toll."

"I don't blame you in the least," said Silverbell; "but the king himself has little to do with all this. It is his ministers. Though he is king there are some he dare not offend."

"That is true. But let me assure you that more than one of those who robbed me have regretted that they ever had a hand in the business. Like Jack Straw, whose deeds I have ever admired, I have taken toll from them, and I have made many a starving man and woman happy. It is needless to say that, if ever Jack Straw desires a score or two of men on whom he can depend, he has only to let me know."

Jack thanked him warmly, and the three then went on.

The residence of Master Latimer was very soon reached, and the three were admitted, with but little delay, by an elderly woman.

She allowed Harkwell to pass in at once, and he returned in a few moments, accompanied by the master of the house.

Latimer was a very old man, but wonderfully erect, and apparently active.

He bade Jack welcome in the warmest of terms, and expressed his pleasure at once more beholding Silverbell.

Harkwell did not remain.

Business of importance, he said, compelled him to take his departure; but he did not go until, once again, he had reminded Jack that, if he required assistance, he had but to communicate with him.

Master Latimer conducted Jack and Silverbell to his own snug chamber, and speedily placed before them the best of wines.

"I have often longed to look upon you, Jack Straw," he said, "and at last my wish has been gratified."

"And the plot you mentioned?"

"Is against the king."

"Against his life, do you mean?"

"Yes, against his life."

"Well, sir, if the plot is successful, many thousands of the people will rejoice."

"What you say is true enough. But they would make a mistake in so rejoicing, for it is not the king himself who grinds them down. It is his advisers."

"First," said Silverbell, "it would be as well to give us the particulars."

"Listen, then. You, of all men, are well aware that, at one time, I was high in favour with the young king. But through meddling lords, who fancied that my influence was becoming too great, I was deposed—in other words, I was expelled from the Court; nay, more, I nearly lost my life.

"The king's enemies, of course, fancied that I was the very man to join them, and they made no secret in broaching the matter.

"I pretended to agree with them, and declared I was ready to assist them in everything. Several times the chiefs have been in this house drawing up their plans."

"Who is the chief?"

"Lord Petersham."

"Ah! And he is supposed to be the king's best friend!"

"He is. Well, several plans have been tried, and the result has been complete failure. But, for the last one, there is every chance of success, and, when I tell it you, you will agree with me.

"It is known to me and one or two others, that the king has had some private dealings with certain foreigners, and has been persuaded to invest money in certain ventures. The result was to be expected—he has lost all. What the total sum is I know not, but it is a very large amount.

"His majesty has tried to raise money in London, but the merchants, knowing well that the security they would get would not be worth anything, refused to lend.

"While in this difficulty, Lord Petersham advised the king to secure certain valuable jewels and raise money on them.

"He told him that he knew of a person who would advance almost any sum he chose to name on the Court jewels he mentioned.

"A long conversation took place, and, in the result, the king has decided to get money on the jewels, and to go himself—in disguise—to the man who is now prepared to advance the money."

"To go himself?" said Silverbell, his face expressing his amazement.

"Ay; Petersham so persuaded him."

"And where is the place?"

"Deptford."

"Proceed," said Jack, "for I am much interested."

"The object of the plotters," continued Latimer, "is, of course, to get him into this house and murder him. Nothing could be easier, and the body could easily be disposed of. The king would disappear as completely as if the earth had opened and swallowed him up.

"Now, you see, Jack Straw, here is a magnificent chance for you. You could save the king from destruction, and then name your reward.

"The justice you have so long tried to get for the poor would be granted at once. Depend upon it, whatever you asked, the king would give you."

"I see all now," said Jack, "yes, now indeed, I understand why you sent for me. By heaven! what you say is indeed correct. What say you, Silverbell?"

"Yes, Jack; now indeed is your chance. Master Latimer is right; the king would grant you anything. When does his majesty set out?"

"To-morrow night. As you know, he is closely watched by day, and there is always a strong guard without his chamber door at night. The king will have a coil of rope ready, and, having assumed the disguise ready placed for him—that of a monk—he will lower himself from the window to the grounds, where one of the plotters will receive him and conduct him to where horses are in waiting."

"I understand. All this is very simple, and, but for you, Master Latimer, it is certain that the king would have lost his life."

"I do not forget many acts of kindness at his hands, neither do I forget that many things he does, and which are obnoxious to the people, he is compelled to do. His hands are forced."

"I will rescue him," said Jack, "and endeavour to capture the plotters. So now give me the full particulars."

*   *   *   *

At dusk on the following evening, four persons had assembled at one of the large houses facing the river, and which was owned by Lord Edgar Petersham, than whom there was no greater favourite of the young and much misdirected king.

The four persons were a portion only of the plotters, but they were the chiefs. Petersham was one, Donald Weldin, a rich City merchant, who found a great deal of the money required, was another; and they were supported by Thomas Morgan and Samuel Rogers, sons of rich land-owners.

Lord Petersham was a tall, finely-built man of about thirty, but his companions were many years older.

Each was attired for travelling.

"Now that we have gone through the first part of our arrangements," said Petersham, "let us think of the final."

"It will take the king two hours to reach Deptford, so that he will arrive at the house between ten and eleven.

"We must be there some considerable time in advance, and therefore, we will set off now."

"It is to be hoped," said Donald Weldin, who was a somewhat fierce-looking man, "that Crawford will make no mistake."

"Mistake?"

"Well, that he will strike hard, and follow the first blow with others, so as to be certain."

Petersham smiled.

"You do not know Crawford so well as I," he said. "When the time comes and he strikes, the king dies instantly. The king has often got out of a diffi-culty, but this time he is doomed. Ere midnight strikes, he will be dead, as sure as my name is Petersham. Then for honours, gentlemen. Next the king's, there will be no greater power than ours. But now as to the jewels."

"What value do you really place on them?" asked Morgan.

"Twenty thousand nobles."

"So much? Truly it is a huge sum. But what shall be done with them?"

"I was approaching that," said Petersham; "and I was about to suggest that we draw lots, and thus ascertain who is to be the possessor of them."

This was agreed to, and the four conspirators drew lots.

The jewels fell to Morgan—if, of course, they fell to anyone.

Petersham at once offered him ten thousand nobles to relinquish his claim, and Morgan agreed.

The fact was, he did not know the actual value of the jewels Petersham had persuaded the king to take with him.

But Petersham did.

He was well aware of the fact that *fifty* thousand nobles did not represent their value.

The disposal of the plunder having been thus arranged, Petersham rang the bell.

The summons was instantly answered by a man-servant.

"Pachman," said Petersham, "see that our horses are in readiness, and mark well what I say: we are about to travel to *Chelsea*. That you well understand?"

"Perfectly, my lord. I assure your lordship that I am not likely to forget."

"So, if anyone inquires, you know what to say."

The man bowed.

"And you will also remember," continued Petersham, "that I travelled to Chelsea entirely alone."

Again the man bowed.

He perfectly understood what was meant, for he had been in Lord Petersham's service a long time, and had been well trained to tell the greatest falsehoods with the gravest of faces.

In a short time the horses were

ready, and the four conspirators left the house, and took their way towards Deptford.

But they were careful to go in a roundabout direction, for they were fearful of being seen.

We must, however, precede their arrival at Deptford.

*　　*　　*　　*

Some hour or more before Petersham and his friends left the Strand, our hero, Silverbell, and Basil were well on their way to Deptford, then simply a little village, with but few inhabitants.

Arrived at the only hostelry the place contained, the three reined up.

The host, whose customers were very few, at once rushed out, and asked in what way he could minister to the comfort of the travellers.

Jack ordered some wine, and this having been brought, he said—

"Where is Larch House, host?"

"Larch House?" replied the host, opening wide his eyes. "Have you business there, gentlemen?"

"Ay," replied Jack, "we would see a friend there. We know he is at Larch House, but have forgotten his name."

"Yonder," said the host, pointing to a dark mass in the distance, "is Larch House; but as to the name of the man—or, I should say, the *men* who live there, I know nothing. They have been there for more than a week, and I have seen but little of them.

"They have issued forth once or twice to exercise their horses, but they never entered my house. Strange-looking men they are, gentlemen, and, I am afraid, mysterious."

"But my friend is a money-lender," said Jack.

"A money-lender? Then you may be assured that he lives not at Larch House. The house is the property of a gentleman abroad, and he, I am sure, is no money-lender. He left the place, with all the furniture, in the possession of a man named Wallis. He disappeared, and the men I speak of made their appearance.

"No doubt you have made some mistake, gentlemen; but still, there will be no harm in calling at the house."

"How many men are there, say you?"

"I know not for certain; but I have seen three or four. Of one I took especial notice. He is a tall, somewhat strange-looking man, of perhaps, fifty. My man tells me he has a great scar down one side of his face, and has lost two of the fingers of his left hand."

The three drank up their wine and departed, Jack saying that no doubt there was some mistake.

But, when out of hearing of the host, he said—

"Did you recognise the description, Silverbell?"

"Assuredly. It is nearly the same as that furnished by Master Latimer. The man described is Crawford."

"Exactly. And the reason he and his companions have not visited this hostelry, is simply because they have been forbidden."

Arrived within bow-shot of Larch House, the three dismounted, led their horses into a field, and secured them to some trees in such a way that the hedge hid them from sight.

Then they approached the house.

They saw that it was surrounded with a rather high, stone wall.

On the right was a small door.

This was open, and, as the three looked, they beheld the figure of a man.

Quickly they saw he was on guard, and that it would be out of all question to attempt to gain an entrance unless the man was removed.

"Listen to me," said Jack; "this man, like the others, is nothing but a common assassin. But, even if he were not, we must not pause. Basil—your bow and one shaft."

Basil unslung the cross-bow he carried, and handed it to Jack, together with an arrow.

Jack watched his opportunity, and, when it came, he took steady aim.

The shot was effective; for the man, without a single cry, threw up his arms, staggered backward and forward a few seconds, and finally fell.

The arrow had pierced his heart.

The three ran forward, seized the body of the man, and carried it to where they had placed their horses.

Then, entering the grounds, which they found somewhat extensive, they crept up to the house.

The whole was in darkness, with the

exception of one window on the ground floor.

Listening, they could hear the sound of voices, but how many men were within, of course it was impossible to tell.

They crept right round the house, and examined it everywhere.

No; there was but one way to gain admittance, and that was by the front.

"Draw your swords," said Jack, "we must make a bold dash for it. We will make a sudden alarm, and as the men rush forth, let us attack them."

This was agreed to, and Jack, picking up a large stone, hurled it with all his force through the window.

Instantly there were loud cries, and a rush was made to the door.

The moment it was open, Jack, Silverbell, and Basil, with terrific fury, attacked the men who showed themselves.

In less than a minute, two of them lay dead on the threshold.

"Surrender, John Crawford!" cried Jack, as he pushed his way into the passage.

"Never!" thundered a tall ruffian as he aimed a blow at Jack's head with a long, heavy sword.

Our hero, however, was too quick for him.

Easily warding off the blow, he leapt forward and sent his sword clean through the man's chest, killing him on the spot.

It was the leading man—Crawford.

Jack rushed into the room followed by Silverbell and Basil.

Two men were there, but they had thrown down their arms.

"'Tis well for you," said Jack. "Had you offered the least resistance it would have cost you your lives."

"Your success," said one, in surly tones, "is only owing to the sudden attack. Had we known what was coming, you would have got something you did not bargain for."

"You will find it as well not to be insolent," said Silverbell, " or you may be deprived of further speech, by having your tongue cut."

"What, would you attack an unarmed man?"

"You are a prisoner now," said Jack; "and— But see," he added, "the hilt of a dagger protrudes from his jerkin. Quick—throw down that weapon!"

Jack was right. The man had concealed a dagger in his jerkin.

However, he quickly threw it down.

"You are not to be trusted," continued Jack; "bind him and let him be taken to an upstairs chamber. Unless I am much mistaken, the branch of a tree and a rope will be his portion."

Hand and foot the man was bound, and Silverbell and Basil carried him upstairs.

Jack turned to the other, a man of about sixty.

Whatever might have been his demeanour previous to the attack on the house, he now presented the appearance of a miserable coward.

"What is your name?" asked Jack.

"James Crawford."

"Crawford! What relation are yo to the man slain—John Crawford?"

"I am his brother."

"You know perfectly well what you were here for?"

"To slay a man who had stolen the Court jewels, and who was about to bring them here, thinking money would be advanced upon them."

"By heaven!" thought Jack, "Petersham and his friends well paved the way; for, if what this man says is correct—and it appears to me to be so —they were not aware that the man to bring the jewels was the king himself.

"You will now do exactly as I tell you," said Jack, aloud; "and, if you obey, I promise you that you shall go from this house uninjured."

To this the man agreed.

"You will now be placed in a room, and the door locked upon you until your services are required," continued Jack; "but you will swear on this cross that you will make no attempt at escape."

James Crawford took the oath, and was then conducted to one of the rooms and locked in.

The bodies of the men slain were then removed, and Basil was placed on duty before the house.

And none too soon, for in less than another quarter of an hour a man, who wore the costume of a monk, made his appearance.

"COME DOWN INSTANTLY AND UNBAR THE DOOR," CRIED JACK.

After but a few words, Basil conducted him to the house, and into the largest of the rooms.

In a few moments Silverbell entered the room. The supposed monk uttered an exclamation of astonishment.

For a moment there was a pause, and then Silverbell said—

"Sire, you may well look surprised, for I am aware that I am the last person you expected to find at this gloomy house."

"Ha! so you know me?"

"I do. Yet I admit that your disguise is such that it would be very difficult for most people to recognise you."

"What is the meaning of your being here?"

"Rather ask, your majesty, what is the reason of *this* person being present."

And he pointed to Jack, who entered the room at the moment.

"Jack Straw, as I'm alive!" cried the king, as, throwing back his mantle, he snatched his blade from its sheath. "I see that I have been led into a trap; but, by the Holy Virgin! I will sell my life dearly."

Jack smiled.

"Put up your blade, sire," he said, "for I assure you, you will have no use for it. It is certainly true that you have been led into a trap, but I am not the layer of it. I, and my friends here, are your deliverers."

"Deliverers? Do you expect me to believe that Jack Straw, who has so often led his men to extract toll from my subjects, and who has often swore to get the people their rights, or die in the attempt, is here to deliver the King of England from a trap?"

"Such is the case," said Silverbell.

"At one time, when you were honoured as our jester, Silverbell," said the king, "we believed a great deal of what you said, and often found it to our advantage so to do; but, since you thought fit to abruptly quit our side, all has altered."

"Listen, your majesty, to the story Jack Straw will tell you, and then judge."

Jack at once told the whole story, which, as may be supposed, had the effect of throwing the king into a state of the greatest excitement.

"Petersham!" he continually muttered; "the base, double-dyed traitor! And I have heaped favour after favour upon his head! May heaven's justice fall upon him!"

On the conclusion of what was really an astounding story, and which was delivered with remarkable smoothness and ease by Jack, the king said—

"And so, Master Latimer, who was supposed to be a traitor, was really the cause of this bloodthirsty plot being frustrated. Good! A far higher position than ever he has yet occupied shall be given to him. As to you, Jack Straw—what reward do you claim? I suppose you would scornfully refuse any?"

"You are wrong, sire. But let us talk of that anon, for, in but a short time, the leaders in this affair will arrive here. Of course, they will expect to see your dead body.

"As it would be as well if you yourself witnessed their entrance, and what they say, you would do well to conceal yourself. Here, sire, is a cabinet."

He tried the doors, but found they were locked.

However, with the aid of a dagger, he opened them.

The cabinet was full of books, of all sorts and sizes.

Assisted by Silverbell, he pulled these out and placed them in an adjoining room.

Plenty of space was thus made for the king to stand.

Having made a few small holes with the point of his dagger, Jack invited the king to enter.

He did so without hesitation, and the doors were closed upon him.

Then Jack gave the man James his instructions, and all was ready.

Jack and Silverbell waited in the next chamber; Basil remained at the outer door on guard; and Crawford waited in the passage.

Certain it was, that Petersham and his companions did not hurry themselves on the road, for nearly another hour passed ere they arrived.

Basil challenged them; Petersham gave a password, and Basil allowed them to proceed.

Crawford received them, and conducted them to the chamber in which the king was concealed.

"Where is John Crawford?" asked Petersham.

"Below, arranging for the disposal of the body," replied the man, without hesitation.

"Soh!" said Petersham, "all is over! Tell us, did he offer resistance?"

"He could not," was the reply, "for he was a dead man within five minutes after his arrival here."

"And the jewels?"

"Are there."

And the man pointed to a box upon the table.

Petersham seized upon it, and found it locked.

"The key is, no doubt, on the body," he said. "Gentlemen, let us take a last farewell of the—"

He paused, as Jack and Silverbell suddenly appeared on the threshold.

Of course, neither Petersham, nor his friends, recognised Jack, but the former immediately recognised Silverbell.

"What is the meaning of this?" he said.

"*I* will answer you," said Jack. "The meaning, my Lord Petersham, is, that the plot against the king's life was discovered in time; that the man Crawford, who was to strike the fatal blow, is slain, and that—"

"Who are *you*?" thundered Petersham, as he and his friends drew their swords and daggers.

"I am Jack Straw."

"Ah! the traitor and robber."

"Not so great a traitor as Petersham—nor am I so great a robber. When I have taken toll from men like you, it has been to give it to the poor; but you would seize upon the Royal jewels to fill your own coffers."

"Stand aside!" thundered Morgan, as he made a dash forward.

The next instant he fell dead, for Basil, standing in the passage, had sent an arrow through his heart.

"I advise you to attempt no resistance," said Jack. "You are foiled, my lord, and the king—"

"Hark you. Think you that the king would believe one word you say?"

"Think you he would believe his *own* ears?"

"His own—"

He stopped, for, at that moment, the doors of the cabinet were thrown open, and the king stepped forth.

There was, for a few seconds, a terrible pause.

Then Petersham cast himself upon his knees, and begged for mercy.

"Mercy!" replied the king, sternly. "Not one atom shall you receive from me—that I swear. You, my lord, are nothing but a brutal, cold-blooded murderer.

"The people shall know what sort of man you are. I will now divulge all. They shall know how much I was in want of money, and how my endeavours to obtain it so nearly cost me my life. I charge each of you to put down your arms."

The three, for a few moments, hesitated.

They were considering whether it would be worth while to make a dash for liberty.

They decided in the negative.

The attitude of Jack Straw, Silverbell, and Basil (who had fitted a fresh arrow to his bow), convinced them that escape was hopeless.

Therefore, when Jack came forward, they at once handed him their arms.

"In this house," continued the king, "you will remain until an escort is sent for you, when you will be conveyed to the Tower."

Petersham was again about to plead for mercy—not for his companions, but for himself—when the king said—

"Do not waste your breath. I do assure you that whatever words you utter will fall on deaf ears. You and your companions have been caught red-handed, and no death would be too terrible for the man who would assassinate his king in cold blood."

In another five minutes the plotters were confined in a strong vault below, and Basil guarded them.

"Now, Jack Straw," said the king, "name your reward."

"For myself I seek no reward, sire, nor do my companions. But, if you would reward my services, then let the honest sons of the soil receive it."

"I understand you. You would benefit them?"

"I would. I would ask you, sire, to

dissolve the infamous yearly tax upon their persons ; to give them liberty of speech ; to let every man hire his ground at State valuation, and not at the price nobles put upon it—for, by doing so, they crush the loyal and honest man, and often make him a rebel and a thief."

" You are right, of that I feel assured. But you must remember that a king is often guided by his ministers. Many of these have such wealth and influence, that the king does not deem it politic to refuse to do this or that. But here I swear that what you have asked shall be done.

" In a day or two you shall call upon me and reduce to writing what you have just said. Somerset will, I believe, assist me ; and, if so, the thing is instantly done."

" I will not fail to wait upon you, sire. And let me tell you that, if what I ask be granted to the poor serfs, more than one proud feather will be placed in your cap. And your majesty will do well to remember that the honest serfs are more to you than your nobles. I say it, though I am a noble."

" *You ?* "

" Yes. I am the son of Lord Linsay."

" Impossible ! "

" Nay, it is true. But of that I will speak at a future time. I say that the serfs are more to you than your nobles—and for this reason, sire : they are the builders-up of the fortunes held by the nobles ; they are the men who, when the peace of the country is threatened by foreigners, fly to arms ; and, on the battle-field, they prove

that they have as much, and more, courage than those who tread upon them with iron heels, and contemptuously call them slaves and hounds."

The king was much struck with this speech, delivered as it was firmly, and with a considerable amount of passion. He took Jack's hand and pressed it, but spoke not.

That action, however, spoke louder than words.

But, after a short pause, during which he placed the box containing the jewels beneath his arm, he said—

" Be assured that I will not rest until I have fulfilled my promise. And now I must away. I return to Whitehall at once, lest my absence be discovered."

" Silverbell and I will accompany you, sire. We will not leave you until we have seen you safely to the palace."

" I accept your offer with thanks."

" With your majesty's permission I have a deal to say to you concerning my father, Lord Linsay, who, for many years, has been supposed dead. Also I would speak of Rochester."

" Most pleased shall I be to listen to you. But tell me—had Rochester's mysterious disappearance anything to do with you ? "

" *All* to do with me, sire."

The man Crawford was now sought for, but it was found that he had decamped.

However, Basil declared that he required no assistance in keeping watch over the prisoners until a guard was sent. And so the king set out, with Jack on his right, and Silverbell on his left.

CHAPTER XX.

HOW ROCHESTER VISITED PENTON HILL—OF WHAT PASSED BETWEEN HIM AND ALDERSON—HOW NELL WAS ABDUCTED—AND OF THE ARRIVAL AT THE ROUND TOWER AT WYCOMBE.

IT was a month after the incidents recorded in the preceding chapter, and Rochester was himself again.

The plot against the king's life was known throughout the length and breadth of the land, and everybody spoke of the rescue by Jack Straw and

his companions, and the reward claimed.

Petersham and his confederates had suffered death, and Master Latimer had been given a very high position at Court.

Most faithfully had the king fulfilled

his promise to Jack, for the down-trodden serfs had obtained what our hero demanded, and loud were they in their praises and expressions of thankfulness.

More than this, Lord Linsay and his wife, were fully recognised and established in the position they had occupied before falling into the clutches of Sir Guibald.

All this only served to embitter Rochester still further against our hero, whose life he swore to take.

But he remained quiet for a long time.

Not inactive though.

He was forming his plans, and these were not only against Jack, but, as the reader will now see—another.

One night, a letter was handed to Rochester.

The contents was as follows—

" My lord is informed that Alderson has returned, and would be pleased to wait upon his lordship, and take what instructions he may be pleased to give him."

For some little time Rochester considered this.

Then he muttered—

" Nay, not here. I will go to him."

Thereupon he himself went to the man who had brought the message.

"Return," he said, "and inform Alderson that I am on the way to him."

Then he ordered his horse to be saddled, and, having placed a couple of bags of money beneath his cloak, he quickly set out.

"Strange indeed will it be, Jack Straw," he muttered, fiercely, "if you escape me this time. You shall die—but I will wring your heart first. By heaven! that girl is the most beautiful creature I ever beheld. Well do I remember her when masquerading as a boy, but now that she has donned a woman's dress, she is more lovely than ever. Mine she shall be—ay, mine."

A little under an hour's ride brought him to Penton Hill (or Pentonville), and at the foot of this he halted, as if uncertain which way to proceed.

It was very dark, the roads were bad, and, in some places, it was dangerous to proceed mounted.

But, suddenly, a man emerged from the darkness.

He looked hard into Rochester's face, and then said—

" There's more than one rabbit in *some* warrens, your worship."

" True," replied Rochester, eagerly. " Lead the way to yours."

The sentence uttered by the man was, of course, a signal or password.

The fellow caught the gold piece thrown to him, and, turning, went down a narrow lane at a quick pace.

At the end he paused, and taking the horse by the bridle, led him across a field.

At the farther end of this was a number of small houses.

At the first he stopped, Rochester dismounted, and the next moment the door opened, and the villain was invited to enter.

He was quickly in the presence of the man he had come to see—a man of the name of Alderson.

He was every bit as tall as Rochester, but he was at least sixty years of age. A more ferocious-looking ruffian could not have been found in England.

He was twirling his enormous moustaches as Rochester entered, and was not very ceremonious in his greeting.

He, however, carefully closed the door, and having placed a chair for his lordship, seated himself opposite.

" I would offer your lordship some wine," he said, " but the truth is that, during my absence, the women-folk have guzzled the whole."

" Do not trouble yourself about wine," replied Rochester—" at least, not on my account. How long have you been in London ? "

" One day only."

" What success did you have in the country ? "

" None at all. Failure—failure—nothing but failure. And I lost five men."

" That is of little importance. What number returned with you ? "

" Fifty."

" Are they here ? "

" All of them. And I may add that they are ready for anything, more especially if they can be assured that they will profit by it, and thus be compensated for what they have lost."

" If my instructions are faithfully

carried out, they will be well paid. That I assure you."

"Your lordship was always liberal, and you may be certain that the men will work for you with pleasure."

"Now listen to me. Have you ever seen Jack Straw?"

"Ay, more than once; and I have every reason to remember him. May the fiends take him, say I."

"What transaction did you have with him?"

"It was in the country some months ago. Do you remember how the Earl of Doughty was robbed?"

"Yes, I remember it. But I had no idea that you had anything to do with it."

"Oh, yes; I had *all* to do with it. We watched for his grace night after night, and when at last we pounced upon him, we had no difficulty in persuading him to deliver up his valuables, which we found amounted to a large sum.

"Within five minutes after this, we suddenly found ourselves face to face with a large body of armed men, and Jack Straw it was who acted as spokesman.

"He very coolly commanded us to deliver up what we had taken from the earl.

"There was no help for it, and we knew that Jack Straw was in the habit of acting promptly, so we handed over what we possessed.

"This, however, did not satisfy him. He thought we were keeping something back, and so everyone of us had to dismount and submit to a search.

"The result was, that we were cleaned out of every coin. I afterwards heard that the money taken was handed over to certain tenants his grace had evicted a few days before."

"Hem! It was a pity that you did not have sufficient men with you to give them battle. But you are, of course, aware that Jack Straw long since disbanded his followers?"

"And came to London. Yes, I am aware of it. I am told that he is in favour with the king."

"Then you have been told what is wrong. He is not in favour, but he has had a few favours granted to him."

"He is an enemy of yours?"

"I have no greater," scowled Rochester. "I have vowed that he shall die."

"And you, perhaps, desire me to put him out of your way?"

"Exactly. But that is not all. Jack Straw is about to marry a young girl. Who she is I know not, nor do I care. But she is exceedingly pretty, and for that reason, I have condescended to notice her. It is my intention to snatch her from Jack Straw, and have her conveyed to my house at Wycombe."

"At Wycombe! I thought your grace had given up that place entirely."

"Nay. It is true I never live there; but that, as well as other places, is sometimes useful. Let me see. How long is it since you had certain *business* there?"

"Two years or more. By Satan! were it fifty years I shall not forget it. I am too well marked for that," grinned Alderson, as he suddenly bared his chest, and showed a long scar.

"That is nothing," said Rochester; "those who get their living, and something more, like you do, must not expect to go scathless."

"Well, on that occasion, I nearly lost my life; and you, your lordship, came very near being placed on your trial."

"Talk—talk!" said Rochester, contemptuously; "who would dare to put *me* on my trial?"

The incident referred to by Alderson was a terrible one.

A well-known and wealthy Frenchman came over to England on matters connected with the French Court, and among others to whom he was introduced, was Rochester.

The latter invited the Frenchman to his residence, and played with him, the stakes being very high.

Rochester was supposed to be clever at the tables, and he made certain that he should win large sums.

But, for once, he had met his match.

The Frenchman won an enormous sum of money from him.

But weeks passed, and Rochester did not pay, so the Frenchman declared that, if the money was not at once forthcoming, he would give the particulars at Court.

Rochester sent him a letter, apologising for the delay, and inviting him to his house at Wycombe, when he would pay all that was due.

The Frenchman accepted the invitation, and went to Wycombe.

He had scarcely crossed the threshold, when he was pounced upon by Alderson.

A fearful struggle ensued, during which Alderson had nearly all his clothes torn from his body, and received a dagger wound in the chest, which nearly terminated his existence.

The Frenchman, was, however, slain by one of Alderson's men, who drove his blade through his body from behind.

The gentleman being missed, the French ambassador made inquiries, and, it having been discovered that the Frenchman was last seen with Rochester, the latter was taken to task.

But he got out of the scrape by declaring, in the most emphatic manner, that he knew nothing of the whereabouts of the man.

"Where is the girl at present staying?" asked Alderson.

"At the house of Elias Leighton, in the Strand. Now I have had the most careful inquiries made, and I find that, to-morrow, Jack Straw and his companions leave London on a matter connected with estates, which are the property of Lord Linsay."

"Who is he?"

"He is Jack Straw's father."

"Never!"

"Such is the report."

"Do you believe it?"

"Yes. I have every reason to believe the report is correct."

"To what part of the country is he going?"

"I cannot say for certain; but, I know that it is nowhere in the direction of Wycombe. In the dead of the night—that is, to-morrow night—you will break into the house, secure the girl, and at once convey her to Wycombe, where I shall await you. So that she will be no trouble to you on the road, take this."

And he handed Alderson a tiny phial.

"That," he added, "contains a powerful drug. If you place a portion of it upon a kerchief, and put it over her face, it will keep her quiet for a few hours.

"And now, I warn you not to use violence towards the other inmates, whoever they are, lest it get to the king's ears."

"And Jack Straw? Will he not at once come to the conclusion that you are the person responsible for the abduction?"

"Certainly he will. He will cause inquiries to be made everywhere, and will, no doubt, get to know where the girl has been conveyed. He will make an attack on the place, and then is your time to capture or slay him; for now that he has disbanded his men, he will not make an attack with any force.

"You will take fifty men with you, and let them know that it is likely they will be away for some few days."

"Good! They will have no objection."

Rochester took the money from his cloak, and placed it upon the table, saying—

"Count that."

Alderson seized upon the bags, and, pouring out the contents, counted the money.

"That is but a first instalment," continued Rochester, "does it satisfy you?"

"Right well. I say again that your lordship was *always* liberal."

Rochester, after giving Alderson still further instructions, and more minute particulars, was conducted outside, and, having mounted, was led to the high road.

The villain's last words to Alderson were—

"Mind—my instructions have been perfect. No mistake can be made; and I warn you—fail at your peril!"

*   *   *   *

How Rochester obtained the information as to our hero being about to leave London, it is impossible to say; but, most certainly it was correct.

He was about to visit certain of his father's estates, the tenants upon which, for years, had acknowledged Sir Guibald as landlord; and the necessary documents to prove Lord Linsay's rights had been procured.

On the afternoon of the day following Rochester's visit to Alderson, Jack,

Silverbell, and Basil, each being in high spirits, set off; leaving Nellie in charge of Elias Leighton.

It was past midnight when Nellie mounted to the pretty chamber which had been set apart for her.

But she did not immediately retire.

She had many things to think of, and the principal, as may easily be guessed, was her approaching marriage.

It being a beautiful night, she opened her window, and, for some little time, stood against it, lost in thought.

Not the faintest idea of danger ever entered her head.

But it was the very worst thing she could have done, when she opened and stood at the window, for she betrayed her whereabouts.

Concealed behind a huge butt which was used for the purpose of catching rain water, was a man.

It was Alderson.

None of his men were near him, but they were close handy. So that they should not attract attention, they were scattered.

But a blast upon a small bugle Alderson carried, would have brought them around him in quick time.

Alderson had watched the windows, and noted the gradual extinguishing of the lights.

He, however, never thought of such luck as Nellie showing herself.

Presently she shut the window, and, a few minutes afterwards, the light went out.

"Half-an-hour," muttered Alderson, "then to work."

From beneath his cloak, he took a bundle of thin iron rods, the end of each being fitted with a socket.

Without the slightest noise, he placed one within the other, until one long rod was made.

Then placing it upon the ground, he whistled softly.

The signal was at once answered by one of his men.

"The rope," said Alderson.

The man took from beneath his cloak, a coil of strong rope.

To one end was attached a somewhat large hook, called by sailors a "grappler."

The hook Alderson attached to the end of the rod, and then he, and the man with him, remained perfectly still for at least half-an-hour.

Then Alderson went forward to the house, and stood beneath the balcony of Nellie's chamber.

He raised the rod, and at once attached the hook to the balcony.

Then he placed all his weight upon it, and, considering it secure, prepared to ascend.

"The moment I'm on the balcony," he said to his man, "follow me."

Alderson was evidently quite accustomed to climbing; at any rate, he went up the rope with, considering his age, remarkable speed.

Reaching the balcony he tried the window.

It was unfastened.

To open it was the work of one moment, and Alderson was within the chamber the next, just as his man reached the balcony.

Yet neither of them made the least noise.

There was just sufficient light to see Nellie lying upon the bed, sound asleep.

Alderson poured some of the contents of the phial given him by Rochester, upon a kerchief.

Then, for a few moments, he deliberated as to whether he should place the kerchief lightly upon Nellie's face, or whether he should suddenly pounce upon her, and forcibly hold it there.

He decided upon the latter.

Creeping to the bedside with the stealthiness of a cat, he placed the kerchief upon Nellie's face, and there held it.

At once the poor girl awoke and commenced to struggle violently.

It was, however, for a few seconds only.

Gradually the bright eyes again closed, and the uplifted hands dropped helplessly to her sides.

"Good!" chuckled Alderson; "the drug has acted well. Pah! throw the kerchief aside, or its fumes will overpower me. What the fiend is the stuff made of? Now here, with this rope, we will tie part of the bedclothes about her. Strike a light and put her garments into a bundle.

"When we get her without the house one of the men must lend his cloak, and with that and the bedclothes, she will not hurt until she is placed in charge of Mother Mason."

"Who's that ?"

"That's the woman Rochester calls his housekeeper. Woman, did I say ? Ho, ho ! What a picture for a painter !"

Having struck a light and lit a taper, the man selected all the clothes he could 'see and tied them together, while Alderson secured the bedclothes about Nellie.

The hook was then thrown off the balcony, the window closed, and the two men prepared to descend.

The man led the way holding aloft the taper, and Alderson followed, carrying Nellie.

"'Tis a thousand pities that Rochester said we must not interfere with the other inmates," muttered Alderson, "for Leighton is a rich man, and we might each have had a pocketful of gold pieces."

The back door was found to be heavily barred, bolted, and chained ; but still no noise was made in removing these protections.

"Leave the door open," whispered Alderson. "Attempt to close it, and you might make a noise."

The door was therefore left open, and consequently the valuable property within the house was at the mercy of any thieves who chanced to pass.

In a short time, Alderson was in the saddle with Nell before him.

He then sounded his bugle, which meant that the men were to go on by different directions to Uxbridge, at which point they would join.

*   *   *   *

The house Rochester owned at Wycombe, was small, but strong ; although it was known to be considerably over a century old.

But, for many years, a great part of it, as well as the wall surrounding it, had been in a dilapidated state, and Rochester made no attempt to repair it.

He never used it as a residence proper, and, therefore, the fact that some parts of it were in ruins, did not trouble him.

It was good enough for the purposes to which he put it, and that was all he cared.

It was not age that had destroyed portions of the Round Tower, as it was called.

Nay, that was caused by one of the greatest and most determined attacks ever made upon a house or castle.

That was when the Round Tower was in the possession of the Earl of Mountjoy.

This young and haughty lord took a fancy to the daughter of one of the City armourers, who was one of the handsomest girls in England.

The girl was betrothed to a young City merchant, and the father, fearing mischief at the hands of the earl, pressed the marriage forward.

This enraged the earl, who caused the girl to be carried off, on the eve of her marriage.

In a day or two, however, it was found he had taken her to Wycombe.

Her betrothed caused the " hue-and-cry " to be raised in the City, and he was joined by four hundred apprentices, who, having armed and provisioned themselves in the best manner possible, marched to Wycombe, which was reached just as night had fallen.

But, in the meantime, the earl had received the intimation that an attack on a large scale was about to be made, and he summoned his friends on all sides, and hired their retainers.

The moment the apprentices came within bow-shot, and before they could make any demand, a flight of arrows were discharged at them, many of the youths being struck.

The next instant, however, several retainers, mounted on the walls and on the roof, were struck down ; for the apprentices treated them to a perfect cloud of arrows.

Then the armourers' and carpenters' apprentices, set themselves to work with their axes, and cut down several of the earl's finest trees, which they used as battering rams, while they were covered by the other apprentices, who picked off every man who dared to show himself.

The rams, in turn, were worked by fifty apprentices, and the effect was, that the thick wall was battered and destroyed in every direction.

Suddenly the gates were opened, and the earl, at the head of fifty men, dashed out.

They were at once met by the apprentices, and a desperate hand-to-hand fight waged for some time.

In the end, the earl, his friends and men were completely defeated—indeed, thirty were slain outright.

The earl succeeded in reaching the tower, and presently appeared on the roof.

He was distinctly seen, for several men, holding links, were beside him.

The apprentices thought he was about to address them.

They were mistaken.

In a few seconds a white figure was led on to the roof, her eyes being bandaged.

It was the unfortunate bridesmaid.

The earl, who now presented a terrible sight, drew his dagger.

Loud cries of horror arose from the apprentices, for clearly enough did they see that he was about to plunge his weapon into the girl's heart.

But, almost simultaneously, the cries of horror changed to ringing cheers; for the earl, suddenly throwing up his arms, dropped at the girl's feet. An arrow, shot by the most expert of all the apprentices—a lad only sixteen years old—had pierced his brain.

The men beside him fled in terror, and the apprentices, again seizing their rams, made for the gates, which they burst open in a few moments, and thus gained admission to the tower.

No further resistance was offered, and the girl was soon in her lover's arms.

It was a great victory, but dearly bought, for many apprentices had fallen to rise no more.

For many, many years the Round Tower remained deserted; but, at last, Rochester bought it, and installed there an old woman, who had been useful to him on many occasions.

This was Mistress, or "Mother" Mason; and, during the few years she had been in charge of the Round Tower, she had assisted in more than one dastardly crime.

Not only did Rochester consider her clever in carrying out any part, or parts of his plans, but he knew that she was a woman who could keep her own counsel.

Also many times, when questioned, she had acted the fool to such perfection, that her questioners considered her three parts insane, and quickly arrived at the conclusion that it was useless to attempt to get anything out of her.

She was between seventy and eighty years of age, and the very incarnation of ugliness.

Surely in all England no other woman could have been found to equal her horrible repulsiveness of look; a great part of which had been caused by the fearful life she had led when a woman of middle age.

It was in the afternoon of the day following Nellie's abduction, that Mother Mason saw a horseman galloping towards the tower, and she hurried to meet him, while Rochester, who had arrived some time before, looked from one of the upper windows.

The man came as messenger to say that Alderson and the other men would reach the tower at nightfall, and he added that the girl had proved a great trouble; that she had slain one man, and that Alderson had had a narrow escape of his life at her hands.

Sure enough, soon after nightfall, the party arrived, and Alderson was received by Rochester.

"Where is the girl?" he asked.

Alderson pointed to a large box, perforated at the top, and which had been placed upon a small cart.

"My lord," he said, "ever since she recovered from the drug, she has been a perfect fury. You see, we made the first halt at a small hostelry, where I knew the host.

"All of a sudden, while we were taking refreshment, she started up, and, snatching a dagger from my side she plunged it into the man I had told off to watch her.

"Then she rushed at me, and, by Satan! I made certain I was a dead man. But, one of the men pushed her aside in the nick of time, and then half-a-dozen more overpowered her.

"So violent was she, that the host suggested that we should gag her, and place her in a box to avoid accidents on the way; and, as you see, I did so. On my soul! I am glad to be rid of her."

"I like a woman of spirit," said Rochester.

"Ay, so do I—at a *distance*."

"Let the men carry the box in, and open it at once. Mother Mason, you will attend upon her."

"With *much* pleasure," grunted the old woman.

"What," whispered Alderson, in Mother Mason's ear, "still as ugly as ever, old woman? On my soul! for long have I had serious thoughts of proposing for your hand."

"Out upon you for a foul-mouthed, drunken sot!" hissed Mother Mason, her sunken eyes flashing fire. "Keep your jests for those who can appreciate them."

"What! Say you would not marry me did I offer you my hand?"

"Dolt!"

"And fortune?" grinned Alderson.

"Begone—hound!"

"Upon my word, you are most ungrateful. I offer my fortune, and you refuse to share it; whereas I am prepared to share yours, and the best part of *your* fortune is your face, which is like that of a battered old witch. Ho, ho!"

"Witch, eh? Know you that, if you further insult me, I will pronounce upon you a spell which will make you curse the hour in which you were born."

"The spells and the curses of ugly, old women," laughed Alderson, "I drink in good liquor; and, when I enter the house, if you do not produce a bottle of good wine, I will not pronounce a *spell* upon you, but I will let you feel the weight of my riding whip."

So saying, Alderson went into the tower.

Into one of the numerous small chambers on the ground floor, the box had been taken.

When Alderson entered, the men were removing the cords, the while Rochester looked on.

In a few moments the lid was removed, and Nellie's beautiful face was seen.

But it was now deathly pale, for she had suffered terribly, not only bodily, but mentally.

An occasional drink was all she had had since she was taken from Leighton's house.

Food she had continually refused.

The bandage was removed, and her hands were untied.

But she made no attempt to leave the box.

For a few seconds she fixed her eyes upon Rochester, and then she said—

"I did not have to be *told* that this outrage was committed by you. I knew it as soon as consciousness returned to me. But wait awhile! You will answer for this to Jack Straw. The next time he meets you, his blade will not pass through your neck, but your base, black heart."

"Fine words, on my soul!" sneered Rochester; "but we are here all prepared for Jack Straw, and sincerely trust he will make his appearance ere long. We shall have a trap laid for him."

"Think not that Jack Straw is in the habit of walking into traps with his eyes shut. Do not think he will come here alone. No, no."

"Who will be foolish enough to come with him?"

"As many as he calls upon. Did he require them, thousands would follow him."

"Wait and see. Mother Mason, into your charge I place this charming girl, who, you will doubtless find, has a doubly-pointed tongue.

"But treat her gently, and allow her to select the daintiest costumes from the wardrobe left her by the lady whose name need not be mentioned, for I have taken a great fancy to her.

"Anon she will learn to love me, and here, in this pretty tower, we shall live most happily."

Nellie did not answer this.

She felt that it was impossible to frame words for a reply.

But her eyes looked the scornful contempt she felt.

The box was once more lifted, and this time carried to the top and placed within a prettily furnished bedchamber.

If any of the things in that bedchamber could have spoken, what horrors they could have told!

Mother Mason followed the men, and when they retired, she produced a long, sharp knife from beneath the folds of her mantle, and cut the cords which fastened the bedclothes about Nellie's body.

Nellie stretched out her hand, saying that she could free herself.

At this Mother Mason grinned.

"Nay, nay, my pretty bird," she said, "weapons such as this are dangerous in the hands of reckless ladies. Besides, on no account must I allow you to distress yourself. I will wait upon you with pleasure. You shall have the choicest wines, the finest foods, and the prettiest costumes that the house contains. These costumes were once worn by a great lady, who for a time lived here. Poor thing! her love for my lord grew so intense, that—"

"Lie not to me," interrupted Nellie. "I am not the person you take me for. I am not a brainless girl, who will believe any story told her. Learn that I am a woman, who has passed through more dangers that most *men*. I am the betrothed wife of Jack Straw, and when he learns where I am, then your occupation will be gone."

"There you mistake. Let me inform you that my lord has here fifty men, well armed, and prepared for anything. The Virgin help anyone who dares to make an attack on this tower. But first, of course, they must learn where you are."

"If this is the prison chamber selected for me, let me be within it alone."

"To be sure. I will only bring you your clothes and a few other things, and then I will begone."

This did not take her long.

She brought plenty of clothes and wine, and other refreshments.

When alone, Nellie shot the bolt of the door.

Then taking the taper, she examined the floor.

It seemed perfect—that is, it did not appear to have a trap-door.

Next, with the greatest care, she proceeded to examine the walls.

Nothing suspicious did she discover until she came to the wall at the foot of the bed.

When she tapped it with her knuckles, it gave out a hollow sound.

She knew a very great deal of secret panels and chambers, and she had no doubt that this was one of the former.

A minute inspection with the taper, convinced her that it was so.

Thereupon she took everything off the bedstead, and, by exerting all her strength, drew the bedstead close against the panel.

Well for her was it she did so, for in little over an hour, she heard the sound of footsteps.

Then there was a noise as of a hand being drawn across the panel, which was then gently pushed.

"Foiled, Rochester!" cried Nellie; "and, by heaven! you will be still further foiled directly."

No reply was returned, but, in a few seconds, she heard Rochester—for he it was—retiring.

CHAPTER XXI.

OF THE ATTACK ON THE ROUND TOWER—OF THE TOTAL DEFEAT OF ROCHESTER, AND RESCUE OF NELLIE.

FORTUNATELY, none of the lawless ruffians who made London their "hunting grounds," passed the house of Elias Leighton, and so neither the contents nor the inmates were disturbed.

But, as soon as Leighton found the door open, he was thrown into a state of the greatest terror.

The very first thing he did was—not to see whether any property had been stolen—but whether Nellie was safe.

He at once saw what had taken place, and, as soon as he could recover from the shock, he went off to St. James', where Lord Linsay and his wife were staying.

"You may depend," said the former, "that Rochester is to do with this dastardly outrage. Fool that I was not to have had her with us."

"It would have happened all the same," said Leighton; "if Rochester makes up his mind to do a thing, he does it at any cost But, what is now to be done?"

Lord Linsay summoned one of the pages, a handsome boy of fourteen.

"Edgar," he said, "I have been told that you are a most excellent rider."

"I' faith, my lord," answered the boy; "I will ride with most of them. Give me a fleet horse, and I will keep on his back over hedge or ditch."

"Do you feel as if you could undertake a long ride?"

"Nothing would suit me better."

"Then see that the groom saddles the fleetest horse, and, while you are getting ready, I will write down the names of the various places through which you will have to pass to get to Kingston, as well as other particulars."

The result of this journey was that, before midnight, the page came upon our hero at a hostelry at Kingston; and he, Silverbell, and Basil at once returned.

They reached St. James' at sunrise, and there learnt the full particulars from Leighton.

"Yes," said Jack, "there cannot be the faintest doubt about it; this is Rochester's doing. And, as sure as there is a heaven above, he shall suffer for it. Poor Nellie! she will be driven to distraction. Where can he have taken her?"

"He has so many places," said Basil.

"And I am acquainted with them," said Silverbell. "Rochester has evidently forgotten that I am still with Jack."

"Where then, think you, has he taken her?"

"My opinion is, that he has taken her to Wycombe."

"If we could but discover who the men are who assisted him!"

"We will make inquiries; but, failing to discover who the men are, we will quickly set out for Wycombe."

"Quick!" said Jack, "let us start at once. If I could but come face to face with the villain, he should not again escape me!"

* * * *

No doubt many thousands of our readers know the little turning in the Strand, close to St. Mary's Church, and which leads to the river.

Strand Lane it is called, and Strand Lane was its name at the period of this romance.

But, how different was then its appearance!

On each side were large houses, which were inhabited by the highest in the land.

At the top of the lane was a great archway, which once boasted a gate; but, during a riot, the gate was smashed, and no one attempted to put another in its place.

At the bottom of the lane, right and left, was a number of wooden sheds, and, at the edge of the river, a kind of wharf.

This was once called the "Strand Ferry," and boats and experienced watermen could be hired at any hour of the day or night.

But, suddenly, the watermen, for a reason which was never learned, disappeared, and, to the astonishment and dismay of the great Strand Lane nobles, the sheds became occupied by a number of men, who defied anyone to interfere with them.

Nevertheless, one of the nobles one day summoned his retainers, and also hired a number of others, and made an attack upon the sheds, offering one hundred nobles for every foe who should be thrown into the river.

But they got more than they had bargained for, as the men fought desperately, and for more than two hours a terrible fight was waged.

The result was, that the retainers were completely beaten, and at last fled in terror.

It was said that the losses on both sides amounted to some forty men.

However, the occupiers of the sheds were interfered with no more.

Some long time after this, Abel Harkwell joined them, and it was quickly found that he was a clever man in many things.

Therefore, when the leader died, it was no wonder that the men unanimously elected him as their chief.

On the night of the day on which Jack returned to London, Harkwell was "at home," if the rotten old shed he called his was home at all.

Entirely alone, he was busy cleaning some arms, though he devoted quite as much attention to a flask of wine beside him.

Suddenly a shrill whistle was heard, and this was followed by another.

"Ay, ay," muttered Harkwell, "that is a visitor. Who can *he* be?"

Another moment, and a man made his appearance.

"Three men," he said, simply— "strangers."

"Did they give a name?"

"Yes; one gives a name well known. It is Jack Straw."

"Jack Straw!" cried Harkwell; "is it possible? Which way did they come?"

"By the river."

"Conduct them hither, and tell Wallace to bring up some wine."

In less than five minutes, Jack, Silverbell, and Basil entered the shed, and were most cordially received by Harkwell.

"I feel assured," he said, "that you seek my services, and very pleased shall I be to lend them. I may say that I am right glad to see you safe and sound. Rochester, you see, has gone into the country, and fifty men from Penton Hill have gone with him—or they have gone to meet him. Hearing this, I at first thought that it was something against you."

"By the Virgin! you thought correctly."

And Jack thereupon told him of Nell's disappearance.

Harkwell was not at all astonished.

"This," he said, "is not the first or the second time that Rochester has carried a lady off. It is more than likely that he has taken the young girl to the same place as the others—that is, to the Round Tower at Wycombe."

"Exactly," said Silverbell, "that is what I had already said."

"It is a serious matter," continued Harkwell, "for everybody knows how violent he is. There is no telling what has happened by now. But, fear it not, I am well prepared to assist you. I can gather together a hundred men within an hour."

"Do so," said Jack, "and we will at once commence the march to Wycombe. Can you procure enough horses?"

"Yes, easily. And you may depend that I will see that every man is well armed. Many of them have served as archers in the army, and are excellent shots. And I can tell you, that an expedition like this will suit them exactly. But, wait a moment, and you shall see a few of the men."

Going without, he placed a small horn to his lips, and blew a shrill blast upon it.

Instantly men began to pour out of the sheds, many of them sword in hand.

The majority of them were tall, powerful-looking fellows of middle age.

They crowded round Harkwell's shed, as if expecting to take an "order."

"Listen, my men," said Harkwell, "I have lately heard many of you complaining that business in London has been very dull of late, and I agree with you—it has.

"But, a chance now presents itself for a journey into the country. Who will go?"

Every man present declared himself ready.

"Well," continued Harkwell, "within an hour, we set out for Wycombe, and you will have a far better leader than me, although I shall be with you. Behold, my men—this is Jack Straw."

At this a ringing cheer (which brought many a servant to the windows of the great houses), burst forth.

"If it is Harkwell's desire, I will lead you," said Jack. "We are about to make an attack on the Round Tower, at Wycombe, which is the property of the villain Rochester.

"The men in his pay have forcibly carried off the young girl to whom I am betrothed, and there can be no doubt she has been taken to Wycombe.

"For the assistance you will render me, you shall be handsomely paid. And, no doubt, you will find much that is valuable in this tower of his.

"Let us get possession of the girl, and then we will sack the tower and raze it to the ground."

Again and again the men cheered.

An expedition like this certainly suited them.

"Arm yourselves thoroughly," continued Jack, "and do not forget that axes are useful."

"We shall not forget something else," said Harkwell.

"What is that?"

"Gunpowder."

"I have had little experience of it.

I was not aware that much had reached this country."

"That is correct, I believe. But I have half-a-dozen small kegs of it. It is a most dangerous compound, but useful in some cases."

"Bring three or four of the kegs with you. It is likely that we may try its powers on the tower walls."

"By the time you have procured your horses," said Harkwell, "we shall be ready."

Sure enough, when they returned, they found the whole of the men ready for departure.

There were over a hundred of them.

It was agreed that they should proceed direct to Pethvell, a village about four miles from Wycombe, where the final plans would be arranged.

*　　*　　*　　*

We now return to the Round Tower.

On the day following the arrival, Nellie saw nothing whatever of Rochester, nor could she get the old woman to say whether he was still within the place.

But she was well aware of the fact that the men were on the alert; for she heard the clank of arms, and the steady tramp of the guards below.

The finest wines and food were placed before her, but she was very careful how she partook of them, lest either were drugged.

At last, when night had come on, her chamber door was opened, and Rochester made his appearance.

"Soh!" he said, "you are looking better—that is well. On my soul, you have a pretty face. I suppose I now find you resigned?"

"Resigned! to what?"

"To remain here with me."

"A strange thing to say to a prisoner."

"I mean that you are willing to stay of your *own* accord."

"I willing? Give me but the chance, and I would fly from this accursed hole as from a pestilence."

"So, then, you would prefer Jack Straw to a noble lord?"

"A what?"

"A noble lord."

"Is that what you call yourself?" asked Nellie, contemptuously.

"It is."

"Then, by the Virgin, you misname yourself. *I* do not call you a noble lord."

"What, then, *do* you call me?"

"A foul murderer and a vile impostor. No other such scoundrel breathes on the face of the earth."

For an instant Rochester's eyes flashed, but the next he forced a smile, as he said—

"Some excuse must be made for a person of *your* position."

"Make what excuse you will, so that you do not pollute this chamber by your presence."

"I see it is useless, by kindness, to attempt to win you over to me; therefore, force will be used."

"Coward! You, who would not meet a man in fair fight, thus threaten a defenceless girl. But, listen to this, and, if you have any spirit at all, you will agree to do as I ask.

"I have been accustomed to the field, and, woman though I am, I well know the use of weapons.

"Give me a dagger, arm yourself with another, and I will fight you to the death."

"Fight with a woman? Impossible!"

"I see—in the case of a woman, you would prefer to quietly assassinate her. Well, then, I must hope on. Something tells me that Jack Straw is already on the road hither."

"Indeed! Well, we are waiting for him. Do not imagine that you were brought here, only because I took a fancy to you. I well knew that Jack Straw—curse him!—would find out where you had been taken, and that he would lose no time in coming here. When he reaches this retreat, he will lose his life."

"Be not too sure of that. It may be *you* who will lose your life."

Rochester approached nearer to Nellie, and was about to hiss something in her ear, when Mother Mason entered the chamber, greatly excited.

She took no notice of Nellie, but whispered a few words in Rochester's ear.

In doing this, her back, for a few seconds, was turned towards our heroine, and she instantly took advantage of it.

"ROCHESTER AND HIS SURVIVING COMRADE UTTERED A CRY OF RAGE, AND ATTACKED JACK WITH INCREASED FURY."

Nellie saw the haft of the old woman's knife protruding from her girdle, and, quietly withdrawing it, she concealed it about her own person.

Rochester hurriedly left the chamber with Mother Mason, who did not forget to lock the door.

But in a few moments she returned.

"Ho, ho!" she leered; "how *quick* you are, my pretty wench! But it will not do to play with me, you see?"

"To play with *you?* What do you mean?"

"You have stolen my knife. Don't deny it; for it was in my girdle."

"Deny it! Why should I?"

"You admit taking it?"

"Assuredly."

"Then return it, or it will be the worse for you."

"It is my intention to keep it. It may presently be of some service to me."

The ugly old woman was astonished at the girl's daring.

"You will not return it?" she said.

"I repeat—no."

"Then I will compel you."

"Keep back!" said Nellie, drawing forth the knife. "If you make the slightest attempt to regain possession of this weapon, I will plunge it into your heart."

Mother Mason drew swiftly back.

She saw that the threat was no idle one.

"No matter," she muttered, "I will get it when she sleeps—if she *does* sleep here again; for there's no telling what may happen if what the man says is correct."

Without another word, she turned and left the chamber.

The words she had uttered in Rochester's ears were—

"One of the men sent out has just returned. He says that a force is on the way hither."

When Rochester descended and entered what, years and years before, had been called, and used as, a "guard-room," he found one of six men he had caused to be attired as ordinary peasants and sent out as spies, surrounded by a number of other men, and being interrogated by Alderson.

As Rochester entered, the man made him a low bow.

"News, my lord," he said. "When I left here I proceeded, as you directed me, straight to Pethvell. I had not been there many minutes, when I saw a large force of horsemen advancing."

"A *large* force! Did you estimate the number?"

"I did; and I should say there are over a hundred men, all mounted and heavily armed. They drew up on the green, and, clambering into a tree, I saw several men—no doubt the leaders —conversing. One I recognised as Abel Harkwell."

"What! Abel Harkwell, of Strand Lane?"

"The same. It was he, I am certain."

"What think you of it, Alderson?"

"There is no doubt that this man is right. Jack Straw has hired Harkwell and his band. Since Abel has ever been against your lordship, there was not much difficulty in that."

"No doubt. But if we can capture him, he shall swing from the highest of the trees that surround this tower. Over a hundred men! Well, we have little to fear. They will be in the open, while we shall be sheltered by these walls, which, though old, will withstand any attack which may be made against them.

"Prepare, Alderson, and see that everywhere is in darkness. Let the best shots go to the upper loopholes; you will remain below while I ascend and direct the archers; then, when we have picked off a number of our enemies, we will sally forth with a rush."

"Will you not don your armour, my lord?" asked Alderson.

"I have already chain armour under my tunic. That will be sufficient in such a paltry affair as this is likely to prove."

"Paltry!" muttered some of the men. "When Jack Straw leads, it is not likely to be a paltry affair."

In a short time every man was at his post, and anxiously waiting to ascertain whether an attack would really be made.

The majority of them devoutly wished that the spy had made a mistake.

Presently was heard the sound of horses' hoofs.

Immediately afterwards rang out the loud and piercing blast of a bugle.

Our hero himself had sounded it, and he rode out from those who followed him.

It was Alderson who replied to the summons.

"Depart!" he roared. "We answer no insolent summonses; or, if we do, it is in one way only."

The words had scarcely left his lips, when a flight of arrows whistled through the air, and three or four saddles were emptied.

But, in shooting, many of Alderson's men had shown themselves, and the result was, that several were stricken down with the arrows shot by Harkwell's skilful followers.

The men were then hurriedly withdrawn into the shelter of the trees.

Jack became impatient, and Silverbell suggested that an attempt should be made to force the gate.

"Yes," said Jack, "we must gain an entrance. Listen: You, Harkwell, get the men with the axes to cut down a couple of the trees. Those within the tower will, of course, fancy that an attack is to be made with battering rams."

"But, while the men are cutting the trees, I will advance to the wall with a couple of kegs of gunpowder."

"By heaven!" said Basil, "that will be too dangerous."

"There *is* danger in it," continued Jack, "but I will undertake it."

Harkwell detached two small kegs which had been slung at his saddle-bow, and Jack dismounted.

"Be careful what you do," said Harkwell. "If you reach the wall in safety, force in the heads of the kegs, and then connect the contents with this rag, which you will light at the farther end."

Jack lay upon his chest, and the kegs were placed crosswise upon his back.

In this way he crawled through the grass and brushwood, and reached the wall in safety.

He had not been seen.

Setting the kegs against the wall, he soon forced in the heads, and then, placing them on their sides, he put one end of the rag against them, and, kindling a light by the aid of flint and steel, returned, as he had come, to his companions, who were watching his operations in breathless silence, and unmoved, though the enemy's arrows were discharged, ever and anon, amid the trees.

Meanwhile there was great activity within the tower.

Rochester was directing the archers above, and Alderson below; though both placed themselves in such positions that they should not be struck by the enemy's arrows.

Loudly and long did Rochester chuckle when he saw the attacking force seek the shelter of the trees; and he it was who urged the men to discharge random shots in the direction of the wood, feeling certain that at least one out of every dozen arrows would be effective.

Then he sent for Alderson, who approached him with the air of a man who already considered himself a victor.

"Presently," said Rochester, "they will no doubt make an attack on the gate, and then— Yes—look! I am correct, they are cutting down the trees to be used as rams. Can't you hear the ring of the axes?"

"Distinctly."

"As soon as the men advance on the gate, shoot back the wicket, and give them a flight of arrows. Then, when they are thrown into confusion, open the gate and dash upon them, sword in hand."

"And you, my lord?"

"I will direct the archers here. If you are careful— But what is that?"

"What?"

"That light at the farther end of the wall to the right?"

"It looks like a lantern."

"Nay, more like furze burning. Ho! ho! surely they are not mad enough to try and burn down a stone wall? But the light grows brighter. Let one of the men—"

He did not conclude the sentence, for he was checked by a brilliant glare of light.

Then there was a noise like the crashing of thunder, and a great part of the solid wall fell inward.

The fall of the stonework was followed by a ringing cheer, and, when Alderson and his men had partially recovered from the confusion into which they had been thrown, they saw a number of the enemy, sword in hand, dashing through the aperture.

Rochester, drawing his blade, called upon the archers to follow him.

Probably thinking that the only way to save their lives was to defeat the attack, they followed, and in a few minutes a fearful hand-to-hand fight was in progress in the courtyard.

A few of Harkwell's men had been directed to cut a pile of furze and fire it beside the wall.

This they did, and a mighty blaze, which illuminated the tower and the country round about, arose.

In less than five minutes it was seen that Rochester and his men would be defeated; for, under Jack Straw (who wielded a heavy battle-axe), Basil, Silverbell, and Harkwell, the men fought like fiends.

"No quarter!" shouted Jack, again and again.

The men following him asked for none, but Alderson quickly began to supplicate for mercy.

Rochester, as soon as he saw that Jack was carrying all before him, slipped away and rushed into the tower.

Just within stood Mother Mason, trembling for her safety.

"Quick!" he said. "Ascend and bring the girl down, while I open the door of the subterranean passage. By Satan! they will not find us there."

But Mother Mason remembered that Nellie was armed.

She would not, however, have told Rochester on any account.

"I may have a difficulty with her," she said.

"Difficulty!" replied Rochester. "If she refuse to come with you, slay her where she stands."

Mother Mason seized an axe and ascended the stairs.

Throwing back the door of the chamber in which Nellie had been placed, she found her mounted on the table, and peering eagerly from the little window.

"Come with me," shouted Mother Mason. "Come—quick!—or you will be lost."

Nellie leapt from the table.

"Here I remain," she said, "until Jack Straw releases me."

"Fool! that is impossible. Come, I say."

And with an oath she rushed upon Nellie, the axe uplifted.

Our heroine, though the knife was in her hand, did not use it.

She seized upon a small but heavy oaken stool, and this, with all her force, she hurled at Mother Mason's head.

The aim was true, for the stool struck the hag fairly in the face, and, with a wild yell, she dropped unconscious at Nellie's feet.

Throwing down the knife Nellie seized the axe, and, without an instant's pause, rushed from the room and down the stairs.

In a few seconds she was almost in the centre of the terrible carnage.

At once she was seen, and a great cheer arose.

But it so happened that Alderson was close to her.

A fearful sight he now presented, for he had received many wounds.

With an oath he rushed forward, and aimed a blow at Nellie with his sword.

But her quick eyes detected the movement, and she stepped nimbly aside.

Then, turning with extraordinary swiftness, she brought her axe down upon Alderson's head, and with such force, that he was killed on the spot.

The battle was at an end.

Another moment, and Nellie was folded to our hero's breast, and again and again did the cheers of the victors roll forth.

"You are not injured, my love?" asked Jack.

"Not at all. And you?"

"A slight wound or two, that is all. Basil, do you take charge of Nellie. Search must be at once made for Rochester."

With Silverbell and Harkwell at his side, followed by fifty men, he entered the tower, and searched every room.

Rochester, however, could not be found.

The fact was, the coward had made his escape by means of a subterranean passage, which had an outlet at some distance from the tower.

Mother Mason was discovered, and taken to the courtyard.

Then came the roll call.

It was found that fifteen of Harkwell's men had been killed, and about the same number wounded.

Of Alderson's men, but five remained alive.

Harkwell's dead were at once taken without the tower and buried, while Alderson's were placed against the walls on the inner side.

Then, once more, the men swarmed into the tower, and took possession of everything of value, which, having spare horses, they could easily carry away.

Then the axes were brought into play, and the furniture in every chamber was reduced almost to splinters, and piled in the centre.

Then, at a signal from Jack, it was fired.

In the bottom of the tower, a heap of wood was placed, and, in the centre, the two other kegs of gunpowder.

Then the whole party mounted and rode away.

At a safe distance they stopped and surveyed the tower, which was speedily a mass of flame from basement to roof.

In a very few minutes, so fierce was the blaze, and to such a height did the flames rise, the country was illuminated for miles around.

Then, suddenly, a terrific explosion was heard, and the blazing wood, as well as masses of stone, was hurled in every direction.

The Round Tower had been destroyed, and the men greeted the fact with loud cheers.

Many persons besides our hero and his companions saw the fire, though they were a mile or two away.

There was one man who stood on the summit of Giant Hill, which was distant some three miles from the tower, and looked down on the burning pile.

That man was Rochester.

Many a bitter imprecation left his lips as he watched the flames, and many a vow of vengeance did he take.

With what result?   We shall see.

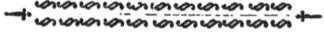

CHAPTER XXII.

OF THE PLOT FORMED BY VALLANCE—OF SILVERBELL'S COUNTERPLOT, AND HOW IT WAS BROUGHT TO A SUCCESSFUL TERMINATION.

THE reader will remember the bargain made between Rochester and Vallance with respect to Mistress Dennison.

But whether Rochester really believed that Vallance would make the attempt to murder her cannot be said.

Vallance, however, was well aware of the fact that, if he succeeded, Rochester would have no hesitation in paying him the promised money, so he at once set to work.

The result of his deliberations was, that he sent for a man of the name of Glenny, an individual who, on many occasions, had been of service to him.

He was a rather short, clean-shaven man of about forty, sharp, active and cunning in the extreme. And, what is more, he was an excellent hand at disguises.

Vallance quickly gave Glenny particulars of what he was to do.

He was to disguise himself as a woman, and keep observation on the White Tower, from the river and elsewhere.

If he saw Mistress Dennison leave the mansion, he was to follow her, as it was important to ascertain whether she visited friends.

Day after day did Glenny watch the tower, but with no result.

Mistress Dennison did not leave it, nor did the servants for any length of time.

One night—the fourth after the successful attack on and total destruction of the Round Tower at Wycombe —Glenny was, as usual, at his post on the river, still disguised as a woman.

He had hired one of the large wherries which plied up and down the river for the carriage of provisions, and from which food or wine could be obtained day or night.

Suddenly a boat drew up alongside of him, and a waterman asked for a bottle of wine.

Glenny replied that he had sold all he had possessed, whereat, a man in the bows closely questioned him as to what he had.

Then, reseating himself, he told the waterman to pull up the river and land him at the next steps.

This was done, and the waterman, being paid, pulled away.

"So," muttered the man as he drew his cloak about him, "I smell a rat sure enough. There can be no mistake. I had a good view of him this time, and I am as certain that he is James Glenny as that my name is Silverbell. My time, fortunately, is not so precious as it was a few days ago.

"I will at once repair to the White Tower; though it is a question whether I shall see its mistress."

A few minutes' walk brought him to the entrance to the tower.

Just as he reached the ponderous door, a servant opened it.

"Sir," she said, "whom do you seek?"

"I seek an interview with Mistress Dennison," was the reply.

The servant shook her head.

"It cannot be," she said. "My mistress interviews no one. If you have any business with her, a letter—"

"One moment," interrupted Silverbell. "Take this to her."

And he handed her a signet ring.

The woman, having carefully closed the door, took the ring to her mistress.

Mistress Dennison uttered a cry of astonishment the moment she beheld it.

"Who can this man be?" she said. "This ring was presented to Master Le Frere by my husband just after our marriage."

"Shall I admit him, or inform him that the hour is too late for an interview?"

"Admit him by all means."

Another few minutes, and Silverbell stood before Mistress Dennison, to whom he bowed in his most ceremonious manner.

Mistress Dennison returned his salutation, while she scanned him closely.

"Tell me, sir," she said, "are you not the bearer of a message from Master Le Frere?"

"Nay," replied Silverbell; "Master Le Frere died long ago in my presence, and, among other things, he gave me that ring."

"Dead?" whispered Mistress Dennison. "Truly your news grieves me beyond expression. No wonder then I have not heard from him for so long. But you—tell me who you are."

"Am I, then, so wonderfully changed? Can you not recognise he who used to be continually at the king's side?"

"Ah! Silverbell! Yes, yes, it is!" cried Mistress Dennison, as she ran forward and clasped Silverbell's hands; "yes, indeed, now I recognise you. But you are most certainly greatly changed."

"You are, of course, aware that for some time I have been closely associated with Jack Straw; and, for the sake of the people (who have now obtained nearly all they asked for), we have undergone many hardships. I do not wonder that I am altered; but I did not think the alteration was so great, that one who used to call me friend failed to recognise me.

"But you must have already thought that something of great importance brings me here.

"Such is the case. Last night, I was proceeding down the river, when I saw someone in a wherry opposite this tower, and thought I recognised him.

"But delay then, to make certain, was not possible, and so to-night I came past the same spot.

"I saw that I was correct. The man, who is disguised as a woman, is a thorough scoundrel, and for a long time has been in the pay of one Vallance, who lives near the Oxford road.

"Now this Vallance is in the pay of Rochester. He it is, I believe, who procures the drugs Rochester might require in his nefarious practices. When I remember what passed between you and Rochester, I cannot help thinking that there is a conspiracy on foot against you."

"I cannot doubt it, and I thank you from the bottom of my heart for thus warning me."

"I will assist you in foiling whatever plans they may have formed against you."

"A thousand thanks," replied Mistress Dennison fervently; "you above all others, I well know, are capable of meeting plot with plot. But, would it not be as well to remain here for the present?"

"It would. If you will let one of your servants convey a note to Jack Straw, that will prevent any uneasiness on the part of my friends."

"Writing materials shall at once be placed before you, and the note shall be taken direct."

The first thing, after writing the note, that Silverbell did, was to set a servant on the watch at the very top of the tower, but in such a position that he would not be observed.

The wherry, however, when morning dawned, had disappeared.

On the following evening, Silverbell, cleverly disguised as a woman-servant, walked for some considerable time in the grounds, as if attending to the various plants, and he took care that he should be distinctly seen in all parts.

Then, just as darkness was coming on, he left the tower, and made his way in the direction of a small hostelry, half-a-mile distant.

His plan had been entirely successful, for he had no sooner entered the hostelry than a man followed.

A side glance convinced him that the man was Glenny.

Yes, he had now cast aside his woman's disguise, and appeared as a well-to-do citizen.

Very glad was Silverbell that no customers were present.

He felt certain that Glenny had followed him for a purpose, and he was correct.

After one or two introductory remarks of a commonplace character, Glenny persisted in paying for Silverbell's wine, and, shortly afterwards, he expressed his admiration as to his appearance; whereat, Silverbell, who imitated the voice of a woman to perfection, pretended to be mightily pleased.

"Ho, ho!" thought Glenny; "here we have a woman from whom, without difficulty, I can obtain any information."

When another bottle of wine had been called for, Glenny said—

"And what is your name? For, by my faith, an you have no objection, I will see you again and again."

"Mary Fallows," replied Silverbell. "And pleased should I be to see you, again. But, alas! I am no longer young."

"What matters that? I am older than you. The fact is, Mary," he added, in confidential tones, "I have just retired from my business—that of a mercer—and am looking out for a decent woman for my wife. Have you been long in service?"

"Not in London. For years I have been in the country. Last I was at Stafford, but my mistress died, and I entered the service of a lady close here—Mistress Dennison, of the White Tower. Mayhap you have served her?"

"Nay, my business was too far citywards. Is she a good mistress?"

"Nay," replied "Mary," contemptuously, "I like her not. She is so secret in everything, and does not treat her servants well."

"Good!" thought Glenny. "By the Virgin! I am in luck's way. I could not have got hold of a better person."

"Mary" continued—

"Why, you see, it is all work and no amusement; for Mistress Dennison is so suspicious, that she will not allow our friends to visit us. More, she will not allow a pedlar to stand at the door. Ho, ho! she little dreams what is done under her very nose. I often smuggle a friend in."

"Good, good!" said Glenny; "and why shouldn't you? Ah, I am the one to amuse you—at least, I and a friend I could bring with me. He is an old man, it is true; but, nevertheless, he is very clever. His tricks are numerous."

"And you could bring him?"

"Easily."

"When?" asked Mary, eagerly.

"Any time you think proper."

"To-morrow night?"

"Ay, to-morrow night. But then,

perhaps, you could not smuggle *both* of us in?"

"I could, without doubt."

"But the other servants?"

"Mistress Dennison keeps but two more now—a man and a woman. But I am the chief, and they would do exactly as I told them. You need have no fear; they are quite as eager to be entertained as am I."

"To-morrow night, then, Mary, I will bring my friend. At what time?"

"Say at ten of the clock."

"Good. And at what part of the tower shall we present ourselves?"

"The river-side. You will see a little archway at the top of the stone steps. The door there leads into the grounds, and once past that, there will be no difficulty."

"Be sure I will be there."

"I will try and find you a good bottle of wine."

"Yes, do; my friend is fond of good wine. But will you not partake of another? Fear not, I have plenty of money."

"Nay, not now. You see, when I get back, my mistress might send for me; so it will be as well if I am able to keep steady on my feet."

"Exactly," replied Glenny.

In another moment or two they left the hostelry, and Glenny did not leave "foolish Mary," as he considered her, until they were close to the White Tower.

Then he made his way to the river, and to where he had left his boat.

Crossing the water, he went with all speed towards the Oxford road.

And many and many a chuckle left his lips as he considered how magnificently he had hoodwinked "the servant."

Vallance, he was certain, would be delighted with him, and would not hesitate when he asked him for an "advance."

He would not have chuckled so merrily, had he been able to see Mary a few moments after he had left her.

Silverbell, having taken off his disguise, informed Mistress Dennison of all that had taken place, and they then proceeded to arrange for the following night.

The servants were already acquainted with the fact that a plot was on foot against their mistress, and they were only too anxious to render any assistance to her in their power.

* * * *

On the following night, almost exactly at ten, Glenny and his friend—who, of course, was no other than Vallance—were at the steps.

"It is a dark night," said Glenny, "and it is certain we shall not be seen as we are smuggled in."

"I trust we shall not be kept here long."

"Nay, fear not, she— Hist! I hear footsteps."

He was right.

Nearer and nearer they came, and, in a few moments the door was unfastened, and Mary appeared.

Despite the darkness she carried no light.

"Follow quietly," she whispered, "for my mistress is in her bedchamber, which faces the grounds here. But it is unfortunate we arranged for to-night."

"Why?"

"My fellow-servants are absent, and will not return until to-morrow."

"That is a pity. But still it is of little importance. We can pass our time with you. The fact is, Mary," he whispered, "I have taken a strong fancy to you."

"Flatterer!"

"Nay, nay; I mean what I say. I swear it."

"Come then—keep close to me."

Soon they were in the kitchen, and Mary informed them that they were safe.

"And," she added, "even if I heard my mistress coming down—which she often does— you would be all right in here."

And she opened an opposite door showing them the wood cellar.

Vallance, as may be supposed, scanned Mary closely.

He had not the faintest suspicion that anything was wrong.

Silverbell acted to perfection the character he represented.

Also, he was exceedingly well disguised, and the voice he assumed could not possibly have been found fault with by anyone as being too masculine for a woman.

Vallance spoke but little, the reason being that all his thoughts were concentrated upon the tragedy he had come there to perpetrate.

But, when wines were placed on the table, he roused himself, and forced a smile upon his face.

Mary now placed three goblets upon the table and filled each.

Vallance and Glenny quickly discovered that the wine was of the finest, and soon swallowed the whole.

Mary, however, left half of hers.

"By the Virgin!" said Glenny, "this wine is splendid. Would that you had more."

"Fear it not," laughed Mary, "I will soon get more. I always have possession of the keys, and my mistress never makes enquiries as to the state of the cellar. At least, she has not done so lately."

"But she *has* made enquiry?"

"She did once."

"And was any missing?"

"Six of the choicest bottles."

"And how did you get out of it?"

"I said that they had been placed on the table in the wine cellar, and that the rats knocked them down. In order to give colour to that, I showed her where it had been spilt. She thought she saw wine, but it was only some water in which strong herbs had been stewed."

"Ho! ho!" grinned Glenny, "truly you *are* clever, Mary."

"Yes," thought Silverbell, "you will consider me *clever* indeed directly."

Aloud he said—

"I will get another bottle. Make no noise while I am gone."

"Be quick," said Glenny.

Mary tripped out of the kitchen, and at once went to another room.

Opening a door here, Silverbell passed into the wood cellar, and approached the opposite door.

He was just in time.

Through the keyhole he saw Vallance empty part of the contents of a phial into his (Silverbell's) goblet.

Then Glenny said—

"What will be the effect?"

"Death!" was the reply."

"But why kill her?"

"The dead will not speak. Suppose I only rendered her unconscious? When she recovered she would remember all, and describe us."

"Ay, true. By all means kill her. The river is close handy, and we can place her in it. When the other servants return and find their mistress murdered and the house robbed, they will, of course, conclude that Mary is the guilty person. Ho, ho! the notion is indeed a good one."

Silverbell returned with the wine and, after some little pleasantry, in which Vallance joined, filled up the two goblets.

Just as he had placed the bottle on the table, he suddenly said—

"Hist! I hear footsteps. Quick! into the cellar with you."

Vallance and Glenny started up at once, and darted into the cellar.

The moment they did so, Silverbell turned his back towards them.

Instantly he swallowed half the contents of Glenny's goblet and refilled it with what was in his own— the wine which had been poisoned.

Then he poured more wine into his own and crept to the door, where he remained some few moments.

Then, returning, he opened the cellar door.

"All is well," he said; "she has not come down. And yet I made sure I heard footsteps."

"Is she above?" asked Vallance.

"Yes, fast asleep, I doubt not; so there is no danger. Here is your healths."

And Silverbell drained his goblet.

Almost immediately afterwards he fell into a chair; then suddenly he started up, and the next instant dropped like a log on the floor.

"All is clear now," said Vallance; "she will die where she is. But no time must be lost. Do you remain where you are while I ascend."

Taking a lantern, he left the kitchen.

Glenny at once swallowed the contents of his goblet, and stood beside the door.

But it was only for the space of a few seconds.

He suddenly placed his hand to his heart, and staggered back to the table, where his hands wandered to his throat.

His appearance was that of a man in the throes of suffocation.

Then again he staggered to the door as if about to shriek for help.

Silverbell, who had been watching him, started up, and, seizing him by the back of the neck, sent him with a crash to the ground.

He did not afterwards move—a proof positive that the poison Vallance had used was a most deadly one.

Then Silverbell prepared to ascend.

Meanwhile, Vallance had cautiously made his way to the first floor of the tower, and made an examination of each room.

He was not only thinking of murder, but plunder also, and he opened his eyes very wide indeed as he saw that each room contained articles of great value.

At the extreme end of the landing was a door, shaded by curtains.

This, he had no doubt, was Mistress Dennison's bedchamber, and he was correct.

Carefully he tried the door, and, finding it unlocked, pushed it open.

A tiny taper burned upon the mantel, an.) by its light he was enabled to see a sleeping figure—at least, so it looked to him—upon the bed.

He placed his hand within his breast, took out a long, thin dagger—a weapon which was afterwards known as a stiletto, from the fact that its inventor was an Italian named Francisco Stiletti—and approached the bed.

Without the slightest hesitation, he raised his hand, and brought the weapon down with all the force he could command.

He was about to bring it down again, when he suddenly paused and bent over the bed.

An instant he looked, and then, with a sharp cry, he drew back the bedclothes.

He at once saw that a trick had been played off against him.

The figure in the bed was not a human being, but a cleverly constructed dummy.

The old villain turned and rushed to the door.

No doubt he was about to call Glenny.

But, before he could reach it, a figure stood upon the threshold—sword in hand.

Back fell the old man—back until he touched the bed.

Then he yelled—

"Silverbell!"

"Yes," was the reply, "after all this time, wretch, we once more come face to face. Yes, I am indeed Silverbell—once the king's jester—and but a little while ago was downstairs. I assumed the character of a woman, and you must admit that I did so successfully."

Plainly enough now, Vallance was beginning to see the way in which he had been checkmated, and a deep groan escaped his lips.

In the very act of slaying, as he had thought, Mistress Dennison, he had been caught.

Being caught red-handed, as it were, what could he say?

Silverbell, in calm tones, continued—

"Under what circumstances we last met I need not say, since there is a lady present, whose blood would almost turn to ice did I give the particulars of the barbarous crime you, in conjunction with others, committed."

As he spoke Mistress Dennison came to the door.

Deathly pale she was, it is true, but that is not to be wondered at, for she was thinking of what *might* have happened had it not been for Silverbell.

But she betrayed no agitation, nor did the servants who were behind her.

Mistress Dennison had wisely decided to leave everything in Silverbell's hands, including Vallance's punishment.

She had resolved that, if the old murderer made an appeal for mercy to her, she would turn a deaf ear to him.

"I need not tell you," said Silverbell, "how I discovered the plot against the life of Mistress Dennison, who is, and has long been, my friend."

"The traitor!" hissed Vallance—"Glenny proved a traitor!"

"You are very much mistaken," replied Silverbell. "Glenny was no traitor to you. You would say so if you saw him at this moment, for he is lying dead in the kitchen."

"Dead!"

"Yes, dead. When I hastily put both of you in the cellar, I changed the goblets, and what you intended for me he drank. You may think, Master Vallance, that it is my intention to place you in the hands of the law. If you *do* so think, throw such an idea to the winds."

"What would you do?" asked Vallance, in hoarse, almost inarticulate tones.

"You will see in a moment. Look here."

He beckoned to the man-servant, who entered the room carrying writing materials.

These Silverbell placed on the table.

"First," he said, "throw down that weapon."

Vallance hesitated.

Might he not want it in an attempt to escape?

But, quickly coming to the conclusion that escape was hopeless, and that perhaps it would be better if he obeyed Silverbell, whom he knew but too well as a stern and most determined man, he threw the dagger down, and it was picked up by the servant.

"Sit down now," continued Silverbell, "and write what is written upon this."

And taking a piece of parchment from his cloak, he held it up and read—

"I, Master Vallance, of the Oxford road, give and bequeath all my property to Silverbell, formerly the king's jester, on condition that he distributes the whole among the poor of London.

"As witness my hand," &c., &c.

"No," yelled Vallance—"never!"

"Write," thundered Silverbell, "or I swear I will send this sword through your body!"

"But if—if I write as you say, shall I be at liberty to depart?"

"Ask no questions, but write."

Vallance saw that there was absolutely no help for it, and so, seating himself, he copied what Silverbell had read.

The document was then witnessed by Mistress Dennison and her servants.

This, of course, made it perfectly legal.

Silverbell, having taken possession of it, said—

"You asked me whether, having written this, you would be at liberty to go. My answer to that is, *no!* But here is another piece of parchment. Now write upon that as I dictate, and be careful to make no mistakes."

Vallance again took up the pen, and Silverbell dictated what he was to write.

When it was complete, it was as follows—

"To Lord Rochester.

"My Lord,—Mistress Dennison has died by my hand. I pray you visit me at ten of the clock to-morrow (Thursday) night, when I will place all the particulars before you."

This Silverbell compelled him to sign in full.

Vallance, as may easily be supposed, was now in a terrible state, and great beads of perspiration stood out upon his face.

It is questionable whether he could have written any more.

After a short pause, Silverbell said—

"Now produce that phial containing the poison."

"Oh, let me go—let me go," whined Vallance. "I entreat you let me go! Mistress Dennison, intercede for me. It was but the love of money which induced—"

"Silence!" interrupted Silverbell. "Can you not see, by a single glance at the lady whom you intended to murder, that any appeal to her will be in vain? Quick! produce the phial."

Vallance placed it upon the table.

Then, from the folds of his cloak, Silverbell took three articles.

The first was a goblet, the second a small bottle of wine, and the third was —a long and strong coil of cord.

These he placed on the table.

Taking up the wine Silverbell half filled the goblet; then he poured into it the whole of the contents of the phial.

And now Vallance saw what was intended, and, with a wild cry, he threw himself upon his knees, and uplifted his hands.

"Mercy!" he cried, "have mercy upon me! Think of my great age."

His appeal fell upon ears that were deaf.

Mistress Dennison was entirely unmoved.

"You will drink the contents of this goblet," said Silverbell. "Have mercy, say you? Have mercy because of your great age? When you planned a foul murder, did you think of your age? Did you think of the age, or the sex, of the person you were about to murder? I repeat—drink this. But there is an alternative."

"Ha!" cried Vallance, eagerly; "that is?"

"This rope. You will drink that poison, or be hanged by this rope. There is no getting away from one or the other. I have sworn it, and, by the heaven above, I will keep my oath!"

The moment was indeed a terrible one, and most trying to Mistress Dennison, who, more than once, felt faint.

For a few seconds, Vallance looked helplessly around the chamber, and at Silverbell's stern face.

Then, suddenly uttering a most awful oath, he seized upon the goblet, drained the contents, and hurled the vessel at Silverbell's face.

Silverbell, however, was too active, for putting up his hands, he caught it.

Again and again did Vallance utter the most terrible oaths and imprecations, but at last he paused.

Acute pains seized him, and he began to stagger backward and forward.

Finally he fell in a heap almost at Silverbell's feet, and not once afterwards did he move.

But no stir was made until fully five minutes had passed, nor was a single word uttered.

Then Silverbell turned Vallance over.

"He is dead," he said, "and Rochester has lost one of his chief allies. But that is not all. This letter will have the effect of bringing Rochester to the house at the Oxford road. And then is the chance for Jack Straw to have a reckoning with him. Mistress Dennison, I ask you to be present."

"Yes, yes; I will be there."

"There will be no poison. There will be a fair fight. But you look faint, and I wonder not at it. Come—let me take you to your chamber below. Presently your servant and I will dispose of the body of yonder murderer and that of his confederate."

* * * *

On the following morning, Silverbell was preparing for departure.

Jack was at St. James', and thither he was about to repair.

He knew that the news he had for him—that the opportunity had come for an uninterrupted reckoning with Rochester—would fill our hero's heart with delight; though he was well aware that he would have to keep the news from Nellie, and from Lord and Lady Linsay.

Entering the pretty withdrawing room, Silverbell found Mistress Dennison standing thoughtfully at one of the windows.

Turning, she welcomed the once popular jester with great warmth.

"I am now about to go to Jack Straw," said Silverbell, "and anon I will send you a message as to the hour you will join us."

"Must you go at once?"

"Ay, 'tis important that I should join Jack Straw as quickly as possible. And the plans which must be drawn up will prevent my seeing you for many hours. I would it were otherwise."

Mistress Dennison made no reply.

Silverbell, after a brief pause, continued—

"Do you know why I would it were otherwise?"

No answer.

"It is because," continued Silverbell, in low and tremulous tones, "that, in the brief space I have been here, I have learned to love you. There can be no harm in telling you this, though I am well aware that it would be impossible for a lady of your position to return the love of a poor jester."

"No, no!" said Mistress Dennison, "it would not be impossible."

"Can it be," said Silverbell, in joyous tones, "that you love me?"

"Yes," replied Mistress Dennison, without hesitation; "I do love you."

"Do you feel that that love would grow and grow, until at last— But no, it cannot be. You have wealth, I have none, or very little."

"I have plenty for both. If I marry you, what I have would be yours."

" *Will* you marry me ? "

"Whenever you ask me ; for I feel that with you I could be happy. With you, once more, the world may be bright, and you may help to disperse the dark clouds which for so long have surrounded me."

" I would do all in my power," replied Silverbell, fervently, as he drew Mistress Dennison to him and kissed her. "No stone would I leave unturned to make you happy."

" I am sure of it."

" But complete happiness can never be yours while Rochester lives. Depend upon it, his time now is very short. Into the trap we shall lay he will certainly fall, and we will take care that he does not get out again."

"He does not deserve to die the death of a gentleman."

"Most true."

"But he may refuse to fight."

"He will be *compelled* to fight. But wait—wait patiently, and you will see. And now I will bid you adieu, and heaven knows, I quit your side with a light and happy heart. What you have said, so far alters my arrangements, that I will return to you in two or three hours."

CHAPTER XXIII.

OF HOW ROCHESTER WALKED INTO THE TRAP SET FOR HIM—OF THE FIGHT BETWEEN HIM AND JACK STRAW, AND THE RESULT.

"BEATEN ! Beaten at all points ! My bitter curse on them ! "

Thus hissed a man seated on a stool outside a small and pretty hostelry at Uxbridge.

The host little thought, as he brought a bottle of wine to the dust-covered traveller, that he was serving "the great Rochester."

Beside his lordship stood the horse he had ridden.

The unfortunate animal looked ready to drop.

Hours upon hours he had been travelling, and the spur had been freely used.

It did not require a second glance at the animal's sides to see this.

"And now," muttered Rochester, "I am without money. Fool that I was, not to have come straight to London after the attack on the tower, instead of staying at Balcombe, and playing and playing until nearly every groat had gone.

"And the delay, of course, has allowed Jack Straw to prepare his plans in London, for he will endeavour to have his revenge for the abduction of the girl.

"No money here though. Piles of it in London. What I am— But ha ! I have it."

Placing his hand within his doublet, he took out of a secret pocket a very beautiful heart of gold, studded with rare and costly diamonds.

"On this I can obtain a fair sum," he thought. "I wonder if there is a Jew hereabouts ? But why seek a Jew ? No doubt the host has money by him."

Thereupon he called him.

" Master Host," said Rochester, "you must know that I am a traveller, who has unfortunately run through all his money.

"Now, I desire to push on to London, which I want to reach by nightfall. But I cannot proceed penniless, and so I want to raise money on this jewel."

And he showed the host the heart.

The host at once saw it was a valuable trinket.

Then he looked hard into Rochester's face.

"I can read your thoughts," said Rochester ; "but, if you fancy that I am a robber, you are in error."

"Nay, I did not so think," replied the host. " I was wondering whether you were aware of the value."

"Oh, yes ; perfectly, as I should be, seeing that I purchased it. Is there a Jew, or a money-lender of any kind hereabouts ? "

"Not that I am aware of ; but I

have a guest upstairs who, I fancy, would lend money on it. He belongs to London."

"Let me see him."

"Nay, that would be impossible, for he put up here this morning on condition that I would see he was not disturbed. But I will take the article to him."

"Ay, do."

"Shall I mention the amount you demand?"

"Nay, see what he will advance."

Upstairs went the host, the trinket in his hand; and, having knocked upon one of the doors, he was directed to enter.

There, at the edge of the bed, and but partially dressed, was no less a person than Abel Harkwell.

Yes, he had left Strand Lane that morning on business at Uxbridge, and having transacted it, he put up at the hostelry for a long rest.

The host explained his errand, and handed Harkwell the heart.

"A pretty toy," said Harkwell. "Tell the gentleman that I will advance him two hundred crowns, and will give him my address in London, so that, by simply paying the interest, he may recover the jewel."

The moment the host had withdrawn, Harkwell darted to the window, and peered out.

It was but for a moment, and he distinctly saw the traveller's face.

"By Heaven!" he muttered, "it is Rochester! How comes he here? Ho! ho! unless I am much mistaken, I will serve him a pretty trick. This jewel shall be mine without payment. He shall have the money, of course, but not for long."

The host quickly returned, and said that the gentleman was content with the amount, on the condition that he could recover the jewel in the course of a day or two.

Thereupon Harkwell picked up a bag, and counted out gold and silver to the amount stated.

Then he wrote down and handed to the host this false address—

"HENRY WESTON,
"Money Changer,
"LOMBARD STREET."

This, and the money, the host took to Rochester, who then called for another goblet of wine.

Harkwell sat down, and hastily wrote some words upon a slip of parchment, and this he placed in his bag.

Then he fully attired himself, and watched at the window until Rochester had mounted and ridden away.

He then called for his horse, and, after a short delay, rode off in the same direction as Rochester.

He soon came in sight of his lordship, who was proceeding very slowly, for neither whip nor spur had now any effect on the tired animal.

Five miles were traversed, and darkness had come on.

Another hostelry was reached, and Rochester did exactly as Harkwell expected, for he drew up, and dismounted.

Not a soul was about, and Rochester entered the hostelry.

At once Harkwell paused, dismounted, and, taking the slip of parchment from the bag, stole silently, yet quickly, to the hostelry.

Rochester he saw in conversation with the host.

Without a moment's hesitation, Harkwell crept up to the horse, took out his dagger, and cut the strap which held to the saddle a leathern bag, into which he had seen Rochester place the two hundred crowns.

Then to the saddle he affixed the parchment, and, darting back to his horse, remounted, and rode at full speed across the fields.

Meanwhile, Rochester had been talking to the host as to a fresh horse.

The latter—not knowing who his visitor was, and thinking, of course, that he was quite an ordinary person—agreed to supply him with a fresh horse, if a deposit were left.

Rochester consented to this, and went without to get the amount required.

He at once saw that the bag had disappeared, and a great cry left his lips.

The host, almost startled out of his wits, rushed to the door, upsetting as he did so a barrel containing wine.

"Robbers!" cried Rochester. "During the few moments I have been speaking with you robbers have been here, and have stolen the money—two hundred crowns—which was attached to my saddle."

"The Virgin guard us! You don't say so?"

"But I *do* say so. I tell you— But what is this?"

He took the slip of parchment from the saddle, and, entering the hostelry, read what was written upon it.

It was as follows—

"My LORD OF ROCHESTER,—

"I advanced you two hundred crowns on the pretty diamond heart—which, by the way, I will not fail to hand to the girl of *my* heart—but being, as you know, a great friend of yours, and thinking that you would be much inconvenienced by so much money, I have relieved you of it.

"Adieu, my lord. I trust that we shall remain, as ever, very firm friends.

"Your servant,

"ABEL HARKWELL."

Rochester, with a fearful oath, thrust the parchment into his bosom.

"One of these days," he hissed, "I will thrust this down his throat! Perdition! To be the victim of a man like this!"

After a long pause, he took a ring from his finger.

"Look," he said to the host, "this, as you see, is worth more than *one* horse. Let me have the animal, and I will leave this with you. You will also have my steed."

"It shall be as you wish," replied the host; "but I am sorry you have lost your money."

"No matter. I have plenty more in London. I shall be inconvenienced only until I get there."

The host quickly produced the horse, which was very fresh, and Rochester, mounting him, rode away at a gallop in the direction of London, the west-end of which he reached in a little over an hour.

He immediately made his way to his own house, where he terrified the servants by the appalling oaths he uttered.

When they considered he had cooled down a little, he was informed that a lad desired to speak with him.

Rochester directed him to be brought before him.

He was a smartly attired, sharp boy, of about fourteen.

"Well," frowned Rochester, "whence come you?"

"From the Oxford road, your lordship."

"Ha! From whom there?"

"Master Vallance."

"Ay, ay. Well?"

"He bade me place this in your hands only, and I have long waited to do so."

"Good. Hand it to me."

The boy handed him a letter.

It was the document Silverbell had forced Vallance to write.

As Rochester read it, a grim smile rested upon his features.

"Soh!" he thought, "he *has* succeeded! Good—good. One whom I certainly feared is removed. How did he accomplish it, I wonder? Well, I shall learn that to-night. Go there! Ay, that will I.

"Say, lad," he said, aloud, "that I will be at the house at the hour named, and if you are there when I arrive, I will present you with a gold piece."

The lad thanked him and departed.

He walked quite a mile in the direction of the Oxford road, but then, suddenly turning, he went back in quite another direction to St. James'.

He ran the whole way to the house in which Lord Linsay was living, and he was at once conducted to Jack.

With Jack was Silverbell, Basil, and Harkwell, who had arrived not long before, and who, of course, had been entertaining them with the account of how he had advanced Rochester the money, and then relieved him of it.

The boy delivered the message, whereat the four were overjoyed.

"Listen now, Harkwell," said Jack. "Proceed to Strand Lane, get half-a-dozen of your picked men, and then go on with all speed to the Oxford road.

"There Silverbell will join you, and conduct you to Vallance's house."

"I shall be there within an hour," replied Harkwell, who then left the house.

Soon after, Silverbell set out for the White Tower.

:"SEE HERE,' SAID JACK, 'HERE IS ANOTHER TREE WHICH HAS BEEN STRUCK BY LIGHTNING!'"

It was arranged that he should conduct Mistress Dennison to the Oxford road.

Then, having made a reasonable excuse, Jack and Basil procured their horses, and rode on as fast as possible to Vallance's house.

They found it in darkness, of course, and every door was securely fastened.

"We must force an entrance by the window," said Jack. "Fortunately there is no one about, and therefore it is not likely we shall be observed. Hold my horse while I stand upon the saddle."

In this way he easily reached the first window, and, with the assistance of his dagger, forced it open.

Then, getting in, he kindled a light, and descending the stairs, opened the door.

"Now," he said, "we must find a place for our horses, for, if they were seen by Rochester, he would probably be suspicious. See! let us place them in yonder field. When the others come up, they can be added."

Accordingly the horses were placed in a field at some considerable distance from the house, which Jack and Basil then entered.

After a short search, they found a couple of large lanterns, as well as a few links and tapers.

Lighting the former, they made an examination of the house.

Never in all their lives had they beheld a place so peculiarly constructed.

Every chamber, too, was filled with a miscellaneous collection of articles.

One would have fancied, to look at the different things, that Vallance was a collector of curiosities.

Such, however, was not the case.

He was simply a man who accepted what he could get, for the "services" he rendered certain persons.

If money were not forthcoming, and he thought there was a possibility of his never getting it, he would take goods.

In this way, his house had been crammed with things, all of them being of value.

One of the rooms at the top was found to be locked, and Jack, with Basil's assistance, forced the door.

They found themselves in a small chamber, heavily draped in black.

The floor was covered with thick rugs, so that there should be no sound of footsteps.

On the right was a lofty, oaken cabinet, elaborately fitted with massive brass.

An ebony table occupied the centre of this extraordinary chamber, and upon it lay many costly articles of jewellery, as well as letters and other documents.

On the left was another, but a smaller cabinet, and beside that what looked like a long box.

This, like the walls, was also heavily draped with black.

Jack pulled off the drapery, and both were horrified to find that it concealed a coffin.

On the top, on a plate of silver, were the words, roughly though distinctly written—

"ELIZABETH PENNING,

"*Aged thirty years.*"

"In heaven's name!" said Basil, starting back, "what can this mean?"

"I think it is plain enough," replied Jack. "There is a body within that."

So saying, he lifted the lid.

There, sure enough, was the body of a woman.

It was in a mummified state, and had evidently been "preserved."

At the foot was a small roll of parchment.

Jack took this up and read—

"I, who have for so long been known as Vallance, declare this to be the body of my wife.

"She disobeyed me, and died by my hand. I leave this in the event of anything happening to me, and request the finder to burn coffin and body."

"The monster!" said Jack.

Basil was too astonished and horrified to make any reply.

"Well," continued Jack, "the villain met a well-deserved end. So, then, his name was really Penning. In what way did she disobey him, I wonder?"

He searched among the papers on the table, but nothing was found which could throw any light on the matter.

The reader, however, may be interested with the facts, which are as follows—

Many years before we introduced him, Vallance (who then called himself an apothecary, as well as an embalmer to the Court) had a house close to Threadneedle Street ; and, even at that time, he received large sums of money for the share he took in the commission of crimes.

But so secret was he, that no one suspected what a scoundrel he was.

The City merchants thought him somewhat eccentric in his movements, but they had no idea whatever that he was otherwise than what he represented himself to be—namely, an apothecary.

He was generally considered to be a quiet, inoffensive man.

He attended a merchant of the name of Penning, and fell in love with the daughter—Elizabeth.

After a time he proposed for her hand and was accepted, the marriage taking place soon afterwards.

Vallance behaved remarkably well towards his wife while the father lived ; for he, being very fond of his daughter, was continually at the house.

Suddenly he fell ill.

Experienced physicians were summoned, but their talents were exercised in vain.

The old man died within six days, and neither of the physicians was able to tell the nature of his disease.

Then it was that Elizabeth found out what sort of a man her husband really was, for she had discovered that he had poisoned her father.

She fled in terror, and was absent for months.

But Vallance, fearing she might divulge what she had discovered, found her out and forced her to return. Afterwards he locked her in one of the rooms.

There, for over a twelvemonth, she remained, never seeing a soul but her husband, though she was well aware of the fact that many people came to the house, and always at night.

At last, Elizabeth, with the aid of a piece of iron she removed from a box, contrived to get out of the room.

Resolved once more to fly, she descended the stairs.

She found her husband in conversation with a man, and learned that he was receiving payment for poisoning a lady of title.

She overheard all that passed between them, and made up her mind to place the conversation before the proper authorities.

But, alas ! she did not get the opportunity.

Vallance, fancying that he heard a noise without the house, suddenly opened the door.

There was no time for his wife to hide herself, and therefore they came face to face.

An instant afterwards she forfeited her life, for Vallance, with a yell of rage, plunged his dagger into her heart.

What his object was in embalming her cannot be said with certainty, but probably he derived some sort of savage satisfaction in occasionally looking upon the body.

The crime was never discovered.

Vallance gave it out that his wife was staying with friends in the country ; and, soon afterwards, he removed to the house near the Oxford road.

"Anon," said Jack, "we will give the body decent interment."

"Let us see what is in these cabinets," said Basil.

After some difficulty they succeeded in forcing them, and found several boxes and bags filled with money.

"For Silverbell," said Jack, "to give to the poor. But, hark ! they have arrived. Let us be quick, for the time when Rochester will be here is rapidly approaching."

Before the house they found Harkwell with the six men, and Silverbell with Mistress Dennison.

The whole of the horses were taken to the field, and then all entered the house.

*   *   *   *

At about half-past nine, Rochester set out for the Oxford road.

He had changed his travel-stained garments, and was now attired in a very handsome costume, which, however, he concealed, as he proceeded, with a long, but light cloak.

He rode slowly, for not only had he much to think of that had passed of late, but also of the future ; and he was also considering a plan in which he thought Vallance would be of assistance to him.

He carried with him a large sum of money, which he intended to hand over to Vallance.

When he reached the house, he knocked upon the door with his riding whip and dismounted.

After a short delay the door was opened by one of Harkwell's men.

He was in his shirt-sleeves, and appeared as if in the act of preparing a meal.

He bowed himself almost to the ground as Rochester presented himself.

His lordship fixed a penetrating glance upon him, but no suspicion that anything was wrong entered his head.

No doubt he considered that this man was one of the two or three poor wretches that Vallance occasionally employed.

"In what chamber is Master Vallance?" asked Rochester.

"He is below in the vaults at present, your lordship," replied the man. "He is engaged in perfecting a special preparation. Will your lordship wait for him, or shall I conduct you below?"

"My time is short. Conduct me below."

Again the man bowed profoundly, and, picking up a lantern, requested Rochester to follow him.

Accordingly, Rochester descended the narrow stairs leading to the vaults, of which there were four, each leading into another.

Three were small, but the fourth was a very large one.

This had contained a number of barrels and boxes, but Jack had had them removed.

Rochester, of course, expected that, his footsteps being heard, Vallance would have come forth to meet him.

As he did not, he asked, in haughty tones—

"Where, then, is Master Vallance?"

"*In his grave!*" thundered a voice.

Rochester, with a loud exclamation, started back, and snatched his blade from its scabbard.

At this instant, Jack made his appearance.

Behind him were two men holding links.

"Jack Straw!" ejaculated Rochester, his face turning deathly pale.

"Ay," said our hero "it is indeed Jack Straw, my Lord of Rochester. And here, you see, is *another* person with whom you are aquainted."

As he spoke, Mistress Dennison came slowly from one of the vaults.

She was followed by Silverbell and Basil.

Rochester uttered not one word.

He could only look from one to the other in utter bewilderment.

"No doubt," said Jack, "you would like to know how it is that we are within this house? I will tell you. Silverbell, here, discovered the plot hatched against Mistress Dennison, and he set himself to foil Vallance and the man in his employment.

"His plans were successful. Glenny, in Mistress Dennison's own house, partook of a poison intended for another; and Vallance was caught with a dagger in his hand, in Mistress Dennison's bedchamber.

"I need not tell you all that passed, for that would take up too much time. But I can tell you that Vallance was forced to sign a paper giving Silverbell all his property for distribution among the poor, and another requesting your attendance at this house.

"He was then given the choice of the manner in which he was to die. One way was by the poison he himself carried, and the other was by the rope.

"He chose the former, and died by his own hand.

"You, of course, by this time, know well why we have been at the trouble to get you here.

"But we do not intend to offer you poison, nor threaten you with the rope, which, however, is the proper way you should die, if but for one thing, and that, the murder of this lady's husband.

"Here, my lord, is a large vault. You will see that it has been well cleared, and that there is plenty of room for a duel to be fought."

"No," said Rochester, in hoarse tones, "I fight not in such a place as that, where, if I were successful, I should no doubt be murdered."

"That, of course, is intended as an

insult to all of us. But let me assure you that *we* do not pass our days and nights in the planning of murders and other crimes as bad. It is you who do that.

"You *will* fight, and in that vault, if you are wise; if you decline, it is our intention to gag and bind you, and, in the dead of the night. convey you to Tyburn, and there on one of the highest trees, hang you."

In such cold, deliberate tones did Jack say this, that Rochester fairly shuddered.

Most certainly he had been caught in a trap.

Was there any chance of escaping from it?

None—none whatever!

He recognised that fact in but a few seconds.

The man who had admitted him now stood at the head of the stairs, a cross-bow in his hand, and an arrow ready fitted to it.

"Is it to be expected that a man is able to fight properly under such circumstances?" asked Rochester, after a pause.

"I should say so," answered Jack. "No one will interfere with you."

"Why is Mistress Dennison here?"

"She is here to see the murderer of her husband fight *fairly*."

"I did not murder him."

"We will not argue about that. Enter the vault."

Rochester made no reply.

For some few moments he stood perfectly motionless, and apparently lost in thought.

Ay, and he had much to think of now.

Many and many a plan had he left undone; many and many a dastardly deed, which, if he could not attend to them, were certain to be discovered.

At last he said—

"In the event of my proving successful?"

"In that case," said Jack, "you will go free."

"You swear that?"

"Ay, I swear it. But let me tell you, my lord, that this is not to be a fight which, in the event of one or the other being wounded, comes to a termination. It is to be a battle to the death."

"And you repeat that, if I am successful, I may go."

"I repeat that I *swear* it; unless, indeed, you would choose to fight with any other here present?"

To this Rochester made no reply.

Rousing himself, he entered the vault.

And he saw around it six men, five of whom held aloft flaming links and drawn swords.

He at once recognised them as Harkwell and his men.

And now, more than ever, he saw how helpless he was.

Harkwell held in his hand a coil of rope, and Rochester knew that, what Jack had threatened would happen if he did not fight.

In a few moments, Jack and Rochester faced each other.

It was a pity that some celebrated painter was not present, for he could have produced one of the most extraordinary pictures the world had ever seen.

An immense vaulted chamber, lit by flaming links, held on high by grim-looking men, who stood with drawn swords against the wall.

On the left, against the door, stood Mistress Dennison, looking pale but firm and determined, and inwardly praying that, at last, vengeance would overtake the man who had brought misery and sorrow to many a score of families.

Beside her, Silverbell, in the well-known attitude he used to assume at Court.

Opposite him, leaning against the wall with folded arms, was Basil.

In the centre of the vault, both bare-headed, were Jack Straw and Rochester, sword in hand.

To complete the scene, the man in his shirt-sleeves, who had stolen down the stairs, was peering in, in a half-stooping attitude, eager to watch the fight.

Such was the picture that could have been painted. and which could have been called—"The last Meeting between Jack Straw and Rochester."

A pause of a few minutes, and the long and heavy blades crossed.

The fight was commenced slowly and guardedly on both sides; but soon.

each warmed to his work until the flashing weapons created a perfect din, and frequently emitted sparks.

There was then a pause, and it was seen that both were wounded, Jack in the wrist, and Rochester in the arm.

Not one word was uttered.

Every man present, indeed, seemed incapable of speech.

They stood like statues, and breathlessly watched the battle.

Not once did Mistress Dennison take her eyes off the combatants.

Eagerly she watched every movement.

It was, of course, impossible to tell who would be the victor, so determinedly did each fight, and yet so carefully.

A pause, and the battle was renewed, with greater determination than before.

Rochester, again and again tried to bring his blade down upon Jack's head.

But he found it impossible.

Jack turned aside every blow, often with such skill, that Harkwell, who had witnessed many a deadly duel, would have applauded had he dared.

At last, Rochester, making certain that his opportunity had arrived, made a thrust at Jack's throat.

But his blade was dashed aside, then lowered by a heavy blow, and, before Rochester could recover himself, Jack's sword passed completely through his heart.

It was one of the most deadly and yet fairest fights ever known.

"Thank heaven!" murmured Mistress Dennison, as she threw herself into Silverbell's arms, "the villain is no more."

"Ay," said Harkwell, who hastily examined him, "he is dead, sure enough, this time. Well, well, never before did my heart beat as it did while this fight was in progress. By the Blessed Virgin! it was a fight with a vengeance! Truly, 'Master Jack Straw, you can wield a blade with marvellous skill. But you are wounded."

This recalled Mistress Dennison to herself.

Tearing off a portion of her garment, she proceeded to bind our hero's wrist.

"It is of but little importance," said Jack. "I have often received many a worse wound than that. But I am anxious to leave this house. Will you, Harkwell, remain in charge for a few hours?"

"Two of my men shall remain. They are trustworthy. But as to the body of Rochester, will it not be as well to bury it in this vault?"

"By no means. To-morrow night we will place it in a large box, and send it to his house. The world must know for certain that the wretch is really dead."

"And in many places," added Silverbell, "there will be great rejoicing."

"But shall you not reveal how he died?" asked Basil,

"Yes," replied Jack. "I will visit the king and tell him all. Silverbel' and Mistress Dennison will accompany me, and bear witness that what I say is true."

Preparations for departure were now made, and soon all (with the exception of the two men left to guard the house) were on their way to St. James'.

It was long past midnight when Lord Linsay's house was reached.

Several servants were seen about the front, and it was soon ascertained that Lord and Lady Linsay and Nellie were in a state bordering on distraction, consequent on Jack's prolonged absence.

Had it not been for Dorothy, she would have left the house in search of him.

Jack quickly explained what had transpired, and loud were the expressions of astonishment and joy.

"It is my intention," added Jack, "to place the particulars before the king."

"Unless I am very much mistaken," said Lord Linsay, "the king will be pleased to hear that Rochester is no more. And the majority of those who, for certain reasons, have called him friend, will also rejoice. He was a terrible ruffian, and the world will never know a tenth part of the atrocious crimes he committed.

"Now I propose that, to celebrate the event, I order a banquet to be prepared. Let us not trouble about the time."

"I cannot join you," said Harkwell, "for I have most important business to attend to. Moreover," he whispered, "I could not allow these men to sit at your table. As you know, though faithful to me, they are none too honest."

"Then come here to-morrow," said Jack, "and you shall be amply paid for the services you have rendered. Nay, refuse me not. I insist upon your being paid, and your men as well."

Harkwell and his men now quitted the house; and, soon afterwards, a sumptuous repast was spread in the largest chamber, full justice being done to the good things placed upon the table.

*   *   *   *

On the following morning, Jack, accompanied by Silverbell, paid a visit to the king, by whom he was warmly received.

He, and the many nobles present, paid the greatest attention to the story Jack told.

It was then seen that Lord Linsay was correct, for the king openly said he was glad that one of the chief causes of anxiety to him was removed.

In spite of his "great popularity," there was not a noble present who did not rejoice that Rochester was no more.

The Duke of Somerset, who was present, then suggested that, in order to prevent any future complications, the king should at once make out a free pardon for the share Jack had taken against the State, and this was done; and the king signified his intention of making over Sir Guibald's property to Jack.

This reminded our hero of the house at Finsbury, and, when evening came on, he and his comrades repaired thither.

Having gained admission, they lit a couple of links, and proceeded to the vault where they had placed Sir Guibald.

They were startled to find that nothing but a mass of bones, and remnants of clothing remained.

"This is remarkable," said Jack; "for if these bones are the remains of Sir Guibald—and, of course, they must be—the flesh has been devoured by rats. If that is so, how is it that my parents did not fall victims to the vermin?"

This question was reasonable enough, and, for some minutes, neither Basil nor Silverbell offered a solution to what appeared to be a mystery.

Then the latter suggested that they should search the vaults.

This was done, and it was then found that a large portion of a wall on the north side of the mansion had fallen down.

The wall divided that part of the house from a broad and deep ditch, which swarmed with rats.

Very glad were the three to leave the place.

"Presently," said Jack, "I will have the building pulled down. It is a disgrace to London. Come—let us return."

*   *   *   *

For a considerable time Jack, with Nellie, resided at his father's house, and with him was Basil.

The latter, however, was very frequently at Elias Leighton's house, and the result was soon known.

He and Dorothy learned to love each other, and when Basil offered her his hand, Dorothy accepted it.

While Basil was engaged in the very pleasing task of making love, Jack was instituting inquiries respecting Nellie's parents.

He found that our heroine had been stolen from them when a baby by her nurse, who did this in revenge for an imaginary wrong.

Both her parents, who belonged to a highly respectable family, were dead.

Silverbell stayed at the house of a friend, and, of course, he was continually at the White Tower.

At last, all arrangements were made, and one splendid morning Jack and Nell, Basil and Dorothy, Silverbell and Mistress Dennison, were married at the pretty church at Whitehall.

Our hero and his beautiful and brave bride took up their residence at Edgware, at which quiet little village a large mansion had been purchased.

With them lived Lord and Lady Linsay. When his lordship died, our hero inherited both his title and estates.

His mother lived to nurse several of her grandchildren.

Silverbell and Mistress Dennison were very happy.

Both were much sought after, for they made themselves popular whereever they went.

It was freely said, and with perfect truth, that a better matched couple could not have been found.

Elias Leighton died some twelve months after his daughter's marriage, and so delighted had he become with Basil, that he left him all his large fortune.

Some years after, the blacksmith, Wat Tyler, rose in rebellion, and was joined by thousands of the lower classes.

Among his leaders was a man of Kent, named Bolin Garveston, who, having admired our hero's deeds, assumed the name of Jack Straw."

Our hero heard this from Basil, and he said, as he clasped his friend's hand—

"The name under which, for so long I fought, is, to all of *us*, dead; but let us hope and trust that he who, for his own purpose, is pleased to revive it, will keep from disgrace the name of—

"Jack Straw."

On Friday, November 7th,

WILL BE PUBLISHED

ONE OF THE MOST INTERESTING STORIES EVER WRITTEN,

ENTITLED

ON AND OFF THE STAGE;

OR,

WHICH WAS RIGHT?

Beautifully Illustrated. 16 Large Pages Weekly.

No. 2 and a Coloured Picture

FOR BINDING WITH THE WORK

WILL BE

Given Away with No. 1.

The Whole in an Illuminated Wrapper, Price 1d.

Orders should be given at once to your Bookseller.
Other Coloured Pictures will be given for
Binding with the work.

www.ingramcontent.com/pod-product-compliance
Lightning Source LLC
Chambersburg PA
CBHW080824250626
47160CB00008B/2850